# THE CROSS OF ST. MARO

A novel by

**E. Kelly Keady**

THE CROSS OF ST. MARO. Copyright ©2004 by E. Kelly Keady.
All rights reserved. Printed in Canada. No part
of this book may be used or reproduced in any manner whatsoever
without written permission except in the case of brief quotations
embodied in critical articles or reviews.
For information, address Magdalene Books, LLC, Suite 4100,
33 South Sixth Street, Minneapolis, MN 55402.

Cover design by Ruthann Oberfoell. Imaging by Paul Kielb.
Cover photo Jurgen Vogt/Getty Images.

www.crossofstmaro.com

Library of Congress Cataloging-in-Publication Data
Library of Congress Control Number: 2004103628

Keady, E. Kelly
The Cross of St. Maro/E. Kelly Keady
ISBN 0-9749738-0-7

First Edition: September 2004
10 9 8 7 6 5 4 3 2 1

*To Maggie,*

# Acknowlegements

To acknowledge everyone who made this happen would not only consume several pages irritating you the reader (unless you were looking for your name), but undoubtedly I would miss someone. Consequently, in the spirit of modern politics, I will take the easy way out and merely try to avoid alienating those people that I will absolutely need for future novels. Of course, this means you Tricia Keady, my sister and editor. Your consistent, "Why didn't you do this..." or more appropriately, "It would be less awkward to say..." reminds me why so many family businesses fail. By the way, the new chapters for the next novel are on the way.

Three other women stand out as well. First, to my sister Maggie and my mother-in-law MaryAnn, who have been there since the beginning doing any odd job to keep this project moving. And of course Mom, whose passion for reading encouraged the writer in me (however, my affinity with reference materials falls on your shoulders, Dad).

To Ann Love, Sachi Watson, Jen Thulen and Ruthann Oberfoell, who not only polished the final material, but transformed it into an actual book. I cannot be more impressed by their professionalism, hard work, and final product, especially given what little they had to start with.

I cannot in good faith say lastly, because so many family and friends have shown their support in so many ways (and you know I will find a way to show my gratitude), but I will say most importantly, to my wife Maggie. Writing requires inspiration, but life requires love. None of which would be possible without you.

*All you have to do is tell them that they
are being attacked, and denounce the pacifists for
lack of patriotism and exposing the country to danger.
It works the same in every country.*

*Hermann Göering*

# THE CROSS OF ST. MARO

# PROLOGUE

*Severna Park, Maryland*

Tasha Dolnick surveyed the bedroom again with her back to the naked body lying motionless on the bathroom floor. Her latex-covered fingers counted as she mentally checked off items on her list. The bag. It was just like his gym bag. Any impressions or fibers left by it would be consistent with the surroundings. The door. Wiped clean. The bed. The sheets replaced and the soiled ones placed in her bag. The condom. Also in the bag. Any remaining traces of her or the chloral hydrate would wash off in the bathtub. The carpet. Vacuumed and the contents of the vacuum cleaner safely in the bag as well. Fingerprints. None. The only things touched were the door, the body, and the sheets. Only he touched the bottle of scotch and the highball. She left both on the counter. Hair, epithelia, and fiber. A shave and a wax two days ago was a start. As for her hair, she kept it pulled back and would not let him handle it. He did not seem to mind. As a precaution, Tasha put the clothes that he had worn earlier in the bag. The vacuum cleaner and the bath took care of the rest.

Now to finish the job.

The disposable synthetic clothing and the light crunching sound as she moved across the bathroom tiles to the tub were far from provocative. Her lightweight Tyvek suit and hood concealed the athletic body and long black hair that seduced the man in the fetal position on the floor. She looked like she was investigating the crime scene, not creating one.

Because he drank more than Tasha realized, he had passed out within minutes of the chloral hydrate entering his system from the condom. What a waste. He was fit for a fifty-year-old. He could have been fun. More importantly, it was inconvenient to move the body. He was not heavy, but awkward, like other bodies on other assignments. She planned that he would only become incapacitated to the point that all she needed to do was guide him to the bathroom. No matter, it was done. Time to finish the assignment.

She turned on the bath water. Hot water. The steam further corrupted any trace evidence. As the water ran, Tasha looked at the bathtub. The body needed to sit at the end of the tub. Lifeless, it would fall back into the water cleansing the body of any transfer evidence or gunshot residue. Removal of the residue on his hand was important. If the residue stayed, it would reveal that her hand partially covered his while pulling the trigger. She left the water on knowing that the bathroom would flood, contaminating any trace evidence left behind.

There would be no mistakes tonight. She had been trained by the best, and this was not her first assignment. She did not make mistakes, but there was always a back up down the line. A lazy clerk, an underpaid cop, an underappreciated lab technician. There was always someone down the line. She had cleaned up others mistakes. But no mistakes tonight.

Tasha propped up the body. Jeffrey Jay Speeter. Age, fifty. Caucasian. Five-foot seven, one hundred fifty pounds. Right-handed. Alcoholic. Recently divorced because of his infidelities. Self-described ladies' man. An easy assignment.

She met Speeter at his gym four days ago. She knew his habits. When he went to the gym. When he left work to go out. Where he drank. What he drank. How much. How late he stayed up.

She asked him if she was using the free weights correctly. A very physical lesson ensued with Speeter copping a feel on every available occasion. The two shared bottled waters afterward. Speeter rambled on about how hard it was to find normal women since his divorce. He gave Tasha his card, complete with home phone number and address. She said that she would call him in a couple of days after she returned from visiting some friends. An intoxicated Speeter was more than pleasantly surprised when she showed up on his doorstep wearing only pumps and a tight black cocktail dress. Some things are too good to be true.

Tasha panned her surroundings a final time. No signs of forced entry. No signs of a struggle. Just a desperate drunk man with a gun and soon to be discovered overwhelming financial difficulties stemming from extensive gambling losses.

She balanced Speeter's body at the edge of the bathtub. The position had to be right. The angle of the bullet's entry had to be consistent with the shot firing first, then falling back into the tub. Blood spatter and brain matter would reveal the angle that the shot had been fired. If she let go of the body first, there could be questions.

Tasha put the gun in Speeter's right hand, placing his index finger on the trigger. She stuck the barrel in his mouth. Speeter's gag reflex caused him to cough slightly and moan. The combination of alcohol and chloral hydrate was beginning to wear off. It did not matter, she was ready.

As she pulled the trigger, Tasha mumbled in her soft Slavic voice, "for Salih."

# PART I

# ONE

"Peter!"

Slightly startled, attorney Peter Farrell stopped, stepped backwards, and stuck his head into the conference room.

"Peter Farrell, this is Paul Simon," introduced Joseph Rosendahl, Peter's boss and mentoring attorney.

"I believe we have spoken on the phone couple of times. It's nice to put a face with the name," remarked Peter. Peter thought to himself that the last thing he needed was a half-hour conversation with Paul Simon and Joe, especially today. Not only was it a gorgeous October Friday afternoon in St. Louis, but the fact that he had only two hours to revise, file, and serve his brief in the Whitmore case weighed heavily on his shoulders.

"Nice to finally meet you, Peter," replied Mr. Simon.

"Peter, why don't you sit down with us for a minute," directed Joe Rosendahl as he closed the conference room door behind Peter.

"This is a lovely view you gentlemen have," remarked Paul Simon, who was one of Golde & Rosendahl's wealthiest clients.

"Actually, this building is the joke of the real estate industry. Everyone says that the view from our International Tower is the best view in the city, because we are the only ones who don't have to look at this eyesore of a building."

Peter politely smiled at Rosendahl's joke, the same joke he had heard at least a dozen times before. Peter sized up Paul Simon. Oddly, he thought he would be a taller man given the big shoes he had to fill. The Simon family was one of the wealthiest families in St. Louis, a true American success story. Paul's father, Thomas Simon, immigrated to the United States in the mid 1920s from what is now called Lebanon. He not only sought economic freedom, but given Christianity's new found power in his homeland, he wanted no part in the once persecuted becoming the persecutors.

Christened Tuma Simon, the twenty-year-old immigrant landed at Ellis Island and changed it to Thomas Simon when he entered the United States of Opportunity. Adaptability would be a key to success in this brave New World. He would not fail. As a peddler of shoelaces, tools, kitchen utensils, fabrics, materials, or anything he could carry, Thomas Simon set forth to make his fortunes. After only six months of eighteen-, nineteen-hour days, young Thomas Simon's hard work had paid off. He saved enough money to allow him to buy a horse and wagon. With this transportation, he established himself as a legitimate businessman. Shortly thereafter he sent for the young woman he had promised to marry two years earlier. Upon her arrival in America, Lillian Habib quickly married her Tuma Simon. The Simons settled in St. Louis, Missouri. Ten months later, Lillian gave birth to a baby girl. The spring baby was appropriately named Rosalind. She was Lillian's "little Rose."

Though the Depression devastated most businesses in the 1930s, Simon managed not only to stay afloat, but also to explore and exploit new areas of merchandising. The young entrepreneur focused on men's clothing. Before long, he owned his own clothing store. That one store grew to three, then five, and soon seven. He convinced other families to immigrate to St. Louis by offering them a share of the business. After only seven years in the clothing industry, Thomas Simon had established himself as the men's clothing store in the St. Louis metropolitan area. Furthermore, he had created the beginning of a Lebanese community in the New World.

Success did have its price. A distance began to grow between Thomas and the two women in his life, which lead to longer hours at work. There were, however, no barriers between Lillian and her little Rose. They were as close as a mother and daughter could be. And by the age of eight, Lillian had taught her daughter to cook, clean, and sew. By nine, Rose was in charge of the housework and practically managed the Simon home.

The honing of Rose's skills could not have been more perfectly timed. For as Rose received her first communion, God blessed her with a baby brother, Paul. The distance between Lillian and Thomas disappeared with the birth of a son.

As the Simon family had grown, so had the family business. Thomas Simon opened additional stores in the St. Louis metropolitan area. In two more years, a factory opened. Then came the big move. A Simon's Men's Store opened in Chicago. By the '60s, Thomas Simon owned stores throughout the Midwest. However Thomas Simon, who built the beginnings of an empire and established a Lebanese community in St. Louis, paid the price of success with his life. At the young age of sixty-seven, Thomas Simon died of a heart attack.

"Before he passed away, my father made me promise that I would take care of the family," Paul Simon remarked with the breath of hesitation.

"As you know, my sister Rose checked into the Cedar Riverside Care Center a year ago after she had suffered a nervous breakdown. You may also know that her breakdown resulted from the separation she was going through with her husband Elias St. Armand. To anyone who has read a newspaper in the last five years, this is no surprise. What the family was able to keep out of papers was the severity of her condition. Elias was able to seal the court records which found her a clear danger to herself and the safety of others. More importantly gentlemen, the court records were sealed because Rose tried to murder Elias St. Armand."

"Tried to murder Elias St. Armand?" Peter couldn't believe that remark just slipped out of his mouth like some summer intern.

"Elias St. Armand is quite a big fish," noted Joe Rosendahl in a self-deprecating voice to cover up for his associate's lack of tact.

What an understatement Peter thought to himself. Elias St. Armand was one of the most powerful men to ever hail from St. Louis, arguably one of the most influential businessmen of our time. Elias St. Armand's name was synonymous with world politics, big business, and special interests. His food conglomerate, the Occidental Group, had annual revenues of over $90 billion. St. Armand's prestige was only matched by his arrogance. He commonly referred to his company as the "World's Kitchen," and he of course was the head chef.

"I have no issues with Elias," Mr. Simon firmly stated. "My concern, which I hope you will alleviate, lies with my sister and the attorneys who represented her during the commitment proceedings."

"Quite frankly, Paul," started the former prosecutor in Joe Rosendahl, "if she tried to kill Elias St. Armand, and she is only staying at Cedar Riverside, I don't know much else an attorney could have accomplished."

"Sealing the records was a coup," chimed Peter, again speaking when he should probably have just been listening.

Ignoring the young attorney's comment, Paul Simon continued. "By no means is Cedar Riverside a maximum security facility, but my sister, realistically, is imprisoned. Although the thought of that sickens me everyday, I know medically, it is for the best. That doesn't put to rest the fact that I still have a scintilla of doubt about her situation. Every time I visit her she rants and raves about how her attorneys cheated and lied to her. If I could have only seen the signs, maybe then I could have helped her sooner. Hell, if her attorneys cheated and lied to her, and the result is having any attempted murder charges go away; I don't care what happened. Still, all of this does not ease the burden of my guilt. And if having you look into any alleged cheating and lying eases her pain, then maybe it will ease my guilt. I am willing to pay whatever it takes for some peace of mind. Mr. Farrell, you look concerned."

Peter Farrell looked at his mentoring attorney first, and then asked, "What firm handled the matter?"

"The Washington D.C. firm, Miller & White," Simon answered.

"They are quite a reputable firm," commented Peter. Glancing again at Joe, Peter continued, "no disrespect intended, but you do know that even making initial inquiries will cause quite a stir."

The retail magnate and Fortune 500 CEO nodded, "I understand where you are going Mr. Farrell and appreciate your candor. Joe, you have a fine young man here. Let me address where you are really going. All I need you to do is talk to my sister, then make a couple inquiries. I want my sister to believe that people believe in her. This seems like a lot of trouble to go through knowing that even making inquiries will cause a stir. You're right. And for what, to play a charade on my sister?"

Peter looked as if he may interrupt again, but Simon continued, "This is a small price to pay for family. You see, Mr. Farrell, there is an old Lebanese proverb that readily comes to mind, 'if you take your clothes off, you will feel cold.'"

Simon paused for an obvious dramatic effect then continued in a slightly condescending tone, "You see, Mr. Farrell, I come from a people who hold family above all else. And Mr. Farrell, if you disregard your family, you will suffer."

"Mr. Simon, I," Peter humbly began to apologize.

"Paul," interjected Peter's boss, "what can we do?"

"Just meet with her as soon as you can and tell me how she reacts. She may want you to review some boxes of documents, too."

"Peter," Joe began again, "what are your plans for tomorrow?"

Knowing full well that watching college football would not be the correct answer, Peter responded, "I will be at Cedar Riverside first thing in the morning."

"Joe," the voice on the intercom was Lois, Aaron Golde's assistant, "is Peter in there?"

"Lois, he's right here," Joe Rosendahl responded.

"Aaron wants him down here if you're finished."

"I think we're done. Is there anything else Paul?"

"No," responded Paul Simon as he shook Joe's hand.

"Then send him down," Lois ordered.

Rosendahl smiled at Paul Simon, "Well, I guess you know who really runs the show here at Golde & Rosendahl."

"Yeah, I better get down there before she comes and grabs me by the ear," said Peter as he stepped toward Simon to shake his hand.

"Has Peter left yet? Aaron is about to leave." It was Lois again.

"I'm on my way."

Peter grabbed his own ear then reached out to shake Paul Simon's hand.

Simon clasped Peter's outstretched hand with both of his hands and pulled him in closer, "You must get my sister to trust you," he squeezed Peter's hand tighter, "we are running out of time."

Simon finally released Peter's hand.

"Peter," Joe reassured his protégé. "I'll be around all weekend if you need anything."

Peter left the conference room and headed down the hall. Obviously, Joe was letting Paul Simon know that the young attorney would not be working on the file by himself. But it was nice to know that Joe would act as a safety net if there were any problems. Be that as it may, Paul Simon's parting words still left Peter with an uneasy feeling. As he walked, Simon's odd handshake left his train of thought. The gold-plated marquee "Golde & Rosendahl" had grabbed Peter's attention. The letters hung above Lois, who guarded the door to Aaron's corner office.

Golde & Rosendahl is the creation of Aaron Golde. The Golde family name is above reproach in St. Louis. Not only because Golde established himself as a pillar in the community, but his father happened to be one of the businessmen who financed Charles Lindbergh's flight over the Atlantic. And in St. Louis, a plume in a family's pedigree went a long way. However, Aaron never traded in on his good name. In fact, Aaron Golde, one of the most-respected attorneys in the country, lied on the very first document he filed with the United States government. As he always retold the story, the fifteen-year-old Golde simply made a mistake on his age when he enlisted in the Army to fight in France. On the rare occasions when Golde relived his colorful past, it was apparent that he battled the Axis powers in nearly every country in central Europe and in the Mediterranean. Upon his return from the war, Golde stayed with the Army and worked in Washington D.C. and Virginia. In the mid '50s, he returned to St. Louis as a special deputy attorney for Hoover's FBI. After ten years of public service, he entered into private practice.

"Is he in?" Peter asked Lois as he peeked in Aaron's office. Aaron Golde was old school. His office reflected that fact. Lining the wall behind his desk were several sets of statutes, reporters, treatises, and hornbooks. Only law books, no computer. In fact, the only technology in his office, other than the lights, was a phone that may have been one of Alexander Graham Bell's original models. A push-button pad had replaced the dial, but everything else clamored turn-of-the-century innovation. He was an old-fashioned gentleman, Mark Twain in a contemporary gray suit. Folksy, without being disingenuous.

"No."

"No?"

Lois rolled her eyes at Peter then tilted her head toward the side door that led out into the outer hallway by the elevator banks.

"He just walked out," she noted before she scolded the young attorney. "I told you he was leaving."

"Aaron?" Peter checked the other hallway and came back to Lois. "Did he say anything?"

Lois shot Peter a deadpan gaze, "He told me to tell you not to screw up the Simon matter."

"Were those his words?"

"I'm a messenger, not a tape recorder."

Message received.

———— ✦ ————

His view had been irreparably altered. Nothing was the same. Nothing will be the same. Now, he thought, more than ever, was the time.

Clutching a grayish-colored cross attached to a thin strap of brown leather, Elias St. Armand turned away from his bay window overlooking the Manhattan skyline and picked up the newspaper from his desk to skim the front page.

*The New York Herald*

**U.S. AID TO LEBANON?**

Associated Press International

*BEIRUT, LEBANON–Secretary of State McKenzie Schofield will meet with Lebanese President Michael Berri and Prime Minister Yusuf Azar today in Beirut only days after a car bomb killed four American business-men and wounded 28 bystanders.*

*The White House maintains that Schofield's scheduled visit relates only to the increased terrorist activities by the Lebanese National Liberal Party, more commonly known as the "Tigers," not the thirty billion-dollar aid package to Lebanon. White House Press Secretary Hugh Oberfoell further denied that the President would endorse the bill.*

*Although the proposed congressional foreign aid package aims at restoring stability to the entire region, ironically, since announcing the aid package last month, the Tigers' terrorist activities have escalated dramatically.*

*Such terrorism had previously prompted sharp criticism of the bill. However, opponents to the package have dwindled, as noted by the defec-tion of Senator Pro Tempore John Jay Knox. The Texas senator had previ-ously called the package "blood money." Despite his earlier statement, he joined Speaker of the House Randolph Sexton in support of the bill last week thus ensuring congressional approval of the package.*

*After two days in Beirut, Secretary of State Schofield will travel to Tel Aviv where she...*

### FEC Official's death not a homicide

*WASHINGTON D.C.–Yesterday afternoon police found the body of Federal Election Committee Commissioner Jeffrey Speeter at his home in Severna Park, Maryland. Speeter, 50, died of a gunshot wound to the head. Police have ruled out homicide, but have been unable to determine whether his death was accidental or suicide.*

*Speeter is best known for his role in last year's Senate campaign finance hearings...*

The green light on his console blinked. St. Armand pressed two other buttons then pressed the blinking one and picked up the phone.

"Yes," St. Armand responded.

"Everything is finished and I am on my way to St. Louis."

The woman's voice was Slavic, St. Armand knew it was Tasha.

"I see," St. Armand picked up the newspaper and set it back down.

"Are you sure there are no issues left unresolved?" he continued.

"The crime scene tape is being taken down as we speak."

"Good," replied St. Armand, "we can move ahead as scheduled."

"I will arrive in St. Louis in a couple of hours."

"You will be meeting someone on Saturday. All the arrangements have been made."

"I prefer to work alone."

"I prefer not to be second guessed."

Elias St. Armand hung up the phone. Another paper had been placed on his desk with a Post-It note attached to the front page stating, "The framed copy will be ready later today."

He picked up the smaller publication and began to read the cover story.

### The Maronite letter

On October 18th, the Cross of St. Maro was bestowed on Elias St. Armand for his outstanding charity and foundation work. Mr. St. Armand is the first U.S. citizen awarded the Cross of St. Maro and the only recipient in the past 20 years. The ceremony...

St. Armand set down the paper. He returned to his bay window and faced the Manhattan skyline with his hands behind his back. The time is now.

# TWO

As Peter Farrell walked through the doors of the same Irish pub he frequented on Friday afternoons for nearly half his life, he immediately spotted his brother John, at the usual table, in the usual corner.

Ever since Peter's mother died, every Friday evening Sean Farrell brought his two sons to O'Shea's, an Irish bar/restaurant on St. Louis' south side. Every Friday, Sean Farrell ordered Irish stew and a pint of stout with his boys usually enjoying burgers and fries. Traditional Irish music always played at O'Shea's. Jigs, reels, and ballads colored the dimly lit rooms of the pub. Although Sean passed away six months ago, his two boys continued the tradition.

"John-John," started Peter.

"Petie," retorted John Farrell using a nickname only he was allowed to, "what is with the Elvis look?"

"Stew I see, you make Pops proud," quipped Peter as he ran his fingers through his hair. His brother was right. It had been quite a while since his last haircut.

"Two pints please, Ann," John Farrell beckoned to Ann Love the bartender.

"How's the Golden Rose?" John asked, using his affectionate name for Peter's law firm, Golde & Rosendahl.

"Thorny as usual, partner."

Peter enjoyed the weekly dinners with his elder brother. Older by three years, but he claimed many more in experience, John had blazed the trail for his younger brother all his life. John taught Peter how to ride a bike while other kids were still on their tricycles. Peter learned algebra from John while most of the other kids just began their multiplication tables. By the time John Farrell graduated law school near the top of his class at Loyola of St. Louis, he had sent his brother off with books, study outlines, old tests, and even interviews with some of the professors.

Although Peter had been given some breaks, he was no slouch. He worked hard to uphold his brother's reputation and to build one of his own. Bucking traditional law school guidelines, Peter accepted less than glamorous administrative jobs with the law school at the request of the Dean. However, the administrative position from his first year of law school not only lead to a clerkship in the second year with the preeminent jurist Judge Patrick Fitzgerald of the Eighth Circuit Court of Appeals, but also a burgeoning friendship with Dean Roger Cosgrove Adams as well.

The two brothers went their separate ways after law school. While John Farrell accepted an associate position at one of St. Louis' largest law firms, Peter joined the litigation boutique of Golde & Rosendahl.

Although Aaron Golde's reputation would lure any young attorney, Peter joined the firm because of Joe Rosendahl. Rosendahl, a friend and classmate of Dean Adams, graduated at the top of his class at Loyola of St. Louis then became a prosecuting attorney. While other baby boomers quickly converted their degrees into dollar signs, Joe Rosendahl prosecuted misdemeanors against pimps, prostitutes, and drug dealers. However fortune smiled quickly on the young attorney. On the first day of a major felony trial, the first chair fell ill. The judge would not continue the trial. That left young Joe Rosendahl to prosecute and convict his first murderer only six months after passing the Missouri bar. Over the next seven years, he compiled an unblemished record, highlighted by murder convictions over a serial killer; a local millionaire who hired someone from the East Side to kill his wife; and the three leaders of the Bloods, the North Side's largest and deadliest gang. These relentless prosecutions attracted the attention of Aaron Golde. Shortly after they met, Golde hired Rosendahl away from the Prosecuting Attorney's Office. Golde referred to Rosendahl as his "bulldog." Rosendahl never quit, no matter what the odds. Peter admired Joe because of his "never give up" attitude.

As the Irish music reeled along, the two Farrell boys enjoyed their pints of stout. A tall red-haired woman with a Polaroid camera strapped over a large bulky navy sweater entered the pub. Her flat tennis shoes and forward lurch concealed her height so as to blend in with the crowd. Her thick brogue captivated happy hour revelers who came in contact with her. Quickly she worked the back room charging two dollars for a snapshot to capture "a lifetime of memories." Although she always refused to "spoil" a picture by having hers taken with some of the happier happy hour crowd, the red-haired woman nevertheless swiftly raked in dollar bills.

"John, I need a favor from you," asked Peter.

"Sure. What do you need?"

"Well, you know my fishing days are numbered with the weather chang-ing and all..."

"Spit it out."

"Tomorrow I meet a new client, and she may have a lot of documents, as in boxes of documents. I was hoping to go south tomorrow night to get some fly fishing in, but if this lady has four or five banker's boxes of documents, I won't be able to fit all that in my car with the gear."

"You mean Pop's car."

"Yeah."

"Peter Joseph Farrell, why are you still driving that piece of crap?"

The day Sean Farrell died was the same day Peter borrowed his father's car because his own had broken down. It had been six months, and Peter had yet to fix his own car. He still preferred to drive the same two-door Monte Carlo his father had used to pick him up from middle school.

"Come on John, I have these two things going on at once."

"Say no more, I will go fishing for you and then that pesky fishing gear won't get in the way of all those boxes."

"Your sarcasm amuses me, but I had in mind that I would go fishing and you would keep the boxes."

"Oh, I see," nodded John, mocking his kid brother as usual. As both broth-ers turned their heads away from the bar toward the band, a flash blinded them.

"Only two dollars for a picture that you two strong handsome lads can share with the lassies," the red-haired woman urged in her enticing raspy voice.

"I don't know if Elvis here qualifies as 'strong and handsome' but I will certainly pose for you. Come on, Pete," demanded John as he threw his arm around his brother and bestowed his sheepish grin for the camera. Knowing the camera was focused on his brother the ham, Peter smiled without bothering to move the hair swapping down from his forehead. The red-haired woman snapped another picture, which was accompanied by another blinding flash.

As the second picture ejected from the Polaroid, John grabbed it and offered, "I'll give you ten for both."

"Thanks Luvs," responded the red-haired woman. As she handed over the pictures, Tasha Dolnick winked at Peter then made her way through the crowd.

The bartender rolled her eyes.

"How about her?" the less then subtle John mentioned to his brother.

"What her? I'm still seeing blue dots from those flashes," responded Peter as he rubbed his eyes.

"Well, I look better in this one, so you can have this one," John handed the first picture to Peter and began to rise from the bar.

"We have no plans all weekend." John continued, "So getting those documents is no problem, just call me."

"Thanks. I will call you tomorrow."

Peter watched his brother begin to walk around the bar to the exit. He picked up the picture, chuckled to himself, and turned to the band as they played an old rebel song about County Derry.

# THREE

The open green lawn inside the gate resembled a governor's mansion or a small college, but definitely not a mental hospital. Once a visitor, who has been previously cleared to visit, enters the main gate, an initial quick, yet thorough, check of the vehicle and its contents, passengers and all, is conducted. Upon parking in an underground garage manned with security cameras every twenty-five feet, the visitor and vehicle are again searched by three guards, two carrying handheld metal detectors, the third holding a German shepherd at bay. An elevator must be taken from the garage to the main level of the facility where once again the visitor and any packages are examined. This time they are examined not only by a walk through an x-ray security machine, but by two guards who rifle through anything not physically attached to the visitor. It may have been labeled a minimum-security facility, but by the time Peter Farrell arrived at the main office, the guards knew the contents of his briefcase and several parts of his anatomy better than he did. Welcome to the Cedar Riverside Care Center.

"Hello, my name is Peter Farrell, here to see Rose St. Armand."

"We have been expecting you, Mr. Farrell."

Who was ever unexpected at this place Peter thought to himself as he opened his briefcase and pulled out a lone document, "Here's a medical authorization to review her records as well."

"That will not be necessary, Mr. Farrell," the robotic clerk responded without motion or emotion. "Mr. Simon faxed the authorization yesterday evening and it was approved this morning. Here are the requested records, but they must be reviewed at this counter. Duplicates will be forwarded to your office the first thing Monday morning."

"Thank you," replied Peter as he opened the Cedar Riverside Care Center's medical file for Rose St. Armand. His new client was not his first "mentally ill and dangerous" or MID client. The other MID patient, Henry Knops, currently lives in East St. Louis, a free man. That is, after Peter was able to gain his release by showing that Knops was not likely to engage in future violent conduct. Poor Henry suffered from a bipolar mood disorder, a chemical imbalance, and an over-zealous prosecutor. The prosecutor, Gregory Taylor, an ex-classmate with a chip on his shoulder larger than the Gateway Arch, convinced a trial judge that Henry Knops assaulted two clerks and tried to kill two police officers. On appeal, Knops' sister hired Peter's firm on a pro bono basis. Peter had the matter remanded back to trial court, where he demonstrated to the judge that Henry was not the madman Taylor had portrayed. Peter explained, using a myriad of expert neurologists that Henry Knops suffered from a chemical imbalance resulting in a progressive seizure.

What really happened was that Henry, having known he needed his medicine when the seizure began, attempted to obtain his prescription at his local drugstore. Unable to communicate in even the simplest manner, he grabbed one of the two clerks and shook him. Frustrated, he attempted to drive himself to the hospital. Henry failed to get even two blocks from the drugstore when he crashed into a police car.

As a six-foot-two, two hundred and fifty-pound African American, unable to speak, convulsing, who had just rammed into a police car, Henry had little chance against the police who quickly cuffed him suspecting he was some crack-crazed lunatic. A simple doctor's examination would have shown that Henry's chemical imbalance and erratic behavior simply required medication, but a young prosecutor sought to fill the city's new jail. Taylor ramrodded the case through the trial court. Fortunately for Henry, the court only institutionalized him whereby he received some treatment. Unfortunately, treatment meant sedation and little else.

After Henry had spent nine months either sedated or restricted by a straight jacket, Henry's sister fired the public defender and hired Peter's firm on a pro bono basis. Peter immediately had Henry examined by a physician, psychiatrist, and neurologist. After only three days of the proper medication, the mild-mannered Henry Knops woke up as Alice did from Wonderland. During Henry's first week awake, Peter spent every possible moment with him. The only family he had was his sister who was ill. Terrified at first, Henry believed his life was over, but his faith in God, then Peter, soon prevailed. Through Aaron Golde's political connections, Henry's appeal fast-tracked. On remand the trial judge not only released Henry, but openly admonished Taylor and the prosecuting attorney's office in the newspapers. The civil suit settled before it ever started.

Rose St. Armand's file resembled Henry's file. She had been diagnosed with the bipolar mood or affective disorder, an anti-social personality disorder, and a chemical dependency, as opposed to Henry's chemical imbalance. The Minnesota Multiphasic Inventory-II, or MMTI-II, confirmed the diagnosis. Pursuant to her file, at her last hearing, the staff psychologist testified that, "Ms. St. Armand is largely in remission from the bipolar disorder due to her medication...despite this, she continues to display symptoms of mood instability and anger, as well as control and behavioral problems," the file noted. Furthermore, she recently provoked an altercation with a nurse who was "viciously attacked" in attempting to medicate Ms. St. Armand. The patient stated she was defending herself because the nurse was "slowly poisoning her." There were at least a dozen other such incidents noted in the file.

Rose St. Armand's case appeared to be a typical MID case. The court's finding of mentally ill and dangerous read like a textbook. She suffered from a substantial psychiatric disorder concerning her mood and perception, which grossly impaired her judgment, behavior, and capacity to recognize reality. Pursuant to the court's findings, the illness is manifested by instances of disturbed behavior and faulty perceptions that her husband and nurses were trying to kill her. The court found that her behavior posed a substantial likelihood of physical harm to herself and others as demonstrated by the attempt on the life of Elias St. Armand and the incidents at the hospital. The commitment and avoidance of jail time fit into a nice little package.

As he walked into the visitor's room, the only thing that bothered Peter about the file was the lack of documented incidents before the murder attempt.

"Who are you?" barked Rose St. Armand in a manner reminiscent of the Spanish inquisition.

"Peter Farrell, Ms. St. Armand. It is a pleasure to make your acquaintance."

"Ms. St. Armand? Now there is a name that has not fallen on these ears in some time," she responded pretending to blush. "Please, call me Rose, just do not call me Rosie like some of these wackos in here."

Peter sat down across the table and studied the woman who must have been in her late sixties. Stripped from the pearls, diamonds, and haute couture, the woman before him bore little resemblance to the paparazzi photos from only a few years ago. The trademark jet-black coif had lost its color, leaving behind a short crop of grayish-white locks. Although she had always appeared petite, the lady before him simply looked like a tiny woman who had aged well beyond her years. Despite the loss of her looks, her wealth, and her liberty, there still was something regal about her.

"Did Paul run out of stuffy New York lawyers, or are you some kind of errand boy?" she continued. "No matter, go back and tell him that you have spoken with me, and that I have been uncooperative as usual."

Rose St. Armand stood, straightened her one-piece jump suit as if it was a thousand-dollar gown, and turned toward the door.

Shocked and afraid he may have lost the firm's richest client, Peter had to say something.

"Why did you do it?"

She stopped.

"Pardon?" she responded in what sounded like a French accent.

"Why did you shoot Elias St. Armand?"

Slowly she turned toward Peter, stared at him sternly, but slightly puzzled.

"You really have no idea, do you?" asked Rose St. Armand.

"No."

"I see it in your eyes. You're telling the truth."

More than slightly skeptical of her omniscient powers, Peter reassured her of his lack of knowledge concerning her attempt to end the life of one of the most powerful men in the country.

"Out of all the doctors and lawyers who say they are here to help me, you are the first to ask that question. Sure, I try and tell them how that bastard has been trying to kill me, yet you are the only one who has ever asked me why."

It was Peter who now had a puzzled look on his face. He could understand a defense lawyer not asking such questions, fearing that a client would actually answer the question and admit to the crime. After that, the lawyer could not allow that defendant to testify. The client would either hang himself by telling the truth or commit perjury. Neither option is acceptable to the criminal defense attorney. However, with all of the psychiatrists and psychologists that probably paraded through the room, surely she was asked about the murder attempt.

"You are surprised, even better. Maybe my brother's errand boy is more than what he appears."

"I don't know whether to take that as a compliment or not, but Ms. St. Armand, Rose, we need to talk."

"No. I need to talk. You need to listen."

"Okay."

"The great Elias St. Armand is not a man. He is the devil incarnate, Lucifer, Elbis. He is incapable of anything good. Whenever I told him that he was going to Hell, he merely would say to me, 'he who has money can eat ice cream in Hell.'"

"To answer your question Mr. Farrell," she continued, "I hated him and wanted him dead. In the beginning, I was under his spell like the rest of the world. The rest of the world, dear Lord, I am surprised that he did not burst into flames receiving the Cross of St. Maro. If I saw him, I would put his eyes out with that cross. Yes, I hate him. I want him dead. He also wants me dead. But I have insurance."

"Insurance?" added Peter looking for an opportunity to get Rose back on focus.

"Yes, insurance," responded Rose as she calmed down. "I met Elias when he was just a Missouri farm boy before the war. He was a farm boy but not a farmer. He lived on a farm, but drove to the city every night for business school classes. It was a two-hour drive to St. Louis and two-hour drive back to the farm. After three hours of classes and twelve hours of chores on the farm, I figured he probably slept only five hours every night. He certainly was a driven individual. I'm not sure if I admired him for that, but I knew my father would. He did. I fell in love with that big, strong, Lebanese farmer who was going places."

"He did go places. Europe for almost five years. I waited longingly, but in hindsight, foolishly. He came back from the war with more medals and stories than one can imagine. Elias even returned with a job. The farm boy left for Europe, returning as a man of the world with the business acumen to match. I have had a lot of time to think about it; yet, I still don't know if it was the war that changed him, or whether it merely washed the dirt off the rugged man I fell in love with. We were married two months after he came home from the war. My father approved of the God-fearing St. Armand and admired the work ethic in Elias."

"The Occidental Group hired Elias upon his return. The St. Louis office was the headquarters for their agribusiness division. I'm no slouch at business Mr. Farrell. All during the war, while my father concentrated on manufacturing uniforms for soldiers, my mother and I held the family business together. So I can appreciate shrewd business acumen. Elias is more than shrewd; he's damn manipulative."

"You are too young to remember white margarine. Margarine was not always yellow, it was white. Because it was white, people would no sooner put margarine on their food than they would soap. Furthermore, for the 'public's best interest,' dairy farmers and their lobbyists had convinced our government leaders that margarine had to be marketed white so that it would not be confused with butter. One of Elias' first triumphs was when he convinced his company to buy as much stock in margarine as they could. Elias bought large shares as well. Elias then influenced congressmen to repeal their restrictions against adding coloring to margarine. I did not know how he was able to influence these politicians until much later. Anyway, yellow dye was added to margarine. The cheaper margarine with yellow dye not only tasted some-what like butter, but because of Elias it also looked like butter. Margarine began to sell at ten times what it had previously sold before it was yellow. Occidental and Elias cleaned up."

"Before I knew it, I was swept across the country, then the world. Each year not only did we travel more and more, but we met congressmen, other politicians, dignitaries, and even royalty. Sure I was taken by the glitter and excitement of everything, but that soon faded. Elias had his extramarital trysts, but there never really was another woman, per se. Our marriage, I mean our arrangement, didn't fail because Elias was just another workaholic husband either. It is hard for me to believe that he ever loved me. I think that I was a perfect ornament for him. I think I merely legitimized him in the eyes of everyone."

"You are a very patient young man." Rose St. Armand stood up, began to walk around the room, then continued, "But a very young man nonetheless. I, on the other hand, have lived many years. However, I have decided that I will not spend my remaining years as a business asset in Elias St. Armand's portfolio."

Peter admittedly had been captivated by Rose St. Armand's tale.

She continued, "My opportunity arose when Elias moved offices to his new Ivory Tower. Elias trusted no one, so about thirty banker's boxes of his confidential documents were stored in our hidden wine cellar during the ten day move. I thought the boxes contained records of offshore accounts in the Caymans, or whatever, maybe even some items the IRS would find interest-ing. I convinced myself that if I had some of this information, Elias would have no choice but to let me go."

"When he left for New York on a two-day trip, I grabbed my chance," Rose clasped her hands together as she stressed the word "chance." After a slight pause, she continued to relive her drama, "I crept down to the basement library and slid open the hidden door in the bookcase to reach the wine cellar. I took one box back upstairs to the kitchen and then another. One of those overnight copying places picked up the two boxes. The next day my husband returned early, at the exact same time the copier called to see if someone was home to receive the copies and originals. I panicked. I called my mother. In a heartbeat, she picked up the four boxes. That night, when Elias went out, we were able to put the originals back in the cellar. The very next morning I put the copies in safety deposit boxes at the bank. I thought I saw the light of a new dawn."

"The flicker of light was snuffed when Elias came home for dinner. My opening a single account for the safety deposit boxes raised red flags right up to the bank's president. So much for confidentiality. Little did I know that Elias' tentacles stretched to every bank and boardroom in the metro area.

Rose stood by the window gazing into the sunlight and continued in a softer tone, almost a whisper, "he summoned me into his library upon returning home from work. Elias had already poured himself a brandy, so I knew he was up to something. At first he said nothing, but only walked the edges of the room as if he were a lion intimidating his prey. Then he exploded by ranting and raving about how I had betrayed him and could no longer be trusted. He confronted me about the documents. I never had a chance to speak."

"I had never heard such rage come from him before. He was crazed. My nerves were frazzled. I grabbed the glass of brandy off the bar and gulped it down. Elias paused for a minute, then continued to break me. This time he started on my 'barren womb,' and my failure to bear him a child to continue his legacy. While he shouted at me, he had also backed me up towards his precious Victorian cherry-wood desk. I maneuvered myself behind it to put space between us."

Rose's voice began to tremble, "Once I was behind the desk, Elias strode over to it. He grabbed a pointer. His voice then began to change. He became calmer, yet crueler. Elias began to bait me about my father. While he hit the pointer on the desk, Elias fired rapid questions at me: how well did I really know my father; what did I know about his death; and did I know why he died. My head was swimming. He told me that his Occidental Group wanted to buy my father's business, but father would not sell. So Elias told me he was chosen, no, volunteered to remove my father. Angered, confused, and frightened, I asked him what he meant. He told me."

With her voice cracking even more, Rose continued, "he said that in this very room, Elias' library, he offered my father one last time to sell the company. When my father refused, Elias shocked him with an electric cattle prod over and over again until his heart stopped. Then Elias pointed the pointer at my heart and imitated a zapping noise."

"I snapped. I pulled the revolver Elias kept in his front desk drawer. Before I knew what happened, I had shot the bastard two or three times. The kitchen staff found me standing there, gun in hand, while Elias lay still on the floor. The staff shuffled me upstairs to the dining room, and then called my brother Paul. Since then, it's been doctors, needles, and lawyers."

Rose stared out the visitor's room window, exhausted, as if a great weight had been lifted off her shoulders. Peter sat still at the table. An awkward moment of silence filled the room. The door unlocking at the end of the hall broke the silence. Footsteps followed.

Hearing the footsteps, Rose quickly sat herself beside Peter and gently spoke, "I still have the documents."

"But you," Peter began to question her.

"Mother had two sets of copies made. You must meet her today after four-thirty mass at St. Maron's."

The visiting room door unlocked and opened, "Rosie, it's time for medicine," interrupted the guard.

Rose St. Armand looked at the guard then turned back to Peter placing her hands on top of the young attorney's hands. She fixed her weary eyes on his, then whispered, "As God wills, I will take care of everything."

# FOUR

Peter pulled into the spot in the parking lot behind St. Maron's Maronite Catholic Church. The small wooden sign marking the parking space read:

*Welcome to your home of St. Maron*

As Peter walked around the car toward the church, he read the reverse side of the sign:

*Have a Blessed Day*

Hopefully, at the end of the day, Peter would be able to count his blessings.

If he timed the meeting with Rose's mother Lillian Simon correctly, he would be able to dump Rose's "secret" documents off on John and be on this way to his favorite trout spot by six o'clock at the latest. Upon reflection, Peter thought to himself that he only gave himself a thirty-minute window for idle chitchat. If Lillian was anything like her daughter, his whole time schedule could be thrown off. This, and a slight touch of inexplicable curiosity, brought the former altar boy to St. Maron's early where he caught part of mass from the last pew.

St. Maron's modest brick exterior bore little resemblance to the extravagant interior. Other than the ivory stone archway, which garnished the entrance, the outside of the small church lacked any ornamentation. On the other side of the archway were stained-glass windows lining the holy chapel on both sides. Instead of the dark stone or cherry-stained wood Peter was used to, the walls were bright white with brilliantly colored flora, birds, animals, and saints dancing about. The altar itself was completely adorned with gold. Even the tapestry was embroidered with gold.

As the priest clasped Peter's folded hands as a sign of peace, Peter surveyed the congregation trying to figure out which member was Lillian Simon.

Acknowledging his ignorance, Peter was surprised by the diversity of these Lebanese Maronites, yet he was unable to recognize an older version of Rose.

*"An ta wah da ka da..."*

Peter genuflected, made the sign of the cross, and exited through the side door.

*"Rabbi anta tariqi..."*

The side door led to a garden. Small evergreens lined the side of the church and a three-foot hedge surrounded the rectangular garden. Peter walked along the pathway past a bronze statue, which centered this quiet place. The three-foot base raised the life-size statue so that it towered over all the bushes and hedges in the garden. The impressive figure cast in bronze was a robed priest, his arms extended and opened. The inscription on the base of the statue read:

"The glory of Lebanon will be given to them"
Isaiah 35:2
dedicated to Msgr. Peter F. Asmar (1936-1966)

"Too young to die," a voice behind Peter began and ended rather matter-of-factly, "he was no older than you."

"Ms. Simon I presume?" Peter addressed the elderly woman in a modest black suit displaying neither jewelry nor baubles. Peter gestured his arm toward her, and she took it into hers tightly.

"Young man, call me Sitti," Lillian Simon instructed Peter in a tone which was more of a command than an invitation.

She led him along the walkway around the statue of Msgr. Asmar and spoke again, "My daughter spoke highly of you."

"I hope I can help."

"You will."

Lillian led Peter to the shady end of the garden, which must have connected to the rectory. Their pace was slow, but deliberate. Neither of them talked as they made their way across the courtyard. As they approached a brick grotto completely engulfed in shade, Lillian released Peter's arm. She entered the grotto. She then pulled from her jacket a black-and-white picture of what appeared to be a little girl in a white dress, maybe a first communion dress. She placed the photo at the feet of the three-foot statue in the grotto with one hand, and then lit one of the tiny candles with her other hand. She knelt. Surprised by himself, Peter knelt beside her. After a quiet moment, Lillian Simon made the sign of the cross and rose, as did Peter.

"You know who this is, son?" Lillian asked the young attorney then continued as if she knew she was sparing Peter the embarrassment of guessing.

"This is St. Jude. St. Jude is the patron saint for those suffering desperate cases of illness. My Rose has suffered too long, and now I know you will bring it all to an end, one way or another, inshalla," she looked up at Peter, "if God wills."

Again she commanded, "Walk with me."

The two walked arm in arm.

"My husband built this church, built this whole community. He was a God-fearing man, who feared no man. I do fear a man, a man you know, Elias St. Armand." Lillian Simon began shaking her head from side to side as she continued, "I do not understand such men. Men who like to destroy. He is like the little children in the spring playing with their Easter eggs. The children use the tip of their eggs as a kind of hammer. The child taps an egg held in another child's hand. One shell breaks, the other does not. The winner is the one who breaks all the eggshells. Elias will not stop until he has broken everyone's eggshell, especially my fragile Rose."

"Mrs. Simon, Sitti," Peter asked, "why me, why are you doing this now?"

"You are the only one Rose has trusted enough to send to me. She called right after your visit with her."

Sitti turned toward the grotto again, then back to Peter and continued, "At first, I thought my daughter was irrational and overzealous because that man received the Cross of St. Maro. She is impulsive at times. I doubted her on the phone. She, however, insisted you are the one. But looking into your eyes, my doubts have vanished. You are the one."

"And the documents?" Peter remembered again that he needed to get on the road if he intended to get any sleep before fishing.

Sitti stopped walking just before the entrance of the rectory.

"They are here."

She continued, "When my husband built this church, he built a secret room behind one of the basement walls to help those immigrants who had a difficult time with the government in this country. Now, only the priests and myself know about the room."

Sitti nodded her head to a young robed priest, who unbeknownst to Peter, had been in the shadows of the arched walkway which ran alongside the church and rectory. The priest disappeared, and a second later, another young priest appeared carrying a white cardboard banker's box, then set the box down underneath the archway. The first priest reappeared a minute later carrying a second banker's box. The first priest set the second box on the top of the first.

"Do you require anything else, Sitti?" the first priest inquired.

Sitti held her right hand over her heart and replied to the young priest, " I am fine, *hamdillah*," then turning to Peter, "I entrust these to you young man. I cannot understand what they contain, but I do know a very powerful man, a very evil man, is willing to kill for them."

For a moment Peter began to believe that he might have been underestimating this whole Simon/St. Armand case, then his train of thought was interrupted by familiar voices.

"Uncle Peter, Uncle Peter," his two nieces grabbed his legs and hugged him.

"Are their any snowbirds in this garden?" asked Catherine as she looked up at her uncle with a Cheshire grin. Every year John and Jenny reminded their girls that snowbirds were watching them for Santa and would report if they had been good or bad.

"Pete, there you are," stated John Farrell and he walked toward his brother.

Confused, Lillian Simon began shaking her head and threw a concerned look at Peter.

Sensing Lillian's concerns Peter quickly interjected, "Lillian Simon, this is my brother John Farrell, and his girls, Catherine and Maggie."

John extended his hand toward Sitti, but she merely nodded at him. The two girls chased one another in the garden.

Peter added, "John came to help me with the documents. I trust him."

Sitti walked away from the brothers toward the parking lot.

"Help me with these," Peter asked his brother as he grabbed the top banker's box full of documents.

"Ooh, she's a treat," whispered John Farrell as he picked up the second box.

"She is something," added Peter. "I just haven't figured out what."

"Dad, where are you and Uncle Peter going?" Catherine asked.

"Yeah Dad, where are you and Uncle Peter going?" Maggie chimed in after her older sister.

"We have to take these out to the cars, come on, but stay on the sidewalk."

The two brothers caught up to Sitti who waited for them at the edge of the parking lot. Sitti stared at Peter with a noticeable concern on her face.

"Do not worry, Sitti, I will take care of everything," the young attorney reassured the revered woman.

"You are in my prayers," Sitti replied.

The elderly woman turned, and then walked back to the church. As Peter's eyes were fixed on her, Lillian "Sitti" Simon entered the church of St. Maron without ever looking back at the Farrell boys.

"Hey, Pete, don't you want to put both boxes in here?" John asked as he held open the hatch door of his hunter-green sports utility vehicle. Catherine and Maggie climbed into their booster seats.

"No," replied Peter as he finally took his eyes off the ivory arched entrance of the church, "I think I will take one with me."

Peter tried to stuff the box in the trunk of his father's Monte Carlo with his camping equipment.

"That car," John remarked while shaking his head.

Abruptly changing his tone, John continued, "Bob Stanmore asked about you this morning."

"Why would your managing partner ask about me?"

"Yeah, I know. I thought he was going to congratulate me for being in the office for the twentieth consecutive Saturday."

"That's not a record John," interjected the younger brother.

"All he wanted to talk about was you and your firm."

"Rosendahl, Golde, Stanmore, Smith and Tweed, I don't like it, too crowded. I think we would have to drop Stanmore and Smith."

"Are you guys gunning for more headlines?"

"I can't think of anything," admitted Peter as he finally repositioned his camping equipment so that he could fit the box of documents in his trunk. Peter slammed the trunk shut.

"Dad, hurry up, you promised we could go to the park," ordered Catherine.

"Yeah Dad, we have to go to the park," Maggie repeated.

"Are those snowbirds over there?" John shouted.

The girls quieted down.

"Well, I am out of here. Give my love to Jenny," Peter continued in a whisper, "and what's the deal about the snowbirds, it's still October?"

Peter waved at Catherine and Maggie. The girls frantically waved, one harder than the other.

"Just wait until you have kids," John yelled to his younger brother as he began to drive off.

"*Inshallah,*" Peter said to himself. "If God wills."

# FIVE

Peter never measured his fishing excursions by the amount of fish that he caught or by the big one that got away. In fact, catching fish was secondary to catching some peace of mind. His father had instilled in his two sons an unyielding work ethic. On the other hand, Peter's mother always made her youngest take time for himself outside. She always said that in order to go forward sometimes you first had to take a step back. Instead of getting caught up in everything, take a walk, clear your head, then move forward. The practice started with long walks the two would take when Peter was only a child. The bonding faded a little during his girl-crazed teenage years, but the memorable walks resumed in college. Sadly, the last moments Peter spent with his mother included the short walk they took together the morning before she lost her short, but volatile, bout with cancer.

Adhering to his mother's advice, the Simon files stayed in the trunk. On the drive down he decided not to even think about work. Although he thoroughly enjoyed his twenty-four hours of peace of mind, Peter was glad to be almost home. It was time to move forward. This was going to be a busy week. Not only did he have the Simon files to review, but he also had depositions scheduled all Wednesday, Thursday, and Friday.

As Peter pulled into the garage, he remembered that he had left a bowl of candy by the door for late night trick-or-treaters. Hopefully, last year's corn nuts episode did not sour the kids, or worse, incite them to toilet paper the house. This year no mistakes: chocolate, chocolate, and chocolate. Peter figured that even if he had a lot of leftovers he would simply give them to the two Anderson kids that lived below in his duplex. Their parents would not mind.

Instead of using the back stairs, Peter walked out of the garage around to the front of the house to check out this year's fashion in Halloween costumes. However, it was nearly eight-thirty and not many kids were out. He saw a large group two houses down, and that was all. As Peter walked up the half winding stairs to his flat, he noticed that his door was ajar. At the landing, Peter laid his hand against the door and slowly opened it to enter the room cautiously. A hundred different reasons swirled through his head as to why the door would be open. At worst, he thought, as he was halfway into his living room, if he had been burglarized, it must have happened late last night and the perpetrator was long gone. After all, there had to be some purpose for his renter's insurance.

The hardwood floor across the room creaked.

Only seconds after hearing the creak from across room, a large body knocked Peter over. Although the sound from across the room enabled Peter to prepare himself slightly for the blow by rolling with the intruder into the bookcase by the door, the intruder still had overtaken Peter. The intruder delivered two sharp blows to Peter's kidneys, rendering him into a quasi-paralyzed fetal position. Peter felt his bronze-plated chameleon fall from the bookcase. He grabbed it and jabbed the statuette up the chin and across the side of the intruder's face. The blow forced him off Peter. Stunned, the intruder began to stand, regaining his composure. Peter lunged, hurling his entire body weight into the intruder. The move knocked both men out the door, sending the two twisted bodies tumbling down the stairs. Fazed, but not incapacitated, Peter felt the intruder grab his arm and neck from behind while beginning to apply pressure with the other arm. Reacting again without thinking, Peter propped his legs up against the wall, using them as a springboard to fling the two through the screen door onto the front walkway.

Shrieks from about a dozen eight- to ten-year-olds surrounded Peter. The vice grip that was placed on Peter's arm and neck quickly released. He rolled over to catch a glimpse of a six-foot-four blond man dressed in navy from head to toe streak through the still screaming kids in the driveway.

"Come along kids," ordered the one mother in the group as she began to corral the kids to cross the street. The mother looked back at Peter with disdain as he tried to stand on his own two feet and snapped, "as if there's not enough violence on television."

As Peter attempted to make his way back inside, he could hear the little girl dressed as a Native American Indian Princess say to her mother, "Mommy, why was the policeman beating that man up?"

"They were just playing," responded the perturbed mother.

Still stunned, Peter looked back for a second. The little girl was right. It did look like a police uniform. What the hell was he doing? Peter wondered as he opened the broken screen door and gingerly climbed his way back up the stairs. Why would someone go to all the trouble to dress up as a policeman just to rob his rinky-dink apartment?

When Peter entered his apartment for the second time, he immediately flipped the light switch. The apartment was in shambles, more than usual. The couch was pulled away from the wall. Everything that had been in the closet now lay on the floor. All files previously in the desk were strewn about the entire apartment. The books had been tossed from the shelves.

Peter cleared off the coffee table and found his phone. There were messages on his voice mail. Before calling the police, Peter dialed in for the messages and punched in his code.

"You have three new messages," chimed the voice mail.

Peter entered the number one to hear the first message.

"Pete, John. The girls got into your box and pulled some things out. It's my fault, but the snowbirds have been alerted, too. All they did is open it and pull one file out. I'm putting everything back now. I don't mean to be nosy, but the names on the files look like a virtual who's who of D.C. Give a call, you have to tell me what you are working on."

"If you would like to save this message, press seven. If you would like to erase this message, press nine."

Peter pressed the number nine.

"Next message."

It was John's voice again, "Pete, me again. This is so wrong, but I'm calling on your files again. I had to because one of the names was someone we both know. This is serious. This stuff that I have come across in these files is unbelievable. I also went over your head and left a message with Joe Rosendahl.

Call me once you get this message."

"If you would like to save this message, press seven. If you would like..."

Peter pressed the number nine again.

"Peter, it's Joe. I am here with your brother. He brought the Simon materials. I have had a chance to review some of the files. There are some disturbing items in here about some individuals which I cannot discuss over the telephone, much less leave a message. It is five-fifteen; John expects that you will be home soon. Listen carefully; you cannot contact anyone, especially the authorities. Trust no one. Just come into the office immediately and bring those Rose Simon documents."

"If you would like to save this message, press seven. If..."

Peter hung up the phone, and speed dialed his office. There was no answer. Peter paced back and forth across the room twice before dashing down the back stairs to the car.

# SIX

In a dimly lit corner of the cobblestone parking lot on the riverfront, a black sports utility vehicle pulled up next to a second black sports utility vehicle so that each driver's door was adjacent to the other. The window of the second vehicle was already rolled down, revealing a figure with long dark hair. The first car's window rolled down exposing the tall blond man in a police uniform.

"Put the box in the back then follow me," a woman's voice ordered from the second sports utility vehicle. The accent was Slavic, it was Tasha.

The blond stared at the woman. He wiped some blood from his chin.

"Andriy now!" Tasha ordered again.

The blond never even blinked.

"Fool! You did not obtain the documents? They will not tolerate failure. Call the number in two hours."

After berating the blond, Tasha Dolnick sped off.

Andriy stared out at the brightly shining Arch towering over the riverfront, touched the dried blood on his neck, and mumbled, "When the time comes for the seventh angel to blow his trumpet, the mysterious plan of God, which he announced to his servants the prophets, shall be accompanied in full."

Racing down Highway 40, Peter forced himself to remember not to miss his exit by placing a Post-It note on the rear view mirror. Mostly Post-Its were part of a mental exercise for Peter Farrell. Even if they contained no messages, the mere fact that it was there triggered his associative memory. In a glimpse of rational thinking, Peter decided not to take Forest Park Parkway downtown. Chances are that with all the adrenaline rushing through his veins, he would be speeding or even run a light. With his luck, tonight would be the night he would be pulled over. And the last thing Peter wanted to encounter was another police officer. Consequently, no taking the parkway to downtown, either. It would be all highway. However the last time he took the highway downtown, he was not paying attention and almost ended up in East St. Louis. Forcing himself to remember the exit was not merely a mental exercise, it was a necessity tonight. He needed all the help he could get to concentrate.

Peter's head was swirling with questions. He was oblivious to the local public radio reports spewing from the Monte Carlo's AM radio. How come no one answered the phone at the office? Is that what they meant by contact no one? And the authorities, Joe had never made a comment like that even when the firm pursued a police brutality case. Was that a real policeman and why didn't he identify himself? None of this made any sense.

> *"In a bizarre shooting incident earlier this evening, two men were killed in a downtown office building...*

Peter turned the radio up.

> *"Authorities determined that at about six this evening, two attorneys were shot to death on the fiftieth floor of the International Tower. Although some hi-tech computer equipment was stolen, authorities are puzzled by such a violent act in the downtown financial and legal district. The International Tower houses over twenty different law firms and over four hundred attorneys. The two slain attorneys have been identified as Joseph Rosendahl and John Farrell."*

Peter took the Post-It off the rear view mirror and headed past the Gateway Arch toward East St. Louis.

⟶•◦•⟵

Across the street from the International Tower stands the newly constructed twenty-floor office tower named for, and housing, the law firm Stanmore, Smith & Tweed. The offices offered an excellent view of the chaos that occurred earlier that evening. Two individuals had watched the events unfold. First, there was one squad car. A few minutes later, two more patrol cars arrived. Within thirty minutes of the first car, no fewer than fifteen police cars surrounded the building. In addition to the police cars, there were two paramedic trucks, a fire engine, and a swat team van.

The swat team left within an hour of the first officer on the scene. Surveillance tapes revealed that only one individual entered and exited during the time of the shooting. The first paramedic team left soon after the swat team. These paramedics exited the building with two body bags. The second set of paramedics and the firemen waited at the scene until officers searched all other floors that had been accessed that afternoon. Within four hours of the initial officer's arrival, almost everyone had left the scene.

"Is it all quiet down there?" asked the middle-aged attorney as he set down the telephone by his desk.

"Just two cars down there now, Bob," the older gentleman responded as he peered out the office suite's window. "They will likely be there until morning."

"Stuart said that he will be making his press conference first thing in the morning," Bob Stanmore added.

"Good," the older gentleman responded.

"The media leak went out a little earlier than expected, but I do not see it as an issue."

"Neither do I."

"It is my understanding that he is already on the run," the attorney began. "Does that concern you?"

"You just keep the money flowing to Stuart, let us handle the rest," the older gentleman answered.

"Then everything is taken care of," assured the attorney.

"Make sure that going east is not an option."

"He's ready if anything happens."

"The game is afoot," the older gentleman muttered as he stared at the two police cars parked outside the International Tower.

# SEVEN

*John, how could this happen?*
*You had the perfect life. Perfect wife. Perfect daughters.*
*This cannot be happening. Jenny, Catherine and Maggie. John, why you?*
*Why not me?*

"If you would like to make a call, please hang up and try again," the automated voice instructed Peter.

He rubbed the tears from his eyes as he held the phone with his other hand. He had to get control of himself.

Peter hung up the phone and reflected on the past ten hours. He wished he could call Jenny, but resisted the urge. He had learned so much since doubling back and driving by the police-quarantined office building where his brother and mentor were slain. Joe's cryptic message, coupled with the attack by the police officer at his apartment and the two patrol cars stationed at the scene, rendered stopping at his office not an option. Furthermore, since the police had been at his apartment, he could not go back there. Peter needed a safe place to stay and sort out his thoughts. After driving around for an hour, he drove back across the bridge and into East St. Louis.

Peter had not seen Henry Knops since last May when he had participated in a free legal clinic that Henry organized on the East Side for "Law Day." Although surprised to see him, Henry welcomed Peter into his home without asking any questions. Peter spent the entire night rummaging through the box of documents Lillian Simon had given him.

At first, he did not understand them. The papers were obviously copies of files. All of the files began with "S," so it appeared that the copies Peter had were part of a much larger filing system. The "S" files mostly contained named files of either people or places. These pages were usually followed by ledger sheets and banking statements. However the bank statements had coded accounts which were transfers from other accounts, and even further transfers from more accounts.

After paging through an inch or two of files, Peter stumbled onto a section that surprised, then sickened him. The first page was the typical photocopy of the outside cover of the file folder. The name on the file folder was the first one Peter recognized. Peter recognized the name because he had read it in the paper on Friday. The name read "Speeter, Jeffrey Jay." Age, fifty. Caucasian. Five-foot seven, one hundred fifty pounds. Right-handed. Alcoholic. Recently divorced because of his infidelities. The next few pages resembled a resumé or curriculum vitae, but more thorough. The fifty-year-old former Air Force pilot rose through the ranks of party politics as a lobbyist and campaign fundraiser before plucking the plumb assignment of Deputy Chief of Staff for Vice President George Algers. Shortly thereafter, he was appointed to the Federal Election Committee. The pages in the file outlined his career from college through last year's congressional hearings on campaign finance reform. In addition to his career, the file outlined his personal and family life with detailed particularity. His routines and favorite restaurants were noted, as was his ex-wife's schedule. Not only were his three daughters identified, but their ages and descriptions were detailed right down to a colorful butterfly tattoo on a less than conspicuous body part. Even their favorite after-school hangouts and class schedules were listed.

The standard bank statements followed the biographical information. The next sections, or Speeter sub-files, Peter had to review twice. There were three sub-files with the same file names but numbered differently:

Speeter: FEC: In the Matter of Fairchild for President Committee and Michael V. Coy as Treasurer: MUR #3309.

Speeter: FEC: In the Matter of Fairchild for President Committee and Michael V. Coy as Treasurer: MUR #3665.

Speeter FEC: In the Matter of Fairchild for President Committee and Michael V. Coy as Treasurer: MUR #4673.

The first two files were stamped closed, the third was not. Each of the files appeared to contain the actual entire Federal Election Committee file including all correspondence, attorneys' notes, investigators' notes, and conciliation agreements. The third file did not contain a conciliation agreement. Even more surprising was the fact that each file contained numerous pages of transcripts of confidential telephone conversations between attorneys, attorneys and investigators, and attorneys and Michael V. Coy, President Fairchild's campaign treasurer.

What alarmed Peter was that, despite overwhelming evidence of campaign finance violations contained in the two closed files, the conciliation agreements called for pitifully small fines. No prosecutorial recommendations. No admonishments. Nothing.

In one of the closed files, several political action committees were identified as having contributed well over their statutory limit on contributions. The other closed file detailed that the Fairchild/Algers ticket vastly exceeded expenditure limits for the Iowa and New Hampshire primaries, yet still received federal matching funds. Once again, despite the clear violations of federal law, Fairchild/Alger's campaign merely received a slap on the wrist, a small fine.

The breach of public trust in both instances was clearly evident: however, complacency with the economy and Fairchild's popularity apparently dictated the FEC's irresponsible action. Backroom politics as usual, but still nothing to commit murder over.

The third file, the open file, shed some light on the past night's events. The file contained only a couple of documents, the beginnings of an investigation into campaign contributions by the Occidental Group to both political parties. The first document proposed an investigation by FEC investigator James Betts. This request for an investigation outlined a two-prong approach. The suggested investigation, according to Betts, should follow the Occidental Group's contributions and their relation to two corporate welfare programs: the Department of Agriculture's Promotional Market Program and the funding of ethanol subsidies.

According to Betts, the Occidental Group had contributed over twelve million dollars in the past three years to 527 groups representing both parties, with several large increments corresponding to renewals for the promotional market program. Betts also noted that even though the campaign contributions seemed extreme, the return on the Occidental Group's investment was staggering. Occidental received more than five hundred million dollars in subsidies over the past three years to promote their agricultural products overseas. Occidental's net of over half a billion dollars of taxpayers' money was worth the millions it spent to get those government officials elected.

The return on investment for the ethanol subsidies was equally unnerving. The Occidental Group had cornered ninety percent of the ethanol market. Consequently, the subsidy of ethanol essentially subsidized the Occidental Group. Betts estimated that this Occidental subsidy alone would cost taxpayers over four billion dollars over the next five years. Again, Occidental had received huge sums of taxpayers' monies.

According to the file, Betts believed he had found a direct correlation between the Occidental contributions through 527 groups and other loopholes and the ethanol subsidy.

Betts believed this relationship could be established in the most recent congressional debate over the subsidy. One month prior to the legislative debate on ethanol, Occidental donated over two million dollars to various key representatives and senators. Despite these extravagant contributions, Senator Milton Stanton of Ohio led a group in opposition to the subsidy. Stanton had support of EPA officials who were willing to testify at the senate hearings that ethanol might actually cause more pollution and be more expensive than any additive derived from natural gas. However, the day before the Senate hearing on the ethanol subsidy, Stanton did a complete about face. At a press conference, the once starch opponent of ethanol stated that after careful thought and "in the interest of all Americans," he would no longer oppose the subsidy. Both the Department of Agriculture's Promotional Market Program and the ethanol subsidy passed by one vote; Vice President George Algers cast the deciding vote once again "in the interest of all Americans." A skeptical Betts believed it was in the interest of the additional one million dollars Stanton's party, the administration's party, received the day before the press conference. Betts noted that he was in the process of securing the testimony of one of Stanton's staff to testify on the "quid pro quo" campaign-money-for-votes scheme. There was another notation that another "official" would be able to get him a memo evidencing that the Occidental money was in fact for the Stanton vote.

The only other document in the file was a memorandum by the FEC General Counsel to Betts that this file was being turned over to the Senate Campaign Finance Committee. Curiously enough, Speeter was copied on the letter. Speeter must have been the "official" Betts was trying to turn against Occidental.

Peter paged through the documents and found a copy of the file labeled "Stanton, Milton F." The bank records in Stanton's file began that same February of the press conference. From this file, it appeared that Betts had only scratched the surface. The Occidental Group had paid Stanton's political party to keep the ethanol subsidy and bribed Stanton as well. From the little Peter knew of the Ohio senator, he just did not seem like a politician for sale. In flipping through the other pages in the Stanton file, Peter confirmed his suspicions. The Stanton file also contained surveillance photos of the sixty-year-old conservative senator in compromising positions with two young male prostitutes. Not exactly the type of photographs that one would bring to the next "family values" luncheon.

Peter did not recognize many of the names or companies in the files. These files basically contained some biographical information, banking statements, ledger sheets, and additional illicit photographs. However, it appeared that various news agencies and newspapers were receiving Occidental money.

The file on Robert Stanmore of St. Louis' own Stanmore, Smith & Tweed, John's law firm, startled Peter. He had met Stanmore on two separate occasions, neither of which were memorable. Stanmore basically was a glorified bookkeeper and as bland as they come. Yet Stanmore had been accepting Occidental money for over twenty years. At the same time, he had been instrumental in campaign financing and promoting Occidental's interests in the Midwest. Stanmore evidently siphoned Occidental money to political parties and political action committees at the state and federal levels. Peter thought to himself that it was no wonder why Bob Stanmore was grilling John about Peter and any new cases he had. Little did John know that Stanmore was neck deep in Occidental and worried about covering his ass. The last page of the file stated that Stanmore reported to someone in St. Louis, but did not name the contact.

Peter recognized Representative John A. Stevens III from Pennsylvania. The conservative congressman had been labeled as the leader of the new breed in Congress in the last conservative sweep of the House of Representatives. The Ivy Leaguer and think-tank pundit had been hand picked for the congressional seat by the retiring, and well respected, Benjamin Harrison. According to Occidental's files, Stevens' campaign received a lot of help from Occidental. On an election campaign that should have been a lock, the Stevens' campaign spent inordinate sums of money to squash an environmentalist, who campaigned across the state in a green bus. Not only were Stevens' campaign coffers and think-tank foundation littered with Occidental money, but his personal account did not suffer either. Stevens' Cayman Island account had received in excess of seven hundred thousand dollars in the past three years. Peter tried to remember whether bribery was listed above or below campaign finance reform in Stevens' Compact with America.

There was a file on Wendell Stevenson, a liberal Wisconsin congressman. Papers showed that Stevenson, and most of his fellow Wisconsin delegation, supported three Indian tribes who wanted to open a new casino in southwestern Wisconsin. Based on their support, the local Office for the Interior Department's Bureau of Indian Affairs approved the application pending final approval by Washington. While the application was pending in Washington, Stevenson flip-flopped his position and convinced a majority of the congressional delegation to oppose the application. Shortly thereafter, the Interior Department denied the application. Peter remembered that the Sunday morning pundits speculated that the sudden switch by Stevenson was due to his discovering that the White House was going to deny the application, therefore Stevenson did not want to appear to come out on the losing side of an issue. The Occidental papers, on the other hand, showed that Stevenson's reelection campaign funds tripled shortly before he flip-flopped on the issue.

Another file contained information on Susan Stone, the California conservative congresswoman. As with Stevens, Stone was another one of the new breed of Congress promising respect with reform. Also, as with the Stevens' file, the Stone file contained similar information on Occidental money distributed into Stone's personal and campaign fund accounts.

The only other file Peter recognized shocked him more than the others because of the obvious implications on his current situation. The Occidental Group had a file on Police Chief Jesse Stuart. Stuart had been on Occidental's payroll for over thirty years. Obviously, Joe Rosendahl and his brother's warning about "the authorities" established that they also knew about Stuart or other police officers who may be corrupt.

Peter's first instinct was to call Aaron Golde, but Aaron was not at home and Peter had no intentions of leaving a message. Peter then called Dean Adams. He had kept in touch with Dean Adams even after the dean left Loyola of St. Louis to become dean of the prestigious Marshall School of Law at the International University in the Georgetown district of our nation's capital. The conversation was short, productive, and comforting. Dean Adams carefully listened to Peter without interruption. Peter's fast-paced recitation of the events from the past couple of hours betrayed his frayed nerves. But for the individuals involved and the bonds between them, Peter would have been told to sleep off whatever he had been drinking or see a professional about his paranoia. Instead Dean Adams instructed Peter to do two things. First, copy the file again and mail it to Aaron Golde by registered mail at his home address. Second, catch the first plane out of St. Louis to D.C. so that Dean Adams could protect him. The dean unassumingly admitted that he had plenty of contacts in Washington that he trusted. After Dean Adams got off the phone with Peter, he would reach out to those contacts. In the meantime, Peter should arrange to fly to the east coast as soon as possible.

Again Peter thought about calling Jenny, but instead phoned Aaron Golde. No answer. Next were the airlines. There was a flight leaving St. Louis for D.C. in six hours; he booked the flight and paid with his credit card. The ticket would be e-mailed to him. He just needed to pull the boarding pass off the Web. In the meantime, he was exhausted, and there was nothing he could do until his flight. He had to get some rest. It was four a.m. Peter told Henry to make sure Peter was awake by seven, that would give him three hours to sleep, if he could sleep. His mind was racing and sleep felt unlikely. At least this craziness would be over by mid-afternoon. By three o'clock, he would be safe in D.C. where he would hand the files to Dean Adams and his D.C. connections to decipher. Then he could call Jenny.

# EIGHT

Dean Roger Cosgrove Adams had lived in Alexandria, Virginia for the past three years. His one-hour commute to the university each day was far from burdensome. As a matter of fact, Dean Adams cherished this transition time between home and the office. Most of the time he listened to audio novels, but lately he had been listening to a self-learning Italian language tape. He and his wife had been planning a twentieth anniversary vacation to Florence, Venice, and Rome this December. He also planned to surprise his wife of twenty years by speaking Italian on the trip. However, this morning there would be no bella language. Dean Adams inserted his London Philharmonic CD in the CD player.

He began every Monday morning commute by washing his car at the "No Brush Car Wush" half a mile from his palatial six-bedroom Victorian house. While Dean Adams sat in his car during the "car wush," he would jot down on a legal pad a weekly to-do list. Every week he started with a clean car and a new list.

At the Car Wush, Dean Adams would review a list he had started earlier that morning. The first item was Peter Farrell. Peter would contact him again by mid-morning. Second was Aaron Golde, who he had not been able to reach. He left a message that Peter had contacted him and further that Peter was on his way to D.C. Aaron would call him as soon as he received the message. The third, fourth, and fifth items were names of individuals he knew and trusted. However, despite this trust, and according to Peter, Dean Adams knew he had to be careful in contacting these individuals. Each of the three individuals was an actual decision maker in this town, not merely wannabes. In addition, each of them had the power to accomplish the two goals he sought: protect Peter; and second, expose the individuals involved with the Occidental Group's influence over government officials. Although he trusted the three individuals listed, Peter was right, he could not be absolutely certain that these individuals were beyond Occidental's reach.

Joe Rosendahl and Peter's brother had already been murdered. The next move must be carefully calculated.

Prior to his legal career, Roger Adams had had a promising math career streamlined by graduating top of his class at MIT. Many peers considered his move into jurisprudence less prudent, yet he never had any regrets. His background in math proved very useful in the logic-based world of law. It also proved effective this morning.

For Dean Adams a math problem consisted of relationships between variables that produced a finite group of answers. If the answer did not fit into the finite group, then one of the variables in the equation was in err. He approached the listed individuals in the same manner. Each of the individuals listed was familiar with some of the events Peter described in the files. With a series of questions, he tested his relationship, and then he would add a new variable into the equation. He offered up information about the Occidental Group. Depending on the person's reaction, he knew whether they could be trusted, or whether further variables or inquiries were required.

Dean Adams reviewed the list again. His conversations with each individual were short, but revealing. He also revised the notes from the telephone calls as he recalled the conversations verbatim.

Andrew L. Hodges was the first of the three names. Roger knew Andy from law school. While Roger veered into academia, the Justice Department drafted Andy. He worked for "justice" for twenty years before a high-powered D.C. firm snatched him up. Although Andrew Hodges was well connected with the D.C. elite, Roger Adams thought he could be particularly helpful because he acted as the special prosecutor four years ago which led to the resignation of one White House official and jail time for two of the official's aides.

"Andy, Roger here."

"Roger, you're lucky I am an early riser. What could you possibly need at 6:00 a.m.?"

"Sorry old man, but this couldn't wait until office hours."

"For you my dear friend, my office is open twenty-four hours a day."

"You are too kind. I need some advice."

"Go ahead."

"Do you remember that Indian gaming case from Wisconsin a couple of years ago?"

"Yes, of course."

"Were you aware of any talk about any illegal influence by the tribes themselves to sway the Interior Department?"

"Actually, there were some discussions around Justice to appoint a special prosecutor to investigate campaign funds donated by the tribes to legislators and even the current administration."

"What happened with the investigation?"

"Never occurred."

"Why?"

"From what I heard, Justice dropped the matter after all the legislators that the tribes had allegedly tried to influence began to oppose the application and then the Interior Department denied the application. It became a non-issue. May I ask how an aborted investigation affects academia the likes of you?"

"Well, Andy, I have been approached by some individuals that suggest brokering influence on such levels is not only possible, but occurring on a grand scale."

The former special prosecutor dispensed with the niceties, "What individuals?"

"You can understand that I cannot name names, but I can use the word 'occidental.'"

There was a long pause before the former special prosecutor spoke again. "Roger how deep are you involved? That's a bad question. Can you offer anything for immunity?"

"Andy, it has not gone that far, I am merely collecting information."

"In a town like this, that is some very dangerous information you are trying to collect. I am still wondering why you, Roger?"

"I honestly do not know."

"I just thought of something. If what you say is true, this is not something we should be discussing over live wires. Where are you calling from?"

"My home."

"Can you meet me at, let's see, at Dixie's for breakfast in two hours?"

"I'll be there."

The next call was to Kathleen Martin, Associate Justice on the United States Supreme Court. Kate Martin was a longtime friend and so was her late husband, the Wall Street wizard Samuel L. Martin.

"Hello?"

"Hello Kate, it's Roger Adams."

"Roger, do you know what time it is?"

"I'm sorry Kate, but I had to speak to you first thing this morning."

"I think it is a little before the first thing, Roger."

"Sorry, Kate." Roger was used to Kate Martin's thorniness. On oral argument, attorneys feared "Cranky Kate" more than any other justice on the bench.

"I need some advice."

"Doesn't that university of yours have any knowledgeable legal minds?"

"None that match yours, your Honor."

"Flattery will get you nowhere. Now that I'm up what can I do for you?"

"Do you remember that EPA case concerning the ethanol mandate?"

"Of course I do. You know I was still on the Court of Appeals when that case was heard."

"Were you on the panel that heard the case?"

"Originally I was, but when I was nominated I recused myself from the case."

"Why?"

"It is none of your damn business Roger, but it was a highly political issue and it seemed inappropriate to many that a recent presidential nominee to the United States Supreme Court sit on the bench to pass judgment on a presidential mandate."

"Why was the mandate to use ethanol stricken?"

"Roger, doesn't that fancy law school of yours carry *Federal Reporters*? My colleagues concluded under the Chevron doctrine, that the EPA lacked authority to promulgate regulations that mandated the use of ethanol additives in gasoline."

"How would you have ruled?"

"I do not respond to hypotheticals, unless I'm proffering the hypo. I will say that I do not disagree with my former colleagues' logic. What is it with all these questions at this ungodly hour?"

"Kate, I have been approached by some individuals that suggest they would be able to influence the Court's decision in this EPA issue or if another similar one arises."

"I am assuming you are not just talking about oral argument."

"No."

"Roger, you are a dear friend and were a dear friend to Sam, but frankly I do not know what you are suggesting. I know the men and women on this bench. Although some of them may act as if they were the ones who drafted the Constitution, especially that damn Franz, none of them would do what you are suggesting, or what I believe you're suggesting. Who would make such a suggestion and why to you?"

"Your Honor, you know I cannot reveal a name..."

"You have an ethical obligation to the Court!" interrupted the Supreme Court Justice.

"And I would report, but I have no specifics. I have merely been approached that such influence may exist, and I assume because of our relationship I was expected to call you."

"Roger, we must talk later today. Meet me at the Biltmore at noon."

"Thank you, Kate."

The third name on Roger Adam's short list was actually a substitution of who would have been the first name on the list. The name not on the list was that of Roland Miller, counselor to the presidents. For the past forty years, Roland Miller had been Washington D.C.'s consummate power broker. Miller advised and represented D.C.'s finest through their good times, but mostly their bad. It had been said that Roland not only knew where all the bodies were buried, but he knew who had the shovels. In his forty years of public and private service, he had either been a confidant to the president or at the very least, consulted on key issues of state. At eighty-five, whispers around the capital began to spread that Roland Miller had slowed down to the point where he could be considered a figurehead. Roger knew better than that. Roland Miller was not only the most celebrated of Loyola of St. Louis alumni, but he had become one of Roger's closest friends. And when Roger relocated out East, Roland introduced his friend to the city. In fact, for the past several years, Roger and Roland lunched together every other week at the Metropolitan. It was the only lunch either of these two busy attorneys ever welcomed.

At last week's lunch, Roland told Roger that a new Middle Eastern client was meeting him in Paris this week. Roger thought to himself that maybe Roland would slow down in his eighties. With Roland in Paris, Roger turned to Roland's protégé, John Kerr. Despite the contrast in their pedigrees, Roland's blue-collar Midwest versus Kerr's Ivy League silver-spoon upbringing, Roland saw in Kerr the same determination and drive that Roland Miller possessed. Although most of the other attorneys at Miller & White were Kerr's senior, Roland Miller ordained Kerr as his protégé and relied on the forty-year-old attorney on all the top cases. In Roland's absence, Roger Adams would now rely on the young protégé.

"Good morning John, Roger Adams here."

"Roger, good to hear from you. What can I do for you?"

"I hope it's not too early for you, John."

"You know me, Roger, never enough hours in a day."

"I know Roland is in Paris, but you know how to contact him."

"Actually, Roger, Roland is on his way to the Middle East. I received a voice mail from him late last night. He told me that he would be "incommunicado" for the next couple of days, but that he would call Wednesday a.m. our time. Is there anything I can help you with?"

"I'm glad you asked, John. I need some advice." Knowing the answer to his next question, Dean Adams continued, "You helped Roland out on that Senate investigation of Speeter last year, is that correct?"

"Both Roland and I worked on that matter."

"If I remember correctly, the Senate cleared Speeter of any wrongdoing, but he had to resign to save face for the President."

"Those are your words Roger, not mine."

"John, with Speeter the battle was over before it began, isn't that correct."

"If what you mean is that the Senate dropped its inquiry early in the proceedings, you're correct."

"In fact, the Senate's committee dropped its investigation within days of Speeter's prepared opening statement."

"Yes."

"Why?"

"Well, our strategy was to turn the tables on the committee members themselves. We wanted to get the trial directed at the committee members and away from Speeter. With a voracious media, we succeeded."

"It must have been more than that."

"Not really, the evidence on Speeter was thin, and we believed several of the committee members merely wanted to grandstand on campaign finance reform since it was a hot issue. We turned the tables on the committee members and informed them that if they wanted to discuss campaign financing, it was going to be discussed about everyone, not just Speeter. With a couple of members up for reelection this year, I guess careful scrutiny into their own re-election monies was more than the senators bargained for."

"There must have been more."

"You know better than to ask such a question, Roger."

"Not to be cold-hearted," he baited, "but your client is not in any position to assert privilege."

"Yes, but his estate still survives. Your questions are starting to cross the line Roger. I think you better get to the point."

"I'm sorry to be so intrusive, John, but you are in a unique position to help me. I have been approached by some individuals who suggested that they were able to intercede on Speeter's behalf with the Senate committee." Dean Adams paused to allow Kerr to interrupt. Kerr said nothing so Dean Adams continued.

"Furthermore, these individuals have suggested that they would be able to exert such influence again should the need arise."

"Sounds a little like a movie, Roger."

The pace of John Kerr's conversation increased as he continued, "What is the source of your information? Is it credible? As far as our defense of Speeter is concerned, I am not aware of any outside influence. Roland was the primary on the case, but you know Roland as well as I do. If your information is credible, and Roland had any idea that such outside influence was participating in his case, he would surely expose it. Roland is untouchable, and frankly Roger, I hope you are not suggesting anything else by your inquiries. What other information do you have?"

"That is basically all of the information I have at this time. It was brought to my attention in the most nonchalant manner."

"Well, I suggest we treat it as such until Roland contacts us Wednesday. Does that sound prudent?"

"Excellent. If Roland calls early, be sure to have him contact me."

"I certainly will, Roger. Keep me informed."

As Dean Roger Adams reflected on the three telephone calls, he began to scribble notations on his list. Then he circled the third name on the list. John Kerr. There was much to do before he met Andy Hodges for breakfast.

# NINE

"Peter, Peter, get up," Henry told a comatose Peter Farrell as he shook his shoulder. "Peter, now!"

"John!" Peter cried out, as he quickly sat up, startled and confused.

"Peter, it's me Henry, you have to get up."

"What time is it?" Peter inquired as he rubbed his eyes and realized it was still dark outside.

"It's six-thirty, but you have to get out of here," instructed the large Henry Knops as he delicately propped Peter in an upright position as if he were a rag doll. "Last night I put us on the watch list, and my beeper just went off, so we probably don't have much time."

"What are you talking about Henry?" Peter asked while still trying to gain full use of his faculties.

"There are only three ways in and out of our tight group of neighborhoods. The four or so dealers have set up "watchers" at those checkpoints. The watcher pages the dealers with messages on their pagers if any trouble is entering the 'hood. When you arrived I pulled in some favors and got us hooked up. Two squad cars just entered from the west, and I figure there is a one out of five chance that they are after you."

"What?"

"I have arranged for a ride for you to the airport. My nephew should be here any minute. You can trust him. He reminds me of you, he wants to be a lawyer."

The back door opened.

"Unc' Hank, yo' driver is here," heralded a voice that entered through the back door.

"Take this too," Henry handed Peter a wad of bills, "you may need some walking money."

"Henry, I don't know what to say?"

"A silver-tongue lawyer like you at a loss for words. Damn, I better check outside to see if this hell froze over."

Henry's nephew entered, he could not have been older than eighteen.

"Peter, this is Jimmy Powell, he will take care of you."

Henry turned and sternly looked at his young nephew, "Jimmy, I am counting on you. The both of you get out of here now." Henry handed Peter his duffel bag and pointed them toward the back door.

"I don't know how to thank you."

"You did that a long time ago, but you must go now," Henry pleaded as he acknowledged Peter.

"Let's go!" Jimmy said, and Peter Farrell followed him out the back door leaving Henry to face whatever unwelcome visitors this early morning would bring.

# TEN

All was quiet this early Monday morning at the "No Brush Car Wush." For the past couple of autumns, since the new football team moved to town, it was always quiet early on Mondays. The only sound was the jet streams of water pulsating against the silver Mercedes. As the jet streams completed their task and a light hot wax was applied, the faint sound of a philharmonic orchestra could be heard from the car wash bay area. When the mechanical arm applying the hot wax ended its rotation, only the sounds of the philharmonic and dripping water remained. The lively symphony emanated from the newly "wushed" silver Mercedes, with blaring horns and sharp, rapid percussion. The driver's side window had been shattered. The water jets had pushed the glass to the edges of the wash bay. Water and glass glistened on the car's dark leather interior. His body slumped over the armrest and sprawled into the passenger side, Dean Roger Cosgrove Adams lay lifeless with two bullet entry wounds in his neck and temple. Behind the counter, with a bullet hole and a stream of blood flowing from his forehead, the clerk had met a similar fate.

A thousand miles away, the police assault on the house of Henry Knops bore little resemblance to any police raid the neighborhood had seen in forty years. It resembled massacres in L.A. or Philadelphia. A pair of officers entered the front and rear of the home by the same method. An assault rifle decimated the hinges and locks on both doors. Upon kicking the remaining splintered wood away, each rifle-toting officer entered the room and littered it with bullets. Each room of the house was searched in a similar manner. The entire onslaught was observed by a single elder and highly decorated officer seated in the back seat of one of the squad cars, Chief of Police Jesse Stuart.

Fearful of entering the home, neighbors avoided it. Henry Knops' body was not discovered until midmorning. His body had been mutilated by scores of bullets, yet his hands clutched a rosary. The day's crime report stated that Mr. Knops had been a victim of gang violence in retribution for his various anti-drug campaigns.

***

Although his morning began earlier than expected, Peter was glad to be on his way. His flight would not be leaving for several hours, which would give him plenty of time to run a couple of errands. First, primarily because Jimmy Powell insisted, Peter had to freshen up. Returning to his apartment was obviously out of the question, so the Gas Mart off of the highway had to do. In the Gas Mart bathroom, Peter discarded his jeans, shirt, and undershirt, which as Jimmy Powell noted over and over again, reeked from his fishing trip. Jimmy gave Peter the white oxford shirt and navy khakis he had in his car. After soaking his head under water and freshening up, Peter also put on the red baseball cap that Jimmy handed him.

As Peter walked out of the gas station bathroom, he glanced over at Jimmy with a smile and said, "Hey, I thought these pants were supposed to fall down to my knees."

"Uncle Hank said you were smart and a good man. Now, I know why he never described you as funny."

"Are you really pre-law?"

"I am pre-everything," answered Jimmy Powell. "I'm only in my first year at State, but the law is something that interests me."

"Why?" inquired Peter.

"Too many rich white lawyers, not enough black ones."

"It's all about money?"

"Hey, money can't hurt."

"Don't bet on that. Come on, we have another stop to make."

Next stop, a twenty-four-hour full copying service center for copying and retrieving the boarding pass from his e-mail. Per Dean Adams' instruction, he would mail the copies to Aaron Golde by registered mail. He paid for the Internet time, copies, and various other office supplies by credit card, saving Henry's cash for an emergency.

As Jimmy and Peter pulled up to the airport, there was a traffic jam leading all the way down the ramp for departures. As they approached the ever-slowing traffic, Jimmy remarked, "Looks like Homeland Security is holding everything up."

"Come again?" Peter's mind had drifted off again, thinking about his brother.

Jimmy pointed to the top of the ramp and explained, "The police set up a road block just at the top where all the sky caps are. All this can't be for you, they must have elevated a terror alert."

"You are probably right," Peter answered, hoping he was right.

"Well for the sake of argument let's say I'm not. Why don't we just make a little adjustment."

Jimmy glanced over his shoulder and exited the long line of cars, then crossed over four lanes and drove down the ramp for "Arrivals." The area was still bustling with traffic, but it was a lot less hectic than the bumper-to-bumper traffic departing directly above, and more importantly, absent of police. "Well, here you are, all safe and sound."

Peter opened the door, stepped out of the car, and looked back, "Thanks, Jimmy."

"Here take this," Jimmy handed him a business card, "in case my humble services are required again."

"E-mail?"

"It's the coffee shop on campus. I pick up messages online there, but who knows the difference. Good luck."

Even without the police barricade outside, the airport would still have been crowded for a Monday morning. The white-collars were starting a new week of making and breaking fortunes with their Wall Street papers tucked safely away under their arms. Meanwhile, the blue-collars were on their way home from a weekend of revelry. Peter mixed in well with the latter in his sunglasses, red baseball cap, white oxford shirt, navy khakis, and duffel bag slung over his shoulder. After a perfunctory examination of his driver's license and e-mail boarding pass, airport security let him follow two other young men rushing to catch their flight. As he entered the terminal, pangs of hunger dictated that some breakfast would be his top priority. Whether he was paranoid or just overly cautious, Peter decided to grab something at the airline club instead of sitting out in the open.

As Peter entered the Frequent Flier Ambassador Club, he flashed his member card quickly to the young woman behind the desk, then immediately detracted the focus of himself by asking the superfluous question of when the flight from Houston was arriving. The attendant typed on her keyboard and informed Peter that the flight would be arriving in thirty minutes. Peter thanked the young woman and made his way to the buffet where he helped himself to a couple of blueberry muffins, orange juice, and a soda. As he sat down to his power breakfast, the cable news program finished up the sports scores. For a moment, Peter felt like a normal traveler waiting for his flight. It lasted less than a minute.

*Good morning. This is Kurt Kenshaw with the morning's top news stories and breaking news from the nation's capital involving a high profile murder. Less than two hours ago, Virginia Police discovered the body of D.C.'s John Marshall School Of Law's Dean Roger Cosgrove Adams at an Alexandria, Virginia gas station. The law school professor and dean had been shot to death prior to this morning's commute. Also found was the body of another man, presumably the gas station attendant. Dean Roger Adams...*

Peter could not believe his ears. John, Joe, and now Dean Adams. He had nowhere to go.

———❦———

Jimmy Powell bit his lip again. Why did he always have to act so cool? He always had to be baddest boy on the block, not into anything. Feigning disinterest had become second nature to him. Uncle Hank always gave him crap about his "attitude." But Big Hank didn't know what it was like these days. Most days Jimmy just felt lucky to be alive, growing up in East St. Louis. Hell, his nineteenth birthday coming next month would be a milestone. Too many of the kids he grew up with, the same kids who dreamed and fantasized aloud of careers in pro basketball, football, or baseball, were either dead or in prison. Some kids, like Jimmy, would graduate high school, but too many others doped themselves into a stupid laziness that would limit the parameter of their existence to the city limits of East St. Louis. Not Jimmy, he was getting out.

Jimmy found his path two years ago in a courthouse across the river. Big Hank jammed himself up. He forgot to take his medication, roughed up a police car, and the man locked him up. But the white man who just stepped out of the car helped free Uncle Hank. And he did it by working with the system, not against it. The idea was so simple, it was a novelty. Too many things in Jimmy's environment steered him into confrontation: us against them; black versus white; down with the man's oppression. Peter Farrell fought the system that wrongfully accused and unjustly punished Uncle Hank by working within it. The idea struck a resonant chord with Jimmy.

For one week over the summer, Jimmy watched, no, scrutinized, every action, every word in the courtroom. For every argument the prosecutor made, Peter had a more polished, succinct counter-argument. Every doctor the state offered was bested by a more thorough, prepared physician called to testify by Peter Farrell. After the first day, Jimmy knew Peter would have his uncle exonerated of all charges. As each day passed, the prosecutor looked more like a junkie rolling out the door of a crack house after a week long stay. Yet Farrell stood straighter, looked fresher, and more alive. By week's end, the judge had chased the prosecutor out of the courtroom with his tail between his legs. Despite their triumph, Peter Farrell did not rejoice or gloat. Jimmy remembered it vividly. Peter extended his hand to Uncle Hank and said softly, "Henry, I am sorry it had to go this far." Then Big Hank hugged the stuffing out of Peter.

Jimmy had wanted to tell Peter Farrell how great he was in the courtroom and thank him for helping when no one else would. During the whole car ride he had planned to tell him how the experience changed his life. How he had brought his grades up. How he planned to make it through college. And most importantly, how he planned to go to law school and become a lawyer just like Farrell. So many questions raced through Jimmy's head to ask Farrell. What college he should go to? What should he study in college? What type of summer jobs would help get him into law school? There was so much advice Jimmy wanted. And the one person he would choose to ask for advice had just stepped out the door. Jimmy, thought to himself, "you blew it." The best he could come up with was a bad-ass attitude and a couple jokes. Try, try again. Maybe Big Hank would hook him up again. If only he could start the conversation over and learn more. What did Farrell say about never having enough copies? Damn, Jimmy, you better not blow it the next time.

# ELEVEN

Focus, focus, focus. Peter had to think straight. He had left the Ambassador Club quickly to get some air and nearly bowled over another frequent flier. Outside the club paranoia overwhelmed him, so he jogged to the bathrooms and locked himself in a stall. Now that he had regained some composure, he again buzzed himself back into the Ambassador Club.

"Welcome again."

"What gate is that Houston flight coming in on?"

The attendant again turned toward her computer screen and punched in the information on the keys. "Gate 34."

"Thank you," responded Peter as he walked into the practically empty coat and baggage check area. Peter noticed two bright red attendant's jackets hanging in the corner. Peter peeked around the wall. The young lady who had helped him with his fictional Houston flight was talking with someone in the room adjacent to the check out counter. Peter tried on the first jacket, which barely slid around his shoulders. The second jacket was too big, but would fit his purpose. He folded the jacket over his duffel bag and snuck out of the Ambassador Club.

The club was located only about ten gates from where his flight to New York was leaving. Even though Peter did not know what he would do if he boarded the plane to New York, he was well aware of the fact that he had to escape St. Louis. Right now the flight to New York was his only option. However, he still had to make sure that it was still an option.

Just before Gate 76, Peter ducked into the bathroom. He turned the water on from the sink, removed his baseball cap, bent down, and began to wet his hair to the point that it was soaking. Using his fingers as a comb, Peter slicked his hair straight back. Peter mixed some soap and water together and applied it to his new hairstyle as if the watery soap was some form of hair gel. With his hair sufficiently slicked back, Peter put the baseball cap in the duffel bag and fitted himself with the oversized bright-red sports jacket. Sufficiently pleased how his new jacket and hairstyle complemented the white oxford and navy khakis, Peter grabbed the duffel bag and made his way to Gate 76.

At Gate 76, Peter hid the duffel bag under some interlocked chairs which rested against the wall. He surveyed the crowd waiting for the arrival of the flight. He needed someone who was traveling alone. The older man in the brown plaid jacket would not do. Neither would the Asian businessman. He thought the man about his age leaning against the far wall would do until his apparent wife with baby in tow snapped the poor guy out of his daydream. Then Peter saw him. A college student two rows back. He was about Peter's size and weight, wearing tan shorts and a green T-shirt stating, "Rugby Players are Better in Bled," whatever that meant.

"Excuse me, sir," Peter interrupted the college student using his best authoritative voice.

Slightly startled, the young man looked up at Peter and set down his sports magazine.

"Excuse me, young man, how would you like to aid our security efforts and win a free round trip ticket anywhere in the continental United States? It will only take five minutes."

"Huh," the young man turned to see that no plane was at the gate yet. "Sure."

"Follow me," Peter directed the young man and briskly walked over to his duffel bag. At the seats over the duffel bag, Peter sat down, pulled the duffel bag out between his legs, extracted about an inch of the documents from the bag, then sorted them by knocking both the vertical and horizontal edges on the seat beside him. The accounting and ledger sheets appeared official enough to impress anyone at a glance.

"Sit down."

The young man sat beside Peter, who took the opportunity to quickly flash the young man his attorney registration card, which once again appeared somewhat official.

"My name is Neil Armstrong and as you know I am with Airport Security.

As you may have noticed with the extra security," Peter paused, "I'm sorry your name is?"

"Steve Peterson."

"S-E-N or S-O-N," Peter asked as he pretended to write the name down.

"S-O-N," Steve Peterson responded.

"S-O-N?"

"S-O-N," Steve Peterson said again, this time a little bit louder.

"Do you fly more than two times a year?" Peter continued.

"Yes."

"Marvelous," Peter again acted as if he kept track of the response. "As you know, we, in cooperation with federal and local law enforcement authorities, are conducting some security exercises today."

"Yeah, quite a mess out front."

"That's Bob Charles' department, and not my responsibility," Peter shot back keeping the young man off guard. "My department maintains and secures access to the aircraft."

The young man stared blankly at Peter, and Peter continued, "The planes that is. I need you to attempt to board a plane without identification."

"What about the free ticket?" Peterson cut to the chase.

Peter handed him the boarding pass he printed off earlier.

"Anywhere in the continental United States and good for one year. I just need you to walk up to Gate 78 and ask for a new boarding pass and give them this one. Do not show any identification. Remember this is a security test. If they ask you for identification, say you forgot it, or your wife has it or something like that. If they give you the ticket just bring it back to me and I will get you your free ticket."

"Gate 78?"

"Yes, Gate 78." Peter pointed diagonally over to Gate 78.

"Peter Farrell?"

"Yes, that's all."

"OK, I'll be right back."

Steve Peterson rose and strolled toward Gate 78 with a big grin on his face thinking of about ten different places he had planned to visit, yet trying to confine himself to only picking one.

Peter watched his unknowing accomplice approach the airline counter for Gate 78. Both of the airline attendants were helping the family of four in line in front of Peterson. Peter realized that he would have to give the kid cash when he came back with the ticket. Three hundred dollars should suffice. No college student in their right mind would turn down three hundred dollars cash in hand. If the kid did make a fuss, Security Officer Armstrong would explain to him that the necessary, no required, paperwork would take about forty-five minutes to complete. After that, the cash wouldn't look so bad.

Peterson made his pitch. The attendant with her hair up in some sort of beehive nodded as Peterson spoke to her. The other attendant just listened. Then it happened. While the beehive lady talked to Peterson, the other attendant stepped behind the screen which separated the boarding walkway from the counter and seating area. Peterson turned back to Peter and smiled. Before Steve Peterson could wipe the sheepish grin off his face, two men swept from behind the screen, grabbed Peterson, and pulled him toward the small office by the gate. As the two men controlled Peterson's flailing arms, the young college student tried in vain to explain who he was as well as his mission for Security Officer Armstrong. Peter quickly discarded the red sports jacket, and fled the Gate 78 area.

Peter figured it would only take ten maybe fifteen minutes before security could straighten out the Steve Peterson situation. Peterson's appearance resembled his own long enough to buy him that much time. After that, there was the slim possibility of an airport shut down or more likely a security blanket by the exits. He needed a plan quickly, very quickly. As Peter turned the corner from the Red Concourse to the Gold Concourse, he had an idea.

Peter entered the large gift shop between the two concourses. The store contained everything from toothbrushes to "Meet Me in St. Louis" sweatshirts. Peter quickly gathered the items he needed, such as a *Wall Street Times*; a *Sports News Illustrated*; a pair of cheap and ugly sunglasses; a pair of faux designer sunglasses; a white polo shirt with the Arch logo; a pair of shorts;

and, a baseball Redbird's T-shirt. He thought of additional items such as some hair gel, rubber bands, a comb, a packet of disposable razors, and a pair of trimming scissors. The clerk, who was more interested in reading her *National Inquisitor* as opposed to waiting on Peter, rang up Peter's items to the amount of one hundred thirty-five dollars and sixteen cents. Thanking the clerk, Peter grabbed the items and walked down the Gold Concourse to the nearest bathroom.

In the Gold Concourse bathroom, Peter began another makeover. He buttoned his oxford to the top button then soaked the gel into his already greasy hair. He combed the gel straight through, and brought his hair back to a point where he could actually shape a little ponytail, which he tied with one of the rubber bands. Peter then put the fake designer sunglasses on and tucked the *Wall Street Times* under his arm. He placed the rest of the items in the duffel bag and exited the bathroom.

Peter knew exactly what he wanted as he walked down the Gold Concourse. Gate 34. No. Gate 35. No. Gates 36 and 37. No, no. Gates 38, 39, 40, 41, and 42. No, no, no, no, and no. Gate 43. There it was. St. Louis to Chicago, Flight 331, departure 10:15 a.m., in twenty-five minutes. The mid-morning Chicago flight always departed from the same gate.

Peter surveyed the Gold Concourse until he spotted his second requirement—an airport bar. There were several groups of men in the bar, who basically all resembled one another. The dress code for the group required blue jeans or shorts; a Chicago or St. Louis Football jersey or T-shirt with matching baseball cap; a beard, mustache, or at the very least a two-day growth; and the ever-present smell of alcohol permeating from their skin.

As with Peterson, Peter searched the barflies for a loner, someone with little to lose and everything to gain. Most of the men were either paired up or in groups of four. No one was alone. Then it happened. One of the pairs split up. One of the men at a small table by the bar left the table, probably to check the flight or to use the restroom. Peter did not have much time. The overweight man in the neon racing T-shirt and jeans would return shortly. Both men had been drinking a long time before they sat down at the airport for their beer and Bloody Marys. The lone man at the table appeared as if he had yet to stop drinking from the previous Friday. The chosen inebriant was slightly taller than Peter, maybe six foot one or two. His short, dark, curly hair did not complement his light brown mustache, nor his over manicured mullet. Peter was unable to tell if the man's beet-red complexion was a result of the sunny weekend or alcohol. Contrasting the color of the man's face was the fellow's green neon racing T-shirt, signed by his favorite race car drivers and their stock car numbers. What really drew Peter to the obvious drunk were his eyes. Not only were they glassy, bloodshot, and partially closed, but his pupils were swimming around, sometimes following flashes of light in two different directions.

"Good morning, my name is Vance Johnson," Peter introduced himself with an intentionally snobbish tone. No response.

"I said 'Good Morning'," Peter repeated. After obtaining disjointed eye contact, Peter continued, "Good morning, let me introduce myself. My name is Vance Johnson."

"What the hell is so good?" retorted the drunk.

"The morning, sir, except for mine," Peter began his sales pitch.

"Who the hell are you?" responded the drunk as he finally became cognitive of the fact that he was actually talking to someone.

"The name is Vance Johnson. I am in somewhat of a predicament and am in need of a Good Samaritan," the pitch continued.

"Good what?"

"Good Samaritan. I need your help and am willing to compensate quite handsomely," continued Peter. "I am scheduled to present a nationwide marketing data research seminar in Chicago in three hours, but I missed my flight."

The man just stared at Peter.

Peter dropped the snobbish tone in his voice and bluntly stated, "I want to pay you a lot of money."

"For what?"

"For your ticket to Chicago."

"How much?"

"Three hundred dollars."

"Five hundred." The man may have been drunk, but he knew Peter was desperate.

"Four hundred."

"Five hundred!"

Obviously not in an ideal negotiating position, Peter carefully took five hundred dollars out of Henry's money. He did not want to make it obvious that he had more money.

"Here, five hundred dollars."

The man pushed his ticket across the table to Peter. "Here is the ticket. I feel too sick to get on that thing anyway."

With ticket in hand and duffel bag in tow, Peter hustled to Gate 43 for the Chicago flight. He gambled that a picture of him had not been circulated, otherwise the Steve Peterson stunt would not have worked. Occidental had tracked him to the airport and to the D.C. flight, but in all likelihood, they could not monitor the boarding of all outgoing flights. They had to depend on airport security to some degree. Without a picture of him, and given that his appearance did not lend itself to profiling, Peter took his chance on airport security. He stood by the gate and waited until the line to board consisted of only a couple of people. When security randomly picked one of the two passengers left in line, Peter stepped behind the remaining traveler. His luck held as the flight attendant only glanced at his driver's license as Peter held his finger over his name. As he handed his ticket and boarding pass to the attendant, the adrenaline that had pulsed through his body for the past twelve hours slightly eased, then returned. He had escaped St. Louis, but had nowhere to go.

Meanwhile the richer, but still inebriated, racing fan folded his arms together and rested his head on the pillow he had made from his forearms. The bartender continued to set the bar up for what he hoped to be a busy Monday for him. More customers, more tips. As he cut the lime wedges, a news bulletin interrupted the local Monday morning talk show.

*Late breaking news on the downtown murders of two prominent St. Louis attorneys. Last night attorney Joseph Rosendahl and John Farrell were gunned down in an office in this downtown skyrise. Another local attorney, Peter Joseph Farrell, brother of one of the victims, is wanted for questioning in the double homicide. St. Louis Police Chief Jesse Stuart had this to say about the shootings:*

> *'The St. Louis police are working in cooperation with the Federal Bureau of Investigation to locate Peter Joseph Farrell concerning this matter.'*

*At the press conference, Captain Stuart also provided the media with this recent photograph.*

The photograph displayed across the television airwaves showed Peter and John Farrell arm and arm against the dark wood interior at O'Shea's pub. The photo had been taken two nights earlier.

# PART II

# TWELVE

Although most of the grand mansions on Manhattan's Upper East Side had been replaced by multimillion-dollar town homes or transformed into Fifth Avenue's Museum Mile, one of America's castles still stands, partially at least, in defiance of the twenty-first century. Half of the enormous structure, known as the north wing, had been lost in a depression-era fire. The rehabilitation of the north wing succumbed to modernization, mimicking the art deco style of the surrounding town homes. However, the "old south" wing, as its blue-blooded Yankee inhabitant affectionately called the preserved portion of the mansion, was not only left in tact, but prevailed over a history colored with an industrial revolution, a depression, two world wars, and countless neighborhood facelifts.

The pride of the "old south" wing was the library on the third floor. The stairs descending into the library gave the impression of entering a cavern despite the fact that the room measured over two full stories. The dark cherrywood paneling, molding, and furniture further inspired the underground effect. The lack of windows or any outside lighting left one basically at the mercy of the various emerald green shaded brass desk lamps situated throughout the library. No fixtures hung from the ceiling. Modern electricity only invaded the library's second level where lights had been encased in the paneling, which hung over the bookcases by about seven or eight inches. Such lighting enabled one to traverse the second story walkway around the inner perimeter of the library and its railing without fear of tumbling to the first level. Yet the second story lighting only illuminated the hundreds of leatherbound volumes and the cherry wood walkway. Little, if any, light escaped below to the first level of the library. The first floor apparently was regulated to the desk lamps adorning the three enormous hand-crafted oak tables aligning the center of the room. In less modern times, it would have taken eight to ten huge men to place the three tables together forming a fifty-foot conference table. Yet modern technology in the form of mechanical runners on the parallel floorboards enabled this task to be completed at the push of a button. The button was of course hidden in the woodwork by the heavy wooden door to the left of the stairs. Behind the heavy door, a spiral staircase ascended to the library's second level walkway. On the exact opposite side of the library, beyond the three conference tables, there was another heavy wooden door. The door was ajar.

The room behind the library was a study. The study was even more dimly lit than the library. The light emerging from the study emanated from only the desk lamp and the roaring fire in the cast iron fireplace. An elderly man sat upright in one of the two burgundy leather chairs close to the fire. Another man, also in his early eighties, stood by a globe, gently revolving the world by his slightest touch.

"Do you believe Elias can handle his little problem?" asked the man with the English accent who sat comfortably by the fireplace.

"You told me he has his best team on it which includes your Ukranian crackpot," responded "old south wing's" blue-blooded Yank as he twirled the globe. He wore an eight-thousand-dollar custom-made Savile Row charcoal gray pinstriped three-piece suit with matching handmade leather shoes from an old well-respected and moderately affluent cobbler located on London's Old Bond Street.

The other gentleman, in his equally expensive dark-blue double-breasted Milanese suit custom tailored on Via Sant' Andrea, shook his head and stated in his Oxford bred tone, "Details do not interest me. My only concern is that our little immigrant," he pauses, "friend, will not be inept in handling this matter."

"Lack of paying attention to details is what got us in this mess."

"We are certain that there is only one man?"

"Yes," responded the Savile Row man.

"And he has no affiliation with any agency?"

"Yes."

"Well, then he should not last more than a few hours."

"Can this affect the election?"

"Elias assures me that it cannot."

"Assurances," the Englishman rolled his eyes.

"No matter, in a matter of days all of this will pass over."

"Have Bonn and Beijing been kept apprised of the situation?"

"Constantly."

"I should hope so."

"Patience old friend, time is on our side."

"Quite right, however, he still must be watched."

As the Savile Row-clad American spun the globe one more time, he ordered, "Keep your man on him."

"I am not requesting permission," snapped the Englishman.

"Permission granted," responded the Savile Row man.

"You are impossible, impossible," the Englishman feigned an Italian accent.

"Don't you have some fashion show to go to?" asked the Savile Row man.

"Just came from one and it was," the Englishman stopped himself, "message received."

The Englishman rose from the burgundy chair.

"I just thought that you needed to get back on your side of the Atlantic." The Savile Row man's attempt of an apology was lame.

"Duly noted, and I do need to return."

"Call me immediately with any news on Elias St. Armand," barked the Savile Row man, "even if it's bad news."

"If I have to talk to you again about Elias, it certainly will not be good news."

The Englishman exited the study into the library.

As the Savile Row man spun the globe one final time, he muttered, "True enough, true enough."

# THIRTEEN

With his T-shirt, khakis, sunglasses, and duffel bag, Peter Farrell resembled any one of the hundreds of thousands of tourists visiting California. His transformation on the crowded flight from St. Louis to Chicago made him feel like a new man, literally. Peter had spent much of the flight in the bathroom with his duffel bag. He spent the time changing his appearance, again. However the time spent in the bathroom came at the expense of the other passengers and flight attendants. On a flight with over one hundred twenty people and only three bathrooms, Peter's hogging the bathroom did not go over well. Peter was well aware of this fact from the constant knocking on the door. Peter even incurred the wrath of the flight attendant who knocked on the door twice, believing he was sick. By the time he left the bathroom, he had left everyone with the impression that they did not want to use that facility for the rest of the flight which is probably what the drunk at the airport would have done anyway.

The time spent in the bathroom was dedicated to the use of two tools. At the time Peter had not thought about the irony in his ability to buy a disposable razor and a small pair of trimming scissors in the concourse's gift shop, even though he would not have been able to pack such items with him. The two items proved indispensable. Using soap from the dispenser and the sink, Peter shaved three days of growth from his face. The close shave refreshed his tired body. Washing the gel from his long hair in the small bathroom quarters proved to be a more difficult task, but not impossible. The most complicated part of this transformation was cutting his hair with the tiny manicure scissors. He'd have finished quickly but for the hair. Peter had never cut anyone's hair, much less his own. He removed the first layer easily enough, but spent twenty minutes evening out both sides and the front. Added to the new clean-cut Peter Farrell was the recently purchased white T-shirt. Everything else went into the duffel bag. Peter spent the remaining ten minutes of the Chicago flight in one of the two empty seats in the back row of the plane.

The next leg of the journey, Chicago to San Francisco, was uneventful. Peter purchased a round trip ticket under his middle name, Joseph, so that the driver's license matched what he told the ticketing agent. However two things differed from his license. Peter used the name Joe instead of Joseph. He also deliberately misspelled his last name. Consequently, on the flight from Chicago to San Francisco there was no Peter Farrell on the manifest, only a Joe Ferrell. In seat 24A by the window and belonging to Joe Ferrell, Peter Farrell slept for almost the entire flight to San Francisco.

Tasha Dolnick thought the flight to San Francisco would be much longer. No matter, there was still plenty of time for her to focus on her next assignment. She did not look forward to missions such as this one. Tasha preferred assignments which required a precise in and out performance on a specific target. She did not mind that this task was complex or that it could very well be her last assignment. No, what troubled her was that there would be too much down time. Too much waiting. Waiting led to thinking. She did not like to think. Thinking led to remembering. And remembering was the one thing she never wanted to do. She trained herself not to remember.

"You must be on some serious business trip," the middle-aged businessman commented as he put his left hand under the tray table to conceal his ring finger.

Tasha was used to such come-ons, especially in first class.

"Nothing out of the ordinary," the lilt in her voice and welcoming smile surprised the frequent flier.

The middle-aged baby boomer removed his ring under the cover of the tray.

"You look like you're very familiar with first class."

There was not a hint of Slavic heritage in Tasha's voice.

"I only fly first class."

"I only get to fly first class as long as my uncle pays my way."

"Well, long live your uncle."

The middle-aged boomer lifted his Bloody Mary and toasted the fictitious uncle.

It all started to come back to her. Sometimes the nightmare would return for no reason. She was only seventeen when the Serbian troops sacked Srebrenica. Forced to evacuate, a column of about five thousand men left Srebrenica. The column included Tasha's father and brother, who had disguised Tasha as a man. The three had agreed that Tasha would cross the countryside through Serbian-controlled territory with other Srebrenican men and boys. The collective fear from the horror stories they had all heard about the women and girls who had been enslaved in the rape camps was reason enough for the deception. Although the rest of the world ignored or remained comfortably ignorant about these Serbian atrocities, she knew the Cetniks and the barbarity associated with them. Along with genocide, rape was another favorite Cetnik ethnic cleansing tool. Rape represented ethnic cleansing at its most dehumanizing degree. It stopped a race from reproducing by dehumanizing, destroying, and disgracing its women.

The Cetnik rebels had attacked the Srebrenican column several times before the UN transport passed the Dolnicks. Tasha's father pleaded with the UN peacekeepers for protection and safe passage to Bosnia. His pleas fell on deaf ears. Tasha would forever remember the UN peacekeeping soldier's words to her father, "We cannot interfere."

Her father's words to the French peacekeeper were equally etched in her memory, "We are not asking you to interfere, but to save us. We have no arms, no food, and no water. All we want is safe passage."

The peacekeeper responded, speeding off. The next day the Serbs overtook the Srebrenican column with little resistance. Despite the fact that Tasha's people immediately surrendered, the Cetniks slaughtered about one fourth of the column. Tasha, her father, brother, and the remaining survivors were taken to either Nova Kasaba or Konjevic Polje. Half to one camp, half to the other camp.

During the transport to Nova Kasaba, the Cetniks had yet to discover Tasha's gender. At Nova Kasaba that changed. At Nova Kasaba, the collective Srebrenican nightmare turned into Tasha's single, relentless horror.

By the time Tasha had discovered her father had been executed by the Cetniks, she had been raped over seventy times by at least twenty of the Cetnik bastards. The number of times and different men blurred together, however one constant element remained. During each violent act, as he climaxed, the Cetnik would exclaim, "Long live the King! Long live Serbia!" as if it were part of some ritualistic act. She could still not recall how many days she was at Nova Kasaba. However Tasha's last two days would never escape her memory.

After days of beating and sexual abuse, the Cetniks led Tasha outside the compound with the remaining Srebrenicans. The captives were stripped of all clothing and led five at a time to the edge of a large crater. The Cetniks ordered their prisoners to face the crater. When Tasha turned to face the crater, she saw her brother Salih's lifeless naked body lying among hundreds of other corpses. The Cetniks then shouted the same chant that Tasha had heard countless times, "Long live the King! Long live Serbia!" before they opened fire on their victims.

Tasha felt a hot liquid stream down her forehead and a stinging sensation in her left arm before she fell into the crater full of corpses. She did not move. The Cetniks ordered another five to the line. "Long live the King! Long live Serbia." Tasha felt a body fall on top of her crushing her ribs, yet she bit her lip and made no sound.

Two more times the Cetniks chanted, "Long live the King! Long live Serbia", and the bodies fell again and again. Finally, they fired several rounds into the crater, riddling the corpses with additional bullet holes. Tasha passed out as the Cetniks left the killing field.

She awoke and lost consciousness several times before she climbed out from under the lifeless bodies. Night had fallen long before Tasha crept out of the crater into the field. Tasha did not even realize that she was naked until she crawled through the pile of clothes that had been shed by the others before they had been executed. She slowly slipped on some trousers and a worn shirt. She continued to crawl through the field into the woods. Under the cover of the woods, Tasha passed out again.

When Tasha Dolnick awoke, she was in a Tuzla hospital. The nurses informed her that she had been in and out of consciousness for the past several weeks. After another month, Tasha's physical healing was nearly complete. However, her emotional state, understandably, never fully healed. In fact, six weeks after she was found in the forest, Tasha's physical and mental health took another unexpectedly expected turn. She was pregnant.

Tasha's pregnancy was no surprise to her Tuzla nurses. They had seen thousands of women like her who had been victims of Serbian mass rapes. During the occupation, thousands of women aborted their pregnancies. They had also seen thousands of women who bore thousands of children. Children commonly called "children of hate."

Months after Tasha decided to keep her baby, she actually felt as if she was getting a life, even her life back together. She could never forget her father, or Salih, or the horrors of Nova Kasaba, but the life inside of her gave her a new lease on life. The hospital allowed Tasha to remain on board as a nurse's aide. The job enabled her to insure the best care for her pregnancy, for her future child, as well as her own journey toward a feeling of self-worth.

For the first six months of her pregnancy, Tasha's tasks at the Tuzla hospital were minimal, but fulfilling to her. She emptied bedpans, redressed wounds, distributed medicine, or whatever she could do, given her condition. The most complicated task Tasha faced during a given day was redressing minor wounds. Most of the wounds belonged to civilians like her, victims of the war known mostly as "collateral damage." On rare occasions, the hospital treated soldiers before they were moved to their new location.

During one such interlude, six Serbian prisoners stayed at the hospital with their two Croat guards. The soldiers awaited a UN peacekeeper escort. Four of the Serbs had lost limbs, the other two suffered from extensive burns. Ignorant of Tasha's recent history, the new charge nurse assigned Tasha to monitor, dress, and redress the burn victims' wounds. Tasha's obvious reluctance did not dissuade the charge nurse. She reminded Tasha how lucky she was, lucky that she was not out on the street as so many other refugees were forced to live. Tasha's fear overwhelmed her. But she could do the task, and would do the task. She could not afford to lose her job.

Slowly, and with extreme focus on her task as opposed to the patient, Tasha removed the soiled bandage on the forearm. She concentrated on the forearm, as if it were attached to nothing. All she could envision was the blistered skin. So focused was Tasha on the burned forearm that she failed to notice the Serbian soldier's other forearm reach for the pair of scissors at the same time Tasha moved her hand to cut strips of bandages for the burned forearm. The Cetnik plunged the scissors into Tasha's belly instantly killing the life inside and screamed, "Long live Serbia!"

Tasha gasped then cried out. The two Croat soldiers were already descending on the Serb. Tasha took several steps backward before the charge nurse caught her falling. As she fell, she stared blankly at the soldiers. As the one Croat restrained the Serb, the other, who was no more than eighteen years old, returned Tasha's stare. The young Croat then pulled his pistol from his holster and shot the Serbian soldier directly in the forehead. Before Tasha passed out, all she could remember was marveling at the ease with which the young Croat soldier snuffed the life out of the Cetnik who stabbed her.

When Tasha awoke after she had been sedated a day and a half, she knew the baby had died, like Salih, and like her father. Tasha felt nothing, no pain, no fear, no life. She dressed herself, and then walked down to the office. The office had been closed several hours, so Tasha unlocked the door with her keys. Tasha used another key to open the bottom desk drawer where she seized all the money in the hospital's petty cash fund as well as an object from the top of the desk. Tasha proceeded to the prisoners' ward. The same young Croat stood on guard alone over the Serbs. Each of the five remaining Serbs had been sedated and strapped to their beds. The lone guard and Tasha's eyes met, but neither balked from their respective duties. Tasha removed the scissors from her coat pocket. The guard blinked and nodded ever so slightly. He left the room. Tasha slit each Serbian soldier's throat from ear to ear.

"Ding!"

"The captain has removed the fasten seat belts sign. You are free to move about the cabin..."

As Tasha Dolnick unfastened her seat belt, she noticed her sweaty hands. She reflected on killing the two attorneys last night. The younger one, who she had approached at the Irish pub, was quite handsome. He could have been an adequate lover. His brother would be good, too. She would like to use him. As a lover..., why did she use the word 'love'. She knew loving was impossible, even living was hard. The only thing that came easy for Tasha Dolnick was killing.

"Would you like to join me in the bathroom?" Tasha asked the boomer as he took another sip of his drink.

The mere suggestion caused the middle-aged businessman to spill his Bloody Mary in his own lap.

Tasha left her seat and her memories behind for the moment.

# FOURTEEN

Feeling the cool crisp mild Pacific air on his face stirred up a host of memories, none of which involved the tragic chain of events of the last twenty-four hours. The fleeting moment quickly passed when Peter recognized a woman waiting by the empty taxi stand. Peter's first instinct beckoned him to head in the opposite direction. However, he could not take his eyes off this woman. She was taller than most, only an inch or two shorter than him. A pair of designer sunglasses held her short black hair away from her eyes. Her pale complexion betrayed her lack of Californian heritage. Dressed in black slacks, a sleeveless vanilla blouse, and her jacket draped over her shoulder, she could be mistaken for a model on a photo shoot.

It took Peter a little bit of time, but he finally placed where he had seen the woman. It was the woman from O'Shea's, the photographer. She seemed taller and thinner, but there was no mistake, it was her. Take away the heels, add the wig, then a bulky sweater; it was her all right. But why? Why her? Why now?

As the woman from O'Shea's loaded her luggage into the available cab, Peter decided to follow her.

"Are you finished with this taxi?" Peter asked the Asian couple removing their carry on luggage.

"Yes, yes," the man responded.

Before Peter could enter the taxi, the driver interjected, "Sorry buddy you're going to have to wait there in line like everyone else."

"Here's fifty dollars to ignore that rule."

Peter peeled a bill from his wadded money and handed it to the cab driver.

Taking the money, the taxi driver responded, "Well, I guess we can bend the rules on this occasion."

"See that cab up ahead pulling away from the curb, follow it!"

"This ain't the movies, Tex."

"My wife is in that car. I just dropped her off so she could go on a business trip to L.A., but as you can see, she isn't exactly getting on any plane."

"You got that right," the cab driver said, noting the obvious.

"I think she is having an affair. There is another fifty in it if you help me out."

"Buddy, you don't need my kind of help."

The driver looked back at the clean cut Peter Farrell, "All right, nothing like a little excitement for a Monday."

After several minutes of following the other cab, Peter's taxi driver pointed at the upcoming exit ramp.

"Looks like she's heading to the Cliff House or the beach."

"Well she sure wasn't dressed for the beach."

"Probably the Cliff House then. They have one of those fancy, schmancy romantic restaurants up there," the driver paused, then caught Peter's eyes in the rear view mirror. "Sorry about that."

"That's all right, the woman in that car is a mystery to me."

Peter waited for the woman to enter the Cliff House before he exited the cab. However, she never entered the building. Instead, she walked along the boardwalk, past vendors and past the Cliff House itself. The woman walked up the sidewalk and finally descended below to what was once the Sutro Baths. Etched out of the cliffs was an open area partially filled with standing water, the only remnants of the once-grand bathhouse just north of the Cliff House. A single pathway lies along the perimeter surrounded by the hills covered in lupine and ice plants. There was no way Peter could discreetly follow the woman into the cave. There was no cover, merely a wide-open natural bay area surrounding the foundation ruins of a turn of the century bathhouse.

Instead of sauntering along the ruins, the woman strode up another path to the mouth of a cave on the north end of the foundation. As the woman walked up the pathway to the cave, Peter spotted two men in suits step out of a cave. The woman appeared to give them orders, but Peter could not tell. All he could see was the woman doing all of the talking. He had to get closer, but there was no way to get down the path without being seen. Even if he could get down the path, there was no way he could get close enough to listen to the threesome.

Peter looked around. Quickly walking along the platform, Peter reached into his pocket, pulled out his keys and some loose change. Rifling through the change, Peter found a quarter and inserted it into one of the telescopes used for viewing the sea lions that gathered on and off Seal Rocks. Aiming his sights on the O'Shea's woman and the two men, he began to understand the exchange between them.

In contrast to the simple elegance of the woman, the two men were dressed in department store suits. One in blue. One in brown. Although one of the men was slightly larger than the other, both resembled one another in their lack of defining features and close-cropped brown hair. The woman still appeared to be barking orders, but now she was counting her fingers as if listing agenda items, needs, or supplies. The blue suit wrote these things down on a small pad.

The brown suit directed the other two to a small deck that was only twenty feet from the mouth of the cave. The brown suit set his briefcase on top of the railing, scouted the area for any passersby or unwanted tourist, then opened his briefcase. Unfortunately it opened in Peter's direction, shielding the contents from anyone.

"Click."

The screen went blank in front of Peter's eyes.

"Damn!" Peter rummaged again through his pockets searching for another quarter. Finding one, he inserted it into the machine. The two suits talked to one another, while the woman appeared impatient. The woman then stepped forward, reached into the briefcase and pulled out a small handgun. Peter, a far cry from a firearm's expert, could only determine that the handgun was some sort of automatic pistol. The pistol also was small enough for the woman to put the gun into her inside coat pocket. Finally, the brown suit handed the woman a set of keys and a wallet then checked the time on his watch. The woman checked her watch as well. The two suits walked up the path toward two cars parked along the roadway that hugged the cliffside. Peter recognized one of the cars, it was a standard government-issued four-door sedan. The plain white plates confirmed that the two men were from the Justice Department. In sharp contrast to Peter's trembling realization that two apparent Federal Agents just gave this mysterious woman a gun, the O'Shea's woman calmly walked up the path and left the scene in the car that had been provided for her.

# FIFTEEN

In her own words, it had been a "shitty" year. Hell, last year was not that great either. Sitting slouched before her terminal, elbows braced on the desk, and her hands holding up her face, Sara Ahrens wondered what else could go wrong. She tried to put her mind in a peaceful place, like that river-rafting outing with the Inner City Kids Program, but she could not make it to the river. Though this year she was no longer on the Sienna Club's Board of Directors, she had continued working eighty-hour weeks for the past year. Between suing the Environmental Protection Agency, again, for failing to set tighter emission standards, enjoining those two bluegrass water treatment plants and the Texas petrochemical facility, as well as the dozen or so other fires that had popped up requiring the "immediate" attention of the chair of the Litigation Committee, Sara's life was all work. It was not just the work, but also the politics. Racing through Sara's mind was the continuing rift and backlash over the vote on the Club's policy concerning U.S. immigration. Although she steadfastly opposed the new policy calling for a reduction of immigration levels, there was no need to play the race card. She told them that even though they live in California and may also be attorneys, there was no reason to smear this environmental issue with racial prejudice. If race never came up she would not have to worry about this defamation suit. To top it all off, the only date she had in the past twelve months was river rafting with a bunch of thirteen-year-old boys. Even then, most of boys were more interested in getting her T-shirt wet as opposed to recognizing the delicacies of the environment around them. There goes her peaceful place. Sara did not even want to go back to the river. What else could go wrong?

"Sara, Sara, are you there?" The voice on the telephone's intercom system sounded confused.

"Yes," Sara mumbled through her hands.

"There's a Joey Sukapukavic on the line for you."

"What? What does he want?"

"Something about the Susan B. Anthony luncheon tomorrow. I don't have you down for a luncheon tomorrow."

Finally lifting her head from her hands and realizing who it was, Sara said, "I will take that call," stressing the "will" with an eager grin on her face.

"Mr. Sukapukavic?" Sara inquired as she picked up and put on her head-set. "Joey Sukapukavic" was a name she had not heard in three years, three months and probably a week. Petie always used that name as a code so her father, the Honorable Douglas Irving Ahrens, never knew the two were romantically involved. Sara disobeyed her father for a couple of years and never regretted a minute she spent with Petie. In fact, Sara knew she had fallen in love the first time she set her eyes on blue-eyed Irishman when Judge Patrick Fitzgerald introduced the young summer law clerk to Sara and her father.

Judge Fitzgerald and her father had been friends for years. They had served together in the Korean war. It was impossible to decipher who saved whose life more times or who became sicker on whose booze more times during their war stories. So when her father accepted a teaching position at Loyola of St. Louis while awaiting his congressional confirmation as a judge on the Ninth Circuit Court of Appeals, it was no surprise that Judge Fitzgerald found an "opening" on his Eighth Circuit's staff for another law clerk. It was not as if Sara was not qualified for the position, top of her class at Berkley and on law review. She knew that as a daughter of one of the old boys in the old boys' network, certain doors would open for her. Walking through those doors was never a problem for Sara, she knew she belonged. The hard part was proving to everyone else beyond a shadow of a doubt, that she belonged. That meant being number one, all the time. Most importantly, number one to the one who had opened those doors for her, her father.

There were only three times her father forbid her to do something. Actually, "forbid" was not the right word. For Judge Douglas Ahrens never denied his only daughter anything. It was not as if he spoiled her, she never asked for anything. He, in turn, never asked anything from her. That is except on three occasions. And when Judge "Ironsides" Ahrens asked for something, he did not ask twice.

The first time her father asked her not to do something, Sara was eight years old. At that time, Sara, her mother, and her father lived near the California coast, a stone's throw from the beach, and a short commute to San Francisco by California standards. The judge enjoyed the solitude, but even more so, he loved the water. He told Sara that because of her Dutch blood, she too would be cursed by an unyielding drive to live by the water. He was right, of course. He always was. Sara never knew a time when her father had been wrong. Her father had asked her not to go down to the beach unless an adult accompanied her. Of course "adult" meant mother, father, or Mr. or Mrs. Foust who lived just across the street. Susie Foust was two years older than Sara. Sara knew very well that Susie was not an adult. However, Susie was the only other kid her age in the area. They did everything together. So on that lazy July morning when Susie wanted to go down to the beach to play in the waves, far be it for Sara to argue with Susie's logic that since she was a lot taller than Sara, Sara could consider her an adult. Sure enough, when playing in the surf, one particular forceful wave swamped the girls, causing them both to choke on water and panic. A beachcomber pulled them from the water. If not for him, Sara feared something tragic could have happened.

The second time her father asked her not to do something, Sara was on her way out the door to her first high school party. Before leaving, she stopped by her father's study. Sara vividly remembered the judge looking over the top of his glasses and right into his daughter's eyes. He made her promise that she would not get into a car if the driver had been drinking. Sara promised, based not so much on the horrors portrayed to her in her driver's education classes, but on the eyes that were fixed on hers as she made the promise. Sure enough, that night at the party some of her friends were drinking, including her ride. Against all social protocols, Sara called her father to pick her up from the party. Unfortunately, this time there was no beachcomber to help Susie. She broke both of her legs and her collarbone while driving home from the party later that night when her Jeep struck the guardrail. The passenger seat was completely smashed by the rollover.

The third time the judge asked her not to do something not only puzzled Sara but tore her apart. Whereas on the first two occasions, the fatherly protection over his daughter was self-evident, the third occasion lacked clarity. Only one month after meeting Peter Farrell, her father asked her not to become involved with him. Her father's rare request shocked her. At first, Sara thought she was more infuriated at her father for trying to dictate her life, her love life. While she understood his protective instinct, she had her own life to live, and Sara wanted Peter in it. What right did her father have to interfere.

As the St. Louis summer progressed, Sara and Peter worked together at the Eighth Circuit Court of Appeals, and Sara tacitly obeyed her father's wishes. Sara and Peter became fast friends. Peter showed her the town, movies, and even several baseball games, a sport Sara had little interest in before the summer she spent in St. Louis. Yet in all the time the two spent together, Sara never defied her father. There were countless chances. Sara knew Peter was interested in more than her friendship, and she was equally attuned to his charms. Despite this, Sara rebuffed his advances over and over again throughout the summer until her last weekend in St. Louis.

The night before she was to leave, Sara, Peter, and several other law clerks celebrated the summer at several of the school's local drinking establishments. After numerous pitchers of beer, more than anyone was willing to admit, Peter, Sara, and two other clerks went for a late night swim over at the Dean's pool, where Peter lived. Sara, not shy of alcohol, still drank more than she knew she should have, as did the others. When the other two clerks were leaving they offered Sara a ride home. In true Ahren fashion she declined, clumsily whispering to Peter that her father told her never to get a ride home from people who had been drinking. Peter told her that her father was right. Sara led Peter upstairs to his carriage house apartment. As they climbed the stairs, she clung to him, knowing that her father was not right about everything. Sara pulled Peter to the bedroom, then onto the bed. After months of wondering how his lips would receive the warm embrace of hers, she kissed him for what seemed like an eternity. Peter gently pulled away, but kept his arms around her. With ease, he lifted her from the edge of the bed to its center. He laid her flat and gazed at her with his affable smirk. Peter moved forward slipping his hand over her eyes, closing the lids by his soft touch. Sara would never forget Peter's lips caressing her forehead then gently saying, "Sleep tonight, there's always tomorrow."

Sara left early in the morning without waking Peter, who lay sound asleep on the sofa. Over the next several weeks they talked every day, more excited than two high school kids on the phone. Even though they spoke daily, they also wrote long letters. Everything Sara did, she wanted to share with Peter. And he with her. Consequently, it was no surprise to Peter when Sara showed up at his door after spending only four weeks back home in California. For the first time in her life she lied to her father, telling him she went to Tahoe with some girlfriends. That weekend Sara and Peter took their friendship to the next level and made love for the first time.

In the ensuing months, Sara and Peter stole weekends together. For over a year, the two trekked across the country to see one another. However, wherever her father could discover the relationship, they were discreet. More than discreet, they were secretive. It was hard enough to disobey her father, but she could not stay away from Peter for any length of time. It was tough on Peter, too. He knew Sara was torn between them, but she insisted on not disclosing their affair to her father. Against his better judgment, he obeyed her wishes. Instead the two designed a code, more like a colorful language, in order to keep their relationship hidden from Judge Ahrens or anyone who could inform him about their relationship. Peter used the name Joey Sukapukavic. He thought it was a silly name, but used it because he also thought what they were doing was silly. Sara picked the name Susan B. Anthony, but dropped the "B." Sara always admired the woman. Moreover, the two had the same initials which made it easy for Sara to remember her code name.

A typical occasion "Joey Sukapukavic" would call "Susan Anthony" when she would be at Sara's work. Certainly Ironside Ahrens and Sienna Club members did not hang around the same social circles, but that never stopped the Judge from popping in on Sara at work. The last thing Sara needed was her father to overhear office gossip, or worse yet be subject to an officemate of hers trying to impress the Judge by talking about Sara's significant other. Not only did the two have code names, but they could have a whole conversation without anyone knowing who or what they were really talking about. For example, to describe a time, like a time to meet, the two used military time, but it was usually used as an address or some other number. If "Joey" called and left a message to pick him up at "1900 Main Street" it really meant to pick him up at seven o'clock. The two of them began to get carried away with their code and used it much more than necessary. It became a game.

However, the game could not last forever. When Sara's mother died, her father became depressed to such a point that Sara moved back home. With her father ailing and needing Sara's time and attention, the undisclosed long distance relationship was put on the back burner. With Peter's reluctant understanding, their relationship entered a state of limbo so Sara could take care of her father. Although she could not admit to herself that her relationship with Peter was over, she knew that her family came first, and that she would not disobey her father again. Slowly but surely the awkward telephone conversations trickled down to unanswered messages left by her former lover.

"Sara, it's been a long time," Joey or Peter said over the phone in his usual understating tone.

"It has. Are you in town on business?" Sara inquired as she began the game Peter had started.

"Actually, you could say I am on a mission. The mission is all business though."

"Where are you staying?"

"At the Wiltshire, room eighteen hundred."

"Nice place if you can afford the two thousand a night price tag."

"It's not that high."

"At least." Sara began to notice that Peter was not his typical playful self, but she understood what he was saying. "Is anything wrong?"

"Wow!" Peter responded.

Sara thought Peter sounded genuinely shocked about her question.

Peter then continued, "I guess you haven't read the papers lately. My company's stock has been taking quite a beating. Anyway I can tell you all about it at the luncheon. I have to run now, but we will talk later."

"Okay, I guess."

Now, it was Sara who was confused.

"Well, I will see you later," Peter ended the conversation abruptly. Bewildered, Sara hung up the receiver. Why would Peter be in the newspaper? She immediately logged onto the Internet to search the name "Peter Farrell." Sara was shocked to see she had over five thousand hits on her search.

# SIXTEEN

With his baseball cap pulled almost completely over his eyes, Peter Farrell walked steadfastly through the Haight's colorful Victorian homes with his hands stuffed deep into his pockets. He hoped that Sara understood his message. He was pretty confident she understood the time and place, but astonished she did not know about the notorious Peter Farrell, the killer lawyer from St. Louis. Worse yet, there his face was again, on a dozen television sets in the storefront window of the electronics shop. If it weren't for his baseball cap and his self-styled haircut, surely everyone would recognize him. In fact, that lady on the bus in Golden Gate Park kept staring at him. He knew he should not have taken something as public as a bus. He had plenty of time before he had to meet Sara at Mission Delores at eight. Stupid, stupid, stupid. He could not afford to be so stupid, and surely he could not afford to be recognized. Hopefully, Peter thought to himself, he was just being paranoid.

Paranoia was no stranger to the neighborhood Peter was walking through. The Haight had its fair share of paranoia in its days. However, as opposed to the drug-induced phobias of the late sixties, Peter's fears were all too real.

"How much?" Peter asked the grocer.

"Apple, one dollar."

The grocer took the bill from Peter's hand and turned back to the small screen TV behind the counter. St. Louis Police Chief Jesse Stuart was holding up computer-generated pictures of Peter. He could not hear what Stuart said, but he knew what he was saying. Good old boy Captain Jesse had called for a national manhunt. A reward has probably been offered. "Too many crazies in this world," the grocer said as he stared at Peter.

He quickly walked out of the store back to the street. A manhunt. Everyone would be looking for him. If he knew that before, he would not have called Sara. He did not want to get Sara involved, but he thought he would be safe out here on the coast, out of St. Louis. But now he knew there was no safe place for him anywhere.

Thanks to the television medium, there was a face to go with this wanted man. His mug would soon be plastered all over the newspapers, too. By this time tomorrow, there would be no place for him to hide. "Damn it," Peter thought to himself, he still had three hours to kill before he was to meet Sara. The more time he was out in public, the more time to be recognized.

Peter passed a twenty-year-old girl in a tattered babydoll dress and dirty feet holding a cat on her lap. Her cardboard sign read, "NEED MONEY TO FEED CAT." She stared at him. Another shopkeeper leaning against his doorframe smoking a cigarette watched the passersby. He stared at Peter.

"It's him," cried a doped-up man lying on the sidewalk, as Peter approached.

Peter put his head down and covered his face with his hand.

"It's him!"

A couple of tourists twenty feet in front of Peter turned around. A window shopper talking on a cellphone by the doped-up man ignored him.

Peter passed the doped up man and the shopper.

"It's him," cried the doped-up man as he sat up, "did ya see that? That was him, Jim Morrison."

Peter threw the half eaten apple in the trash as he walked past the Psychedelic Head Shoppe. He wished that all of this was really just a bad LSD trip. Reality sucked.

———◆———

"Nelson!" lashed out San Francisco's Mission Precinct Detective First Class Martinez to her junior detective.

"Yeah boss," responded the equally young and naive Larry Nelson.

Holding a fax in front of her, Detective Martinez spoke sternly to her apprentice, "When did this come in?"

"About an hour ago, around five."

"How come you didn't bring it to me right away?"

"You were in a meeting and I didn't think I should interrupt you."

"A bulletin comes in that a serial murder suspect may be in our jurisdiction and you don't think you should interrupt me?"

"Well, it said downtown was handling it with the Bureau."

"When is the last time downtown handled anything?" Martinez facetiously asked her junior partner as she reviewed the fax again. "And what is this, this guy is wanted for questioning for two murders yesterday afternoon in St. Louis and a couple more this morning in Virginia. Now they believe he's here. What is this guy, a superman, flying across the country with a red cape on? No one could get around like that."

"What if he had a private plane?"

The senior detective glowered at Nelson and continued, "And this guy 'may' be involved in three murders, yet there are no warnings that he 'may' be armed and dangerous. All the vics were shot, were they not?" Detective Martinez folded up the fax and put it in her coat pocket.

"What are we going to do about it?"

Martinez tossed Nelson his coat, and motioned to him to follow her, "'We' are not going to do anything. But I am going to get some answers from downtown."

# SEVENTEEN

On the Friday before Palm Sunday, the feast of the Seven Dolors of Mary, some of the first colonists to the bay area settled on a serene knoll surrounded by woodlands, a stream, and a tiny lake. In recognition of the timing of their arrival and in tribute to the Blessed Virgin, the colonists christened their settlement "Dolores." The settlers soon established a mission. It was dedicated on October 9, 1776, three months after the signing of the Declaration Of Independence. Two centuries later lies a four-lane divided boulevard lined with thirty-foot palm trees. The old mission, with its white-washed western simplistic exterior and redwood timbered and tiled roof, still stands defiantly in contrast to the area's colorful Edwardian homes. Adjacent to the mission towers the Parish Church with its two uneven steeples. Services are held in the Basilica, but the reverence of the mission escapes no one.

The mission's four-foot-thick adobe walls measure only twenty-two feet by one hundred fourteen feet. Native Americans baptized two centuries ago decorated the mission with diamond patterns of white, yellow, red, and blue. The wood-carved pews, golden altar, and venerated baptismal font exemplified the simplistic charm of the interior of the old parish. Through the doors of the old parish, one gains access to one of the most hallowed places in the bay area, the cemetery at the Mission of San Francisco de Asis.

Peter had an excellent view of the entire cemetery from just inside the Lourdes Grotto for the Forgotten Dead. The garden was in full bloom. The full, green firs provided much shade. However the setting sun provided more than enough shadows to ease Peter's ongoing paranoia about being identified in the public light.

Peter had shown up much too early for his liking. He had walked up and down the palm-lined Dolores Street twice "casing" the place. Once inside the church, Peter still had almost an hour to wait. He spent half of that time kneeling at a pew praying, no talking, to God. Peter went to mass regularly, semi-regularly. However, he prayed all of the time. Peter would pray for John and his family, for the souls of his Mom and Dad, himself, and more often than not, Sara. Despite his prayers, it had been a long time since he really talked to God, the last occasion being his father's funeral. Peter had spent over an hour before the services having a one-way conversation with God, asking him to take care of his father. At Dolores, Peter once again had a one-way conversation with God, this time about John. Peter asked God to take good care of his brother. He also needed him to send an angel to watch over Jenny and the kids. Finally, Peter requested an angel to watch over him, if God had one to spare.

Peter thought the vision entering the cemetery was that angel.

She was a vision. At about five foot eight, Sara Ahrens was taller than most. But she was always guarded about her appearance. Peter had called her the poster girl for the California girl-next-door image, only to embarrass and offend the humble blond. Her khakis and sleeveless navy blue button-down blouse reflected her classic taste. Her father consistently remarked that his daughter carried herself with a simple elegance. Peter thought Sara was gorgeous.

"Sara," Peter spoke in a hushed voice lower than normal tone but more than a whisper.

"Peter?"

"You cut your hair," Peter longingly admired his former lover remembering the long locks which had been replaced by a shoulder-length haircut.

"What the hell is going on!" Sara retorted, having replaced the longing she felt with anxiety from the numerous articles she had read on the Internet about the events that had occurred in the past twenty-four hours.

"Lies."

"They have to be. I know that you couldn't kill anyone, much less John. What is going on?"

"I don't know. What do you know?"

"I know you are in trouble and way over your head. You need help, Peter."

"No, no, no. What did you read?"

"They say you killed John, some other lawyer, and maybe even Dean Adams. No, that is not exactly it. You're wanted for questioning in those murders is what the FBI says, but most just say you killed them. How could they say this about you? Peter, they are ready to shoot you on sight."

Sara began to betray her usual calm demeanor. Realizing his surroundings and sensing her alarm, Peter took Sara's arm and put it around his and guided her down the back path of the garden. He sought as little attention as possible. Emotion in a cemetery was not unusual, but highly unlikely when the gravestones date back two centuries.

"I'm alright." Sara assured her friend and former lover. "I just need to know what is going on. We need to arrange for you to get out of this manhunt safely."

"One thing at a time. You said they want me for questioning, but some people want me killed?"

"The FBI says that you may have knowledge about all three murders and that you are wanted for questioning. That is what the St. Louis and Maryland authorities are saying, too."

"Who says they want to kill me?"

"The crazies on the net. You are all over the place. It is like one big chat room and you are the main course. Some say you are a crazed serial murderer and will be shot on site. Others say you are a CIA hit man who has gone over to the other side, whatever that means. Some even think you are a hero for killing all the lawyers. They call you 'Shakespeare.'"

"Cute."

"Your picture is even all over the net."

"This is crazy."

"Did you see who killed them? Why are they after you?"

"What else do you know?"

"Nothing. Peter, why would anyone say you killed your brother or the Dean? Did you see the person who did this and know why they're after you? I know people who can keep you safe. So do you."

"I don't know anyone who can keep me safe, and I should never have called you."

"Peter, I know, my father knows people in the Bureau. They can put you in a safe house."

"I can't. You don't understand."

"It's very easy, Peter."

"Sara you don't understand. I am not a witness."

Sara stared at him, confused.

"I was nowhere near any of these murders. First, Sunday I was fishing and about a hundred miles from St. Louis when John and Joe were killed. Second, I have not been east of the Mississippi, except for Chicago, in the past year. I wasn't in D.C. Third, finally, someone, or some group, is after me because of these documents."

Peter let the duffel bag slide off his shoulders and opened it revealing the bulk of documents among the clothing.

"What?" Sara began then looked at Peter confusingly.

"You know the Occidental Group?"

"The world's grocer or something like that."

"They are bigger than that. Agribusiness is only one facet. Banking, construction, dozens of other fields all have Occidental ties."

"I know them from their ethanol work."

"Exactly, that's all a part of this."

"Peter, let's just go see my father. He can help."

"You don't understand Sara, I don't know if anyone can help."

"Let's back up for a second," Peter continued.

The two had walked to the far corner of the cemetery, which ran along Dolores Street. The large bushes, flowers, gravestones, and statues had almost completely blocked the entrance from the mission where Sara first entered. Peter set the duffel bag down and rummaged through the Occidental papers.

"Here it is," he found the file he wanted.

"Peter," Sara began again to plead with him.

"Just look at this," Peter pulled out the Occidental papers. The file in his hand contained the Speeter FEC file. "This is a copy of a Federal Election Committee file on an investigation of the President's campaign treasurer.

Actually it is an investigation of funds going to both parties. See this, this, and this," Peter pointed to various columns detailing dollar figures, "these represent contributions by the Occidental Group to both political parties."

"Wait a second, that's millions of dollars," the environmental activist noted.

"Exactly. The FEC investigator, a guy named Betts, tracked this money to congressional votes on two agribusiness issues, one being the ethanol subsidy. The picture is not too tough to paint: Occidental gave about ten million to the campaigns of key senators and congressmen and received subsidies of over four billion dollars."

"Four billion dollars paid by Joe and Jane taxpayer."

"Exactly. But this guy Betts was able to find a direct link between Occidental and the ethanol subsidy vote. Senator Milton Stanton."

"Senator Flip Flop," chided Sara.

"Stanton and others in his party received one million dollars the day he was supposed to kill the subsidy in Senate hearings..."

"But he gets the vote and rubber stamps the ethanol subsidy from Occidental."

"That's not the end of it, look at this."

Peter pulled another group of papers out, "I don't know if Betts knew this or not, but Occidental had these photos of Senator Milton with these two kids."

"Well if you are going to be blackmailed, at least it's nice to get a million dollars to soothe the pain," Sara sarcastically remarked.

"There are a dozen files like this describing Occidental's payoffs or black-mail. Look at this, Representative Stevenson sold out on an Indian Gaming issue. Stevens, sell out. Even your own congresswoman Stone, sold out." Peter began stacking sets of the papers on the ground. "Sara, these are just the 'S's', who knows how far this goes."

Sara began to page through the documents. "Stewart, that's that Nazi who's after you."

"You see. I don't know who is Occidental and who isn't."

"That bastard!"

"What?"

"Randy Sexton," Sara answered as she pulled some of the papers from the duffel bag.

"Speaker of the House Randolph Sexton."

"These are Occidental payments," Sara pointed to a column with dollar signs while Peter nodded, "so he is on Occidental's payroll."

"He is corrupt, too."

"He attacked the Sienna Club as a tax-deductible entity that is politically active when he should have known that wasn't true. That smear hurt us in the last elections. And here is good old Congressman Randy Sexton being paid to vote on certain issues. No wonder he has such a horrible environmental record, we could never afford to pay him what Occidental pays him. Furthermore, he's a pervert. Look at these pictures."

Peter appreciated the little bit of levity.

Sara continued, "Peter where did you get these Occidental papers?"

"I can't tell you."

"People are trying to frame you for murder and you cannot tell me?"

"Client confidentiality."

Puzzled, Sara asked, "Does your firm represent these people?"

"No, no, no."

"Then who?"

"Sara, John had a box of these files when he was killed. He was killed because he was holding them for me. I think the Dean was killed because he was asking too many questions about Occidental. I told him about these files and now he is dead. Everyone who is coming in contact with these files is in jeopardy, and I am sorry I brought you into this mess." Peter paused and continued, "I had nowhere to turn. I tried to contact Aaron Golde, but wasn't able to get him. Now I think they know I will call him, like they knew I'd call Dean Adams. Nobody knows about you. I guess that is one thing I can thank your father for. I figured you could help me contact Aaron."

"Whatever you need."

"No." Peter said sharply, "Not 'whatever I need.' Your involvement starts and stops with one phone call."

Sara returned Peter's sharp tone, "My father knows more federal and state law enforcement officers in the State of California than anyone, except for the Governor."

"Sara."

"No, Peter, you listen. My father has good friends in the Bureau. With these documents we can turn them upside down, they won't know what hit them."

"Sara, this is not some crusade. You and Aaron Golde are about the only people I can trust. These people are everywhere. I don't know how deep this goes. Look at the Dean, he is no different then your father, and he is dead. Aaron, on the other hand, has experience dealing with corrupt politicians. He will know what to do. I have already sent him a copy of these documents, but he will not get them until tomorrow. I have to send him a message that they are coming. This is the only way. It has to be my way."

Opposite the back end of the cemetery and Dolores Street, only twenty or so feet from Peter and Sara, a small Philippine woman wearing a smock exited the mission's gift shop to survey the cemetery for customers. Dusk began to set, and the shopkeeper looked forward to the end of the day.

As both Peter and Sara knelt above the duffel bag, Peter took Sara's hand in his, "Sara, I couldn't live with myself if anything happened to you or your father. Let's just get ahold of Aaron, he has taken on corruption his whole career. He will know what to do."

"Aaiiee, gun!" the shopkeeper shrieked.

Peter turned and looked down the pathway at the woman. She stood motionless with her hands covering her mouth, facing the opposite path which ran alongside the mission. Peter peered over the gravestone between him and the motionless shopkeeper. He immediately recognized the two suits who must have just entered the cemetery from the mission. It was the two FBI agents from this afternoon. The brown suit had already drawn his government issued weapon, while the blue unholstered his gun, evidently in response to the shopkeeper's shriek. As Peter identified the G-men, the brown suit spotted Farrell, aimed, and fired two shots directly in the headstone for the Carey family. The gun's silencer muffled the gunfire until it ricocheted off the stone. Peter flung himself over Sara.

"Farrell!" the brown suit called out. "All we want are the documents and to talk to you. Just put your hands up and turn over the documents."

"What? Who are they?" Sara nervously whispered to Peter.

"Did I forget to tell you someone is trying to kill me?" Peter dryly answered.

"Farrell, do you have the documents?" shouted the brown suit as the shop-keeper still stood motionless.

While still crouched down behind the gravestones, Peter began to gather together the papers. Speeter, Stanton, Stevens, Stevenson, and Stone. Peter then folded the papers and stuffed them into his pockets. Sara followed suit, folding Sexton's papers, then shoving them into her front khaki pocket.

"Farrell!" The voice was closer.

Peter looked at Sara and then grabbed the duffel bag. Peter shuffled the Occidental papers, loosening them from one another. Staring at Sara, Peter lifted the bag up and nodded in the direction of the shopkeeper. Sara returned Peter's nod.

"Farrell!"

The voice was now only twenty or thirty feet away, thought Peter.

"If you want the documents here they are!" shouted Peter as he threw the unzipped duffel bag with all his might high into the air towards the voice. The Occidental papers flew all over the cemetery grounds as a breeze swirled them around the headstones. Peter pushed Sara in the direction of the shop-keeper. They sprinted as fast as their legs could carry them. Both the blue suit and brown suit were dumbfounded by the Occidental papers whirling about the cemetery grounds. The blue suit darted to collect the fallen duffel bag, which still had papers blowing from it. The brown suit grabbed papers which had made their way down to earth. Belatedly realizing both Peter and Sara were racing to the gift shop, the agent in the brown suit fired two shots toward the couple. Peter shoved Sara through the gift shop archway, then forced the shopkeeper back into the store. Once all three were inside, Peter locked the door behind them by pulling the large two-by-four through the iron braces. The shopkeeper, whose terror had now turned into panic, ran through the front door out onto Dolores Street.

"Where is your car?" Peter shouted at Sara as he grabbed her by both arms. Three blasts rang out around the door handle, but the six-inches of nineteenth century oak did not give.

"Around the corner."

Peter rushed Sara through the same door the little shop woman had escaped through. Outside, Peter and Sara encountered a mob of nicely dressed people descending upon Dolores Street. The evening mass for All Saint's Day had just let out. The flock of churchgoers, bulletins in hand, made their way to their respective cars. The Holy Day of Obligation offered the perfect cover for Peter and Sara to escape.

"Walk with that group to the corner and your car," commanded Peter.

"Where are you going?"

"I'll lead them away."

"Peter."

"Just get going, but don't go home. Stay with people and in crowds. Go to your office. There are at least a dozen people there twenty-four hours a day."

"Call me in half an hour."

"No, I'll e-mail you. Your office e-mail."

"Be careful!"

"Hurry up and catch that group!"

Peter watched Sara scurry up to a bunch of students who happened to be walking in the same direction as her car. Sara blended in perfectly. As he watched her, Peter momentarily slipped back into that world where he and Sara had planned to grow old together.

The door behind Peter slammed against the adobe wall and the sound of splintering wood yanked him back to reality. Without looking back, Peter raced in the opposite direction Sara had gone.

"There he is!" Peter heard a voice behind him. For the first twenty to thirty feet Peter pushed his way through the crowd receiving scowls from all those who had so recently been deep in prayer, forgiveness, and repentance. As the crowd dissipated, Peter sprinted to the next corner where he turned right. Before he was halfway down Eighteenth Street, he realized he had covered several blocks. He turned to see if he was being followed. Neither agent was behind him, only people milling in and out of shops or coffee houses. Two blocks ahead there were more crowds of people. If he could just make it up there, he would be able to lose anyone in the crowds.

Once Peter made it to the corner where all the people were stirring along the street, he bent over, hands on his knees, sucking in as much air as possible. While still hunched over, he made a mental note that he just had better get in shape. Peter straightened up, looked back down the street then stretched his back by bending backwards, hands on his hips. When he finally opened his eyes, he realized where he was. The Castro.

——◆——

Realizing that she had just run a red light on Market Street while speeding along at fifty miles per hour, Sara eased her foot on the brakes to meet the speed limit. This whole thing was crazy. Those were real bullets. Oh my God, Peter! What the hell is going on?

Sara prided herself on remaining calm while others panicked. Not that it was usually hard. She knew a trick. Not even a trick, she later learned, but a mental exercise. But when her father taught her how not to be afraid of the dark and to make the monsters under her bed disappear, it was a trick. Exercising a tender side that anyone rarely saw, Judge Ahrens always took his time in tucking his little girl in for the night. After reading together, the frightened Sara would beg her father to stay. Her father stayed long enough to teach her the trick. Judge Ahrens had Sara name animals that started with the letters of the alphabet. The two would always start at "aardvark," then "baboon," then "canary," then "dog." but the Judge invariably made Sara pick another "D." Dog was too easy. Sara would be fast asleep by the time she hit "llama." Even by herself in the dark, her trick made her forget that she was alone or frightened, or just lonely. Sara could never remember a time she actually made it all the way to "zebra."

"Queensland hairy-nosed wombat..."

Sara had upgraded her animal alphabet to endangered species.

"Ruwenzori otter-shrew..."

Already at the letter "R" and Sara could not calm herself down. It was all too surreal. Those were real bullets.

"Sonoran pronghorn..."

Would these people really be trying to kill Peter to cover up four billion dollars in subsidies? Well, that is a stupid question. We started a war over oil in the Middle East.

"Tipton kangaroo rat..."

Sara thought to herself, if they are trying to kill Peter, now they are both targets because of the documents.

"Oh my God!" Sara remembered as she pulled the loose pieces of papers from her pants. She still had a handful of Occidental papers. She almost swerved off the road as she glanced at the name on the top of the paper: "Sexton, Representative Randall." "Uhh, Utah prairie dog..."

Sara had never made it to the letter "U" before, but she had looked up some names to use if she ever got that far. Someone just tried to kill her. The thoughts still raced through her head. Shots fired, the short, stout Filipino woman screaming. Peter pushing her through the door. Peter. Is he all right? What is next?

"T... U... V... Virginia Northern flying squirrel..."

Peter had to be all right. He always knew what to do. What to say. When to listen. When to speak. He was always right. And he knew it. Sara never considered him arrogant. But he never lacked self-confidence. That was for sure. "Nothing is impossible," he always said, "it just hasn't been done yet."

What is next?

"W... W... W..."

If Peter is right about this, then going to the police or anyone like that is out of the question. He said trust no one. Just go to the office and wait for him. Wait.

"Whooping crane... X... X..."

There has to be something else to do other than wait. Her father would know what to do. Dad is the only one to trust.

"X... X..."

There had to be people out there who could help, and the Judge would know those people. That had to be the answer.

"Damn it, I never did an X. Y, Yunnan snub-nosed monkey."

Peter said no one and that he would handle everything, but he just doesn't have the experience the Judge has. The Judge will know what to do. Sara picked up her car phone, but before she hit her speed dial she paused and said aloud "Z, Zanzibar red colubus."

# EIGHTEEN

As he hung up the phone, Judge Ahrens thought of his father. He never knew his father, only knew of him. But all he knew he admired. He now wondered whether his daughter could ever feel that way about him.

What he knew about his father, Douglas Ahrens had learned through survivors. Years of research formed the patchwork which enabled him to picture the man who brought him into the world. Public records were of little help since most had been destroyed in the war. It was the survivors who told the story of Isaac Ahrens, one of the original leaders of the Dutch Underground.

Long before the Nazi occupation, before the stripping of Dutch civil liberties, before labor camps, before Auschwitz, a young law student married his school sweetheart, Rachael Van Oostertang. After school and marriage, a promising career in law awaited Isaac Ahrens. After a few years of civil service in Amsterdam, the couple grew restless in the big city. The timing could not have been better for a change. Isaac's uncle passed away, leaving Isaac his private practice in the small country town of Hoogeveen in Drenthe. The "big city lawyer" had no trouble fitting into the new small-town lifestyle. His reputation in the region as a fair and just man grew. This reputation, and some very influential client landowners, soon won him the region's judgeship.

Because of the uneasiness of the economic times, Isaac and Rachael waited to have children. But Rachael could wait no longer. The pregnancy was difficult on Rachael, but Abraham Ahrens was born on July 2, 1932. His parents affectionately called him Bram.

The world around Bram changed quickly and dramatically as the economic depression of the late '20s and early '30s led to the rise of Fascist regimes. The most significant impact to the newborn's life, to his parents' lives, to the whole world, was the appointment of Hitler as Chancellor of Germany. Hitler's rise to power led to devastating consequences for Jews in the Netherlands. While Jewish mortality rates under Nazi occupation were shocking in Belgium (forty percent) and France (twenty-five percent), nothing compared to the staggering seventy-three percent mortality rate Jews faced in the Netherlands. Of the more than 140,000 Jews living in the pre-war Netherlands, at least 102,000 were murdered or died in Nazi camps. With Hitler in power, to be born a Dutch Jew was tantamount to being given a death sentence.

Isaac Ahrens and his family remained sheltered from the ugliness thirty miles away across the border in Germany where the Nazi regime began to swell and propagate anti-Semitism. The simple country life suited Isaac, Rachael, and Bram. The town in Hoogeveen was only a few miles away for necessities or just to see neighbors. Furthermore, Assen was not that far if Isaac was ever required for a special appearance. The Ahrens' country home was not lavish, but it definitely provided more creature comforts than other homes in the area. Many of their "neighbors" were farmers living within several miles of Hoogeveen. Life in the country remained peaceful.

Yet in Drenthe, Isaac noticed a significant change. Jewish refugees began to cross the border. At first only a few, but by 1938 refugees numbered into the thousands. In the middle of nowhere between Assen and Hoogeveen, the Dutch government built a refugee camp to house the Jews fleeing Germany in Westerbork. As one of the region's judicial leaders, Isaac visited Westerbork. Appalled at the conditions at the refugee camp, he lent whatever political clout he could to establish the Centrale Commissie Vluchtelingenvraagstukken (Central Committee for Refugee Questions). The Committee helped refugees, but it did not take long to overwhelm the system. Things were changing. Despite the Westerbork refugee camp twelve miles to the north and Hitler's Nazi regime thirty miles to the east, the Ahrens' country life still remained peaceful, but not for long.

On May 9, 1940, German tanks and troops raced across the Dutch border. Isaac barely kept ahead of the ensuing army as he fled Drenthe to be with his family. The Third Reich captured the Netherlands in five short days.

At the time of the surrender, Rachael was pregnant with her second child.

Most Dutch viewed the German occupation as an inconvenience that would only last a short time. This war would be a short one, people would say. The Germans would be gone soon and everything would return as it was. What the Dutch underestimated was this was not just a German military occupation, it was an annexation. Holland was to become a part of Germany. On May 29, 1940, a Reichkommissar was appointed to head the Dutch administrative apparatus which had been left in place. Such a maneuver demonstrated that in Holland, as opposed to other German advancements, the Nazis were not concerned with Allied borders or military targets. The Nazis in Holland were extending the German borders. And within the German borders, not only was Judaism not tolerated, it was to be obliterated.

Many of those who heard horror stories from refugees were pleasantly surprised that little had changed in their lives after the Nazi occupation. Their fears had subsided. Unlike his countrymen, Isaac Ahrens' fears turned to mistrust. Isaac, Rachael, and Bram still lived their secluded life. Isaac had his duties to attend, but Rachael and Bram, at Isaac's instruction, rarely left the country house. They were never allowed into town. Isaac had to protect his family. And the only way he knew how to was to shield them from the outside world. In addition, he had to shield his unborn child from the Nazis. The best way to accomplish this was to conceal Rachel's pregnancy. Rachael chastised her husband at first, but she loved and trusted him. She knew that Isaac always had their best interests at heart. Rachael and Bram remained in the country with only themselves to keep them company.

In town, life grew worse every day. Liberties which Jews had enjoyed, and Isaac had championed and upheld throughout his career, were stripped one by one.

Every week it was something new. Nothing dramatic at first. It was always gradual to ensure compliance with as little objection as possible. The Nazi plan worked perfectly on the naïve Dutch people. Each day the Dutch Jews told themselves that living without this or living without that was only an inconvenience. So when Jews were required to register for identification purposes it was only an inconvenience. They could live with it. The war would be over soon. Then the next week, or next month, it would be something different. A liberty once enjoyed, or taken for granted, would be lost. What neither Isaac Ahrens nor the Dutch Jewry in general imagined was that these "minor inconveniences" were all part of Endlosung, the Final Solution: identification, isolation, deportation, and extermination.

Isaac Abrams' legal career ended with a Nazi edict in October 1940 requiring all government officials to sign affidavits that they were not Jewish. By filing a non-Aryan Form B, officials were dismissed, as was Isaac Ahrens. Even the Dutch High Court's President was dismissed. No longer would Isaac Ahrens be able to protect peoples' rights under the law, even if these rights had dwindled with every passing day.

On November 11, 1940, Douglas Ahrens was born, although no records reflect that fact. Isaac Ahrens had one of his trusted neighbors, Mirjam van Galen, a widowed farmer who lived a mile south of them, midwife for Rachael. Isaac swore her to secrecy. This was no problem for Mirjam, who had last been to town five years ago to bury her husband. Isaac did not record the birth. Since Rachael had kept her pregnancy secret, it was as if Douglas Ahrens was never born.

In the following spring, Isaac received a letter from the Joodse Raad voor Amsterdam. The Council requested that he return to Amsterdam and serve an appropriate administrative position within the Council. Isaac declined. Isaac had little interest in subjecting his family to the turmoil that existed in Amsterdam.

A few months later, Isaac received another letter from the Joodse Raad voor Amsterdam. The Council now requested that he serve with the Jewish Council in Drenthe. By this time, the Nazis had banned all Jews from owning radios. Isaac's radio in his office in Hoogeveen was the only link to the outside world. If it was found, there was the threat of being sent to the punishment camp at Mouthausen. In order to keep apprised of the war and avoid imprisonment, Isaac discarded his radio and joined the Jewish Council. The Joodse Raad clearly only had their own self-interests in mind, as opposed to the interests of their Jewish brothers and sisters. However, as a member of the Council, Isaac did have his hand on the pulse of the war effort in the Netherlands. It was obvious that the Jewish people were being isolated and excluded from the rest of the Dutch society based upon the various edicts and decrees handed down. Doctors, lawyers, and other professionals were banned from the stock and other commodity exchanges. Public parks, swimming pools and beaches all became segregated. Even some schools became segregated. After segregation, Jews were forbidden in those public places as well as libraries, movie theatres, hotels, etc. However, the regulations that tipped Isaac off were the various orders requiring Jews to register all their assets: stocks, bank accounts, land, anything of value. As the orders passed over his desk, Isaac feared the worst.

June 26, 1942, confirmed Isaac Ahrens' worst fears. On that day, the Jewish Council received notification of the beginning of deportation. Within days he was notified that the SS would take over the supervision of Camp Westerbork. From that point on, all he could think of was that his wife and two sons were within miles of the SS. Several weeks later, Isaac discovered information that only the highest echelons of the Jewish Council knew. Deportations began from Westerbork to a final destination, Auschwitz.

As far as Isaac was concerned, deportation equaled death. He had heard enough stories from German and Polish Jewish refugees to know that once a Jew left on a German train, in all likelihood he would not return. Fortunately, being on the Jewish Council had its benefits. First and foremost, council members, their families, staff, and other "indispensable people" were exempt from deportation. The Council dispensed numbered stamps to indispensables. The numbered stamps, a life vest more than a commodity, were few and far between. Isaac, of course, was issued a stamp. So were Rachael and Bram. Bram had a stamp; even at only ten years old he had no identification papers, but had a stamp. These were not times to take risks. However, little Douglas was a risk. There would be no stamp for the infant because as far as the Third Reich was concerned, he did not exist. Rachael and Bram discussed registering him, but Isaac's mistrust of the Nazis prevailed. From his experience on the Council, Isaac knew that whatever concession the

Reichskommissariat granted with the right hand, they soon retracted with the left. Little Doug Ahrens would remain a non-person. For him, there would be no official stamp.

Of the fifteen thousand holders of Jewish Council exemption stamps, Dutch Jews in Amsterdam held fourteen thousand. The Provinces received only a thousand. Of that thousand, Isaac was able to finagle two hundred stamps for his province, an extraordinary amount considering the location and population of Drenthe. However, Isaac knew he had to help whoever he could, and the most needy were already in Westerbork, the last stop in Holland before Auschwitz.

Isaac Ahrens knew the area of Westerbork better than most, and certainly better than the Germans who ran the camp. Its location served its purpose well. As an isolated campground in the middle of nowhere, the detention center favored its custodian in defending attacks or identifying mass defections. In achieving the Endlosung, the SS was more concerned with volume rather than individual defections. It was not easy to escape Westerbork. However it was easy to gain access to its detainees. That is all that Isaac required.

Old Mirjam van Galen's farm extended to within a mile and a half of Westerbork. From the north end of her fields, it was only two miles to the Westerbork Detention Center. Between Mirjam's fields and the Detention Center lay one mile of woodlands and another mile of barren wasteland. From Mirjam's farm it was easy to access the Detention Center without being detected. Time and patience were required, but one could get up to the fences easily without being detected. It would require a young person's endurance and agility, but the two miles could be covered in a half an hour.

New detainees entered the Westerbork Detention center by the south entrance and were processed on the south side as well. Usually, due to the relatively slow nature of bureaucracy, new deportees were held overnight in two barricades, again located on the south side. During this final processing, deportees had one last chance to prove that deportation was a mistake. It was one last chance to prove they were not a Jew, or a baptized Jew, or a mixed marriage Jew, or a Jew that held a Jewish Council exemption stamp. One last chance to avoid Auschwitz.

With his own money, Isaac bribed a low-level Drenthe SS Vatersturmfuhrer to obtain train schedules for deportations. He received information the day the train was to arrive at Westerbork. However, for Isaac's plan, that was all the information he required.

With more money and exemption stamps, Isaac enlisted three sets of runners, mostly Jews, who sought stamps for themselves or their families, and one gentile. There were four criteria for a runner. First, one had to be desperate enough to risk being caught and sent to the prison camp at Manthausen. Second, one had to be fast, or it did not matter how desperate they were. Third, a runner had to know how to read and write. Finally, and most importantly, Isaac had to trust them.

Every day, one of the SS Vatersturmfuhrer would deliver reports, orders, decrees, or just news. If a train was arriving in Westerbork that day, the soldier would include a schedule detailing the estimated arrival of the train. Isaac would memorize the schedule, then burn it. He then would drive home by way of Mirjam's farm. Isaac would tell Mirjam when the next train was due and leave with some of her produce. An hour before the train, Mirjam rode out to the northwest corner of her fields to burn a bundle of old crops. The small bonfire was a signal to the runners. There were three sets of two runners. Deportation trains only ran on Tuesdays, Wednesdays, and Fridays. A set of runners was assigned to each day. The pair would hide in the woodlands north of Mirjam's farm. Upon seeing the signal, they would race through the woods and the fields to Westerbork Detention Center. From the fields, there was about a hundred yards that they would have to crawl on all fours to remain under cover of the brush. It was relatively easy to sneak all the way up to the fence and remain hidden from any guards. The hard part was maintaining one's patience and composure while the deportees were unloaded and herded into the courtyard. Further control was required to wait for a couple of the deportees to roam by the fence. The first few stragglers would win the lottery. The runners would take down their names and addresses and give them the exemption stamps for their identification cards. Each runner had two or three stamps; any more would raise suspicion and the SS deportation personnel would realize what was happening. After obtaining the information and delivering the stamps, the runners would flee. The next day another pair of runners would station themselves in the woods by Mirjam's farm, while the runners from the day before would visit Isaac Ahrens for more stamps and to deliver the names and addresses. Isaac wired this information to Amsterdam to be included on his exemption list. As lucky deportees wandered into town, the region filled with whispers of angels who descended upon them delivering freedom.

For each mission a runner completed, he would get one stamp for himself and his family. Isaac gave two extra stamps to a runner with a larger family. The gentile used his stamps to help his neighbors. After eight weeks, Isaac had given the runners one hundred thirty-five exemption stamps. The remainder he used for his family, friends, and staff. In dispensing the stamps, he admonished each individual not to depend on the exemption. He encouraged them to become an onderduikerrs and go underground. Isaac knew that the stamps could afford only immediate, limited protection. However, for some, especially those who were able to avoid the train from Westerbork to Auschwitz, the exemption stamp proved essential to life.

When all the stamps had been dispensed and the names gathered for exemption lists, Isaac prepared his family to go underground. The hardest part, he knew, would be to explain to Rachael that they would have to leave Bram and Doug. The boys would have a better chance surviving with a Catholic family. Through his resources, Isaac found a family up in Friesland by Heerebveen who would care for the boys. It would not be easy, but Isaac knew that soon they would have no other choice. There would come a time he would have to say goodbye to his boys. Although he would never tell Rachael this, he knew that that goodbye would probably be the last time they saw their children.

That pain was felt again in the next generation. As Douglas "Ironsides" Ahrens removed his clenched fists from his weeping eyes, he knew that he could have seen his daughter for the last time. He wanted one more chance to say goodbye and that he loved her. For what he had to do, if called upon, would sever the family bond again.

# NINETEEN

The Castro was in full swing. Although the party had died down considerably since Halloween, Monday night in the Castro compared to Friday or Saturday in any other city. The Castro was always colorful, and tonight was no exception. The setting sun allowed the street to be illuminated by neon lights, which further illustrated the exuberance emanating from the neighborhood. Rich blue, red, and pink lights lit up the neighborhood. Each shop also was colorfully decorated with rainbow gay liberation flags or rainbow-themed displays.

In addition to the festive light show provided by the Castro, sounds of pulsating and pumping music from the various open-air bars and discos filled the atmosphere. And, of course, coupled with the Castro regulars milling in and out of the numerous shops, boutiques, bars, discos, and theaters, there was no doubt the nightlife was vibrant. Peter could not decide if it was the people, more than the lights or music, who breathed life into this San Francisco neighborhood.

Obviously many of the Castro's natives were openly gay, men holding hands, women arm in arm. Mostly, there were groups, three or four men together, some women, but mostly men. Big men in short shorts walking tiny dogs. Thin men with fine features and precision haircuts laughed and smoked at the entrance of every bar. Club boys on street corners handing out fliers for dance clubs. There also was a fair share of tourists descending on one of the Bay Area's hot spots. Peter, a single, physically fit young man dressed in a T-shirt and khakis fit right in with the crowd whose wardrobe of choice was basically T-shirts and jeans. Peter's shoes, however, were not at nice as many of the pairs walking the Castro.

Also working the Castro were several groups of young men who were either still decked out from the night before or who felt one night of Halloween was not enough. One group, which included costumes of a Native American, cowboy, motorcycle cop, army man, and a construction worker, strutted down the street singing "Y... M... C..." They were too far ahead of Peter for him to hear the rest. A few leather-clad S & M groups walked by asking "Trick or Trick?" Peter would never forget the giant bunny rabbit hopping down the street. A man, probably in his late twenties, stood six-foot-six, as he paraded down the street scantily dressed in baby blue rabbit ears, a choke collar with a shiny brass bell attached, fuzzy blue mittens, a matching fuzzy pair of shorts with a large cotton tail and fish-net stockings. Peter almost wished he had a carrot.

Peter thought he blended into the crowd well despite being in the minority of straight men on the block. The two suits who had been following him would stick out like sore thumbs in this crowd. Considering his attire, separating Peter from the he rest of the crowd would be like finding a needle in a haystack. Confident he was safe for the time being, Peter strolled the Castro thinking of what had to be done.

He was still distracted. The large number of couples only made Peter think of Sara. He was confident she had escaped. By the time the two suits had begun following him, Sara had rounded the corner in the opposite direction. However, that only accounts for the blue suit and the brown suit. What if there were other suits, agents? And what about the woman? Where was she and what was she doing? Also what was in that package she had? Drugs? Money? Sara better be all right or he would never forgive himself.

Peter knew that Sara would be expecting an e-mail in about fifteen to twenty minutes. He needed to find one of those full-service copy centers or a library or something soon. For that, a telephone book would be the key, preferably yellow pages. A phone book required a public phone. Contrary to his inbred-latent-ever-so-minimal-but-still-present-midwestern-homophobic fears, this required Peter to enter one of the Castro's lively establishments.

"Here we go," Peter quietly said to himself as he pensively walked into Babs' Boys, one of the many bars/discos on Castro Street. He was not sure what alarmed him more, the dull red lights and fire engine-red wall, or the pulsating, no throbbing, club music. It sure was not the men in the bar, because there was hardly a soul in the place. The room was fairly wide open with chairs and tables at one end, stools and mirrors lining the sides and a dance floor separating everyone from the bar. "Everyone" included three men by the window, a couple at the bar, and the bartender. Peter approached the bar.

"What can I do for youuu?" the bartender asked, as he looked Peter up and down.

"Do you have a phone and a directory?" Peter asked.

"But of course, just by the little boys' room there is a pay phone with a yellow pages."

"Thank you."

"Anything else and I'll be here."

Although still uncomfortable, Peter almost felt flattered that the bartender was hitting on him. As Peter turned the corner toward the restrooms, the overbearing red lights changed to purple from the black and white light bulbs illuminating the hallway. Peter's white T-shirt and shorts were now purple. Peter pulled the phone book from the shelf, paging through it for libraries or a copy center. Nothing was in the area. As Peter aimlessly flipped through the book he remembered that Jimmy Powell said that he picked his e-mail up at one of the coffee houses on campus. Quickly turning the pages back, Peter found exactly what he wanted and it was only about seven blocks away–CJ's Cyber Java.

Just as Peter closed the telephone book, he was thrown by a kick delivered to his ribs sending him to the floor writhing in pain. Unable to regain his composure, two more kicks rocked Peter's ribs, then another to his groin left him incapacitated and gasping for air.

"Get up."

Peter heard a voice.

"Get up now."

The voice was a woman's voice, but Peter could barely get to his hands and knees to see who it was.

"There is a gun aimed directly at the base of your skull, so no sudden movements," the woman's voice commanded as she ran her fingers through his hair.

Peter turned his head and was not surprised by who he saw. He was surprised by her ability to incapacitate him so quickly. It was the woman from O'Shea's and the Cliff House. Her gloved hand pointed a handgun directly at his head.

"I see you moved up from photography."

Tasha smiled as Peter rolled over onto his side.

"Get up now!"

The smile vanished when she aimed the gun directly at his face.

"You are either going to kill me now or later, so what's the hurry?"

The woman fired a shot into the wall directly over Peter's head. Although the music was extremely loud, it could not muffle the sound of the gunshot. Stunned but obedient, Peter began to rise to his knees.

A man flung open the bathroom door while another stood directly behind him.

"What the hell is going on here!" demanded the first man, who was well built, balding, had a goatee, and stood about six-foot-four dressed in his boots, blue jeans, a plain white T-shirt, and a sweater vest. The man behind him was slightly shorter than the first, trim and wearing a white oxford over a black tank top, and again, blue jeans.

Peter reacted quickly and whimpered, "Don't hurt me."

The line confused Tasha.

"Listen bitch..." The man with the goatee pushed Tasha against the wall. Before Tasha could react, Peter lunged at her and the man with the goatee knocking all three of them to the ground. The handgun slid down the hall towards the dance floor. Both Peter and Tasha watched the gun slide along the floor. Finally gaining her composure, Tasha kneed the man with the goatee in the groin, but before she could escape the tangled threesome, the other man jumped on the pile elbowing her in the head. Peter rolled away and scrambled down the hall to the gun. Glancing back to see Tasha manhandle the two Bab's Boys patrons, Peter grabbed the gun, bumped into the bartender who had come to see the commotion, and raced out the door.

———⊷•⊰———

Back at Mission Dolores, Detective Martinez surveyed both ends of Dolores Street. Police cars had blocked off one hundred feet north and south of the street. Of course the media had arrived before she had been able to get to the scene. Interviews had been taking place for the past ten minutes, but no one had seen anything. Typical.

"Detective?"

A young officer approached Detective Martinez.

"Yes."

"The older woman over there, Mrs. Marcos, runs the gift shop. You will want to bring her in. She said two Caucasian men, late thirties, early forties shot at a couple in the cemetery and chased them all outside."

"Can she ID the shooters?"

"No, just white and wearing suits."

"Suits?"

"Coat, tie, slacks."

"Take her in for a statement and have her look at some books."

Detective Larry Nelson exited the gift shop and made way to Martinez.

"Looks like we got ourselves a live one," Detective Nelson shouted.

"Come again?" responded Martinez.

"Some reporter was talking with some of the witnesses and they are saying the 'Shakespeare' killer was here."

"'Shakespeare'?"

"That English writer."

"I know who Shakespeare is."

"You know, Shakespeare, 'let's kill all the lawyers.'"

"Yes. Once again I know who Shakespeare is."

"That guy we got the bulletin on. The one wanted for killing those two lawyers in St. Louis and the Dean of that law school."

"What was a reporter doing talking to our witnesses?"

"They just got here before I did."

"Where is the reporter?"

"She left, but some of the other networks are here. They are all going with that story tonight."

"Nelson," Martinez was about to give her junior detective a lecture when she stopped herself. "Nelson, if this Shakespeare was this killer, how come he wasn't doing the shooting, but being shot at?"

"Bounty hunters."

The junior detective felt pretty confident about his response.

"What?"

"That's what they are saying, bounty hunters tracked him here."

"Bounty hunters wearing suits?"

"I'm just telling you what I heard through the witnesses and reporters."

"Nelson, ever think of doing a little investigating yourself?" Martinez stared at her apprentice. "Forget it, let me talk to that Marcos woman."

None of this made any sense to Martinez. More importantly, she was not going to let the media dictate her investigation. Shakespeare? These people will say anything to liven up a story.

"Who's Marcos?"

Martinez looked around and noticed skeletons and ghosts on windows across the street. "Don't worry your pretty little head about that Nelson, you have bigger things to fear?"

"What's that boss?"

The eager detective looked up at his supervisor as she ascended the stairs of the gift shop.

"Tomorrow is Day of the Dead."

# TWENTY

Although only seven blocks from the Babs' Boys, it had taken Peter over an hour and a half to reach CJ's Cyber Java. A series of alleys, dimly lit streets, and fifteen minutes of paranoia casing the coffee house out in order to assure himself that no one could have followed him there, prevented him from arriving earlier.

CJ's Cyber Java was exactly what it was called, a coffee house with about a dozen personal computers hooked up to the Internet. A patron could enjoy a nice imported blend while on some Internet chat line. The terminals, bolted on top of a select group of tables, were scattered throughout the coffee house. Ceiling fans hung between the exposed HVAC system circulated the air in the dark blue, gray, and black open room. A large black chalkboard identified the espressos, coffees, cappuccinos, mochas, and imported sodas offered in colored chalk. The cafe even had two beat-up sofas, several used armchairs, and a bookshelf containing a library of books ranging from Kafka to Dr. Seuss. The black-clad girl behind the counter wore square spectacles with aquamarine-tinted hair. Intentionally or not, the hair matched the blue-green coffee tables and plastic chairs. CJ's was relatively empty. Peter, the clerk, and two young men having coffee on one of the sofas were the only ones in the coffee house. The alternative music befit the decorum.

Peter set himself up at terminal number seven. It was in a corner by a window where he could view the outside and see both the front entrance and the back exit. Peter logged on and checked the CNC Web page to see if there had been any new developments. There was. CNC was running with a story from an anonymous source that he and Jenny may have been having an affair. The source further speculated that envy over his brother's life started this killing spree. The story was so full of holes and conjecture that he could not believe that someone was printing it. Worse yet, Jenny and the kids would soon be swamped by the media. Meanwhile CNC was bragging that they were the first ones with the story. Sure they were, they made it up.

Feeling completely disgusted, he contacted the Sienna Club's Web page.

| | |
|---|---|
| *To:* | *Sara Ahrens* |
| *Message:* | *Worried about you.* |
| | *- J. Sukapukavic* |

Peter received an immediate response.

| | |
|---|---|
| *To:* | *Sukapukavic* |
| *Message:* | *Where have you been? Are you all right?* |
| *To:* | *Sara* |
| *Message:* | *Yes. Sorry, I couldn't get to you sooner. Long story. Have you talked to anyone?* |
| *To:* | *Sukapukavic* |
| *Message:* | *Yes. When I hadn't heard from you I contacted the Judge.* |

Damn! Peter thought to himself. The message continued.

> *You took so long that I didn't know what to do. I told him not to do anything until I called him back. He believes you, Peter and I know he can help. He said he would do so on your terms. He has some ideas and wants to talk to you. I have to call him back. What should I do?*

Peter thought while he digested the fact that he was now endangering another person in this mess. The worst-case scenario is that he now put her in danger. Even if she was not in danger, she could be smeared all over the media like Jenny had been. He could not undo what Sara had done, but he could limit how far the Judge would get involved which would limit Sara's further risk.

| | |
|---|---|
| *To:* | *Sara* |
| *Message:* | *When you call him back, have him pick you up and stay at his house tonight. You will be safer there. Tell the Judge I will meet him tomorrow. I miss you. I want you safe.* |

| To: | Sukapukavic |
|---|---|
| Message: | *I will be fine and I miss you, too. We will get through this. Where can we pick you up?* |

Peter needed food, a shower, new clothes, and sleep, but staying the night with Sara and the Judge was out of the question. After what happened at the mission and the Castro, Peter could not afford another encounter with the two suits or the woman from O'Shea's.

| To: | Sara |
|---|---|
| Message: | *No, I will meet you tomorrow.* |
| To: | Sukapukavic |
| Message: | *Just stay with us, it will be safer.* |
| To: | Sara |
| Message: | *No, I still have to run a couple of errands.* |

Peter had stuffed the gun in his sock before he had entered CJ's. He tied a thin strip of cloth around it to keep it in place. Now the makeshift holster itched. Fearing he would shoot his foot off, Peter carefully scratched his leg then continued.

| | *You just stay with the Judge and I will meet him tomorrow morning at Union Square at 8:00.* |
|---|---|
| To: | Sukapukavic |
| Message: | *That doesn't make any sense. Where will you stay tonight? Just let us pick you up.* |

After the mission and the Castro, Peter's paranoia had hit an all-time high. The only way someone could find him is if they followed Sara to him. That means they could be watching the Judge, too. If he showed up at the Judge's, surely they would all be in danger. They were after him and him alone. The further he stayed away from Sara the safer she would be. If they were to meet, Sara could not be there, only the Judge. It also had to be in a public place. That would be more natural. Less conspicuous. Then and only then could he be sure that the Judge was not being followed.

| To: | Sara |
|---|---|
| Message: | *I will talk to the Judge, but it has to be him alone. Promise that you will not come.* |

Peter waited several minutes before he received a response.

| | |
|---|---|
| *To:* | *Mr. Sukapukavic* |
| *Message:* | *I will not go with the Judge. But you need to promise me something, too. Promise me that I will see you again. I miss you, Peter.* |
| *To:* | *Sara* |
| *Message:* | *Sara, you know there's always tomorrow.* |

# TWENTY-ONE

1 am Election Day.

The large handcrafted cherry-wood grandfather clock rang with one chime. The chain slightly rattled in the silent, dimly lit study as he pulled his gold pocket watch from his vest. The elderly man compared the settings on both timepieces.

"Running late again."

The sharply dressed man, in another tailor-made Savile Row navy blue pinstriped three-piece suit closed the lid of his pocket watch. He gave the globe a twirl for good measure and walked to the desk. The Savile Row man picked up the phone and stated to the person on the other end of the line.

"Put the call through now."

A moment or two passed.

"Sir," the voice from the speakerphone answered, "your call is ready."

The voice on the speakerphone was distinctly British.

"Well my good friend, out late at the clubs again?" chided the Englishman.

"In these dire times, I cannot afford to indulge the cavalier, bohemian lifestyle you enjoy," retorted the Savile Row man.

"Get me off that damn squawk box of yours!" demanded the Englishman.

The Savile Row man rolled his eyes and picked up the phone.

"Are you pleased now?"

*"Grazzi."*

*"Prego."*

"Now, where are we with our little Lebanese friend?" the Englishman continued after the exchange of pleasantries.

"I have been told that everything is going according to plan."

"What does our man say?"

"Nothing I can ever understand."

"You cannot deny his effectiveness."

"He did say that what was lost will be found tomorrow, or something like that."

"Maybe I should be speaking with him."

"Help yourself."

"My friend, you need not be so terse with me. He can be odd, but his effectiveness is undeniable. He knows what to do, and nothing will interfere with him accomplishing his task. Nothing has before. *Niente.*"

"*Niente?* What about Paris?" snapped the Savile Row man.

"Paris, Paris, Paris. Sometimes I think you are going French on me."

"We lost a good man there."

"Lost is not the appropriate word, but you digress my friend. Back to the issue at hand, when will everything be resolved?" inquired the Englishman.

"Well before your nightly entertainment begins."

"Please do not take this in the wrong light my friend, but you are not charming at this hour. Keep me informed."

"I always do." The Savile Row man hung up the phone and again pulled out his pocket watch, checked it against the grandfather clock, then snapped it shut.

Peter Farrell had been wandering the streets of San Francisco for hours. He was tired but not sleepy. Knowing that Sara was safe put his mind at ease somewhat, but he still second-guessed himself for getting her involved in the first place. He wanted to be with her so much right now, but he knew his presence would only endanger her. One thing he never forgot about Sara, actually he remembered almost every moment they spent together, was how safe he felt in her arms. In her arms an outside world did not exist. It was only the two of them. No tests, no studies, no work, no stress, just comfort. She was a safe haven to escape to whenever the world started to close in on him. He wanted to feel that safe haven now.

Peter tried to draw as little attention to himself as possible. The easy part about being inconspicuous in the middle of the night was that essentially no one was out that could recognize him. Furthermore, it was easier to spot squad cars with their searchlights roaming the alleyways. On the downside, there was hardly anyone to blend in with. The tourists and busybodied shoppers had long since retired for the evening. The streets were practically empty. Practically, that is. Because after the tourists and shoppers retire, the city's some odd fifteen thousand homeless own the streets. To survive the night Peter needed to blend in.

Peter had two goals for the night. Survive and end up by Union Square in the morning. Hotels were out of the question. First, at this time of night he may not get a room even if he risked it. Second, the risks were too great. He would stand out registering for a room. There would be no hustle or bustle or commotion where he could conceal himself in the shuffle of people. At this hour he would stick out like a sore thumb. It was easy at first when no one knew the infamous "Shakespeare Killer" was in town. By now, every local news station would have covered the mission shooting incident and broadcast his picture throughout the city. The police would have notified all the cab stations by now. And cabbies listen to police ban radios anyway. Cabs were out of the question. With the MUNI down at this hour, that pretty much left walking.

Walking north on Valencia, Peter gradually changed his appearance with each block. First he completely untucked his shirt. Next he pulled his baseball cap further over his eyes. He then started to slouch more when he walked. Then he slowed his slouched walk to a shuffle. By the time he reached Market Street, no one gave him a second look or questioned why he would be on the streets at this hour. That is until he reached the Civic Center. Eight blocks west of Union Square, Peter found himself in United Nation's Plaza, the middle of the Civic Center District. The area contained a plethora of beaux arts buildings, one of the finest collections in the country. Their splendor is further illustrated when illuminated at night. There is City Hall, built in 1914, displaying its extravagant baroque revival. At the south end of the plaza there is Bill Graham Civic Auditorium, pre-dating City Hall by a year. Then there are the nearly identical Veterans Auditorium Building and the War Memorial Opera House. Finally, across the street from the sculpture garden is the spectacular modern glass-walled home of the San Francisco Symphony orchestra, the Louise M. Davis Symphony Hall.

"Littered," as the many tuxedo clad and bejeweled would term it, among these beautiful beaux art buildings lie many of the city's ragged homeless. With their belongings in shopping carts, bags, or tied to them, street people milled about the plaza. Some were obviously inebriated ranting or raving, but most minded their own business, what little of it they had. Many appeared on their own, like Peter, but some huddled together. Some slept, some roamed, some just sat and talked. One man saw Peter and flapped his arms up and down.

"Hey, are you a cop?" he yelled at Peter, still flapping.

Peter walked by the stairs, heckled by those in the bleachers.

"No citation here, cop," yelled the man, "I'm not doing nothin'. I'm invisible."

Peter started to walk a bit faster.

A second man stood up and began to walk the stairs, following Peter.

"Hey, pig! The mayor goin' to have you kick us off these steps. I used to pay taxes for these steps."

The first man shouted to a group of men at the bottom of the stairs in front of Peter, "Hey, Dogman's picking a fight with a cop."

The man at the other end of the steps now took notice of Peter. The first man began to follow Dogman along the step, parallel with Peter. Just before Peter reached the group of men, a squad car turned up the street toward them. If some kind of scuffle broke out or the squad car had any reason to stop, surely Peter would be caught. The plaza area was too wide open.

"I'm not a cop," Peter shouted up to Dogman, but making sure the group in front of him also heard him say, "I am a reporter."

Dogman stopped and put his hands on his hips as if he had just vanquished the enemy.

"So that's why you're dressed like that," he said.

"That's no cop," one of the three men at the end of the steps commented.

"I knew you were some kind of undercover something dressed like that."

"Dressed like what?" Peter had thought he had disguised himself well.

"New shoes, your clothes look clean, no one would believe you belong down here," Dogman said.

"Yeah, no one," Dogman's sidekick repeated.

Dogman wore a black tank top covered by a worn blue jean jacket which matched his blue jeans. What stood out were his black, cracked cowboy boots. He walked bowlegged as if he had been working on the ranch all day. His face was hidden beneath a burly, unkept, nicotine-stained moustache and beard that was a mixture of sandy brown and gray. Not a tall man, Dogman's bowlegged stance made him appear even shorter than he actually was.

"Have I got a story to tell you," the man who trailed Dogman began. He was a short man, dressed similar to Dogman in worn jeans but wore a pair of ragged tennis shoes instead of cowboy boots. Although both men were Caucasian, their tanned leather faces suggested a Native American quality.

"Shuddup Squeezer," Dogman barked at the second man.

"Yeah, shuddup Squeezer," the large African American in front of Peter said.

The squad car slowed in front of the group of men who waved as if it was a cruise ship just embarking on its maiden voyage. The squad car sped off as the men giggled.

"What was that all about?" Peter asked.

Dogman answered while the others men laughed, "Just a little game we play with them. We are all invisible tonight. They only see us when they want to see us. Sometimes they stop and start handing out citations like lottery tickets; other times they see right through us, won't answer a question or nothing. So sometimes me and the boys wave our arms around to see if we're invisible. Tonight we're invisible."

Squeezer finished his snorted laughter and stepped in front of Peter.

"I want to tell you my story. I've been working on it."

"Working on it?" asked Peter.

"Oh yeah. It's really good now."

"What do you mean?"

"I've added more stuff like you said."

Peter was obviously confused.

"Some reporter the other week came down here and was writing a story," Dogman began. "He talked to Squeezer and Squeezer gave him a real good story, but the guy said he couldn't give him any money."

Dogman glanced down at Squeezer then back at Peter.

"So since that time he has been working on his story."

"I don't think it works that way," Peter told Squeezer.

"I told you Squeezer. Nobody is going to buy your story," Dogman chided.

"Yeah, nobody will buy your story," the other man chimed in.

"Actually, for my story, I am trying to find the shelter where you guys stay."

"If we stayed in a shelter we would not be talking to you right now," the large African American bluntly told Peter.

"Here is where I stay," Dogman pulled a credit card from his pocket.

"It's good at a hundred locations," Squeezer said as he began to snort and laugh again.

Once again Peter obviously looked confused.

"This is my hotel key. I can get into any ATM booth in the city."

"They're great on a cold night," Squeezer chimed in.

The large man said, "If you are looking for a shelter, there's one down there a couple blocks, then take a right," he pointed down the street, "but you have to sign up for a bed before noon and they won't tell if they have one until after three."

"Thanks," Peter said as he started to walk where the homeless man had pointed. After taking two steps, Peter walked back and gave each of them a twenty and told Squeezer he would come back for his story some time.

After Peter had walked a couple blocks in the direction he was told, he stopped thinking about avoiding the police for a block or two. Peter had found himself entering the Tenderloin, San Francisco's Red Light District. It was completely different from where he had seen Dogman and the others. Among the beaux arts architecture the homeless appeared out of place, like innocent trespassers. But in the Tenderloin, which consists of couples with prostitutes, drug dealers, and other unsavory characters, the homeless melted into the surroundings. One man slept in a doorway. A ragged couple used each other as props to sleep by a garbage can; another man was rolled around the foot of a stoop. Peter found himself looking straight ahead or down at the ground. With just the street or street light in his view, Peter understood why Dogman believed he could be invisible.

Another patrol car passed two streets ahead, and Peter decided to walk north out of the neighborhood and away from the cops. He was tired again, and sleepy and cold. After two blocks, he ran into O'Farrell Street and considered it a good omen. He took a right thinking Union Square would only be a few blocks away. At the end of the block, Peter discovered that good fortune had found him. He saw an ATM booth and reached into his pocket for his "hotel key." Dogman's trick would let him get a couple hours of sleep before meeting the Judge in the morning.

# TWENTY-TWO

It was a quarter after eight, and the heart of San Francisco bustled in the early morning rush hour activity. Union Square only slowed in the wee hours, where even then patrons of the many surrounding hotels staggered back to their rooms. The fact that it was Election Day added to the early morning excitement. Lawyers, brokers, and financial advisers, and even the non-professionals made their mark. Several sets of construction workers dined on donuts and washed them down with coffee from stainless steel thermoses. A pair of older twins clad in matching red suits and bonnets marched through the Square while a camera crew filmed them for a commercial. The early morning crowd enjoyed entertainment by one of the Square's regulars who performed show tunes and lounge songs on her portable karaoke machine. And of course, many of the city's forgotten homeless manned their treasured shopping carts, begged for money, or just slept on the grassy knolls surrounding the cement square.

Ninth Circuit Appellate Justice Douglas Irving Ahrens paced the Square. They called him Ironsides because his principles, courtroom, and overall demeanor were always the same. He always ran a tight ship, always on course, always on time. His courtroom was a no-nonsense courtroom. He never tolerated tardiness. His appointment was late, extremely late, but he had no choice in the matter. He had to wait. Ironsides was not in control of the situation. Neither was his appointment.

The judge walked back toward the street. Why did Sara have to get involved with someone on the list? She had to be protected. He would do whatever he could to ensure that the poison that infected him did not spread to her.

"Your Honor," beckoned a voice behind the judge.

The judge turned around and saw no one. A man blanketed in newspapers lying on the grassy knoll by a bench began to rise and speak, "Your Honor."

"Farrell?"

"If it may please the court."

"You look like hell."

Turning his head toward some of the homeless, Peter Farrell replied, "As you can see, personal hygiene is a privilege, not a right."

"You are a bastard for getting my daughter involved in this..."

"Wait a second," Peter held his arms to avoid any attempt of physical confrontation by the angry judge. "She only was supposed to make one phone call for me. That's it. What happened in the..."

"How many lives have you destroyed with your selfishness?" interrupted the judge as he feigned to lunge at Farrell, but regained his composure.

"But."

"You never, never should have contacted her!"

Judge Ahrens stressed the second "never" emphatically.

"I cannot undo what has already been done," Peter pleaded.

"But I can clean up some of this mess."

"Judge, I do not mean to be disrespectful, but I don't think you alone can deal with these people. I need you to contact..."

"Don't you tell me what I can and cannot handle. I know exactly who you are dealing with and what must be done."

"What are you talking about?"

"Come with me."

"Judge Ahrens, we need to contact Aaron Golde in St. Louis. He can..."

Again interrupting the young attorney, Judge Ahrens ordered, "Come with me, now young man."

Peter followed the Ninth Circuit Justice across Union Square Park as if the judge was leading him back to chambers for a scolding out of the ears of a jury. Peter hated the fact that Sara was now involved in this mess. The last thing he wanted was to endanger the woman he still loved, but no one could have foreseen what had happened in the cemetery. Peter understood that the judge had every right to be furious with him, but none of that was going to help the situation now. Aaron Golde must have received the Occidental papers by this morning. If Peter could just safely contact Aaron to explain what the documents were and how the Occidental people were after him, Sara would be safe. In fact, no one would have to know about her. Peter could enter some type of witness protection program while Aaron Golde and his political connections would weed out the Occidental infestation in Washington. It would be Aaron's greatest case. Triumph of all triumphs. But first, Peter had to contact Aaron.

"Judge, your Honor, what we need to do is contact Aaron Golde, then..."

"What 'we' need to do?" the Judge turned about face to Peter. "How dare you say 'we.' I will do what 'we' need to do."

The two approached Stockton Street where Judge Ahrens stopped beside the passenger side of a black van. "Get in," commanded Judge Ironsides.

Peter opened the passenger door and was shocked to see Tasha Dolnick with a gun pointed directly at his face.

"Peter!" Sara cried from the back seat.

Judge Ahrens almost knocked Peter to the floor of car as he pushed his way into the vehicle to see his daughter held at gunpoint in the back seat. The large blond man did not bother to acknowledge the judge's presence. His eyes remained fixed on the target in the backseat.

"This was not part of the deal!" objected Judge Ironsides. "Your people said they would leave her alone."

Tasha Dolnick kept her gun pointed directly at Peter, but directed her comments to the judge, "Old man, back away from the car. As you can see your daughter is fine," she paused, "for now."

Old Ironsides was reduced to only a shell of a man.

"Now, back away from the car," she continued in her Slavic accent. "You will be contacted later today."

"Sara, are you all right?" Peter asked in order to elicit an affirmative response. If the judge did something crazy he feared the man in the back seat would not hesitate to kill her.

"I'm sorry Peter."

Sara was obviously frightened.

Calmly, Peter again looked into Sara's eyes.

"Sara?"

"I'm fine. I am fine."

"You see old man," Tasha appeared to enjoy the torn family, "your daughter is fine. Now, you get in the car, next to me. Behave and I will be gentle with you."

Peter climbed into the seat and closed the passenger's door. The black van slowly pulled away from the parking spot and left Union Square. Judge Ahrens stood on the sidewalk motionless as his shoulders sunk, his arms dropped to his sides. His little red "I voted" sticker, which had already begun to peel off his jacket, fell to the ground.

Tasha pulled her headset microphone down to her mouth and spoke softly, "We have the package."

Tasha gave Peter a little wink as they left the city.

# TWENTY-THREE

"I thought they would be here by now," barked St. Louis Police Chief Jesse Stuart.

"Patience my friend," assured the voice from behind the burgundy chair.

Stuart stared out the window at the ocean.

"I'm just anxious for the press conference. I brought the full dress uniform."

"And I am sure you will look very authoritative," responded Elias St. Armand who had yet to turn his leather chair to face Chief Stuart.

Stuart shrugged off St. Armand's indifferent behavior. The Chief's mind was elsewhere, dressed in full blues, on one of those morning shows, describing the capture of the fugitive "Shakespeare Killer."

---

Fear and tension consumed the ride. Peter sensed that no one in the car cared to be in the same vehicle as the large blond man. Sara, with a gun pointed at her by the blond man, certainly had no warm feelings for him. Peter could still feel the bruises on his back from tumbling down the stairs with the man and gained no comfort in the fact that the same man now held a gun. Interestingly enough, the Slavic woman spoke tersely to the blond man, like she was reprimanding him or telling him never to do something again. She spoke Russian or some Slavic language that Peter could not understand. Peter did understand the tone in her voice, and it was not complimentary. The blond man ignored her.

Peter looked back again at Sara. Her face betrayed fear. But Peter also recognized the anger in her eyes. He hoped that Sara was only using anger to quell her fear. Sara was not the type to do something wild and crazy like reach for the gun. However, Peter also was fairly certain that this was the first time that Sara had a gun pointed at her. People were not always predictable when faced with a new situation, much less one involving a gun.

"Face forward," ordered Tasha Dolnick.

"Are you going to kill us?" Sara bluntly asked.

Good question, Peter thought.

"If I were going to kill you, you would already be dead," she answered.

Good answer.

"I think," Peter started.

"Shut that pretty little trap of yours, or I will have to do it," ordered Tasha as she reached for her holstered sidearm. Tasha's raised eyebrows and a slight turn of her head toward him compounded the overstated gesture meant for Peter's benefit. In an instant her facial expression changed. She barked another order to the blond man, but again in the Slavic language they shared.

An uneasy silence again filled the black van.

Then the blond man spoke.

"And Joseph, seeing that the child was vigorous in mind and body, again resolved that He should not remain ignorant of the letters, and took Him away, and handed Him over to another teacher. And the teacher said to Joseph: I shall first teach him the Greek letters, and then the Hebrew. For the teacher was aware of the trial that had been made of the child, and was afraid of Him. Nevertheless, he wrote out the alphabet, and gave Him all his attention for a long time, and He made him no answer. And Jesus said to him: If thou art really a teacher, and art well acquainted with the letters, tell me the power of the Alpha, and I will tell thee the power of the Beta. And the teacher was enraged by this, and struck Him on the head. And the child being in pain, cursed him; and immediately he swooned away, and fell to the ground on his face. And the child returned to Joseph's house; and Joseph was grieved, and gave orders to His mother, saying: 'Do not let Him go outside the door, because those who make him angry die'."

After the large blond man's parable, no one spoke.

———➤•◦•◄———

"What time is it?" the Englishman hoarsely inquired.

"Exactly seventeen minutes from the time your man answered the phone," the Savile Row man sharply answered as he snapped shut his gold pocket watch.

"You should be kinder with me my friend, I have a heavy head this morning."

"Maybe you should consider tempering your lifestyle."

"A suggestion I will certainly take to heart this morning, but unfortunately will discard this evening."

"You're impossible."

"I cannot disappoint my nieces, the beautiful girls *signorine*."

The conversation paused and then the Englishman continued, "And my beauty sleep was interrupted for what reason?"

"They have the package and that young attorney."

"So all is well, I shall return to my deep slumber."

"Not so fast."

"There is more."

"Our Lebanese friend has begun to question our man."

"Oh?"

"Actually the choice of the word 'question' may not be entirely appropriate."

"Come again?"

"Our Lebanese friend specifically told me his confidence is waning in our man."

"He retrieved the documents and the man, what else could he want? Does he suspect?"

"Maybe."

"Shall we pull him out of there now that all is in order?"

"No, let us leave the decision to our man."

"You knew I would agree."

"Yes, but you talk to him. He mumbled something about someone seeking something until they found it and became troubled and astonished."

"I will speak with him."

"Go back to your beauty sleep. You need it."

"You're cruel my friend. Very cruel."

As he hung up the telephone the Savile Row man turned the sound on the television set up. It was Election Day, and all the politicians were out voting for themselves.

# TWENTY-FOUR

Located on San Francisco's northern shoreline with a picturesque view of the Golden Gate Bridge, the Marina Yacht Club sheltered the West Coast's elite. Although dwarfed by its San Diego neighbor to the South, the Marina Yacht Club made no apologies. It did not have to. The Pan Pacific elite harbored their opulence, affluence, and decadence in the Marina. Armani sports coats and tailored slacks were de rigueur while khakis and light blue oxfords were regulated inland. The prevailing laid-back San Franciscans did not encroach onto the Marina docks, and guests were not encouraged. Unfortunately for Sara Ahrens and Peter Farrell, on this occasion an exception had been made.

Although the Cedars of Lebanon was not the flagship of Elias St. Armand's various yachts, she matched, or overmatched any rival in the Marina. The lavish decor aboard the Cedars of Lebanon, of course, was made to intimidate, not impress. Peter was intimidated. Moreover, Peter was scared. The strange and silent blond who attacked him on Halloween and the woman from O'Shea's boarded the grand yacht with them. Predictably, the two FBI agents, brown suit and blue suit, lead the contingent. The brown suit entered the main cabin followed by the rest. Both the blue suit and the brown suit remained on guard at the cabin's entrance.

The main cabin did not disappoint the wayward visitor. Lavished in a white pine and navy blue finish, the room put any office Peter had seen to shame. Covering the center of the hardwood floors lay a twenty-by-thirty-foot handmade Persian rug with the most intricate of designs. Along the outside appeared to be depictions of various battle scenes, as if it was telling thousands of stories throughout the textile. At the center of the rug appeared a lone cedar tree colored in a deep, almost regal, burgundy. On the other side of the Persian rug stood a grand cherry-wood desk. Behind the desk, facing away from the visitors, a man sat in his leather chair.

"The wily Peter Farrell, finally."

Still standing with the Persian rug between himself and the desk, Peter responded, "I wish I could say it was a pleasure to meet you Mr. St. Armand."

The burgundy leather chair swiveled around so that the host could view his guests.

"Please Mr. Farrell, you have read enough about me. You must call me Elias. I certainly hope you will extend me the same courtesy."

Elias St. Armand stood. The first thing that came to Peter's mind was that Elias St. Armand was taller than he expected. Rumors circulated that St. Armand was an egomaniac to such extent that he surrounded himself with people shorter than himself to make him appear more statuesque, a Napoleon of sorts. However, St. Armand was tall, eye-to-eye with Peter. Elias St. Armand also was a robust man, not portly, but solid. His thick black hair, although receding, must have been one of the greatest Helsinki treatments ever. Peter figured that St. Armand had to be almost seventy, but his thick mane was someone's half his age. The tightly wound skin of his face, although tanned, must have been purchased as well.

The billionaire spoke again, "I will not belittle you by explaining why you are here. You have something of mine and I expect its return."

Looking at Sara, Peter asked without asking, "Let her go."

"Oh come now Peter, I expected more from you. You know I will use the girl for whatever value she may have then divest myself of her. Her fate is a foregone conclusion. She is irrelevant for the purpose of our negotiation. The term we must negotiate is the price you are willing to pay for returning to me what is mine."

"The price I am going to pay."

"Surely, Peter, you did not think that the trouble you have cost me would go unpunished."

Peter stared sternly into Elias St. Armand's eyes.

"I've paid enough."

The billionaire feigned a quizzical look then responded, "Oh, your brother, clever fellow, but in the end he could not close the deal. The same goes with that other fellow... what was his name?"

"Joe Rosendahl," Peter responded.

"Ah yes, the Jew. Tasha does excellent work."

St. Armand lifted a brandy snifter towards Tasha Dolnick as if toasting her at a banquet. He sipped from it, then worked his way around the desk.

"But I digress. We still need to work out our deal."

Peter raised his eyebrows.

"Deal?"

"Yes. Deal, contract, closing, whatever you lawyers call it. Let us get down to brass tacks," St. Armand stated with a Cheshire grin.

"The way I see it you have three choices, two of which are far less pleasant than the third."

"Choices. For what?"

"This is not a question-answer session, young man. Interruptions are unbecoming."

Interrupting again, Peter acted as if he did not know what Elias St. Armand was talking about.

"What could I have left?"

Peter dug in his pockets to pull out a few sheets of the Occidental papers he pocketed at the mission. He tossed them on the Persian rug, landing on the burgundy cedar tree.

"Here, what else could you want?"

"Please young man, again you are disappointing me." Picking up the papers that had been tossed to the ground, St. Armand continued, "There is another set of my documents. You have it, I do not. I want my property returned."

"What other set?"

"Mr. Farrell, you made another set when you left St. Louis."

Puzzled, Peter could not understand how St. Armand knew about the copies of the Occidental papers he made for Aaron Golde.

Recognizing the young attorney's surprised reaction, Elias St. Armand continued, "Oh Peter, Peter, Peter. I thought a young man in your field would be able to think beyond your little yellow legal pad. This is the information age, a new millennium. Every time someone swipes your debit or credit card, that information is recorded. Every time you make a telephone call, that information is recorded. Every time you log onto your computer, that information is recorded. And young man, all that information is for sale as long as you can pay the price. You, young man, purchased over eleven hundred copies yesterday morning for about ninety dollars on your credit card. I have one set of copies, now I want to know what you did with the other set of copies."

"I don't have them."

"Being that you stand here before me, that is obvious. Whom did you give them to?"

St. Armand's information stunned Peter, but it was his lack of knowledge that gave Peter hope. It was clear that St. Armand did not know about Jimmy Powell or the Occidental papers Powell mailed to Aaron Golde. Peter also knew that if St. Armand did know about Powell and Golde, surely he and Sara would already be dead. This fact was Peter's only hope.

"The documents are safe, but if anything happens to me, all of the papers will be leaked to the media," bargained Peter.

"I doubt that," St. Armand quickly responded, "but I might have to take that chance."

"What?"

"As I stated before, you basically have three choices. The first choice is that I kill you and take my chances with your 'leaking to the media.' Second, I torture you and your lady friend until you tell me what I need to know. This could very well lead back to option number one, but my only preference is to get back my files."

"And the third?"

"The third is much more desirable. Simply put, you join my organization."

"Join you?"

"Not officially, of course, but you would be on Occidental's payroll."

"Why me?"

"We are not so different, young man. We both have rich ethnic backgrounds. You Irish, myself Lebanese. Our ancestors were generally poor and oppressed. Living off a land that did not always produce strengthened our heritage. The Turkish Empire abusing my people and the British Empire's stranglehold on your people only fortified our resolve. Despite all this, the cream has risen to the top in this adopted nation of ours."

Elias St. Armand had worked his way over to a cabin window during his monologue.

"This is the land of opportunity." St. Armand stared out the window and continued, "Mr. Farrell, I am giving you an opportunity of a lifetime. My organization transcends traditional corporate boundaries. I represent the new age of transnational corporations. No longer will it be necessary to lobby, buy, or frame politicians. As of today, America is entering a new world order. Of course, there will be loose ends to tie up, but those things get ironed out over time."

St. Armand turned away from the window toward Peter.

"I am sorry, I digress. You see Mr. Farrell, Occidental is in a unique position for the millennium. My corporation controls, no owns, various nations across this globe. Now American politics are mine. For years, Occidental candidates have been positioning themselves in various governmental offices. Yes, at first we depended on traditional methods, which should not surprise you. But now, this election represents the first time that a majority of candidates are actually Occidental candidates. Today, in a majority of the elections, whether someone votes liberal or conservative is irrelevant because they are voting Occidental."

Elias approached Peter.

"So now you see what I can do for you. I am a kingmaker and I have been told that you have the potential to become a king. Of course, we would start you out slowly as a representative. Maybe even a junior senator. In years to come you could author a bill to research a cure for something. I don't care what it is. The bill will pass, of course. The cure would be found because of the Farrell Act. Instant national name recognition. You will have to go to mass on Saturday night for a full year, because you will be booked on all the Sunday morning shows."

"I sense your reluctance, Peter. Actually I am quite sure you loathe me. Be that as it may, you know you must fully assess your options. What good are you dead? None. Alive on the other hand, anything is possible. Besides, Occidental is not the devil. We have served our country well. My foundations have cured more diseases, averted more wars and alleviated more financial crises than even you could guess. Imagine what you could do with that kind of power behind you. It has to be tempting?"

Peter did not respond. The man standing before him admitted he had his brother killed. The woman that had killed his brother now held a gun on Sara, the woman he loved.

"And what about her?" Peter inquired.

As a teacher scolding a young student Elias St. Armand responded, "As I told you before, the woman's fate is sealed. She is irrelevant to our negotiation."

"She is the daughter of a Ninth Circuit Appellate Justice."

"And Kennedy was President of the United States. Mr. Farrell, Peter, I do not enjoy wasting time on non-negotiable items. What say you?"

"I say that you are a crazy egomaniac."

"Crazy!" Elias St. Armand shattered his snifter on his desk.

Peter had struck a cord.

Regrouping himself and checking his Rolex, Elias St. Armand continued, "Young man, you are wasting all of our time. What say you?"

Throughout his capture, Peter wondered why no one ever searched him for Tasha's gun he had grabbed in the Castro. Maybe she did not realize Peter had taken the handgun from the bar. Whatever the case, it was still tucked inside his sock tied to his leg. The time had to be right.

"I say that your maniacal fantasies extend well beyond any grasp of the real world," responded Peter, antagonizing the billionaire.

"Son, you are naïve," retorted St. Armand, still with a crazed look in his eyes. "How does the United States of America go to war in the Mideast? The United States exercises power in the Mideast because I say so."

"Even before 9/11, the U.S. Senate approved of the First Gulf War by only five votes. Why? Some had Occidental's best interest in mind, but others I had to convince or manipulate. The Senate and the American public were subjected to endless stories about the atrocities inflicted upon the Kuwaiti people. Some were true, but the best ones I created. Like the Kuwaiti girl who sobbingly described to the American public the killing of hundreds of babies in an Iraqi children's hospital. Or in the Second Gulf War, the 'imminent' threat of weapons of mass destruction. How can you be so naïve? Of all people, I did not think that you would swallow everything that was spoon-fed to you."

Still very worked up, the billionaire stared at Peter.

"Even if I believed you, believed that you can do what you say, or even allow me to do everything I want, I would not sell my soul to my brother's killer."

"So be it, I was extending the offer as a favor to a friend anyway," the billionaire simply said as he began to leave the main cabin room. Turning back, Elias St. Armand commented, "You do know I will use all efforts to get the information I need."

Elias took several steps and then bellowed, "Captain Stuart! Mr. Farrell, you do know Captain Stuart? He is a skilled interrogator."

St. Louis Police Chief Jesse Stuart sauntered down the steps on the other side of the cabin.

St. Armand continued, "Andriy, come with me. Let us leave the good Captain to his work. Start with the girl, Mr. Farrell seems to hold quite an affection for her."

Elias St. Armand and the silent blond called Andriy left the cabin of the Cedars of Lebanon, leaving Peter and Sara with Stuart, Tasha Dolnick, and the two FBI agents. Dolnick still had her gun drawn on Sara while both FBI agents remained behind Peter. Police Chief Stuart approached the rest from beyond the desk. Everyone remained silent for a moment or two.

"This will be fun," the fully dressed Police Chief Stuart calmly stated as he crossed onto the Persian rug.

The boat jolted as it departed from dock.

"Where are we going?" Sara asked.

Ignoring Sara, Stuart uttered a command to the two FBI agents, "Get the tarp from below, we can use any excess blood to lure sharks."

Both blue suit and brown suit scrambled off.

With the two FBI agents below deck, Peter knew his odds would not get better. Taking advantage of those odds, Peter baited the police commander,

"Now it makes sense how such a stupid bigot such as yourself could remain police chief for so long. When Elias St. Armand owns the city, I guess he can make any monkey head of law enforcement in his home town."

Stuart merely laughed as he approached Peter Farrell. The St. Louis police chief stopped face-to-face before the young attorney and grinned from ear to ear.

Slapping the "to protect and serve" badge off the Captain's uniform, Peter taunted, "You don't deserve to wear this."

Stunned, the police commander's toothless grin quickly disappeared. "Pick it up," Stuart ordered.

Peter stood motionless.

"Now!" the police chief ordered again.

This time Peter released a defiant smirk.

With a quickness defying his age, Stuart punched Peter in the stomach, causing him to double over in pain.

"I gave an order, son."

Still gasping for air, Peter on his knees stared at the commander's badge with its pin propping the shield on end. With both hands grasping the badge, Peter thrust the shield, pin first into the commander's groin. With Stuart reeling in pain between him and Tasha Dolnick, Peter clumsily pulled up his pant leg and grabbed the handgun from his sock. Crouched over the slumping Stuart, Peter pointed the gun at the police chief's back.

"Back off and drop the gun!" he shouted at Tasha Dolnick.

Dolnick had her gun drawn and aimed directly at Peter.

"Drop it, I will shoot him!"

Dolnick did not respond.

For the first time in his life, Peter discharged a firearm, shattering the police chief's kneecap with one shot.

Dolnick threw her gun to the floor. Sara raced over to Peter. Grabbing her arm, Peter guided Sara up the stairs of the cabin. Looking at his gun in disbelief, Peter tossed it to the ground. Reaching the deck, the two fugitives saw that the boat had only just cleared the pier.

Starting to climb the rail, Peter directed Sara, "We've got to jump."

Peter helped Sara over the rail and they both jumped into the bay.

———<><>———

Back aboard the Cedars of Lebanon, St. Louis Police Chief Jesse Stuart writhed in pain as he bled all over the Persian rug. Gasping, he kept shouting for help as Tasha Dolnick talked on her cellphone. The blue suited and brown suited FBI agents finally returned with the tarp in hand.

"They just left and the gun is here," Tasha Dolnick closed her cellphone.

Acknowledging the agents, she continued, "Spread the tarp over the rug."

As the agents opened the tarp, Dolnick walked over to the cabin entry stairs where Peter had thrown down his gun. Dolnick withdrew a plastic glove from her jacket and put it on her hand.

"Put the old man on the tarp," Dolnick ordered the two agents.

"No, no, you can't do this," pleaded the wounded police chief as the two agents lifted him onto the center of the tarp.

Tasha Dolnick, a woman who despised military authoritative figures, picked up Peter's gun with her gloved hand, raised the Sig Saurer P-228 9mm, a handgun she used often, and fired one shot into the head of the weeping corrupt police commander. Shocked and stunned, blue suit and brown suit looked at one another. Without lowering the weapon, Tasha fired two more shots. The two agents dropped neatly to the tarp with Stuart's corpse. Tasha pulled out her cellphone.

———<><>———

Pulling away from the Marina Yacht Club and resting comfortably in his stretch limousine, Elias St. Armand put his cellphone back into his double-breasted Armani coat pocket.

"Well my strong and silent shadow, you can report back to your superiors that everything is going according to plan," St. Armand chatted across the limo to Andriy Kravenko.

Again addressing the individual sitting across from him, "Listen Kravenko, you are being quite dull today. Don't you have any of your mysterious cryptic sayings for me?"

Kravenko stared at St. Armand and then finally stated without any emotion, "Blessed is the lion which becomes man when consumed by man; and cursed is the man whom the lion consumes, and the lion becomes man."

"I like that, lions eating man," St. Armand nodded in agreement.

"I like that."

# TWENTY-FIVE

The chambers and courtrooms for the Ninth Circuit Court of Appeals are some of the most modern facilities in the land. The dark cherry or oak wood-paneled courtrooms that personified a stodgy, almost elitist, form of the law had no place in these new California courtrooms. Light colors and a white pine interior are used to exemplify the openness of a Court of Law in California.

Back in chambers, Judge Ironsides Ahrens worked at a feverish pace scanning documents and frantically typing. Every document scanned and every short explanatory memo he typed was saved not only on his hard drive and disk but also on the network itself. He had kept up the rabid pace for hours and was almost complete. He knew he had gathered enough information, but wanted to make sure he did not forget anything. He would not have a second chance to set things right.

The judge picked up a picture of his wife Lin with Sara when she was a toddler. How blessedly naïve he was back then. How things have changed.

Occidental changed him.

Occidental changed everything.

It was all too vivid for Judge Ahrens, a new bright-eyed judge sitting on a superior court in San Francisco. His legal career blossomed so quickly affording his family a lifestyle that enabled them to have a place in the city and their home on the coast. Douglas Ahrens wanted to give something back. Not only out of a sense of community service, but also out of a love for his adopted country, the United States. Douglas Ahrens regarded his United States citizenship as his highest honor and public service as his duty. His service in Korea did not fulfill his sense of public duty. On a campaign he financed himself, he was elected to the bench for a six-year term.

His first term quickly opened his eyes. While he did not suffer in the process, all he did in private practice was enable the rich to get richer. Although he did not blindly believe he would be handing down earth-shattering jurisprudence decisions on a daily basis, he did not expect the mundane number-crunching machine he encountered in the criminal judicial system. His entire professional life had been based on the fact that the United States legal system was the best in the world. His parents, family, and heritage had been victims of Fascists who stripped them of all their civil liberties. But in America, they would rather have ten guilty men go free than one innocent man stripped of his liberty. Even Great Britain paled in comparison to the United States, whose exclusionary rules of evidence prohibit the government from using evidence it wrongfully obtained to try to convict someone. Even "fruit of the poisonous tree" evidence, evidence obtained from unlawfully obtained evidence, was generally forbidden. Nowhere were civil liberties protected more than in the United States criminal justice system. Although he held the system high on a white marble pedestal, after his first term that white marble had been muddied up a bit.

Everyone always wanted to blame the defense attorneys for getting their clients "off." To this, Judge Ahrens always responded that if prosecutors and judges worked as hard as defense lawyers, there would be a lot fewer people getting "off." By no means did Judge Ahrens hold a tender spot for the defense bar, he just wanted to hold everyone up to the same high standard of justice. He earned his nickname, "Ironsides," by wielding a swift sword of justice on everyone; defense lawyers merely had the benefit of being less accountable in the eyes of Judge Ahrens.

Judge Ahrens encountered what he believed to be three problems with the system. The three parties, or problems, that needed to be fixed were the police, the prosecutors, and the judges. Criminals walked not because of defense lawyers. More than likely they were set free in spite of defense lawyers. Judge Ahrens viewed laziness on the part of police officers, prosecutors, and judges alike as the reason behind all these evening news stories concerning murders committed by someone with a history of violence. Police too often took shortcuts on arrests and investigations. Prosecutors were quick to deal to get a file off their desk or failed to adequately prepare if the case went to trial. And judges accepted too many plea agreements without asking questions in order to clear their docket or presided over a trial with as much interest as a sea lion napping on a rock.

Judge Ahrens' courtroom was different. Lawyers had to be prepared or face ridicule. However his nickname was not earned by chastising lawyers in his courtroom, that only enhanced the moniker. He was given the name Ironsides by the County Attorney's Office after having one prosecuting attorney for lunch. Before lunch, the prosecuting attorney and a public defender retired to Judge Ahrens' chambers to discuss a number of plea agreements and a sentencing recommendation. Judge Ahrens had asked to see the police report for the sentencing recommendation. The prosecuting attorney said that it had been misplaced. Judge Ahrens, mildly annoyed, told the attorney to find it and that he and the defense attorney, who had a couple more cases before the judge, should meet him in his chambers to go over these matters during lunch. Judge Ahrens routinely worked through his lunch and did not see it as an imposition to ask the attorneys to do so every now and then. In chambers, the prosecuting attorney brought the file to Ahrens who was sitting behind his desk eating a sandwich. The judge asked for the file. The prosecuting attorney said that he could easily sum up the file for him. Judge Ahrens said that was not necessary and held out his hand. The prosecuting attorney then started summing up the file. The judge firmly told the attorney to hand over the file. While reading the file the judge stopped eating; he had lost his appetite.

"What is this?" Judge Ahrens calmly asked.

"What is what?" the prosecuting attorney coyly replied.

"The defendant's name is the same, but there is no mention of disorderly conduct. This is a sex crime. Is this a prior conviction?"

"No."

"Then explain this to me. That man just pled guilty to disorderly conduct, but this is a sex crime."

The prosecuting attorney stood up and pointed to one of the last paragraphs in the police report.

"I have to say this out loud because I do not believe what I am seeing," began the judge.

"Two college students go to a party in a dorm. The defendant is admittedly high on cocaine and offers cocaine to a female student. The female student accompanies the defendant back to his dorm room where the defendant again uses cocaine. The defendant attempts to have sexual intercourse with the female student who rebuffs him. The defendant persists, rips off her blouse, throws her on the bed, and tries to force himself on her. The female student is able to strike the defendant on the head and struggle free."

"And here is the sentence you point out to me." Judge Ahrens read from the police report, "In a rage he stormed out of the room and put his fist through a hallway window."

For over an hour Judge Ahrens berated the attorney for trying to pull something over on him. He was so loud that the other attorneys, clerks, and others who gathered in the courtroom for the afternoon session could hear him. From that time on the Prosecuting Attorney's Office dubbed him "Ironsides." But also from that time on, rarely did a prosecutor approach Judge Ironsides Ahrens with a plea agreement that did not comport with the crime committed.

Ironsides' second six-year term on the superior court was again filled with mixed emotion. Judge Ahrens cherished the system that he took an oath to uphold, but time and time again people in that system let him down. The judge never believed it was the system itself to blame, only people let the system down. Unfortunately, for Superior Court Judge Douglas Ahrens, some of those people were justices above him on California's First District Court of Appeals. Although Judge Ahrens held the Bill of Rights and the Constitution with the utmost regard, he did not see that it was his place to rewrite the rights enumerated therein. Time and again the appellate courts were expanding the rights of the accused, giving little regard to victims or the community. Legal technicalities and loopholes became the rule not the exception. One such case pushed Douglas Ahrens over the limit. The case came before the judge toward the end of his second term. He had spent ten years on the bench. Because of this case, he began to contemplate other career moves rather another six-year term.

The case itself was simple. A white supremacist killed two thirteen-year-old African-American teenage girls on their way home from school. The white supremacist, one Robert Raymond Williams, who went by the name "Ray," had confessed to the murders, twice. While waiting for detectives to question him, Ray asked the desk sergeant if he could get something off his chest. The desk sergeant told him he could, but also said that he had to advise him of his rights. The desk sergeant looked for a Miranda card, but could not find one so he summed up the Miranda rights for Williams. Williams confessed to the murders. The sergeant then took Williams to the detectives. The sergeant informed the detectives that Williams had something to confess. The detectives read Williams his Miranda rights again. And once again Williams confessed to brutally killing the two girls.

It was expected that after the confessions that Williams would enter a plea agreement. Ahrens would have agreed to life without parole, but he never had a chance to approve such a plea. The white supremacist group, Resistance by Aryan Whites, or RAW, took up Williams' cause. In fact, Williams had no cause. He was an ignorant white man who committed an evil act. In his confession he said that the girls had been taunting him for months. However, no such evidence was entered at trial. Williams was obviously a bigot who thought he'd been provoked into an evil act that he believed was justified. In Williams, RAW found a martyr and enough free media to espouse their cause.

The defense attorneys hired by RAW, of course, argued that both confessions should be excluded from the evidence at trial. Judge Ahrens denied the motions. While the motions to exclude the confessions were not completely far-fetched, the intent of the law did not waiver. In the first confession, the desk sergeant did not use every word in the Miranda warning, but the substance of the warning was not in dispute. Furthermore, Williams confessed twice. More importantly, the second confession came after a word for word reading of the Miranda warning.

The confessions alone were compelling, but by far not the only evidence against Williams. A crossing guard testified that on at least two occasions within the week of the murders, she spotted Williams' orange pick-up truck parked by the school. She also testified that the same pick-up truck was parked on a street by the school the day the murders were committed. The truck, already a bright orange, was further identified by the Rebel Flag painted on its hood. A friend of Williams reluctantly testified that he was going to get the "two teenage black whores that had been teasing him." There was no evidence of rape, but the prosecution concluded that the girls had been so badly beaten that Williams decided not to rape them. The Crime Scene Unit had a field day with the case. Williams' fingerprints matched prints on the bloody bat found from the confessions. The blood on the bat was positively identified as coming from the girls. The girls' blood was also found in Williams' apartment. According to his confession, he had burned his clothes. Carpet fibers from Williams' apartment were found at the crime scene, a field a half-mile away from Williams' apartment.

The jury convicted Williams in less than an hour.

The Resistance by Aryan Whites financed Williams' appeal. He won.

California's First District Court of Appeals reversed Williams' conviction stating that Williams was not properly read his rights for the first confession and that the second confession was a product of the first confession because the desk sergeant told the detectives in front of Williams that Williams had confessed. Consequently, the appellate court threw out both confessions. Without the confessions, the Court of Appeals further stated, the jury would not have convicted Williams.

The Court of Appeal's decision crippled the Prosecuting Attorney's Office. Without the confessions they were left with the testimony of the crossing guard, Williams' friend, the bloody bat, the girls' blood in the apartment, and fibers from the apartment carpeting at the crime scene. However, Skinheads from RAW persuaded the crossing guard not to testify again. Williams' friend could no longer be found. And because the bloody bat was obtained from the confession, it was "fruit from the poisonous tree" and could not be used at trial. All that was left was evidence of the girls' blood in Williams' apartment and fibers from the apartment's carpeting at the crime scene. All that proved was that Williams walked through the field the girls were murdered in before he was arrested. The Prosecutor's Office did not want to go forward. Judge Ahrens could not blame them. All anyone could hope for was that some other witness would come forward before Williams could be "provoked" again.

It did not happen that way. Four months after his release, police arrested Williams for the murder of an African-American schoolgirl. In his confession, he admitted to not only this murder, but to another that was still filed under missing persons. Consequently, overturning the conviction resulted in two additional, preventable murders.

To say that Judge Ironsides Ahrens was outraged was an understatement. Risking disbarment, Judge Ahrens publicly commented on the "travesty of justice." He was admonished by the Bar Association and put on probation pursuant to the Code of Judicial Conduct.

Shortly thereafter, Occidental approached him. It was not as if some long arm of the corporation gave him a bag full of money. It happened gradually. Judge Ahrens was approached by a lobbyist, not on behalf of any special interest, but to inform him that people shared his views and wished to see his career move forward. Next came whispers that he was being considered for the seat of a retiring justice on the First District Court of Appeals. The whispers persisted until they were part of conversations during cocktail parties. Before Judge Ahrens even decided that he wanted to be considered for the appellate bench, the governor summoned him to Sacramento. Judge Ahrens remembered the meeting well.

Judge Ahrens had spent enough time at cocktail parties not to be intimidated by the governor's interest in him. He was impressed and flattered, but not intimidated. Furthermore, it was not as if the governor had the mandate of the people of California. The governor had just won a tough re-election campaign largely on part of his campaign promise to be tough on crime. It was undisputed that Ironsides Ahrens was tough on crime, and thanks to his public outrage on the Williams' case, voters knew that fact. Ahrens was a smart choice and a popular choice. The governor said as much at the meeting. The only thing that struck Judge Ahrens as odd was that a young attorney sat in on the meeting. Ahrens later learn that the man in the room was John Kerr of the Washington, D.C. power broker firm Miller & White. Ahrens would see Kerr again.

After appointment by the governor, a justice on the court of appeals serves a twelve-year term subject to voter approval. Voter approval is usually a perfunctory matter. A justice is re-elected because no one usually challenges the justice or the challenge is by some nobody. Judge Ahrens' re-election became the exception. A former pro-football star, who worked as an attorney in the Attorney General's office, decided to challenge Ahrens for his seat on the bench. The football star not only had the name recognition to defeat Ahrens, but the campaign money to do it as well. Before Ahrens knew it, he found himself behind in the polls. That is when John Kerr resurfaced. The former governor had become a senator and sent Kerr to assist Ahrens in getting re-elected. Ahrens was informed that Washington had high hopes for Ahrens as a Federal Judge or even a seat on the United States Court of Appeals for the Ninth Circuit. Losing this election would wash away any hopes of such an appointment. Ahrens was admittedly swept up by these political aspirations, but even more so, he was doing good work on the bench and did not want to see that come to an end. When Kerr came on board so did the money. With a heavily financed campaign, Ahrens was easily re-elected. Ahrens learned later that Occidental financed the entire campaign violating nearly every campaign financing law on the California books. Ahrens also learned that Occidental had financed the campaign of his adversary as well. In fact, Occidental engineered his adversary's campaign in order to get Ahrens to accept help out of desperation.

When Ahrens first learned that Occidental had bought the election for him, he was in denial. He had been insulated from the financing and thought election laws could not affect him. Kerr explained to Ahrens what Ahrens already knew—i.e., even the appearance of impropriety would tarnish his career. Kerr also revealed that while Occidental had been financing his campaign, a case had come before Ahrens on the Court of Appeals which involved an Occidental subsidiary. In a two-to-one ruling, Ahrens had ruled in favor of the Occidental subsidiary. Although Ahrens had not known about Occidental funding his campaign or that the case before him involved Occidental, the decision would be scrutinized under a microscope. Everything could snowball into questioning his every decision on the Court of Appeals and the Superior Court. Judge Ahrens worried whether another Williams-type case could be reversed because of the Occidental financing. If some other kid died because the Judge wanted to come clean, the Judge knew he could not live with himself. He rationalized that absolving his own guilty conscience was not worth the price. The judge failed to realize that Occidental had only begun to erode his principles.

Over the years, Judge Ahrens had several Occidental-related cases come before him on the bench. He ruled in favor of Occidental on all of them. He believed that he would have ruled that way whether or not Occidental exercised its influence over him. In time, he was appointed to the Ninth Circuit Court of Appeals. Only a few Occidental-related cases came before him on that bench. Again he ruled in favor of Occidental, and again he believed the law justified his decisions.

After a number of years on the Federal bench, Ahrens was introduced to the political think tank called the Council on International Relations. Political heavyweights of all kinds gathered to discuss domestic and foreign policy issues. Every meeting was like a virtual "Who's Who" of the world's political and economical power brokers. Senators, cabinet members, bankers, royalty, and even two members of the United States Supreme Court were present. Occidental's Elias St. Armand was there with Kerr by his side. By the third or fourth meeting, Ahrens felt his discussions with CIR members affected policy. Only six months after giving a presentation to the Council on Hate Crimes, a bill was introduced in Congress concerning hate crimes legislation. As he had intended with each step in his career, he felt he was accomplishing something positive. But at what price?

Judge Ironsides Ahrens put down the photo of him, his wife, and Sara. It was time to pay that price.

# TWENTY-SIX

Still soaked from her Pacific Ocean swim, Sara Ahrens had not spoken a word during the forty-five minute cab ride. Peter thought she might be in shock from the threat against her life, being shot at yesterday, the cold water, everything. Sara Ahrens was not in shock. She was mad, not just mad, but pissed off. Pissed off at her father, Elias St. Armand, herself, and even Peter. Her whole life had been a lie. She had believed that her father had raised her on uncompromising principles. She believed that her work affected change for a better world. She believed she made a difference. During the course of one twenty-four-hour period, one day, all of her beliefs had been shattered.

Whether her father planned to have her taken captive with Peter did not matter. She gave him the benefit of the doubt that he did not know that his actions would put her and Peter's lives in jeopardy. But what never could be excused was the fact her father had sold out. There was no other explanation. Her father was bought and paid for, just like all the others Elias St. Armand had purchased. But none of those other people in Peter's Occidental papers were her father. The person who had raised her. The person who had taught her values. The person who had loved her mother. Why did her father have to be this person?

And Elias St. Armand, that bastard. Could everything he was telling Peter be true? If he owned her father, he could own all those other people. Peter's Occidental papers seemed to confirm her deepest fears. A shadow corporate government. Why bother with her endless petitions, injunctions, and mandamus actions. Everything would be decided at the next board meeting. Congressional votes, hearings, committees would be illusory. Hell, she had seen enough lobbying and campaign finance abuses to make her think that Elias St. Armand's puppet government could have been going on for years. She had wasted her entire adult life believing she had been curbing corporate America's assault on the environment, only to find out that any victories she may have had were mere morsels thrown to the floor from Elias St. Armand's scrap table.

And damn it, Peter. Why did he have to open her eyes to this world of corruption and deceit? Oblivious to these Occidental revelations, Sara's life had purpose and principle. Now that Peter had re-entered it, her world has been turned upside down. Sara knew it was not Peter's fault, but her anger engulfed everything and everyone she knew. Albeit unjustified, this included Peter as well. She knew she could not be mad at Peter, but everything was so confusing. This was not Peter's fault. Peter was merely an alarm clock that woke Sara up from a deep sleep. Unfortunately, there was no snooze button here. Sara was wide awake, more awake than she had ever been.

Peter had no idea where they were heading. As soon as they convinced a cab driver that they were not some kind of freaks, but had money for a fare, Sara directed the cabby. The cabby lent Sara a blanket to warm her, but Sara did not say anything when Peter put the blanket around her. The only words Peter heard Sara utter were directions over the Golden Gate and past the Marin Headlands.

"Take a left and go up the hill," Sara told the cab driver.

"Sara?" Peter inquired.

"Yes?" she responded in a controlled voice.

"Are you all right?"

"Yes." Again the response was short.

"But you haven't said anything this whole time."

"Take another left at the fork up ahead," Sara directed the cabbie.

"Sara."

"Peter what do you want me to say?" Sara snapped. "Yes, I am fine with the fact that my father is corrupt. I am kosher with the fact that everything I have worked for in my life has been worth nothing. Do you want me to say everything is hunky-dory even though my whole life has been turned upside down since you called me yesterday?"

Squeezing her shoulder Peter softly said, "Sara, I'm sorry. I never should have involved you."

"Oh Peter, it's not you, it's everything else. My head is spinning."

"Ma'am," interrupted the cab driver.

"I'm sorry," Sara wiped a tear off her cheek and continued to give directions, "left again. It winds all the way up to a cabin."

"Where are we going?" Peter asked.

"To a friend's." Sara confidently looked at Peter. "He's untouchable."

"Untouchable?"

"I know I may not be a great judge of character, given my father and all, but other than you, this is the only person I can trust. Right now I can't see any better options."

"We still have Aaron Golde."

"With everyone else in that city on Occidental's payroll, I'm not willing to entrust my life to just anyone."

"Aaron Golde is not just anyone. He has fought corruption his entire life."

"And yet in all those years he never knew about your old friend the police chief back on the boat that you crippled."

Not waiting for a response Sara continued, "No, I don't want to have anything to do with that city."

"Sara."

"There," pointing up the hill for the cab driver.

"Who lives here?"

"You'll see."

As the cab pulled in front of the one-story elongated cabin, Peter noticed two things. First, the enormous redwoods virtually camouflaged the cabin from anyone who was not within fifty feet of the building. Second, despite its traditional rustic log exterior, a large auburn satellite dish extended from the back of the structure.

When the cab stopped, Sara exited quickly, running to an old man who stood on the porch. The man, dressed in jean overalls covering a red and black-checkered flannel shirt, looked like he was actually smoking a corncob pipe. After Peter paid the cab driver with five wet twenty-dollar bills, he was able to get a closer look. The build of his body resembled that of a fit fifty-year-old, fifty-five if you pushed it. His weathered face told a different story. Bearded, yet no mustache, the old man smiled, revealing even more deep wrinkles. Piercing this leather exterior were his two charcoal black eyes. Peter almost thought that his eyes were fully dilated, but these black pearls surveyed everything. Although the old man behaved as if this were a meeting with old friends, his ever-moving eyes disclosed a slight uneasiness.

Sara hugged the old man.

"Redwood, I've missed you."

Embracing her, Redwood said, "Sweet Sara, it has been far too long. I began to fear that such a pretty young thing such as you no longer took comfort in the company of a decrepit old soul as myself."

"Nonsense."

Indeed it was, thought Peter. Judging from the stump, ax, and splintered wood it appeared that the "decrepit old soul" had spent the morning chopping half a cord of wood.

"And who is your young and equally soggy friend?"

"Peter, I would like you to meet my oldest and dearest friend, Redwood," Sara said before she turned and walked onto the porch.

"My pleasure," Peter responded wincing from the old man's powerful grip.

"It would be my pleasure if the two of you would come in, change out of those damp clothes, and warm yourselves by the fire."

Half expecting to find some quilts, a rocking chair, and some hunting trophies, Peter was surprised by the old man's lair. The entire cabin, every room, was covered with books. Bookcase after bookcase gave the impression that one was deep in the basement of a university library, not in a log cabin in the middle of the woods. The books themselves revealed no consistent theme about their owner. In what appeared to be the den, there were books ranging from such Ancient Greek writers as Homer, Aeschylus, Sophocles, Plato, Aristotle, and Cicero to Roman writers as Vergil, Horace, Quintillian, Plutarch, and Lucian. A long hallway contained the Manyoshu and Kokinshu anthologies to more modern Japanese works by Emperor Hirohito. Along the west side of the long hallway contained numerous Confucist, Buddhist, and

Taoist writers. Peter was even impressed by the extensive collection of Irish literature, but felt it would be in poor taste to question why the works of William Butler Yeats, George Bernard Shaw, James Joyce, and Sean O'Faolain were located in the bathroom.

Far in the back of the cabin in a cozy room with several chairs and a fireplace, fully changed, Sara and Peter warmed themselves kneeling by the fire. Once again, books after books lined the walls of the room. Judging from the shelves of works on Christianity, Judaism, and Islamic teachings, a religious theme prevailed at this end of the cabin.

"Thank you for the dry clothes," stated Peter, breaking the silence.

Sara remained gazing into the fire.

"Oh, I keep a closet of extras around for visitors. Flannel suits you young man."

Putting her hand on Peter's knee, and faking a smile, Sara said, "It would be hard to find something that doesn't suit Peter."

Sara gazed into the fire again.

The old man leaned against the doorframe. His posture invited his guests to reveal, with ease, whatever brought them to his doorstep.

After another bout of silence, Peter cleared his throat as if to tell the old man enough of a story so that the two could move along.

Sensing Peter's impatience, Sara jumped up, and with an unrecognizable enthusiasm given the day's events said, "Redwood I am just famished. Could we trouble you..."

The old man smiled at the young blond.

Taking Redwood's arm, Sara continued, "But I insist on helping you with everything. It will be just like old times."

As Sara pulled the old man into the kitchen, Peter rose and walked over to one of the few windows in the cabin. Staring at the towering redwoods which were undoubtedly hundreds of years old, Peter felt dwarfed by his surroundings, and the knowledge that he forever scarred Sara's life.

# TWENTY-SEVEN

Judge Ironsides Ahrens sat behind his dark cherry-wood desk in his chambers at the Ninth Circuit Court of Appeals, his head in his hands. A single envelope lay in the middle of the desk. Only the small lamp on the desk was on, leaving most of the room in the dark or hidden in motionless shadows. Things had not been so desperate since Holland with Bram.

Three months after the boys had been sent to live in hiding up in Heerenveen, Isaac and Rachel Ahrens were swept up in a raid gathering Jews for deportation. The two were sent to Westerbork. Their exemption stamps offered no protection. Sometimes Council members still received special attention with their papers; however, on this given day at this given time, no such special treatment was afforded to the Ahrens. *Endlosung.* They were herded with the others for "resettlement in the East." Isaac Ahrens knew what that meant—Auschwitz.

The two boys fared far better in Heerenveen. It was similar to their life in Hoogeveen. Their foster parents were the Pressers, a couple in their late forties who lived on a small potato farm just outside Heerenveen in Friesland. Obviously, the arrangement suited the boys. They could be hidden in the open, yet safe from deportation. The Pressers would have taken in any children, but obtaining a boy who could help out on the farm was a practical bonus. There also was an emotional bonus. The Pressers had lost their son in the war and had struggled managing the farm and their grief on their own. Admittedly, the struggle had more to do with the loss of their child than losing additional labor; however, the two Ahrens boys would soon relieve both.

There was much work for the pre-teen Bram. To prepare for winter, firewood had to be stockpiled, kindling gathered, and wood for the bake oven needed to be sorted. Bram was also in charge of the potshellon, the compost piles. Bram gathered and composted straw and heather with cattle manure to fertilize the fields. The Pressers also assigned him less glamorous chores: cleaning the barn, feeding the cattle, herding the cattle, mending fences, as well as his normal household chores.

On every errand, every chore, and at almost every moment, Doug, or "Dougie" as Bram affectionately called his younger brother, was at his side. When he gathered firewood, Dougie was nearby trying to roll a log along the ground. If Bram gathered heather for compost, Dougie was at his side with two fistfuls. The two were inseparable. Wherever Bram went, his little brother shadowed him. Bram did not mind. He knew deep down that all the two had in this world were each other.

Bram did like the Pressers, though. And whatever Bram liked, Dougie liked. The Pressers were nice people; however, they were not the Ahrens boys' parents. Even though the Pressers were very affectionate with the Ahrens boys, this affection could not replace the love of the boys' parents. The Pressers knew this, so did Bram, and whatever Bram felt, so did little Doug Ahrens. Bram also thought the Pressers were fun. Every evening after a hard day's work, dinner, and chores, Mrs. Presser would play spelling and word games with Bram and Doug, who always shouted out the exact same thing as Bram. Bram did think that one thing was strange or odd about the Pressers. Every evening they would move a hutch which covered the entrance to their basement then go downstairs to listen to the radio. The boys were not allowed down into the basement. Furthermore, the boys were instructed to rush down into the basement only if they saw any visitors or soldiers coming. Bram rarely saw visitors and never saw soldiers. That is until *Dolle Disdang.*

On Monday, September 4, 1944, a report was sent out over Allied radio channels that the Allies had liberated the Dutch town of Breda and would soon be freeing all of Holland from Nazi Germany. Upon hearing the report, the Pressers, and the rest of Holland, went crazy. The following day, *Dolle Disdang* or "Mad Tuesday," Dutch citizens everywhere took to the streets. They danced. They sang. They cheered and waved Dutch flags. The war was over, the Dutch were free. The Pressers were no different. On Tuesday morning they woke up late, they had actually slept in for the first time in years.

The Ahrens boys had already left to mend the fences, but Bram's note said that they would return at lunchtime to tend to the barn. Mrs. Presser wanted to bake. She never wasted sugar on such a needless thing as baking, but she simply had to. The boys would love cookies. Cookies would be an ideal way to break the news of the end of the war. Mr. Presser scrambled up to the attic to find his Dutch National Flag that he hid, under threat of punishment of *Reichskommissariat* law, to remember his son. He would fly the flag high in memory of his son. The Pressers, and all of Holland, were caught up in the craziness of *Dolle Disdang.*

Unfortunately, the report was false.

The Allies had not liberated Holland. The behavior of the Dutch people on Dolle Disdang, coupled with a railway strike, infuriated the *Reichskommissariat* and the Nazis. Although some German troops fell under the same spell as the Dutch people and began to desert the occupied territory, orders were given to squash the celebrations.

The three soldiers who spotted the Pressers' flag from the road were not aware of the Allied radio report or even the *Reichskommisariat's* orders. For these soldiers, none of that mattered. They simply saw the flag and sought to punish those who flew the Dutch flag in defiance of the *Wehrmacht.* The jeep transport for these three soldiers had no room for prisoners.

Bram and his sidekick Dougie returned from the fields to a gruesome site. As they entered the kitchen they found the lifeless body of Mrs. Presser strewn about on the kitchen floor in a pool of blood. Walking past the body and tracking blood into the hallway, the two found the body of Mr. Presser at the front door. Both his body and the hallway had been riddled with bullets. The Dutch flag had been shredded and thrown on top of the body. The two bodies detracted from the fact that the house had been ransacked from top to bottom.

With his little brother holding his hand, Bram walked around the house twice. He then walked to the barn, then back up to the house again. At the barn, Bram had picked up a spade. Behind the house he dug two large graves. Doug played in the dirt that Bram had piled up by the holes. Bram then dragged the body of Mrs. Presser by her feet into the backyard to the side of the hole. Bram then rolled the body into the hole. Doug carried her arm as if he had half the load. Bram also tried to drag the body of Mr. Presser. He was too heavy. All Bram could manage was moving his legs to shut the front door. The two boys piled dirt on top of Mrs. Presser, then covered the grave with flowers they picked from Mrs. Presser's garden. That evening Bram nailed both the front doors and hallway door shut, as if Mr. Presser's body were contained in a mausoleum.

Finally, the boys moved their belongings, bedding, and all the blankets into the barn.

For the first week the boys did no chores, not even straightening up their beds or bathing. After the food from the kitchen ran out, they basically lived off of eggs, milk, and boiled potatoes. Dougie developed a cough. Sensing a need for order, Bram returned to their same routines as when they were living with Pressers. Dougie felt better with the daily routines. However, after about three more weeks, little Dougie started to cry more often at night. This led to whining during the day. Soon, every day Doug would ask his brother if they could go back to Hoogeveen, back to their parents. Day after day Doug would beg, whine, then cry. Finally, Bram capitulated. He agreed that they would go back to Hoogeveen to find their parents. Six weeks had passed since they had moved into the barn.

Bram understood that in order to travel, he needed money. But he had none. Bram had not been inside the house in several weeks, ever since the food ran out. He had forgotten how little it resembled the home he had lived in for fourteen months. The place was in shambles. Pictures were slashed, their frames broken and most of them discarded on the floor. The furniture fared no better. Legs of chairs were broken, cushions slashed with stuffing and padding strewn about, empty drawers with their contents emptied on the floors. Much of the china and other porcelain items had been broken. The only things Bram noticed were missing were a couple of clocks and a neck-lace Mrs. Presser wore on Sundays.

The kitchen floor was still stained with dried blood. Bram's attempt of cleaning the blood by pouring a pail of water over it had miserably failed six weeks ago. However, Bram did notice that the stain by the hutch was irregular. The stain was on one side of the hutch but not the other. It was then that Bram remembered how Mr. and Mrs. Presser listened to the radio down in the basement. Bram pushed the hutch a couple feet over, then lifted the basement door. Doug's eyes were as wide as they could be. Neither Bram nor Doug had ever been down in the basement. Bram took one step before returning to the kitchen to retrieve a candle and matches from a kitchen drawer.

The basement steps were steep. Bram held the candle with one hand and little Dougie's hand with the other. The basement was dark and bare. Against one wall there was a bookshelf with two chairs in front of it. Bram and Doug, guided by candlelight, walked to the bookcase. Doug, more at ease than Bram, sat in one of the chairs. In the middle of the bookcase was the radio. Bram knew his parents had to get rid of their radio, and the Pressers probably would have wanted them to have it. So Bram gave the candle to Doug and lifted the radio up. There was something behind the radio. It was a small box. Bram set the radio down on the chair. Doug's eyes remained transfixed on the flame of the candle he was holding. In the dim candlelight, Bram slowly took hold of the small box. The small cigar box was like nothing he had ever seen before. The wood was dark and polished. It also had a metal clasp on the front. Bram unhooked the clasp. Inside there were bills after bills after bills. Bram found what he was looking for—money.

The trip to Hoogeveen began with a quarter mile walk up to the road. From the road, Bram figured they could get a ride to Hoogeveen. After a hearty breakfast, the two set out on their adventure. By the end of the driveway little Dougie was too tired to carry the radio. He started to cry. The next day the two set out again, this time Bram pulled his brother and the radio behind him in a little wagon that had belonged to the Pressers.

Bram headed south. He knew he had to go south and east. He figured he would walk one day south and one day east, and he would probably be there. By the evening of the first day, the Ahrens boys had made little progress, only about three miles to just north of Wolvega on their sixty-mile trip. Doug had eaten most of the food they had brought with them. Their biggest excitement was crossing train tracks and seeing a train from far away.

About an hour after dusk with little Dougie asleep in the wagon, Bram saw his first car. It actually was a truck. Bram flapped his arms wildly. The truck flashed its lights.

As the truck pulled up beside the weary young travelers, Bram shook his brother awake. The truck driver opened the door and leaned out of the cab. "What are the two of you doing here?"

Bram had practiced his lines for ten hours. He stood as straight as he could and recited, "Kind sir, we are on our way to Hoogeveen back to our parents and need transportation. I have a stamp."

As he finished, Bram pulled his exemption stamp from his pocket and showed the truck driver.

The truck driver climbed out of the cab. He was only a foot taller than Bram. He took the stamp from Bram's hand and flung it in front of the truck.

"Boy, is your head crazy? Having one of these stamps is going to get you killed. It's worthless. If you really want to see something, look at these."

The short man unfolded some papers and showed the boy, "These are *Wehrmacht* Papers. They say I'm driving for the Germans. I can go any-where."

Bram ran in front of the truck and by the light of the headlamps found the exemption stamp his father had given him. It was the last thing his father had given him. The only thing he had to remember him by.

"You don't want that stamp," repeated the truck driver.

Pushing the stamp deep down in his pocket, Bram said, "Kind sir, we are on our way to Hoogeveen back to our parents and we need a ride. Would a kind man like you please drive us back to our parents?"

"I am going to Amsterdam. I have to deliver my potatoes."

"But kind sir, we need," Bram overstressed the word 'need,' "to go to Hoogeveen to our parents."

"Nothing in Hoogeveen."

"But kind sir."

"Your parents won't be in Hoogeveen. If anywhere, they would be in Amsterdam."

"Is Amsterdam on the way to Hoogeveen?" Bram asked the truck driver.

"For you, Amsterdam is on the way to Hoogeveen."

With that, the truck driver loaded Bram and his drowsy little brother into the cab of the truck. He put the blankets, radio and wagon back with the potatoes. Within minutes Bram joined his brother in a deep sleep.

"Son, son, wake up."

Bram recognized the voice of the truck driver.

"Come on, son, get up."

"Yes." Bram began to rub his eyes, "Yes, kind sir."

"I need you and your brother to get out of my cab for a couple of hours."

"Can't we just sleep?"

"No. I have to deliver my potatoes to the Germans. And you two can't go there."

"Is this your home?" Bram inquired.

"Yes, but you cannot go in there. My wife won't let me take anyone in."

Bram just stared at the truck driver. His brother still lay asleep leaning against the door.

"Don't worry, kid. I will come back for you in one hour."

"But where will we go?" Bram began to wake up.

"Don't worry. I will take you to some of your people. I bring them potatoes all the time."

"You are not Dutch?"

The truck driver's Jewish reference was lost on young Abraham Ahrens.

"People like your Mom and Dad. People who use that, that stamp of yours."

Again Bram did not understand, but he did understand Mom and Dad.

"You will take us to Mom and Dad?"

Just wanting to get the kids out of the truck, the truck driver said, "Yes."

Bram climbed out of the truck. The driver lifted Doug and laid the sleeping child down on the stoop by his brother. The driver then took a sack from behind the driver's seat. Walking back to the load of potatoes, he filled the sack.

Setting the sack of potatoes on the other side of Bram, the driver told him, "I have your wagon and radio with me. Now you have a sack of my potatoes. When I come back, we will trade back. You will give back my potatoes and I will give you back your wagon and radio. OK?"

Bram again just stared at the truck driver and asked, "What's your name?"

"Joop. Call me Joop."

As the trucker climbed back into the cab of his truck, Joop glanced down at the boys and said, "Remember, in one hour we will trade back."

Before he drove away, Bram shouted out to the man, "Mr. Joop, where are we?"

"Son, you are in Amsterdam." With that, Joop sped off in his truck.

After a couple of hours and as morning broke, Doug woke up. Bram was tired but he did not want to miss Joop if he drove by. Soon he recognized that he had to sleep. Pointing and waving his finger at little Dougie in the same way Mrs. Presser or his Mom did when it was something really important, Bram instructed his brother to stay right by his side and to wake him if Joop came back.

A woman's voice caused Bram to stir from his sound sleep. He thought it was his mother. It had been five hours since Joop left the two boys. Bram had been asleep for nearly two hours. Bram rubbed the sleep from his eyes. He could tell the woman playing with Doug was not his mother. However, she did resemble his mother. A thin, worn-out, and tired version of his mother.

The woman introduced herself as Beatrix van Ruisdael. She told the two boys that they could not stay on the streets and had to come with her. Bram protested. They had to wait for Joop because Joop was going to take them to their parents in Hoogeveen. Realizing that the children would not leave, Beatrix knew she had to mislead the kids to get them off the street. She told Bram that Joop had sent her to pick the kids up. Beatrix further told the kids that Joop wanted them to stay with her for a couple of days.

Bram relented. The three then walked ten blocks to a neighborhood which appeared to be deserted. Most of the windows were broken, and many of the homes did not have doors. The home they entered resembled the neighborhood, abandoned and forsaken. There were large gaping holes in most of the walls. The banister for the stairs had been torn off. Bram could see right through to the upstairs since many of the second level's floorboards had been removed. As they walked down the hallway, the two wide-eyed children passed rooms that had no doors or furniture. At the end of the dark hallway, Beatrix told the boys to wait. She entered the room and lit some candles. The cozy little room had been a large kitchen. But now it was divided in half by a curtain with the kitchen and wood stove on one half and a cot and chair on the other half. Beatrix told the boys to sit on the bed while she boiled some of the potatoes.

The three lived as a family through the *Hongerwinter*. The Germans had prevented or diverted any food or fuel from entering Amsterdam. Coupled with the harshness of the weather, many citizens perished from hunger, cold, or disease. Without the shelter provided by Beatrix van Ruisdael, there is little doubt the Ahrens boys would not have survived the *Hongerwinter*. Bram, on the other hand, ensured Beatrix van Ruisdael's survival. Every other day he peddled at least ten miles on one of the van Ruisdael's old bikes to the country. He traveled at night and in the snow. The bike had no tires. Bram used the Presser's money to buy food from farmers in the country. When the money ran out, Bram had to beg or steal food. In the beginning, Bram had been able to buy brown beans, flour, and even bacon. By March, Bram had to steal beets or dig up tulip bulbs. By the end of the winter Bram had been getting sick more often than not. He had not been taking care of himself, but still made his trips to the country. Beatrix, who had lost her only child to pneumonia, feared that neither child would make it through the winter. Fortunately, the change in seasons brought more food into the city.

On May 5, 1944, the Allies liberated Holland. Canadian soldiers patrolled the streets of Amsterdam. The city was once again alive with joy. Everyone hugged everyone. Everyone sang with everyone. Everyone forgave everyone. Joop Wielek had even tracked down Bram to return Doug's little red wagon.

With the streets littered with flowers and confetti and the hustle and bustle of people pulling their lives together, Beatrix held Bram's hand. With his other hand, Bram pulled Doug in his little red wagon. They walked to the train station. Joop, who had turned a little profit during the war, bought train tickets for Bram and Doug to Meppel where a friend of his would drive them to Hoogeveen. Beatrix went with the children, knowing full well what they would find in Hoogeveen.

Although it had been only a day since the Allies liberated the city, its people were consumed in delirium. Some old men were drunk and sang by the Grand Canal. Couples walked hand in hand trading kisses every few feet. And children played. Bram could not remember the last time he saw children at play. Some boys and girls rode bicycles in circles. About a half-dozen boys kicked a ball toward a makeshift goal. Some girls picked weeds as if they were the most prized tulips in the land. A lone boy about Bram's age threw rocks into the canal.

The boy skipping stones was the last clear vision Bram saw before the sniper's shot caught him in the chest. Beatrix let go of his hand at the sound of the shot. Little girls screamed. The boy skipping stones turned to see Bram fall back into the wagon with his brother. Doug did not move as the Canadian soldiers repeatedly fired upon the third-story window. Bram's outstretched arms clung to Doug's shirt. With his right hand, he set his father's exemption stamp in Doug's hands. The only memory Douglas Ironsides Ahrens has of his brother is of Bram closing his eyes.

Judge Ahrens opened his eyes and unclenched his fist. Within the palm of his hand was a laminated card. In the center of the card was his father's exemption stamp safely protected from the elements and human touch by clear plastic. The judge moved the laminated card between his fingers, then wrote his note.

> *Dear Sara,*
>
> *You will never know how much I love you even if you cannot fathom such an emotion. Everything I have ever done I have done out of love for you to ensure that you and your children would not have to endure what your grandparents and relatives had to bear. I have labored to make the world a place where*

*you and your children would be safe. Safe from the horrors of oppression, Fascism, and Nazism. I have discovered no greater horrors in life than those suffered by your Grandfather, Grandmother, your Uncle Bram, and all who suffered at the hands of the Nazis. That is until now.*

*Having your child taken from you rips apart your soul. Before, I only imagined the pain suffered by Bram and all the rest. Today, I felt it. I pray that you never have to experience it.*

*I have taken steps to ensure your safety now and in the future. I have sent an encrypted e-mail to an old friend of your mother, you know who it is. My analysis contained therein will implicate them on such a scale that they cannot afford to take any chances with harming you. They know that. So does your old friend. He will know what buttons to push.*

*I cannot ever hope for you to understand what I have done. I chose the path I did in life knowing that it was not virtuous. However, I believed that my path was necessary to achieve a greater good. There is so much evil in this world that I sought to correct, that I failed to see the evil in front of me. I can no longer be a part of that evil. With me around, the information I left for you can only be discredited. Without me, you will be safe.*

*I leave knowing that you will be safe. I also leave knowing that we will never be the same. I will take knowing you are safe with me.*

*Always your loving father*

With his last stroke of the pen, Judge Ahrens sighed a deep breath. Despite the many pauses he took, he remained stoic throughout his composition. His time for reflection had ended. He had made his peace. Douglas Irving Ahrens, son of Isaac Ahrens, brother of Abraham Ahrens, clipped the 1942 Jewish Council Exemption stamp to his letter to Sara. Judge "Ironsides" Ahrens then pulled the revolver from his top desk drawer.

# TWENTY-EIGHT

Off the coast of Black Point Battery, a familiar site of uniformed policemen gathered around two waterlogged bodies. Several of the officers taped off the area, discouraging the growing crowd of tourists and locals. Off the shore, divers bobbed up and down in the ocean waves. The two bodies, surrounded by policemen, lie on the beach like driftwood or rotten fish the ocean had spit back onto the shore. Having not had time to decay, or even be picked apart by the creatures of the sea, the bodies were easily recognizable. St. Louis Police Chief Jesse Stuart lay dead; next to him was one of the FBI agents in his familiar blue suit.

"We got another one!" yelled one of the divers to shore.

With her plastic gloves on, Detective Martinez knelt over the body of the slain police commander and gently examined the dead man's knee.

Detective Nelson stood over his superior and inquired, "Do you know who this is?"

"Yes," she replied.

"It's that police chief from St. Louis that was on TV."

"I know."

"He's the one who was after the Shakespeare Killer."

"I know."

"The other guy is from the Bureau."

"I know."

"This Shakespeare guy has gone over the edge. Killing lawyers he could get away with, but a federal agent and a police chief? He'll never get a trial."

"What makes you think it was your Shakespeare guy?"

"Easy, the hunted becomes the hunter."

"That's ridiculous," Martinez responded.

"Why?"

"Because your 'hunter' will now have every law enforcement officer after him."

"So?"

"So, it does not make sense."

"Maybe he wants to go out in a bang of glory."

Martinez questioned her junior detective.

"If he wanted to do that, why didn't he just get into a big shootout at the mission? If he is shooting everyone else, how come he did not fire a shot at the cemetery?"

"I don't know."

"I know. There are too many unanswered questions. Second, these killings are not even consistent with your Shakespeare theory. They are not lawyers. Third, this one fits the description of one of your well-dressed bounty hunters at the mission."

A uniformed officer scurried down the hill toward the detectives.

"Detective Martinez?"

"Right here."

"Detective Martinez, there is another body," stated the young uniformed policeman.

"I know, they are fishing him out right now."

"No, not here. Downtown."

"Downtown?"

"A federal judge from the appeals court."

Looking directly at his superior, Nelson smirked and said, "Back on track, another lawyer."

———<>———

Andriy Kravenko stood by the edge of the parking lot atop Telegraph Hill, the highest point in San Francisco. Long before the Golden Gate Bridge guarded the harbor, a lookout was posted where Coit Tower stands. The lookout could view the entire bay and easily spot approaching ships. Once spotted, the lookout hoisted the ship's colors, the national flag of the ship. From this point, the lookout could watch a ship leave the harbor, sail and disappear for months, or quite possibly, forever. Kravenko took an envelope from his blazer. Opening it, he pushed aside a disk with his finger and removed a folded piece of paper from the package. It had been a shame that all of the judge's electronic communications were intercepted. Whatever secrets he wished to reveal were trapped safely on the disk. Kravenko opened the letter and again read Judge Ahrens' last words to his daughter. The letter crumpled in the wind as he read it over and over. As he refolded it, returned it to the envelope, and secured it in his inside pocket, Kravenko mumbled to himself, "Blessed are they who have been persecuted within themselves; it is they who have truly come to know the Father."

# TWENTY-NINE

After failing to reach Aaron Golde by telephone, Peter watched Sara intently as she retold the events of the past day to Redwood. He was careful not to interrupt, not that it would even be necessary. Skilled as a litigator, Sara's presentation of what had happened resembled a closing statement rather than a plea for help. Of course, it was both. Whoever this Redwood was, Peter knew that the old man had to be convinced that they were in trouble, and not just a couple of ranting paranoids. Sara was effective, but Peter could only think of Sara's first reaction to everything. If Sara were reluctant to believe Peter, how would this tree man react? Redwood did not react. When Sara finished, the old man left for the kitchen to "fetch everyone some hot cocoa." A cup of hot chocolate would hit the spot, but that was not the reaction one would expect. Peter worried that Sara may have overplayed her hand to her old friend.

"Do you think you should have told him everything?" Peter inquired.

"If I did not think I should have told him everything, I would not have."

Withdrawing a bit, Peter continued, "Who is this guy?"

"My most trusted friend," replied Sara.

"Most?"

"I have known Redwood all my life, which is a lot longer than I have known you."

Peter was relieved that Sara almost seemed playful.

"But really, who is he and what is up with all of these books?"

"Ever since I have known Redwood he has lived here with all of his books. I think he is fluent in about ten languages. He taught me Dutch before I reached the age of eight. Shocked the hell out of my parents when I began speaking Dutch to them on my eighth birthday. Redwood was a friend of Mom. I know what you are thinking. He was not close with my father. Father never came up here. In fact, I cannot think of a time that I saw Redwood and the Judge together. I don't think either ever spoke ill of one another, they just never spoke about one another. Almost like a non-recognition status."

"Mom loved Redwood. For years I hoped that he was my grandfather. Mom said that she had hoped for the same thing when she was a girl. I know he does not look it, but he has to be at least eighty. Anyone up here will tell you, 'if you cut old Redwood in half you'd find a thousand rings to count.'"

"I don't know what he does or what he did for a living. He is very evasive about his past and always steers the conversation away from himself. What I do know is that he knows everyone and everything. I mean it, Peter. In the past, whenever I have been jammed up at Sienna, as a last resort I would call Redwood. Ol' Redwood always knew which button to push. If I should call one senator or another, or what congressman I should put under pressure. He was able to get me and a couple of other Sienna members into a state dinner when the Brazilian president was in D.C. You know how hard it is to get into one of those things, much less sit people from our club together with people destroying rain forests. I don't think I'll be invited back too soon, but it was worth it."

Redwood entered the room again carrying a book.

"Here it is."

"Here what is," asked Sara.

"That parable you mentioned, about Jesus as a child," Redwood pointed the passage in the book to Sara.

"What is this?" asked Sara.

"The Gospel of Thomas, the first Greek version."

"Now I would hardly like to put my years as an altar boy up against your library, but I do not recall a Gospel of Thomas in the Bible."

"Because there is no Gospel of Thomas in the Bible," Redwood responded.

"And your point is," Peter waved his hand to his elder as if giving him a chance to continue.

"There is no point, just that the passage was from the Gospel of Thomas."

"But there is no Gospel of Thomas in the Bible," Peter reiterated.

"Son, the Bible does not contain all early Christian writings. There are a number of Gospels that never made the final version. The Bible is a book, a book containing holy scripture, but a book nonetheless. Its editors did not include every Christian writing. Many of the Gnostic teachings were specifically excluded. Just imagine how different the world would be if the Bible did contain different passages, like the passage of the angered young Jesus."

Peter was still confused.

"Anyone for cocoa?" asked Redwood as he exited the room without waiting for a response.

Sara paged through Redwood's book for a minute, ignoring Peter shaking his head in bewilderment.

"This is exactly what that man said, word for word."

"Sara, we tell this guy that part of our government is corrupt to the core, and about three or four sets of people are trying to kill us and all he comes up with is a story that got left on the Bible's cutting room floor," Peter stated with the look of confusion still on his face.

"Peter, I know you probably don't trust my judgment anymore, especially after this morning, but you have no choice. If you cannot contact Aaron Golde, and you don't want to leave him a message, I am your only hope. More importantly, I have a say in this now. My life is on the line, and that being so there is no one I would rather have in my corner than Redwood."

"A resounding endorsement, dear Sara," Redwood said as he entered the room carrying a tray holding the three steaming mugs of cocoa. "But your friend has a point, he does not know me from Adam. Judging from his experiences in the last three days, I do not blame him for a lack of blind faith."

"No disrespect sir," Peter apologized as he took a mug from the tray.

"None taken," retorted the old man, "but you can learn a thing or two about who you are up against given the fact that this man has the ability to quote, verbatim, from the Gospel of Thomas, or even what that Gospel says about the man himself. He does not sound like your average thug. There may be more to him than what you believe. You have to trust all the facts, not just the perceptions of a random few. More importantly, at some point you are going to have to trust someone other than yourself, or you will never learn the whole truth."

"Quite frankly, sir..."

"Call me Redwood," the old man interrupted.

"Redwood," Peter continued, "I don't know the good guys from the bad guys out there."

"Interesting," the old man said as he sipped his chocolate.

Taken aback, Peter responded, "It is more than interesting, it's devastating. If Elias St. Armand and Occidental can control congressmen, senators, police, and FBI agents, where does it end? Are there any good people out there?"

"What makes you so sure your Aaron Golde is good?"

The old man struck a cord with Peter. Peter knew he could trust Aaron. Before the attorney in Peter could strike back the old man continued, "Young man, do you know who Mencius is?"

"Menshee what?"

"Mencius."

Opening his eyes wide and holding his arms open, Peter's whole body questioned the old man.

"Mencius was a Confucian philosopher in the third century before Christ. Mencius wholeheartedly believed and preached that human nature is inherently good. According to Mencius, there were four germs, or seeds, of human character. Those seeds, if properly nurtured, mature into the virtues of benevolence, rightness, propriety, and wisdom."

The old man paused for a few minutes, sipped some more cocoa, then looked Peter directly in the eyes.

"Mr. Farrell, have your seeds been properly nurtured?"

"What?" Peter said with an expression of bewilderment.

"That is the question you should be asking, not whether someone, anyone, is good, but whether one has been properly nurtured to extol the virtues of benevolence, rightness, propriety, and wisdom. How can anyone tell if anyone is good? A handshake, a sit down for coffee, camping for a week, work with someone for a year or a couple of years? Anyone can act 'good,' because the seeds have always been there. However, actually being good we have to examine the nurturing of the seed."

Peter interrupted, "No disrespect, Mr. Redwood, but..."

"Young man," continued Redwood, "you are grilling yourself trying to figure out who you can trust, who is good."

"Yes."

"I am telling you that you are not going to be able to tell if someone is good because there is some good in everyone. What you should ask yourself is, 'how can I find the good in people and how can I nurture that good?'"

"Once again, I mean no disrespect, but what does that have to do with..."

Before Peter could finish, the old man continued, "You see impatient one, your enemy is merely anti-Menscian, or is that Amenscian, he is simply looking for the bad seed in people and nurturing it. You, on the other hand, need to stop looking for good people and start nurturing the good in people."

"Wait a minute, I think you have something."

Both Sara and Redwood stopped and looked at Peter.

"I'm sorry, it's not exactly what you are talking about, but I think I have something. It's along that planting a seed line and nurturing it. Sara, do you still have those papers from the cemetery?"

"Yes, I set them by the clothes to dry."

Sara rose from her chair and gathered the papers that had been hanging over a chair by the fire. She handed them to Peter.

"Here they are."

"Now if we just had a fax machine."

Redwood rose, walked over to what Peter had thought was paneling and opened the sliding doors, "Would a scanner and e-mail work?"

Both Peter and Sara looked at one another in disbelief.

The old man responded, "I do some reading on the Internet as well."

Peter scanned in the documents detailing Speaker of the House "Randy" Randall Sexton's illicit affair with several "escorts". The file was incomplete. Many of the documents had been lost at Mission Dolores; however, what Peter had was enough. Peter scanned several sworn affidavits by hotel managers, bellboys, and even the girls themselves, hotel receipts, phone records, and the coup de grace, compromising photographs of the congressman.

Logging onto the Internet, using his firm's password, Peter e-mailed the Sexton file to all the online national news media. Once again using his firm's address, Peter typed that the scanned information was from "Shakespeare."

"I don't know if you should have signed it that way."

"I figured it would give all the surfers something to hit. I didn't think anybody would have understood it if I used Francis Bacon."

"Amusing," Redwood grinned at the literary reference.

"Now that the bait is on the hook, time to throw the line into the water."

"What are you doing?" Sara asked.

"It is time to negotiate with Occidental, this time on my terms. I need to bluff St. Armand. He will have to back off or I will plaster all the Occidental papers over the web.

Returning to the lawyer in her, Sara commented, "Sounds fine, except for the fact that you do not have any more files."

"That would be the 'bluff' part that I was talking about. He doesn't know what I have. Besides, Aaron Golde has them, or should have them soon."

"How are you going to negotiate, conference call?"

Failing to catch the humor, Peter, was very serious.

"No, I have jeopardized enough people's lives, this I have to do on my own."

"What do you mean?"

"I'll meet him."

"That's crazy."

"Not as crazy as getting both of you killed. Sara, I have caused you enough harm, it's time that I move along."

"That does not make any sense."

"It makes perfect sense. If something happens, I'll know that you are safe. Besides, spread out like this, I always know that I have backup out there."

"Peter."

"The young man has a point," interjected Redwood.

Peter drifted back into his work. He had to send a message to Elias St. Armand. Unfortunately, the CEO of the multinational corporation did not have an e-mail address. Telephoning was out of the question, of course. Peter decided to e-mail Occidental's San Francisco office and leave it in their general mail, hoping it was being monitored. Now all Peter had to do was leave enough keywords in the message to ensure that his message would be found. Peter typed:

*Sexton first, more to follow unless ESA meets alone. Farrell.*

Too conspicuous, Peter typed again:

*One down, more to follow. Meet alone. Mission Dolores. I will find you.*

*P. F. Sexton*

Peter thought that would get the point across.

"Peter, I am going with you."

"No. If they see you with me they know I will not be able to back up my threats. With you hidden, they will assume you have the documents and with one push of the button the Occidental papers are all over the net."

"But I just have this gut feeling."

"Sara," Peter stood and held her hands, "You have known me for over four years, have I ever been wrong?"

"You let me get away."

"OK, once," said Peter as he kissed her forehead.

He put his arms around, squeezed her tightly, and whispered into her ear, "but never again."

Recovering from the moment, Peter looked at Redwood and asked, "Do you have a car I can borrow?"

"Take the jeep."

Redwood handed a set of keys to Peter.

Before leaving, Peter looked back at Sara.

More command than wish, she said, "Be careful."

Peter was out the door.

As he drove away, Sara complained, "Why can't we go in hiding? With your help no one would ever find us in these hills. Why does he have to be some kind of hero?"

Redwood watched the brakes of his jeep fade off into the forest and calmly stated, "Evil triumphs when good men do nothing."

# THIRTY

Attorney John Kerr hated to wait. He took it as a slap in the face, a show of disrespect. By arriving late, for whatever reason, the individual informed Kerr that he or she did not value John Kerr's time. Such an affront to him had proven costly on more than one occasion. Kerr's lack of tolerance for such behavior had driven him to leave meetings before they had started, publicly berate the violating party, or cancel deals because a representative was late for a closing. However, Kerr's rigid policy was not without exceptions. His perceived mentor, Roland Miller, of course could keep his underling waiting for any length of time. After all, who could reprimand the counselor to presidents, except of course the President himself? If ever kept waiting by Miller, Kerr could only stew on the inside while graciously accepting the elder statesman's feeble apologies.

Kerr also would wait for CIA Assistant Director Oscar Watson, if that situation ever presented itself. It had not. Yet. Assistant Director Watson waited for Kerr at their monthly meetings at D.C.'s Marbury Hotel. It was not as if John Kerr ever arrived past the prearranged time, heaven forbid. It was that Watson always arrived early. Given that any meeting the Director had with anyone, much less with one of D.C.'s high-powered attorneys, was public news, the discretion on the Director's part was understood.

And of course, John Kerr would wait for Elias St. Armand. What Kerr failed to realize until years later was how long he had waited for Elias St. Armand.

Straight out of law school, John Kerr was on a hot streak. He landed an associate position with the top lobbyist firm Miller & White. The D.C. elite labeled it a lobbyist firm, though it actually was a law firm. When members of the Hill routinely entered and exited the large glass doors of Miller & White, there was no doubt in anyone's mind that policy issues, as opposed to legal problems, dominated in the conference rooms. Then, of course, there was the first name on the firm's letterhead. Miller. Roland Miller. Counselor to presidents. This firm did not handle DUI's, that is, unless they involved a senator's son whose bill would pass by only two votes unless he decided to withdraw it and reintroduce it in the next session where it could become filibuster-proof. This was no ordinary law firm.

After two years with Miller & White, John Kerr had yet to distinguish himself. Yet the only pressure put on the young Kerr was by himself. There was no expectation that a first-, second-, or even third-year associate would, or even could, bring in the type of business Miller & White enjoyed. Kerr, on the other hand, wanted to raise the bar. So when a friend of a friend contacted him about some international holding companies needing assistance in acquiring and managing some U.S. banks, Kerr jumped at the chance to make a name for himself.

It was not until about two months into his negotiations to acquire three Georgia banks that Kerr began to realize that there was more to his new business partners than met the eye.

His friend, Casey Rappaport, had introduced him to some other attorneys who introduced Kerr to attorneys out of Houston. The Texas attorneys were from the firm Baker, Culver, Carr & Irving. The attorneys at "Baker Culver," as they were known, clicked with Kerr. They spoke the same language, an argot that centered on money and power. Kerr toiled through weeks of sixteen-, seventeen-, eighteen-hour days to impress his Texas associates. It worked. Baker Culver lavished Kerr with such praise that Kerr wanted to jump ship. But Baker Culver made it clear to him that Kerr's association with Miller & White was paramount to their business dealings. Kerr began to realize that his expertise in acquisitions, mergers, and banking regulations ranked below the fact that every letter Kerr wrote, or call he received, or conference he held, carried the credentials of the Miller & White firm. This became important as Kerr began to peel away at who his client really was.

Kerr was used to corporations and wealthy individuals trying to hide something from the government, and all the cat and mouse games associated with those clients. However, he was amazed at the extent at which these new clients tried to hide things. All financing for shares to acquire any bank originated from various holding companies. Yet "originate" may not have been the best word to describe where the financing actually originated. The various holding companies were also put in place by other holding companies. Clearly Kerr had been hired by Baker Culver to cloak these bank purchases with Miller & White's legitimacy as a preemptive measure against any federal regulators. It worked and Kerr knew it.

With this knowledge, Kerr sought a larger piece of the pie. It was given to him along with many other things, the least of which was the knowledge of the depth Baker Culver maneuvered these holding companies. Baker Culver revealed themselves to Kerr in a manner as if describing ordinary transactions as opposed to an admission of guilt. The admission was that the holding companies financed various arm sales to Iran and Iraq, as well as various other terrorist organizations, laundered drug money or funds from these illegal arms sales through their newly acquired U.S. banks, supplemented and even provided the financial income for various Mideast officials, and even provided financial assistance to assist the builders of the Pakistani nuclear bomb in order to increase arms sales to India.

Many of the activities simply involved the ability to broker deals, the lawyers at Baker Culver explained. For example, the United States, contrary to the law signed by the president and passed by Congress in the Boland Amendment, wanted to sell arms to Iran. Iran wanted to buy arms from the U.S. The key was that neither party trusted one another in this illegal sale. The Israelis acted as the middleman, but that had little impact on the trust factor. The Americans wanted their money from the Israelis as soon as they gave their arms to the Israelis, whereas the Iranians would not pay for the arms until they physically reached them. A banker was required. That is where the Baker Culver holding companies stepped into the illegal arms deals. For a front-end fee and an exorbitant interest rate for the few days that were required for the transaction, Baker Culver's holding companies would pay the Israelis who paid the Americans. Payment from the Iranians followed shortly thereafter.

Eventually Kerr learned through peeling away all the various layers of holding companies, subsidiaries, and offshore accounts that his client was in fact one of the largest multinational corporations in the world. His client was, and still is, the Occidental Group.

It was not the excitement of Baker Culver's out-maneuvering federal regulators that enticed Kerr. Half the work in avoiding investigation was in hiring former government officials and cashing in on the old boys' network connections. Nor was the money a factor. Nevertheless, Baker Culver made John Kerr a rich man with stock options and nonrecourse loans to invest in a booming junk bond business.

It was always the power.

Kerr had been caught hook, line, and sinker in the revelation meeting where Baker Culver described their involvement in the illicit banking activities. But it was not the illegal arms sale that convinced Kerr to join forces with Baker Culver. It was the power they wielded in the timing of the sale. As part of the negotiation, Baker Culver demanded that any release of the U.S. hostages held in Iran could not take place until after the November election. Baker Culver did not back the incumbent president, and did not envision four more years of reform in their future. If the hostages were released before the election, certainly the incumbent would be able to claim a victory that could spill over into the election. On the other hand, if the U.S. hostages were not released until after the election, not only would the incumbent be robbed of any glory, but the incoming president could claim the release as a mandate on foreign policy. Baker Culver's backing the right horse had ushered them into the innermost chambers of American politics. John Kerr would not be denied this access.

As part of this unfettered access, Kerr enjoyed a burgeoning relationship with the CIA. That is with Oscar Watson in particular. Watson had been deputy director and a key player in the arms sales to Iran. American arms sales to Iran, of course, required CIA approval. Watson oversaw the entire operation. The CIA was well aware of Baker Culver's illegal activities with their holding companies. Nevertheless, these offshore accounts served a purpose.

As Watson had stated on many occasions, these offshore banking accounts were vital to maintaining national security. The translation was simple: the CIA used Baker Culver and vice versa. In fact, through John Kerr's relationship with Assistant Director Watson, the Baker Culver offshore accounts developed into the unofficial bank of the CIA. If the CIA needed funds for a covert operation, Watson contacted Kerr. Kerr arranged that any accounting be kept off the books. At a monthly meeting at D.C.'s Marbury Hotel, Watson would review the CIA's unofficial account and establish any further lines of credit. Although the money found its way to bribes, illegal arms sales, or even "black op" missions, the two could have been mistaken as businessmen discussing restructuring of debt or a company's future expansion into new markets. Business was business.

Watson also provided Kerr with the ultimate power: life or death. With a phone call and sufficient justification, Kerr could have someone disappear or just killed in a matter of minutes. This power was rarely used, but certainly at his disposal given the occasion. Dean Roger Cosgrove Adam's potential exposure of Occidental provided such an occasion. In addition, a path had to be blocked. Business was business.

John Kerr did not meet Elias St. Armand until he had established himself with Baker Culver. It was a natural progression. Kerr impressed Baker Culver, so Baker Culver introduced Kerr to its contacts at Occidental. Shortly thereafter, Kerr met Elias St. Armand. The first meeting was uneventful, merely a pat on the back "'atta boy" at a cocktail party. St. Armand was never present at Baker Culver meetings. The purpose of having Occidental subsidiaries and holding companies was to avoid any perception that Occidental was involved with such financial activities. Elias St. Armand had little interest in exposing this pretense. Therefore, needless appearances, much less any appearance, were unwarranted. Consequently, over the first several years, John Kerr had little contact with Elias St. Armand.

After several years, Kerr spent less time in Houston, or at his Georgia or Florida banks, and more and more time in D.C. and New York concentrating on Miller & White business. After cultivating so much business for the firm through all his new banking connections, the partners in the firm awarded Kerr with a partnership. More importantly, with his new political alliances blossoming, Roland took notice of the young attorney's initiative. Kerr never fully understood if Miller simply was oblivious to his shady business dealings, or if Miller simply took a blind eye to the matters because of the benefits for the firm. Nevertheless, the results were the same; Kerr had achieved most valuable-attorney status at the firm. That meant Roland would open more doors for him, if Kerr wanted to step through them.

It was at this same time that Kerr had his first crucial meeting with Elias St. Armand. John Kerr had flown up to New York on the belief one of his banks faced potential investigation by the U.S. Attorney for the Southern District of New York. Kerr had been offered a deal for testimony. Kerr rejected the deal. After meeting with a bogus assistant U.S. Attorney, the ruse was revealed to Kerr by Elias St. Armand himself. St. Armand explained to Kerr that he had just been tested, and passed. St. Armand explained to Kerr that Kerr's sphere of influence would be expanding. St. Armand further encouraged Kerr to cultivate his relationship with Miller. In the end, just as foretold by Elias St. Armand, Kerr's relationship with Miller blossomed, as did Kerr's sphere of influence.

As Kerr became a player, he met more regularly with Elias St. Armand. Given Miller's presence in American politics, meetings with St. Armand were always discreet, unless they had a "chance" meeting at a fundraiser. Miller and St. Armand walked in the same political circles, but neither cared to be in the same room as the other. There was a mutual dislike between St. Armand and Miller, but Kerr never delved into the matter. For, if Kerr intended to pursue his interests in the world of Occidental and Elias St. Armand, he had to keep his Occidental world hidden from Miller. However, soon it would be a moot point.

That would be the case if his contact ever arrived. This tardiness was inexcusable.

Kerr could feel his jacket pocket vibrate. It was his cellphone.

"Yes," Kerr answered his phone.

The woman's voice on the other end instructed Kerr to feel under the table for a package.

"What?"

The voice repeated the instruction.

Kerr felt under the table. While his left hand felt some hardened gum, his right hand discovered a paper envelope taped underneath the tabletop. Kerr discreetly removed the envelope from the table. It felt like there was nothing in it. He opened the envelope and pulled out the key card. After the key card was safely in his jacket pocket, Kerr placed the entire envelope in his leather briefcase.

Soon all of this would be a moot point.

———•◦•———

The CNC news anchor appeared almost disheveled, but definitely flabbergasted, as he reported the "Special News Report,"

> *This has been one of the biggest single news days this anchor has seen since 9-11. Again, we have this late breaking news. An hour ago we reported unsubstantiated reports that Speaker of the House Randall Sexton had several affairs, some with professional prostitutes, during the course of the last several years. The Speaker has been known for his conservative fiscal agenda and conservative social agenda which included his affiliation with several of the religious right's coalitions.*
>
> *CNC has this late breaking news that Speaker of the House Randall Sexton will retire effective immediately. His office issued a press release announcing the decision just moments ago. The statement from his office also stated that as of now, no press conference is scheduled, but the Speaker has spoken with the President and the Speaker's own caucus, all of which have accepted his resignation.*
>
> *Once again, amid numerous reports of illicit sexual affairs, Speaker of the House Randall Sexton has retired and resigned from office.*
>
> *This news is on top of the news that the serial killer dubbed as the*

*"Shakespeare Killer' has struck again in San Francisco. Unofficial reports have linked the murders of a St. Louis Police Chief and two FBI agents to the "Shakespeare Killer," who tracked the fugitive to San Francisco. This would bring the unofficial "Shakespeare Killer" count to six.*

*The Shakespeare murders began in St. Louis with the deaths of two attorneys. Peter Joseph Farrell, the brother of one of the attorneys shot to death in St. Louis, is the primary suspect in all six murders...*

The television screen flashed to a composite sketch of what Peter may look like now, as well as the photographs Tasha Dolnick took of him at O'Shea's.

*Peter Joseph Farrell had been dubbed the "Shakespeare Killer" after he had been linked to the death of a former law professor who had been shot to death near his home in Virginia.*

*The St. Louis Police Chief and the unidentified FBI agents were part of the nationwide manhunt for Peter Joseph Farrell.*

*We will go to our local affiliate in San Francisco and then back to Washington D.C. for more on Speaker of the House Randall Sexton...*

# THIRTY-ONE

Peter had picked the mission area for two reasons. First, he still knew the area like the back of his hand. Peter spent many a day walking the streets in Sara's early days at the Sienna Club. Second, and more importantly, today was November 2nd, *Dia de los Muertos*, the Day of the Dead. Sara had brought him to this celebration once and the Latino festivity fascinated Peter. For the festival, the Hispanic Catholic neighborhood decorates itself in skulls, skeletons, banners, grotesque costumes, and merry dances. Drums beat in the streets. The faithful marched.  Peter had likened it to a New Orleans jazz funeral at first.

"*Listos!*" shouted one of the parade leaders. "*Vamanos con los muertos!*"

A large procession marched down Dolores Street. The abundance of revelers provided Peter with ample camouflage. It was almost nine, and the procession would allow him to pass by the mission to determine if Elias St. Armand was alone. Although his pale Irish skin betrayed him somewhat, the large banner of the Virgin of Guadeloupe he held partially covering his head helped.

Staring at the two men by his side, one blowing fervently into a large conch shell, the other in an elaborate headdress forged from flowers, Peter began to remember more of what Sara had told him about Day of the Dead. Despite the black attire, painted skull faces, and frightful imagery, the celebration had more to do with Memorial Day than Halloween. The celebration honored those who had passed along before the rest of us. The skeleton imagery depicted the dead that are with us who have come to join the living. One of the centerpieces of the celebration was the procession honoring the dead. For the procession, some revelers dressed all in black, painted their faces as skulls; others carried skeletons, wreaths with marigold blossoms, the flower of the dead, or religious imagery such as the Virgin of Guadeloupe. Even the direction of the procession has spiritual meaning: to the west to honor *las mujeres*, all the women who have died; to the south for *los angelitos,* the little angels, children and infants who had died before they had time to experience life; and to the east to honor *los guerreros*, the warriors, men who have died. Peter wondered if he would be honored as one of *los guerreros*.

As the procession proceeded toward the mission, Peter could not see Elias St. Armand. Peter had envisioned the robust Lebanese, three-piece suit and all, pacing the Mission stairs. Unfortunately, all that adorned the church's stairs were hundreds of marigold wreaths, as well as other flowers littering the steps. No Elias St. Armand, no meeting. Several people milled around the Mission Dolores, but no one resembling the illustrious Elias St. Armand. Two boys in baseball caps beat drums, one trying to do so faster than the other. Four women also gathered, clothed in traditional Aztec or Mayan dress, discussing whatever the important issue of the day had been while intermittently placing marigold blossoms by a statuette of the Virgin of Guadeloupe. A lone man also stood before the Mission. He, however, was clad entirely in black with his face painted as a white skull. Peter could not imagine the CEO of a multinational corporation committing himself to face painting. Besides that fact, this man was taller and thinner than St. Armand. No Elias St. Armand.

"*Vamanos*," the man beside Peter with the conch shell shouted as he knocked Peter in the arm with his elbow.

"*Vamanos*," Peter shouted back.

The man smiled and then blew extra hard into his conch shell.

The procession arrived in front of the Mission Basilica. Peter thrust his banner of the Virgin of Guadeloupe up high, and took a hard look over at the Basilica. There he was underneath the archway. In his navy blue, double-breasted blazer, black slacks, and wing tips, the corporate giant Elias St. Armand stood alone smoking a cigarette, ambivalent to the festivities around him. Other than the single man, kids, and women, Elias appeared to be alone. Peter shoved his way horizontally through the crowd and away from the conch shell man. The revelers did not mind his intrusion. It was a loose group of followers, chanting, singing and dancing. On the outer edge of the procession, Peter felt his arm being pulled behind his back. Before he could react, a moist cloth covered his face.

"*Santa Maria, madre de Dios...*" the crowd's chant began to fade.

Peter grew dizzy as he realized that some type of chloroform drained him of his consciousness. As he drifted off into a stream of unconsciousness he realized—Sara was right.

# THIRTY-TWO

"Where the hell have you been?" bellowed the distinctly English, but obviously angry, voice.

Sitting with his feet up on his desk in his study while sipping a hundred-year-old cognac and still clad in his sharply tailored tuxedo, the Savile Row man calmly responded, "Awfully early in the morning for you my friend."

"Quite early. But even more disturbing is the fact that I have been languishing on this line waiting for you since half seven."

"I apologize for the inconvenience, but once I was made aware of your call I had my driver summoned immediately. It is unlike you to be so impetuous at this hour. What is so important?"

"Our little theologian rang me about an hour ago."

"And?"

"Something is wrong."

The Savile Row man rose from his chair and walked over to the globe. He found Paris.

"I gathered that once that pervert Sexton resigned, which, might I add, may not be so bad in the long run."

"It is along those lines."

"I am growing impatient by your operatic buildup, get to the point."

"They lost him again."

"Farrell?"

"This all was supposed to be wrapped up by tomorrow. What happened?"

"As my messages to you earlier stated, a meeting had been set and the matter would be settled by tonight."

"Again with the dramatics my friend." The Savile Row man set down his crystal snifter of cognac and gave the globe a spin, "get to the point."

"This little thorn in Elias' side never revealed its prickly self."

"Come again?"

"Farrell was a no show."

For a brief moment only silence filled the lines between the two worldly men. The Savile Row man broke the silence.

"This thorn in St. Armand's side, as you put it, is quickly causing an infection."

"St. Armand has assured our man that Congressman Sexton will be the only casualty."

"How can you be sure of that?"

"He has not said why. Apparently all he tells our friend is that it will all be over tonight."

"If he knows where Farrell is, why doesn't he just let our man take care of the problem? I do not like all of these games he is playing. That Lebanese farm boy will answer to the Board for this fiasco."

"You think we should convene?"

"We need to rid ourselves of Elias and his shenanigans once and for all."

"My friend, I think you are jumping the gun, as you say, in reconvening the Board for this nuisance."

"Nuisance? Your English heritage is betraying your Renaissance persona. This is more than a nuisance. The Speaker of the House of Representatives had to resign. I despised the man, but that depraved congressman had been useful to us before. Very useful."

"But to assemble everyone together?"

"We will do what we have to do. I just want to make sure we are all on the same page."

"It is settled then, I will ring the others. It may take several hours, but I will contact you by seven in the morning, your time."

"That leaves Elias St. Armand with six hours, he better use them wisely."

"Good night, my friend."

The Englishman disconnected the line.

The Savile Row man once again pulled from his vest pocket his gold pocket watch.

"Six hours."

# THIRTY-THREE

"Damn it, Roland! I can't believe you had a chance to get rid of Occidental years ago, but you didn't," a familiar midwestern voice chided.

"Those were different times, Bob," a softer voice responded.

"Hell, they weren't that different," the familiar voice reprimanded.

"The Cold War was very expensive."

"I think the word you mean is 'costly.'"

"Yes," the softer voice calmly stated, "very costly."

"Damn costly," the Midwesterner shot back. "And look what it cost us now, another scandal in Washington. Just what the nation needs, another black eye. I despised the man, but we don't need this, don't need to go through all that crap again."

"I agree, but this was not our doing. It was out of everyone's control."

"Bullshit!"

"Excuse me?"

"What do you have, wax in your ears, or something? You heard me." The familiar voice paused, then continued, "Well, look what we have here. It looks like our sleeping beauty is waking."

The voices had become clearer to Peter as he woke. His head throbbed. The inside of his mouth felt like it needed to be shaved. Peter felt hungover, as if this was the morning after too many pints of stout.

"Young man, do not try to rise too quickly," cautioned the calm voice.

"I know what you mean," replied Peter as he held his head firmly with his hands as if to push it back together.

"You were out much longer than we expected," the calm voice explained.

Remembering what had happened to him, Peter wryly commented, "That's what three days without sleep and a whole lot of chemicals buys you these days."

Peter looked up to see a large man in a dark blue suit wearing an earpiece.

It was the man with the conch shell.

The conch shell man glanced at Peter then turned to the voices and noted, "It was a standard dosage sir."

"Yeah, yeah, standard for an elephant," the bullish voice resounded.

As the conscious world became clearer and clearer to Peter, so did the familiar voice. After rubbing them a time or two, Peter's eyes did not betray his ears. Peter finally addressed the man behind the voice, "Mr. President?"

"Well, I guess that junk you were on did not rot your noggin' completely," commented President Robert Hamilton Fairchild, Ohio's native son. The President's bullish demeanor depicted on television rang true with him in person as well. A fiscal conservative who masqueraded his liberal social views under a steady stream of one-liners, President Fairchild's midwestern charm was lost on only a precious few. Even some members of the Press Corps called him "Bob" when the cameras were not rolling. Of course, not to his face. Known for his quick retorts, the President when asked what he would do if his son told him he was gay, stated 'I don't care who my son brings home for dinner as long as under my roof he abides by my rules: dinner is always at six; no foul language at the table; and when I have gas everyone agrees it's really the dog.' The Ohio governor barely survived the primaries and garnered an even narrower victory in his first presidential election. After four years of his razor sharp wit and a sharper economy, Bob Fairchild was re-elected in a landslide. Bob was now bending over, hands behind his back, to examine the young attorney.

"Where am I?" Peter inquired of the President.

"The Kensington," replied the President. "San Francisco's oldest and most prestigious respected blah blah blah establishments."

"So I'm still in San Francisco."

"You're quick."

"What time is it?" Peter asked.

"Its almost eleven-thirty, son, but you need not concern yourself with time. You're not going anywhere too soon. Furthermore, your Q and A session is over. It's time to start answering some of my questions."

"Bob, let us take this slow," intervened the calm voice. Peter had a hard enough time just concentrating on the President, that he had forgotten about the man with the soft voice. Turning his head, Peter recognized him immediately. The voice belonged to Roland Miller, mentor, counselor and confidant to the presidency. Establishing himself early in the post-war era, Roland Miller became one of the key men behind the scenes during the Cold War. Miller drafted the legislation establishing the Central Intelligence Agency. Whenever a scandal, storm, or situation broke over the White House, Roland Miller was called in "to advise." He was no pollster, political consultant, nor spin meister; Roland Miller belonged to the old world of statesmen, men whose reputation and honor were a calling card, not a commodity. There were few men in Washington like Miller, and none with his credentials.

"Bob, let us take this slow. We need to get a lot accomplished in a short time. If we rush the young man, we may miss or overlook something that will be invaluable to us later."

"Bullshit," the President rebuffed his counselor. "I just need the answer to one question: where the hell are those documents?"

Without trying to be deliberately evasive, Peter asked, "How do you know about the documents? For that matter, how did you find me?"

Peter tried to rise but fell back onto the couch.

The elder statesman quickly maneuvered to Peter's side on the couch.

"Bob, I asked you to go slow." Miller addressed Peter as Peter began to rub his eyes again, "Son, we may be privy to certain knowledge that may seem to be surprising to you, but you have to understand that you are involved in a very delicate situation. Bob, would you get the young man some water?"

President Fairchild rolled his eyes, picked up the water pitcher from the coffee table, poured Peter a glass, and handed it to him.

"Thank you," Peter responded. He took the glass, guzzled the water, then asked for another.

Roland Miller leaned over Peter.

"Do you feel better?"

Peter stared sharply at Roland Miller, then redirected his eyes toward the President.

"I'll feel better when you answer my questions. What do you know about the documents and how did you find me?"

Taken slightly by surprise, Roland Miller straightened himself and rose from the couch. The President grinned from ear to ear.

"I like him," the President smiled at Miller. "As far as finding you, you made that easy once you pulled that little Internet stunt."

"The government monitors that?"

"What else do you think those freaks at NSA do? The story behind the documents is a little more complicated though."

Roland Miller interrupted, "Mr. President, do you think it is necessary to go into all of this with him?"

"If there was a guy who deserved, no earned, an explanation, it is this guy here. We can read a license plate from thousands of miles in the sky, but we can't find a lawyer who has no black-bag experience for three days. Hell, I thought Occidental would have killed you long ago."

The President noticed Peter cringe at the mention of Occidental.

"Yes, I know about Occidental, Roland knows about Occidental. Occidental and the CIR. Do you know who the CIR is?"

"No."

The President glanced over to Roland Miller.

"Maybe he wasn't on any fast track up the CIR ranks."

Miller shrugged his shoulders.

Returning to Peter the President continued, "CIR, the Council on International Relations. Roland, what is it they call themselves, a 'global think tank'?"

"A consortium which represents global interests."

"Consortium, that's right. In this world of haves and have-nots, there are those that have it all: money and power."

"If you will, Mr. President," interrupted the elder statesman.

"That's right Roland, you used to be one of them."

"After the United States refused to join the League of Nations following World War I, representatives of American financial dynasties met with their

British counterparts. Some say that the point of the meeting was to pursue ideas on global stability. The crash of the Market led to further meetings and to the formation of what we now call the Council on International Relations. The Council was, and is, backed by blue bloods on both sides of the Atlantic. In the beginning they sought to ensure global stability to promote their own financial stability. With the development of both sides of the Atlantic through World War II and the Cold War, the Council flourished. Its members include the wealthiest and most influential people in the world."

"And you two are not members?"

"Hell no!" shouted the President.

"It is hard to explain. Many of the 'members' are just that, members. They get together out of the public spotlight to discuss important issues and policies. Some of the President's cabinet are such members. A free exchange of ideas, off the record, free from political gamesmanship or pressures."

"So?" Peter responded.

"Exactly. Except, that is, for the fact that a core of the Council of International Relations actually implements these policies. All is well and good if the idea is to stop a famine in Africa, but you can understand our concern when such influence can take the United States into an armed conflict."

"How do you deal with these people?" asked Peter.

"We just do," responded the President.

"That's no answer."

"It is the only answer."

"What does this have to do with Occidental?"

"As one of the largest companies in the world, in fact one of the top fifty economies in the world, Occidental wields significant global influence."

"Not to mention American influence," Peter interrupted again.

"The Occidental Papers," chimed in the President.

"We believe Elias St. Armand is trying to become part of the CIR core or take it over."

"How do you know all of this?" Peter inquired.

Obviously disturbed about what he was about to say, the President walked over to the bar and poured a drink, "Roland may no longer be a CIR member, but he keeps an open dialogue for me."

The President paused, took a sip, and continued, "Be that as it may, I still need to know where those documents are."

"I don't have them."

"What?"

The President slammed his bourbon on the bar, then composed himself.

"Obviously," he continued, "you mean that you don't have them with you."

"They are not in my control."

"This is not a lawyer's deposition where you can evade the question," snapped the President. As he composed himself again, he continued, "What do you mean, not in your control? You either know where they are or do not know where they are."

"Some of St. Armand's men have the original copies, except for the Sexton papers which I assume everyone has seen by now."

The President and Miller were visibly disappointed.

Peter continued, "Then there is another set I sent off for safekeeping."

"Another set, I love it," mused the President.

"Where is this other set?" the President and Miller asked simultaneously.

Sensing a moment in the whirlwind of events, Peter realized it was time for him to make a decision.

After taking a breath, Peter responded to the their inquiry, "The other copy is with a senior partner of my law firm, Aaron Golde."

"What?" answered the shocked president.

Confused, Peter turned toward Roland Miller who had his head in his hands.

The elder statesman took his head from his hands, blankly looked at Peter and coldly stated, "Aaron Golde has been a member of the CIR for thirty years."

Elias St. Armand rested comfortably in one of his three St. Louis mansions. This estate represented the old-world charm and prestige of his adopted hometown. Located in midtown, along Lindell Boulevard, the area had given the turn-of-the-century elite a comfortable distance from the hustle and bustle of downtown. Now the strip represented a trophy case to display the city's wealthiest families. Rightly so, no trophy was grander than the St. Armand mansion.

The St. Armand parlour room was consistent with the rest of the mansion, relying on an understated opulence with a turn of the century motif. A Van Gogh, two Monets and some paintings from pointillists that Elias had never bothered to learn the names of adorned the walls. Two Degas sculptures also were prominently displayed in the parlour room. And of course, there was the stained-glass rose window at the end of the room which Elias had yet to replace. Despite all the treasures, Elias St. Armand was always drawn to one item, a handcrafted bronze chess set featuring figurines from the Crusades. Most of the time he played against himself, but there was a standing game every other Tuesday, today.

Of course, when Elias played chess against an adversary, especially this adversary, Elias was always the Christian Crusaders. As Elias lifted his finger from one of the knights, he mouthed the word "check" to his adversary who had been talking on the phone.

"Excellent work. You will be well compensated. So they will meet tomorrow at one-twenty."

Elias' adversary hung the phone back on its antique stand by the chessboard.

"It is on for tomorrow. Here is the number."

He set a piece of paper by the phone.

"Excellent," Elias responded. "You did hear me, I said 'check.'"

"Yes, I heard you Elias," Elias' chess adversary replied as he picked up his queen, moved her, then continued, "my desert lady says checkmate."

"Damn!" Elias exclaimed. "Thirty years and you never let me win."

"My dear friend, there are a lot of other games in which you excel. I am sure tomorrow will be no different."

"Oh, tomorrow will be different Aaron, very different."

Elias smiled as he and Aaron Golde reset the pieces for another game.

---

Kerr checked his watch. Twenty more minutes.

Even at this late hour, the Kensington's lobby bar was half full. The busy bartender tended his flock as the television aired election results every ten minutes. Most of the patrons resembled John Kerr, the lawyer. Professionals were out late this election night, drowning sorrows or celebrating.

Kerr motioned to the bartender and ordered a single malt scotch. The bartender nodded then grabbed the bottle from the top shelf.

Locating Farrell and the girl just fell right into his lap, but he was not going to look a gift horse in the mouth. Miller, on the other hand, was not a part of the original plan, but everyone knew that there would be some fallout.

The bartender returned with the scotch.

"Put it on my tab," Kerr instructed. He had not finished the first drink, but wanted to make sure he left one at the bar while he went upstairs. Kerr eyed his leather briefcase, then checked his watch again.

Fifteen minutes.

Soon there would be no more waiting.

# THIRTY-FOUR

The friendly Texas lunch hour crowd watched the motorcade proceed toward the book depository down the expressway. On that mild November afternoon the President waved to the onlookers. The sound of a shot, then another, altered the speed of the procession for the next few seconds. The third shot appeared to be in slow motion as the President's head...

Redwood woke up in a sweat.

The man was not frail, but he needed to rest every now and again. He required short naps throughout the day not as a result of his age, but because he had not had an entire night's sleep in almost forty years. The fresh basin of water beside the bed was born of necessity. The cool water extinguished beads of sweat caused by his "rest." As he slowly walked down the hall, he could see that Sara had been furiously working on the computer. Small piles of printouts were carefully stacked in the den.

"A moment's rest would do you some good, Sara."

"Oh, I'm fine Redwood. Look at this."

Sara handed Redwood a page she had printed off the computer.

"Look what I found surfing."

"I am sorry dear, I do not have my glasses."

Redwood handed the piece of paper back to Sara.

Sara explained, "I think it's a message to Peter."

"My dear, I am sure a lot of people on the Internet have messages for people they believe are serial killers. I think they are mostly marriage proposals."

"No, this is different."

"How so?"

"Well, most of the message is gibberish, but in the first sentence the name 'Henry' is used. Then, in the second sentence, the word 'knots' is misspelled as 'knops.' Finally, the message is from 'Big Hank's Nephew.' I think this is from Jimmy Powell, the kid who drove Peter to the airport yesterday. Get it? Henry Knop's nephew, Big Hank's Nephew."

"Sara, I think you need to slow down."

"After I found that message, I started to print off any other messages I could find."

Sara folded up the "Big Hank's Nephew" message and put it in her pocket. She then proceeded to page through the other stacks.

"And this one, no this one is it." Sara looked confused as she read to herself one of the other messages.

Ol' Redwood sat down Indian style next to Sara.

"Sara, we need to talk," he began.

As she paged through the other printouts, she dismissed her elder, "There is too much to do. Too much is going wrong here."

Redwood grabbed both of her hands and gently made her set down the papers. He softly said to her, "Sara, we need to talk about your father."

"I don't have a father. I don't even know who that man was. I hate him."

"Let me explain who he was."

"I don't need explanations. His actions speak louder than anything you or he could say."

"Sara, I am not going to justify your father's actions. I would not and cannot. There is no justification for what these people are doing. I just want you to understand your father a little better. You already know that there are many horrible things that you do not know about him, that I did not know about him. We may not know the man he became, but I can help you understand. Hopefully understanding can help you focus your pain."

"Focus my pain. I can't focus on anything. Everything is so wrong, my father, these Occidental people who run everything. The world is wrong."

Sara was close to bursting into tears.

"Have you heard of Seicho No Ie?"

"What?"

"Say-choh No ee-yay. It is a new age religious movement in Japan. Its followers believe that health, happiness, and prosperity are all made possible through the power of freeing the mind of all negativism."

"What does that have to do with me?" snapped the young woman.

"Young lady, you do realize the negative energy flowing from you?"

"There hasn't been a whole lot positive about my day today."

"Hear me out. Those who follow Seicho No Ie believe that sin and guilt are not real. Sin was not created in the real world as we know it. Sin is a misguided sense of reality which produces afflictions which are perceived to be real."

"You mean none of this is real."

"Not exactly, the uncertainty of the phenomenal world is only the appearance of a shadow of our mind."

"Phenomenal shadow of what?"

Redwood knew Sara was mocking him, but he enjoyed the fact that she had lightened the moment up.

Without revealing his smile, Redwood continued, "Seicho No Ie teaches one to be reconciled with everything in the universe. In this reconciliation, we would be grateful to all things in the whole universe."

"Redwood, you must be joking."

"Too many people, too many religions, focus on sin, evil as opposed to good. Too much focus is on bad people going to hell and good people going to heaven. According to Seicho No Ie, sin is imperfect, therefore not real. You should not fear what is not real. Concentrate, reconciliate, with the reality that you know."

Redwood sensed that he was beginning to lose Sara.

"Sara, your father spent his life concentrating on evil. He spent his whole life trying to reconcile his life with the horrors of the Holocaust."

Sara's attention span changed when Redwood began talking about her father.

Redwood continued, "As a war baby, your father lives with guilt. The guilt of a survivor, knowing that so many died so that he could live. He had let this guilt consume him. This guilt has cast a cloud, or shadow if you will, changing many of his perceptions of reality. He wears his guilt like one would a pair of sunglasses. With or without the sunglasses he is the same man. However, with those sunglasses on, his perceptions are changed. He does things that he would not do when he is not wearing the glasses."

"Are you saying my father is delusional?"

"Not the medical definition which you are thinking of my dear. We are all delusional to a degree. There is no perfect objective perception of reality. You see a half-eaten burrito discarded on the sidewalk. You probably think, how could someone litter like that? However, to a homeless person who has not eaten in days, the sight of the same burrito would feel like he won the lottery."

"Guilt is no excuse for what my father has done. His whole life was a lie."

"You are missing the point, Sara. Guilt has made your father do some things that he would have not normally done. You peel away the guilt, like removing the sunglasses, you find the father you loved and respected. You peel away the things he may or may not have done for Occidental, you still have your father."

"I cannot separate the truth like that. I cannot do your Say no Key peeling away layers."

"It is more than that, Sara. Seicho No Ie teaches that all things and all people must be appreciated, especially our parents and ancestors who went through the difficult task of earthly life on behalf of succeeding generations. In fact..." Redwood paused.

"What?"

"Oh, I thought I heard something. What was your question?"

"Your Japanese religion."

"It is not my religion. It just helps relating some points to you. Are you sure you did not hear anything?"

———⹂◆⹁———

John Kerr inserted the key card, waited for the green light, and opened the door to room number 1122.

"You're early," scowled Tasha wearing only her bra and panties as she grabbed her wrinkled dress that had been balled up beside the bed.

Noticing the half-clothed man on the bed, Kerr berated the assassin,

"What are you doing? What is he naked for?"

Tasha strutted to the other side of the bed letting her dress drag behind her. She picked up a harness from the nightstand and unholstered the agent's Sig Saurer P-228 9mm automatic pistol.

"Here it is," Tasha calmly stated as she tossed the weapon a few feet to John Kerr.

Kerr bobbled the gun before gaining a grip on the pistol. He bent over to put it in his briefcase.

"What are you doing?" Tasha remarked as she let her dress that she held in one hand fall to the floor. Her disdain for him was evident by her condescending tone. As she passed him to go into the bathroom, she ordered, "Stop."

The puzzled look on Kerr's face changed back to his standard manic self when he glanced at his watch.

Tasha threw a hand towel from the bathroom to Kerr, "Wipe it down."

Trying to get control that he lost when he entered the room, the attorney went on the offensive, "Who is going to clean up this mess? There's not much time."

"You concentrate on what you have to do. Besides, I'm told it does not have to be perfect."

"Just don't be late," warned Kerr as he opened the door and left the room.

Tasha detested the attorney with the little pecker. Fortunately, he did not have to do much, so there was little for him to screw up. Tasha walked backed to the half-naked man on the bed.

Secret Service Agent Robert James Clinton. Age, thirty-eight. Caucasian. Six-foot-one, one hundred eighty five pounds. Right-handed. Sexaholic. Never married. An easy assignment.

She met Agent Clinton, or "Bob", two months ago at a strip club downtown. Clinton had been sent for reconnaissance for an upcoming tour of California by Vice President Algers. Tasha knew Bob would be in that club on that night before Agent Clinton ever knew he would be assigned to the detail. She spent several nights with him then, as well as several nights and days when he returned ten days ago. One of the reasons Bob recommended the Kensington was because he knew a stripper who also was a chambermaid at the hotel. To someone who thought about sex all the time, convenience overcame reason on occasion. In his mind, all he was doing was getting in a little quickie when nothing was going on. He did not get drunk or gamble or get into fights, Bob just needed a little physical contact now and then. Furthermore, he was not even on the presidential detail. Agent Clinton had some time off and volunteered to go back out to San Francisco when a couple agents contracted food poisoning from a mushroom pizza and were not fit for duty. He was just an extra, nobody would miss him.

Tasha put Bob's pants back on. She just needed to get him dressed and make it appear as if a struggle occurred. There was no struggle. Bob was putty in her hands. In a fleeting moment, her sensual massage of Bob's neck ended in a snap and the agent fell limp on the bed. As she fastened his belt, Tasha smiled. Some men did not know how to keep their pants on.

# THIRTY-FIVE

Aaron Golde had left the St. Armand estate over an hour ago, yet the sting of defeat still burned deep inside Elias. Aaron was right though, there were many other games that Elias St. Armand had no equals. But this was not a game. It was revenge. It was retribution. It was rewriting history the way it should have been written in the first place. All the pieces were in place. All the moves had been carefully planned, and anticipation of countermeasures had been even more thorough. His sacrificial knight was in place. He had been manipulating his adversary's bishop with ease. More gratifying was his ability to use his prized pawn to the very end.

Elias picked up one of the infantrymen from his prized chess set and held it in his hand. He then punched the number Aaron had given him.

"Good evening," the mild-mannered voice answered on the other end.

Using the speakerphone Elias barked, "Is he in?"

"Whom may I ask is telephoning?"

"Elias St. Armand, and I do not have much time or patience."

The servant did not respond. There was only silence for a moment or two. The calm and condescending voice of the Savile Row man finally responded, "Elias, what do you want and how the hell did you get this number?"

Elias kept it short and to the point.

"There is a board meeting tomorrow at one-twenty, and I demand to be heard at the meeting."

"Need I remind you that you have other issues that should be garnering your full attention at the moment?"

"They will resolve themselves."

"They will resolve themselves?" repeated the Savile Row man.

There was a long pause.

"What kind of answer is that? We were told that you could not find Farrell. Is that true?"

"By morning, that will resolve itself."

Growing annoyed, the Savile Row man shot back, "What kind of answer is that? And Sexton, what about that? Is he a part of 'resolving themselves?' Your little games cost us the Speaker of the House."

"He was a pawn that had outlived his usefulness anyway."

Elias would not give his adversary any ground.

"A pawn? Are you crazy? He was the Speaker of the House of the United States of America, you idiot. You will have to explain your actions."

"Then let me be heard tomorrow before the board."

"You will come before the board when your presence is requested."

Elias raised his voice, "I demand to be heard before the board."

"You are in no position to demand anything. I am tired of this conversation."

"You have more to lose than I do if the board does not hear me out."

"Elias, are you threatening me?"

"I am stating a fact."

Silence followed Elias' statement. Elias could not even hear a breath from the other end. He knew the Savile Row man was consulting with someone else on the other line. Elias knew that the men on the other line had no choice but to meet with him. They still believed the Occidental files were still missing. They knew that Speaker Sexton could be just the tip of the iceberg. The board could not afford to so easily dismiss Occidental's influence over American politics, or even any remote chance that their influence would be exposed on such a grand scale. Elias knew the board would meet with him. They had no choice.

The Savile Row man broke the silence, "Elias, against my better judgment, the board will meet with you. However, heed some cautionary advice. Your explanation better be meritworthy, and it better be short, we have much to accomplish tomorrow."

"Excellent, then, until tomorrow."

With a push of a button Elias turned the speakerphone off. Turning back to his chess set, Elias placed the infantryman down on the board by the opposition's king, then muttered aloud, "They had no choice. Check."

If the President had been high-strung before, the news about Aaron Golde having the other set of Occidental papers did little to soothe his nerves. The President poured another bourbon.

"Why can't you just start an investigation against Occidental?" Peter naively asked.

"It's not that simple," replied Roland Miller.

"You two are basically the most powerful men in the country, the world. Why can't you make it that simple?"

"To put it into the simplest terms possible, no one knows where Occidental's influence in the government starts and ends. The two are inexplicably intertwined. Tearing Occidental and the CIR from the government would cripple the nation."

The President interrupted, "That's why those files you had were so important. We could have been able to weed out the most corrupt elements while still keeping Occidental at bay."

"I don't think the files I had would have helped that much, all I had were the S's. It would have been a start but..."

"Just the S's? We never would have made a dent in their organization."

The President became even more despondent.

"Bob, it would have been a start. First, we weed out the undesirables, then choke off the money," chimed in Roland Miller.

Roland Miller further explained, "One of the ways Occidental exercises its authority over congressmen and the like is actually quite legal. Occidental pours millions of dollars into 527 groups and other legal loopholes. It's not about ideology; the money simply guarantees that Occidental will always have access through government channels. In return for getting elected and re-elected, more and more often Occidental gets corporate welfare in the form of special tax breaks."

"There was something in the file on the ethanol bill and a guy named Betts," interrupted Peter.

"Jim Betts?" President Fairchild joined the conversation.

"Yeah. A James Betts, an FEC investigator," answered Peter.

"Roland, Betts is the investigator I had looking into Occidental's ethanol subsidy. They were making money hand over fist, it was costing my taxpayers billions," President Fairchild always personalized taxes, knowing full well his constituents always voted their pocketbooks.

He continued, "Betts? I thought you said you had the S's not the B's."

"Betts was in the Speeter file."

"Jeff Speeter?"

"Yes, from the FEC."

"I appointed him to the Federal Election Committee."

"Well sir, he was Occidental, and it looks like Senator Stanton is also on the Occidental payroll."

"That was what Betts was looking into, Stanton's flip-flop on the ethanol subsidy. He thought he could convince Speeter to testify against Stanton and Occidental."

Again Peter questioned the two powerful men, "If everything you say is true..."

"I know where you are going," interrupted the elder statesman, "but rooting out Occidental is not going to happen as long as big money calls the shots. Bribery and extortion are only the tip of the iceberg. The status quo still allows Occidental and others to pour hundreds of millions of dollars into elections rendering candidates beholden to them."

Playing the part of devil's advocate, Peter countered, "But money is just a form of freedom of speech."

"Bullshit!" President Fairchild exclaimed, then shot off as if he were lecturing law students, "Buckley v. Valeo explicitly stated that there is a compelling government interest in curbing such speech because large contributions can be given, or appear to be given, 'to secure a political quid pro quo from current and potential officeholders which undermines the integrity of our system of representative democracy.'"

The President paused then continued his speech, "That is why I am still pushing campaign finance legislation to have tighter guidelines on public disclosure of all contributions. I am also going to replace that weasel speaker with someone who is going to implement reform."

Again the devil's advocate, "Great speech sir, but with all due respect, isn't it slightly more than ironic that you, of all people, are crusading like this?" Peter continued without taking heed of the looks of warning from Roland Miller, "after all, obviously you and your party have benefited directly or indirectly from Occidental money or other contributions."

"It's all right Roland."

The President had obviously come to terms with himself and the fact that such a question would arise.

"Someone has to say stop. It is also true that as a president in my second term that campaign contributions are irrelevant to me. But I am president and no other person is better situated to stop this insanity of buying elections."

"Gentlemen," Roland Miller stopped the debate, "we need to figure out what we are going to do. After all, Mr. Farrell is an alleged serial killer and currently residing in the presidential suite with the President."

"He's no problem," the President responded. "In fact, if we get those files, this young man is going to help us beat back the Occidental monster. Won't you?"

"Of course," Peter replied. Then with Sara always on his mind he continued, "there is also the matter of two other people."

Before Peter could finish, the Miller reassured him, "that has already been taken care of. Now let's get those documents."

Just as the President finished, the presidential suite's door opened, both Secret Service men stood motionless, but sharply alert. Obviously nothing suspicious had been wired to them through their ever-present earpieces. Through the door, Roland Miller's protégé John Kerr entered.

"Ah, John," Miller greeted his right hand man, "did you bring the materials for tomorrow morning's press conference that you dragged me out here for?"

Kerr was visibly shocked and surprised at the sight of Peter Farrell.

Playing upon Kerr's obvious astonishment, the President bellowed, "C'mon Kerr, when's the last time you got to shake hands with a serial killer?"

Roland intervened, "I am sorry for the surprise, John. You no doubt recognize Peter Farrell. Peter will be helping us in a couple of matters."

Peter introduced himself, "Peter Farrell," shaking Kerr's hand he added, "I'm really not a serial killer."

Still having fun, the President continued, "C'mon Kerr, cheer up, you always want to be 'in'. What's more 'in' than being in the same room with Roland Miller, the President, and the most notorious man in America? What's it they call you Farrell, the Shakespeare Killer, 'kill all the lawyers'? You're a lawyer Kerr, aren't you?"

Kerr looked at the President and muttered, "Shouldn't we call someone?"

Roland assured his protègé, "It is all under control."

"Don't worry Kerr," the President chimed in, "I pardoned him. Do you have Manson's or Bundy's numbers?"

"Well here are the drafts." Kerr ignored the President and regained his composure. Setting the documents down he noted, "I'll just leave them over here by the table."

"Thanks John," Miller responded as Kerr also set a leather satchel down by the breakfast nook table.

"I also sent a car to pick the two individuals at the cabin," he continued. "Do you need my help with this situation?" offered the eager assistant.

"No, John." Roland Miller continued, "Get some sleep. We will handle this matter. We will see you in the morning."

As quick as he entered the suite, Kerr left.

As soon as the door shut the President began, "Roland, I never knew what you ever saw in Kerr. He's too eager to please. Not like Farrell here who has been a pain in the ass since I first heard his name. Now, where were we..."

# THIRTY-SIX

Tasha Dolnick never enjoyed "dressing up." She adjusted her stockings and refastened her garter belt. Lace and lingerie never bode well with her, but she always played the part. And this would be her greatest part.

After adjusting her skimpy waitress outfit, Tasha checked her makeup again. Another luxury, yet this was not as frivolous as the other accessories. Tasha actually liked makeup. Not the caked on face paint used if she had to play a prostitute, but a simple blush, some eyeliner and lipstick were fine. It was one of the few things that made her feel normal. It made her feel pretty.

However, Tasha's favorite accessory was always wigs or extensions. With new hair she became a new person, someone other than Tasha Dolnick, the person who had been raped, tortured, robbed of her family, her heritage, and her life, left only to kill those who had stolen everything from her. And kill again.

In a secured room one floor beneath the presidential suite, Tasha made one final adjustment to the lace netting decorating her wig, stared directly into her reflection in the mirror and softly told herself, "for Salih."

---

This time the creak from the front porch was obvious to both Redwood and Sara as they sat motionless in the living room. Redwood motioned for Sara to follow him as they both quickly tiptoed into the computer room. Ever so gently, Redwood slid the hidden bookcase door closed. Once the door had been closed completely, Redwood turned to Sara, put his finger to his lips commanding silence. Redwood then took both of Sara's shoulders and positioned her against the wall. He moved the chair away from the desk. Before any other redecorating, Redwood took the disk out of his computer and put it in a sleeve which he then put into a backpack. Redwood then opened the desk drawer to grab another disk. Redwood put the other disk in the drive, shut the computer down, and then rebooted it.

Ever so slowly, Redwood bent down to the ground. He motioned to Sara to help him roll up the Persian rug. Underneath the rug Sara saw the trap door.

---

Still within the confines of Kensington's underground garage, John Kerr sat comfortably in the leather interior of his BMW. For the third time, he checked the always accurate Swiss timing on his watch. Only four minutes had passed since the last time he had checked, but it should give her enough time.

As he waited, he wondered. If Farrell was here, who was at the cabin with the girl? He hated loose ends. It would not matter in a couple of minutes; it would just be another body. They were professionals; they knew how to handle it. Still, this was too perfect. Farrell was already there. It could not have been set up better.

Kerr pulled his cellphone from his jacket pocket. He also took out his handkerchief. Folding the handkerchief over, Kerr covered the mouthpiece on a disposable cellphone and dialed 9-1-1. And in the worst masquerade of his voice imaginable, spoke to the emergency operator, "My name is Jim Phillips. I'm one of the bellmen working at the Kensington. I have some information on that fugitive guy, Peter Farrell, the one killing all those lawyers. He's here."

---

Peter was exhausted. He also still felt like crap from the drug the conch shell man gave him, but he continued to answer President Bob Fairchild's questions, "I don't know."

"So, other than for you, you have no idea why Elias St. Armand was in San Francisco?"

"No." Peter thought to himself how far off the media and the general public were about their highest elected official. The common consensus was to view the President as a parental figure seeking only to protect his children, the tax-payers. The man standing before Peter was a much more complex than Peter had believed. His questioning of Peter was concise and thorough. His follow-up questions were even more polished than the initial questions. Query after query, the president demonstrated an intelligence and thought process that belied his folksy image as a midwestern farm boy who didn't understand why the other political party wanted to always confuse the American public and himself with issues other than what "real people" wanted to hear. The President knew exactly what was going on, and Peter needed a break from his relentless questioning.

"I have to freshen up."

Peter rose and made his way to the suite's bathroom.

The President turned his attention to Roland Miller who had been listening attentively.

"Roland, we're not getting very far here. I think we are going to have to resort to calling them."

"Are you sure that is advisable," responded the President's friend and confidant.

"I don't think we have any other recourse."

"You told me last term, no more deals with the devil."

"I think we have to rid ourselves of this serpent. Elias St. Armand has to go. With the Sexton scandal and whatever else may arise, the CIR has to agree. Elias St. Armand has to have outlived any usefulness he had for them. They have to deal. Golde can give us the documents, and all of us can be rid of Occidental forever."

"If they will not agree?"

"It's an option for them. He's expendable. They have to believe that now is the time."

"You're probably right."

"I know I am," the President confidently stated.

Peter stared at his reflection in the bathroom mirror. He did look like hell. Just look at what three days without sleep and a bunch of drugs can get you these days he thought to himself again. Although his head was pounding, he still heard the President bellow from the other room.

"Roland, get them on the line right now. We've wasted too much time already."

Peter turned the faucet on and let the cold water chill a little bit longer.

"I know they won't talk to me, but tell them I want all of this resolved in the next twenty-four hours."

Peter splashed the cold water on his face.

There was a knock on the suite's door. One of the two Secret Service men opened the door.

"Call them right now Roland. I've had enough of this crap."

Peter splashed some more water onto his face and out of reflex, glanced over at the cart that was wheeled in by the long-legged room service lady.

"Wait," the President shouted another command to Roland. "What the hell else did I want to tell them?"

As the President barked orders at Roland Miller, visions of the past couple of days' events popped in and out of his head as the water soothed his eyes and face. Peter's flashbacks included him and John at O'Shea's, Rose and Sitti, the policeman who wrestled him in front of the trick-or-treaters, the shoot-out at the cemetery, Elias St. Armand, and jumping off the boat with Sara. The more water Peter splashed on his face the clearer the images became. Now there were the sudden images of him and John and the red-haired woman at the bar; the same woman at the airport and Cliff House with black hair; then the same woman again, this time ready to shoot him in the Castro and on St. Armand's boat; then there was the vision of the blonde woman wheeling the silver dinner cart into the suite.

The President continued to list items out loud, "and tell them that they are not going to override my veto on that Lebanon money."

All the images of women ran together for Peter, and once again he envisioned the woman who had just wheeled in the room service.

Without turning off the water, Peter shouted, "No!" and ran to the bathroom's door.

By the time Peter shouted, Tasha had reached the breakfast nook table and Kerr's satchel carrying the late Secret Service Agent Clinton's Sig Saurer P-228 9mm automatic pistol.

Alarmed by Peter's cry, the Secret Service man by the door had drawn his firearm and started at Peter. The other Secret Service agent, the conch shell man, who had been standing at attention by the entertainment center, began to pull his gun from his holster. The President, who had been standing behind the couch by Roland Miller, turned his head toward the bathroom suite. Roland Miller turned toward Tasha Dolnick.

Within seconds of Peter's cry, Tasha Dolnick had gotten off five rounds. Two rounds had entered into the chest of the conch shell man. The third round hit the other Secret Service man in the leg, starting his stumble. The fourth went through his neck, the fifth hit him squarely in the temple, and sent him sprawling to the ground.

Before Tasha could get off another shot, Roland scrambled over the sofa toward the President. Behind the President, Peter dove toward the stricken agent's gun. Tasha fixed on the President and fired two rounds as Roland thrust his friend Bob Fairchild to the floor. With the President and Miller on the ground, Peter had a clear sight of the person who had killed his brother. He fired three, four, then a fifth shot, sending Tasha Dolnick's body backwards, shattering the glass breakfast table.

After being frozen in his shooting position for what felt like several minutes, yet actually only seconds, Peter began to hear the rustling around him. The conch shell man was gasping for air right behind him. No movement came from the other agent. The explanation came from the pool of blood leaking from his body. Muted shouts from down the hall grew closer and closer. Peter rose.

He was aware the President and Roland Miller lay sprawled on the other side of the couch. He heard some movement, but it did not register. Peter slowly walked to the body of Tasha Dolnick. He did not know the woman. The only things he knew, he hated. She had tried to kill Sara, tried to kill him, and had killed John. Now Peter had killed her. There was no chance to think. Feelings of guilt ran through him as he reflected on the fact that John had never entered his mind as he fired the gun. As Peter lifted the gun and aimed it again at the lifeless bloody body of the assassin, he thought of John and only John.

"Farrell! Farrell!" Miller shouted at Peter.

Peter snapped out of the trance and scrambled over to Roland Miller and the President.

"We have to stop the bleeding!" yelled the elder statesman.

As Peter stood over the fallen body of President Bob Fairchild, Roland Miller, who had spent a lifetime holding the office of the President together, vainly tried to stop the bleeding from the President's head. Peter did not hear the other Secret Service agents burst into the room, but he had already dropped the gun to the floor as he blankly stared at the two lifelong friends. As the agents tackled Peter to the ground, Peter's stare never left Roland Miller's bloody hands that were pressed tightly against the President's head. Peter knew what Miller feared. The President was dead.

---

Not too far away in the quiet Mission District, with the strike of midnight, the last of the revelers had left the streets. Into their beds they climbed, *Dia de los Muertos,* the Day of the Dead, had ended.

# THIRTY-SEVEN

Sara had taken the bright lights of the city for granted. Her life had been dedicated to preserving forests just like this, but lately, she had spent too much time in the office and not enough time outdoors. The pitch-black woods seemed foreign to her. It would take a minute to get acclimated. But if not for the stars in the sky and Ol' Redwood's tight grip on her wrist, she would be frightfully lost.

"Sara, nothing above a whisper," ordered Redwood.

"Are you sure someone is at the cabin?"

"Shhh."

Redwood led Sara to a small clump of bushes and sat her down. From his pouch, Redwood pulled a small pair of odd-looking binoculars and gave them to Sara. Sara looked confused. She opened her mouth to explain she was having enough trouble seeing something two feet in front of her, much less fifty yards up the hill. Redwood placed his hand on her mouth and lifted the binoculars to her face.

Sara could not believe her eyes. She could actually see everything. The binoculars must have been infrared. There was an owl, a pair of deer, and a raccoon. It was just like the wildlife cable channels. The raccoon walked around as if it were on a midnight stroll. She felt Redwood's hands adjust her head, pointing it up the hill. There it was, Redwood's cabin. His porch, the woodpile, the... Something moved on the porch. A figure. It was standing still but it was someone. Wide-eyed, Sara pitched the binoculars back to Redwood.

Redwood grabbed Sara's wrist again and led her down the hill away from the cabin. His grip was firm, but not too hard. Her shoes slipped twice on the damp leaves, but with only a minor adjustment in his pace, Redwood kept Sara from falling. The two had walked for fifteen minutes before a word was spoken. Sara knew she would not be the first to speak.

"It should be all right to talk now," assured Redwood.

"I can stay quiet," Sara retorted.

"Keep it low, to a minimum."

"Anything you say."

"Do you know where we are?"

"California still, I hope."

"Do you know how to get to the road?"

"If you let go of me, I don't know if I could find you."

"Sara, have more confidence. Trust your senses."

"But I can't see anything."

"Sara, you know better than that. Is sight your only sense?"

"No, but I need to see to know where I am going."

"I am glad you are working with the Sienna Club instead of with the EEOC."

Knowing that she had just been ridiculed, but not knowing why, Sara remained silent.

"Sara, how does a sightless person know how to cross the street?"

"A dog, no, those beepers on the crossing lights."

"How does a sightless person know an elevator door has opened?"

"He hears the door open."

"How does..."

"OK, I get the point."

"Do you? Sara, your mind is clouded with negative thoughts. It is not as open as it usually is to new ideas, new ways of thinking. Dwelling on your past will cloud your future. Peter needs your help, but you cannot help if you cannot open your mind."

"Hey, I am one of the most liberal, open-minded people I know."

"Then how come you can only see with your eyes?" snapped the woodsman.

The two remained quiet for the next several minutes. Sara fumed. She knew Redwood was right. Her anger had clouded her thoughts. But Redwood didn't have to be so harsh. He used to be so much subtler in making his point. Direct confrontation was not his style. Sara concluded that even Redwood might be worried about everything that was going on with Occidental. He was right though, she had not been thinking clearly.

"What am I listening for?"

"Just listen."

Sara hated it when he did this. She listened. She had heard an owl for about the last five minutes. There was a slight breeze which rustled the leaves, but at this altitude there was always a breeze or a gust. Crickets. It sounded like any other forest. Then she heard it. About ten or twenty yards to their left was a bubbling, churning sound. A stream.

"There is a stream to our left."

"What do streams do?"

Sara thought to herself. It rains. A stream forms. A stream runs into another stream.

"The stream runs downhill into the creek that we drove over on our way up."

Redwood stopped and let go of her wrist.

"Follow the stream. It will lead you to the road. You can actually reach the road walking as fast as you can driving because it winds around the other side so much."

"Aren't you going with?"

"No, I need to go back to the cabin."

"You can't do that, they'll still be there."

"I am counting on that. If they are looking for you I will need to slow them down so you can make it to the road."

"Why can't we stay in the woods until morning?"

"Sara, Peter needs you. Find him."

Before Sara could let out a "but," Redwood hugged her tight. He released her, turned, and walked back up the hill.

Without turning around to face her he reiterated, "Remember, trust your senses."

With those last words, Ol' Redwood disappeared into the forest. Sara was all alone.

# THIRTY-EIGHT

"Release him," barked Roland Miller to the Secret Service men. "Shut the door and secure the perimeter."

With military precision, the agents moved. The suite doors were secured. The curtains drawn. Peter still lay on the floor with one agent over him with his weapon drawn.

"Get away from him," commanded Miller.

"Sir, is he...," asked the agent who directed the others.

"How many agents heard the shots?"

There was no mistake that Miller was in charge.

"Just us."

"Outside contact?"

"Sir, I radioed in that we were responding to shots fired."

"Cancel that now!"

"Sir?"

"Now!"

The lead agent turned from the others and spoke into his sleeve as he moved toward Miller.

Another, obviously the youngest of the four, asked, "Shouldn't we contact Lil' Tex?"

"Negative!" Roland Miller yelled at the two agents.

The lead agent, now only a couple feet from Miller, turned to him and calmly said, "Back up has been called off, but you are not running the show."

"You're Nash aren't you?" Miller addressed the lead agent who was at least fifteen years the senior of the other agents.

"Yes, sir."

"This is worse than it looks," the President's best friend assured Nash.

"Another shooter?" Nash inquired.

"No, only the woman."

"How far does this go, sir?"

"It could be a Johnson scenario. Something is terribly wrong here, and it could not have happened without some of your men."

Nash remained expressionless. It was not a threat, just an observation. A correct observation.

"Find out where Kerr is. Indiscreetly, I mean indiscreetly. And do you know where all your agents are?"

Nash stared straight into the eyes of Miller, "What do I tell my men?"

"Nothing. Everyone is re-assigned after this. We will also need some cleaners."

"How much time?"

"Twenty-four hours, thirty-six would be a plus."

Miller responded to Nash, both understood the cover-up they were planning.

"What is the secured position for tonight?"

"San Francisco General."

"Then take him to the second."

"Sir," for the first time Nash took the initiative, "I suggest the fourth at Mercy. I know the staff there and inquiries may go beyond San Francisco General."

"You're right, Nash," glancing over at the other agents Miller continued, "and them."

"My men will be fine. Him?"

The agent pointed at Farrell.

Miller, still in charge, "He's with me. We will need to get out of here."

"No problem. The floor is secured and the service elevator is available. Just a second."

Nash listened intently to information fed to him through his earpiece.

"What is it?" asked Miller.

"An agent has not reported in. Special Agent Clinton."

"Never heard of him."

"He's on loan from the VP's detail since they were here a week and a half ago."

Miller grimaced while his right hand clenched in an ever-tightening fist, "I need time."

"Sir," an agent standing by Tasha's corpse wanted his superior's attention. He pointed at the gun and continued, "This is one of ours."

Roland Miller, presidential advisor, kingmaker, and survivor stood over the slain body of President Robert Fairchild, glanced down at his fallen leader, shook his head, and looked at Nash, "Thirty-six hours. Nash, I need thirty-six hours."

---

Detective Martinez could not believe herself. This was the bottom of the barrel, the lowest of the low. Martinez had stooped lower than even her junior partner would have dropped. On her night off, she was on a stakeout, by herself. Not just any stakeout, this one was based on a hunch. No tip, no lead, just a gut feeling. How pathetic, she thought. Police work had no room for "gut feelings." A good investigation resulted from hard work: tracking down leads, interviewing witnesses, canvassing neighborhoods, background checks, endless hours on phones, and eliminating all other possibilities except what actually happened. The last time she heard Nelson admit he had "a gut feeling" she told him it was probably just a bad tamale. Gut feelings and hunches belonged in the casinos or at the racetracks, but never in police work.

Despite this, here she was, parked in a garage. This was no hunch; this was a social life that had gone completely down the tubes. Ever since Pedro left for college, the house seemed big and empty. For eighteen years, her brothers and sisters had been her life. She never resented the fact that her adult life had revolved completely around raising her six brothers and sisters. However, since Pedro, the baby, left for Michigan University on a scholarship two months ago, she wished she had prepared herself a little better for the loneliness, the emptiness, and how much bigger her house grew every day.

The three-bedroom, one-and-a-half story, stucco house just a block and a half off Van Ness, used to be quite small. Nearly twenty years ago, seventeen-year-old Maria Angela Martinez, her parents, grandmother, Nana, and five brothers and sisters, Miguel, Carlos, Pilar, Gina, and Jimmy (her mother had a thing for that nice man who was president) all lived in the one house. Her parents and baby Jimmy slept in the small room on the first floor. Maria, Pilar, and Nana slept in the larger bedroom on the same floor as their parents. The younger kids all slept upstairs in the large room which doubled as the playroom. Even though her mother was five months pregnant, which meant Maria and Pilar would have to share their room with another person soon, it was a happy, busy home.

In particular, it was probably Maria who was happiest of all at that time. She had just received her Scholastic Aptitude Test scores. By scoring in the ninety-fifth percentile, she knew she would be able to obtain a full scholarship at one of the finest West Coast schools. She had researched everything. She would be able to pay for her complete college education at three schools. All three were in California. Of course, she wanted to move away from home (only one roommate to share a bathroom with, imagine that), but not too far. All three schools also had top programs in law enforcement and criminal behavioral sciences. She, of course, would graduate top of her class, then join the academy in Quantico. Maria Angela Martinez would be an FBI agent.

Unfortunately, fate had other plans for Maria Angela Martinez.

The hit-and-run accident shattered Maria's dreams and forever changed her life. A man, Caucasian, mid to late forties, expensively dressed, and driving a sports car, ran a red light. To avoid having the oncoming traffic damage his precious vehicle, he careened onto the sidewalk striking Maria's parents. Her father was killed instantly. The paramedics arriving on the scene kept Maria's mother alive long enough to reach the emergency room. Crying out for the doctors to save her baby, Maria's mother clung to life long enough to give birth to Pedro, the lone survivor.

To pay bills and make ends meet, Maria dropped out of high school. She was able to get a job in law enforcement, but it was only a janitorial position at the local precinct. She also found a job filing papers and doing other general office work for a small-time street lawyer, Poncho "I'll get you out of the big Casa" Hernandez, who specialized in criminal defense and civil rights cases. To this day, Maria is one of only a few people who knew Poncho's real name was George.

Maria berated herself for her selfish thoughts at the time. She went from hanging out at the tequillaras, playing soccer, and dreaming about college to working two jobs and taking care of her whole family. It would have been the easy way to just let Social Services split them all up, but Nana would have none of that. The family was the cornerstone of life. From that cornerstone, society emerges. And Nana said it wasn't going to be her family that they could blame the fall of society on.

So Maria worked. So Carlos worked. And so did Miguel. Their combined income paid the bills and kept the family together. Society would not go to hell on Maria's watch.

Gina married and moved to Los Angeles. Miguel started his own construction company, remodeling wherever the new gentrification tide hit in the city. Carlos went to work for Miguel and started a family and rebuilt a home only two blocks from where they all grew up. Pilar did something in the fashion industry downtown, but Maria was never quite sure what she actually did. Jimmy, the rich one in the family, lived in San Jose and worked in Silicon Valley. And now Pedro had moved to Michigan to start college. Maria was all alone.

Well, not completely alone. Detective Martinez had her work. She had her hunch. And she had been sitting in her car for almost an hour in the Kensington's underground parking garage without having a single Secret Service agent bother her. Not exactly the tightest protection of a national security interest. She had positioned herself well. The main elevators were in plain view with a turn of her head to the left. With her car windows open she could hear any vehicle entering the garage from behind her. Directly in front of her were the service elevators.

Her hunch was simple, but unrealistic. If someone wanted everyone to believe that this "Shakespeare killer" or killers wanted to kill all the lawyers, then why not cut off the head of the snake? The President was a lawyer. During his campaign for the presidency, he championed his down-home law practice as if he were a modern-day Abe Lincoln. It was no secret that he had vetoed several bills calling for tort reform, and he was frequently criticized for having the Trial Lawyers Association and the National Bar Association in his hip pocket. If someone was trying to send a message about killing lawyers, and they were in San Francisco, it would not require a great leap of faith to believe they might target the President.

Obviously the security was lax enough. Martinez wondered if the President was even at the Kensington. She recognized some Secret Service agents stationed by the elaborate entrance of the hotel and the entrance to the underground parking, but no one actually on this level of the parking garage. In fact, the only person she had seen was that Caucasian, five-foot-ten, short black hair, male dressed in an expensive suit depart the elevator twenty minutes ago.

A squad car pulled into the garage.

Detective Martinez stepped out of her car and flagged the patrol car down. The patrol car pulled up in front of her.

Flashing her gold shield, Detective Martinez inquired, "What brings you here?"

"A crank call," responded one of the uniformed officers.

"Yeah, some crackpot called in that they saw that Shakespeare killer here," added the other officer.

"I have a couple lawyers I know that I wish he'd take a crack at," interjected the first officer causing both policemen to chuckle.

"Was the Secret Service notified?"

"Oh yeah, right away. Dispatch said that they said they have everything under control."

Martinez took charge and asked, "Then why are you here?"

"After the past two days, Sarge has us checking dogs that bark too loudly."

"When did the call come in?"

"Must have been almost ten minutes ago. We were just down the street."

"Why are you here Detective?" inquired one of the officers, turning the tables on Detective Martinez.

Before the detective could answer, the service elevator doors opened. With the detective and two uniformed police officers staring directly at them from only ten feet away, the only thing Peter could muster was, "Oh shit."

———————

Redwood watched for a minute as the patrol car left slowly, still keeping its lights off. The car must have been parked down the hill while the two men snuck up to the cabin through the woods. He counted three individuals total. One left with the car. One was inside the cabin. And one stood guard by the woodpile.

He had done it over a hundred times; it had just been a long time since he had to act like an animal. His fittest days were behind him, but he was far from feeble. Hours of chopping wood and hiking in the forest left little room for body fat. If Ol' Redwood's body was a temple, then he had the best rabbi available taking care of it. However, his mind was his greatest asset. He had spent so much time in the woods that he knew every noise, every smell, and every taste. He had spent years walking among the creatures of the forest as an equal, not as a tourist, or worse yet, a pillager. More importantly, a lifetime ago this was his job. Therefore, sneaking up on the intruder and incapacitating him made about as much noise as an owl flying through the night sky. One down.

The intruder inside the cabin would be much different. There it was again. Redwood counted to himself for the fourth time. The intruder was right on the other side of the front door pacing back and forth. He must have been waiting for a signal or a response. Possibly, but doubtfully, that signal should be coming from the man lying behind the woodpile. That man had no communication equipment on him. What he did have on him bothered him more than his ability, or inability, to contact anyone else. Although he was not in uniform, the man carried police identification with him. The badge was authentic. He was no imposter, he was one of San Francisco's finest. Redwood assumed the man inside was also a police officer. But that was all he could assume. Redwood knew from experience that local officers were often used to tie up loose ends at the last minute if a professional crew was unavailable. Whether they were willing participants or merely pawns, they had been given orders. Redwood could not take a chance that those orders included harming Sara.

Redwood heard the faint creak again. One, two, three, four. Redwood flung the full force of his body against the door and crashed into the intruder who had been pacing just inside the door. Before the stunned man could regain his wits, Redwood pummeled him with his two powerful fists. The man was out cold. Redwood reached into the intruder's pant pocket pulling out a small leather billfold. Flipping it open revealed another San Francisco police badge. No surprise. Redwood rose and walked over to the cellphone, knocked from the intruder's hands by Redwood's forceful entry. Redwood punched "Star Six Nine." Nothing. Something was hanging out of the intruder's shirt pocket. It was a picture of Sara.

Redwood dropped the phone and ran out the door clenching Sara's picture in his hand.

<hr />

Trust your senses he said. It had only been a couple of minutes since Redwood left, yet the only sense that she was aware of was that it was cold. A lot colder since Redwood turned around. But there it was, just as he pointed out to her. The stream had led to the creek and the creek had led to the road. Redwood had forgotten to mention that the road was pitch black. There was a slight decline in the direction to the left. To the right definitely went back up into the hills. So Sara proceeded on the road to the left, down the hill toward town.

Cold, dark, and wet. That is what her senses were telling her. The evening air condensed and patches of fog appeared. Sara had noticed the fog by the creek. Now that she was on the elevated road, the fog was more prevalent. It wove in and out of the trees and slithered as if it were alive. The weaving fog also made it appear as if the trees were moving, following her down the road. The owls, raccoons, and other nocturnal animals had disappeared. Only the fog and trees followed Sara down the dark road.

To alleviate her wandering mind, Sara once again adopted Ol' Redwood's advice. There was no forgetting what her father did. Sara did not blame him for endangering her life. That could be rationalized by a father doing anything to save his daughter. Occidental probably threatened her life if her father did not hand Peter over. It may not have been the smartest or most courageous act, but it could be rationalized. Father did not know he would be double-crossed. Again not the smartest move, but forgivable.

What Sara could not forgive was the lie. As far as Sara was concerned, her father's whole life was a lie. He was not the man he purported to be. He was not the admired and respected jurist, Ironsides Ahrens, being groomed for the United States Supreme Court. He was not the man of principle, man of justice, man of law. He was not the man Sara had looked up to her entire life. A man bigger than life itself, a living legend. No, he was just a pawn. A pawn for Occidental. The lie would live, the legacy would die.

Redwood had helped her start to come to grips with her hatred for her father. She still hated him. There would be no forgiveness. However, the word had never been dropped. She would see him some day, some day in prison. Not in the near future, but it would happen someday.

Sara looked up from her feet which she had been staring at for the past several minutes. The fog and trees still followed her descent down the road. The fog had grown thicker, the air cooler.

Down the road, Sara could now see that there actually was a bend or turn in the road. It began to light up. The light on the bend in the road intensified. As it intensified, it narrowed into two high beams. As the car turned, Sara began to run down the center of the road. The car climbed the hill while Sara ran towards the oncoming vehicle with her arms flailing around. With the car only a hundred yards away and slowing down, Sara stopped running, but continued to wave her arms. The car stopped directly in front of Sara. The man in the car shined a high-powered light directly into Sara's face. Then he turned on the familiar blue and red flashing lights.

"After this, I'll be wearing one of those gold shields in no time."

The second officer sounded almost giddy as he pressed Peter's body up against the cement wall to cuff him.

The elder first officer began, "This is our collar, stressing the word 'our.'

Both uniformed officers stared at one another for a minute.

"Before you promote each other to captain, I suggest you check his identification," Detective Martinez suggested as she nodded to Roland Miller. The older uniformed police officer obliged the detective's request and pulled the elder statesman's billfold from his jacket pocket.

"His driver's license says he is 'Roland Miller.'"

"Try the other side," Martinez instructed.

The officer flipped the billfold around, "This is a White House security pass."

"Gentlemen, I would like to introduce you to former ambassador, former secretary of state, and presently chief advisor to the president, Roland Miller."

"What?"

Both officers were shocked.

"Thank you, detective."

Roland rubbed his wrists after the officer had dropped his arm in dismay.

"Not so fast, sir."

Detective Martinez was only beginning.

"Keep him cuffed," she ordered. "Now Mr. Miller, would you care to explain why you are sneaking around an underground garage with an alleged serial killer?"

Standing straighter to personify and project dignity and respect, one of the most powerful men in the world simply stated, "These are national security concerns and we must be on our way."

"Wrong answer," interjected Martinez. "Put them both in the back of the squad car."

The police officers obeyed the senior officer on the scene and began taking Peter and Miller to the car.

"You will regret this, detective," threatened Miller.

"I doubt it," retorted Martinez.

Peter could not risk being taken to the police station. Sara was still out there, plus who knows what could happen. He would be a sitting duck. How many law enforcement officials had already tried to kill him. He had to act now.

"The President has been shot."

"Peter!" Miller angrily shouted at the young attorney.

"The twenty-first floor, he has been shot."

Martinez finally lost her cool.

"What the hell is going on here!"

Miller responded, "The President has been shot, yes. As we speak, he is being airlifted out of the hotel. His condition is not critical, but we cannot take any chances."

"The perpetrator?" the detective inquired while regaining her composure.

"She is dead. Your officers can verify all of this upstairs. Ask for Nash. Tell him that Roland Miller authorized your participation."

"Go up there," ordered Martinez. "Give me one of your radios."

Before the service elevator door closed, the young uniformed officer flipped his radio to the detective.

Either skeptical or overwhelmed, Martinez continued to question Miller.

"How does he fit into all of this?" pointing at the still handcuffed Peter Farrell.

"He saved the President's life and my life. The assassin did kill two agents, though."

"A serial killer simply walks into the President's suite and throws his body in front of an assassination attempt?"

"Hey, let's drop this serial killer bullshit. I'm standing right here."

Raising his hand to direct the young man to settle down, the President's advisor explained, "Mr. Farrell is not a serial killer. To the best of my knowledge he has not killed anyone other than the assassin upstairs. He has been framed for those other murders on TV, and now he is the only living person who can link the assassin to those who hired her."

"To the best of your knowledge..."

"Silence, Peter," reprimanded the elder statesman. "I need him alive and I need to take him to Washington."

"Let's take him down to the precinct."

Martinez turned toward her car.

"No," Peter interjected again.

"That is part of the problem, officer. Detective, your local law enforcement as well as some federal agents have been compromised. To be blunt, we do not know who is dirty and who is not."

"Then how are you going to protect him?"

Before Roland Miller could respond, the radio broke in, "Detective?"

"I'm here," Martinez answered the call.

"It is a mess up here. Two agents down and a gunman, gunwoman."

"Any sign of the President?"

"Negative."

Suddenly there was a new voice on the other end, "Detective, this is Special Agent Nash. We need to maintain radio silence on this one, so do you have everything you need?"

"Affirmative."

"Satisfied?" Miller asked.

"Not completely."

"With the President's condition, Farrell's notoriety, and the people responsible for this still at large, national security dictates that we must be on our way."

"Where?"

"The airport."

"OK, but I am escorting you there."

"Fine."

"No, not the airport." Peter had just realized that Sara could still be in trouble and turned to Miller, "Who did you tell to pick up Sara and her friend."

"Any bags to check?" the attendant asked.

With his carry-on in hand, John Kerr responded, "No."

"We just started pre-boarding, so you can board whenever you want."

"Is the flight on time?"

"It is running twenty minutes behind, but that will be made up before landing at LaGuardia, weather permitting," responded the clerk.

"Will the weather affect the time?" asked Kerr.

"No, it shouldn't, they just want me to say that."

Kerr left the counter and boarded the plane to New York City. Elias preferred that he take a commercial flight. If need be, he would send the jet for him, but it did not look like there would be any problems. Everything was running on time. As it should be.

# THIRTY-NINE

"Did your car stall up the road, Miss?" the patrolman inquired.

Sara did not know what to do.

"Are you all right?" the patrolman asked as he raised his flashlight, shining it in Sara's face.

"I am just out for a walk," Sara responded.

"This is not a good road to be walking, Miss."

"Thank you," Sara nodded. "I will take the path back up to my cabin."

"Why were you waving your arms?"

Sara thought quickly and said, "Oh, I thought you were my husband."

Another patrol car pulled up across the road. The second officer shined his flashlight on Sara, then on the other patrolman. He kept the light in front of his face, shielding his identity.

"Fred is that you?" asked the first patrolman shielding his eyes from the light.

"I will handle this, you can go now," ordered the second officer.

"Who are you?"

The first patrolman unholstered his firearm.

Sara stood motionless.

"I will handle this," he said again.

Before the first patrolman could react, the second officer fired. The shot knocked the patrolman back causing him to fall. The bullet lodged in his shoulder, but the fall twisted his leg. He stretched but could not reach his gun. The second officer aimed his gun and flashlight at Sara as he walked over to the patrolman.

With his eyes still focused on Sara he bent down to pick up the patrolman's gun. Just as he turned his eyes from Sara, a blur knocked him down to the ground. His flashlight rolled around on the ground. The second officer was down, he would not get up.

The flashlight rose from the ground.

"Sara, are you all right."

"Redwood!"

She ran over and hugged her old friend.

"We have to help this man," instructed Redwood as he guided Sara over to the first patrolman.

---

The car ride to the airport was not a long ride; it only seemed long. Miller called his agents and instructed them to get up to the cabin as soon as possible. Martinez radioed in that assistance would be needed in that area. She also found out that backup was already responding to an officer down accompanied by two civilians: a young woman and an older man. Peter felt helpless.

The deafening silence in the car did not help.

"You look nervous, but not guilty," reassured Detective Martinez as if reading his mind.

The silence was broken.

"Under the circumstances, this is the last place I would expect to be or should be," Peter responded.

"Your friends are fine," interjected Roland Miller.

"He's right," Martinez assured the young attorney.

Silence overcame the car until Martinez changed the subject.

"Maybe I'm having problems digesting all of this, but you cannot expect me to sit idly by."

"That is exactly what I expect for the next two days," ordered Roland Miller.

"A string of murders criss-crosses the country and ends up with an assassination attempt on the President, and I am supposed to sit by."

"Exactly."

"That's insane."

"What is insane is a city detective delving into national security matters as if she were going to head up a congressional investigation."

"Would you like me to turn this car around?"

"No," interjected Peter.

"What I mean is that I need to determine the level of involvement and participation," Miller continued.

"What you mean is 'how high does this go up?'" Martinez paraphrased the elder statesman.

"Farrell is the only person who can tie the assassin to the conspirators. I need to keep him alive."

"Thanks for your personal interest in my life," interjected Peter.

"However," Miller continued, "if the conspirators believe Mr. Farrell is still out there, coupled with the lack of contact with the assassin and no report on the President, the conspirators are bound to ask questions to the wrong people."

"How do you know Farrell and the conspirators are not linked?"

"The assassin for one. She had been chasing Farrell for two days."

"Maybe 'chasing' is the wrong word," Martinez inquired.

"What do you mean?" asked Peter.

"If this woman was able to get past Secret Service to take pot shots at the President, I doubt you could give her a run for her money. It sounds to me like you were steered in this direction. It makes sense, too. Who better to kill the President than some wacko bent on killing lawyers?"

"You are very perceptive, detective," complimented Miller.

"What an idiot I've been," Peter stated as the light bulb went off in his head.

"What do you mean Farrell?" asked the elder statesman.

"Come on," Peter bemoaned, "who is really going to believe a conspiracy theory coming from a lone gunman implicated for assassinating the President."

Detective Martinez stared at Peter in the rear view mirror. Roland Miller squinted his eyes as if he wanted to say something.

Peter broke the silence again.

"That's what they were planning this whole time. I was supposed to come out to California. I am supposed to be some kind of a patsy."

"If you ask me," interjected the detective, "you can leave out the 'some kind of.'"

---

"He is on his way," the distinctively British voice reported over the speakerphone.

"And when will you arrive?" inquired the blue-blooded Savile Row man.

"First thing in the morning," responded the Brit.

"Whose morning?"

"Your time, of course. Times like these call for patience."

"Patience is the most overrated virtue."

"I prefer sins myself; virtues tend to be so boring."

"You will be here at once."

"My valet is packing as we speak. Shall I bring my clubs?"

"You are testing my patience."

"I thought you had none. No matter, I have enough for all."

"Are you certain Kravenko is the right man?"

"He is the only man. He may be an odd sort, but he has been invaluable so far."

"But he can clean up this mess?"

"That is if another calling, let us say from a higher order, does not sidetrack our man."

"Do not even joke about such matters, especially with him," rebuked the Savile Row man.

"A little levity lightens the lingering, licentious Elias legend."

"Will you be serious for one moment? Elias has something up his sleeve. The Farrell matter is the least of our worries."

"I concur."

"If Elias is pounding his chest, it means that he has something or has done something of which we are not aware."

"I concur again."

"He is not the bluffing type. Something is going on, I just wish we had better information. Kravenko had no insight?"

"Unfortunately, he was involved only in the retrieval of the Occidental files. I believe he just wanted to borrow him as a gesture of good faith, an insurance policy, if you will."

"What about the Tasha girl he has been using? Did Kravenko get close to her?"

"Again, he was of little assistance in that area. Apparently they did not have a love connection."

"What the hell has he been good for?" ranted the increasingly agitated Savile Row man.

"Communication skills are not his forte. As you know his talents lie elsewhere."

"I know. I despise the fact that Elias believes he has the upper hand."

"Tomorrow we will know what little mischief he has been up to."

---

Aboard his private Lear jet, shoes off, glasses still on but gently resting on his nose, Elias St. Armand rested his eyes. A young lady entered the cabin, glanced at her employer, then began to straighten the cabin. First, she closed the liquor cabinet. Next, she carefully lifted the crystal snifter and coaster from the table by Mr. St. Armand. After the coaster and snifter had been safely put away, the young lady walked to the cabin door. She stood at the door for a moment, then glanced at her watch. Turning around, she again stood motionless for a moment, dreading the inevitable. She took one step, hesitated, then proceeded toward her sole passenger.

Gently setting her hand on Elias St. Armand's shoulder, the young lady softly said, "Sir, sir. I am sorry to wake you but the captain says we will be landing soon, so you should buckle up."

With his eyes still closed and remaining motionless, St. Armand calmly responded, "I am not asleep, young lady. I am merely resting my eyes. Thank you for your concern."

The flight assistant exited the cabin without having her boss see her roll her eyes.

Elias St. Armand checked his Rolex. It was almost 2 a.m. Tasha should have called by now. No matter, there may have been some adjustments to the schedule. If she were unable to report right away, she would do so first thing in the morning. Elias wanted to hear the news first, whether good or bad. He had been accused of "micromanaging" on many occasions. Elias never considered this an accusation. He knew he was always the best person to close a deal. It was like accusing him of being one of the most wealthy and powerful men in the world. So what?

After tomorrow, he would be the most powerful man in the world. Step one was complete. The President was dead. Step two, his successor, George W. Algers, would be sworn into office. Elias had never owned a president before. Congressmen and senators are penny-ante peons now that he owns the presidency. Congress was not completely worthless. He needed legislation passed, stricken, or just tied up in committee. But with the presidency, no more vetoes. A whole new judicial system could be appointed. And above all else, the collective will of the country would be his. So follow the sheep as the shepherd leads. And lead he will. Finally, he will lead his crusade into the Middle East. Step three: the U.S. will invade Lebanon and establish Beirut as the capital of the New Middle East. Victory over the infidels would be his. The world would bask in his triumph over terrorism.

---

Martinez had no problem getting the trio through airport security. Miller held up his end in obtaining access to the military field. However, Peter was the reluctant one out of the three.

"I am not getting on a plane without Sara," demanded Peter.

"She is on her way, but will not be able to get here for another forty-five minutes," Miller responded.

"So?"

"They will have another plane ready for when she gets here. We have to leave now."

Martinez answered her cellphone.

"Not without Sara."

"Plans need to be made. I cannot do this from here. I need to get to New York City."

Peter took no pleasure in the frustration he caused Roland Miller.

"That was the girl," Martinez interjected. "She said that she and Redwood are fine and that she will catch up to you in New York City."

"Let us be on our way," commanded the former secretary of state.

"Why didn't you let me speak with her?"

"She was talking to an officer and the officer was talking with me." Martinez continued, "They will not be here for another forty-five minutes, maybe longer."

Peter stared at the detective.

"She also said that Susan Anthony was fine," Martinez said with a grin.

"Now get on the plane."

# PART III

# FORTY

Most people assume, mistakenly, that St. Anthony founded Christian monasticism. However, the credit more accurately belongs to St. Pachomius. It is true that eremitical monks followed St. Anthony through the desert before Pachomius founded his monastery. But Pachomius' monastery was coenobitical. Finally, with Pachomius, a communal life had been established for monks. No longer would hermit monks wander through the desert. The monastery, as we know it, was born.

Born of heathen parents in 292, in the Upper Thebaid region of the Nile, Pachomius' early years were no different than other children raised in Egypt. After conscription in the emperor's army, he enrolled in the catechumens. Upon his baptism into the Christian church, Pachomius sought spiritual guidance from an old desert hermit called Palaemon. The two led a life of extreme austerity. Pachomius and Palaemon's nourishment consisted mostly of water, bread, and salt. Prayer and manual labor filled their hours, sometimes passing the whole night without sleep. While wandering the desert, a voice called to Pachomius to build a monastery on the banks of the Nile at a place called Tabennisi. In only a short while, the monks at Tabennisi numbered a hundred. Pachomius taught the monks the austere life of Palaemon which was a method of obtaining enlightenment through prayer and reflection. He set no rigid physical standards, measuring each monk by his own capacity. Pachomius, as the ultimate example, never lay down to sleep. He only allowed himself short rests while sitting on a stone. Pachomius also never ate a full meal, only rations from time to time to sustain his body's need for nourishment. His rigorous example of life and prayer was followed and embraced by hundreds, then thousands of others. By the time of Pachomius' death in 348, he had over three thousand Tabennisi monks in the nine monasteries under his charge.

The Tabennisi monks became the keepers of all the sacred Christian texts, dutifully copying them through all hours of the day and night. Their library comprised the most comprehensive collection of Jewish and Christian scriptures ever compiled, consisting of the commonly accepted Old and New Testament scriptures, as well as later Christian Apocrypha, the Gnostic scriptures, and even the Jewish pseudepigrapha which included the Dead Sea Scrolls. The monks spent endless hours copying the texts and translating scriptures from Greek to Coptic. Unfortunately, the sacred library was short-lived. Around the year 370, the Archbishop of Alexandria denounced all texts other than the conventional Bible as heresy. All Tabennisi texts were banned and destroyed. In a desperate attempt to save their treasured library, monks hid many of the texts in the desert in places such as Nag Hammadi. Others accompanied pilgrimages out of the reach of the prohibition. These monks were hunted down as heretics. Only a few survived.

One pilgrimage found its way across the Mediterranean Sea, through the Cyclades Islands and the Aegean Sea, past Constantinople and into the Black Sea, to land in Tiras, south of present day Odessa in the Ukraine. The monks traveled up the Dniester River to the foothills of the Carpathian Mountains. Seeking asylum and refuge, the Tabennisi monks rebuilt their monastery thousands of miles from their homeland, high in the Carpathian Mountains, just north of Hovr Hoverla. The Tabennisiot fortress hovered over Trans-Carpathia on thousand-foot cliff, accessible only by a unique pulley system. The restricted access staved off intruders as well as worshipers. Rarely did the monks descend from the cliffs, and no one visited the monastery. That is, except for children abandoned by nearby villagers.

Andriy Kravenko was one of these children. At first glance, the infant Kravenko was no different than the thousands of other little boys who had been left at the base of the monastery over the years. In fact, the very existence of the monastery depended on the abandonment of these children. And the children depended on the monastery.

Ukraine literally means, "border land." Throughout history, the Ukraine, and Trans-Carpathia in particular, has consistently achieved a state of statelessness. The Slavic descendants have been conquered and assimilated by the

Kievan Rus, Hungarians, Poles, Lithuanians, the Ottoman Empire, Transylvanians, the Austrian-Hungarian Empire, Czechoslovakians, Germans, and the Soviets. To the victor of Trans-Carpathia belonged not only the spoils of land, but the spoils of its people. The offspring of conquerors and conquered became further casualties of war. Most of these children were not only unwanted, but discarded. Out of shame, self-preservation, and even love, a few of these children were placed in a basket to rise a thousand feet above to the Tabennesiot monastery, never to be heard or seen again. Over fifty years ago, Andriy Kravenko had been placed in that basket and hoisted up the cliff to the monastery.

Andriy Kravenko, son of Lina Kravenko and grandson of the Ukrainian patriot Andrii Volodymir Kravenko, knew little of his family history. His legacy began in 1890, with Andrii Volodymer Kravenko, the son of a farmer from a village just outside Khust. The village fell under the rule of a lord-lieutenant appointed by, and responsible to, the Hungarian Royal Government in Budapest. After the outbreak of World War I, Ukrainian nationalism swept the western countryside. This fever diminished under Czechoslovakian rule. Far from relinquishing his dreams of an independent Ukrainian free state, young Andrii joined the OUN, the Organization of Ukrainian Nationals, and rose through the nationalist ranks quickly. At the pinnacle of both his career and his dreams, his Western region rejected Soviet rule and defied Hungary by achieving independence in February 1939. Rewarding years of service, Andrii Volodymir Kravenko was appointed to a cabinet position in the Voloshyn government for the newly created state of Carpatho-Ukraine. As leaders of the newest and smallest state in the area, many nationalists held both state and military positions. Kravenko was no exception. Andrii Volodymir Kravenko was one of the field generals in the Carpathian Sich, an army of only five thousand soldiers. The Carpatho-Ukrainian independence was short-lived. In a secret pact between Nazi Germany and Hungary, Hitler agreed to the Hungarian occupation of all of Transcarpathia. After only a month of existence, on March 14, 1939, the Hungarian army swept across the Carpatho-Ukrainian borders soundly defeating the Carpathian Sich.

Killed in battle, Andrii Volodymir Kravenko was survived by his daughter, Lina Kravenko.

The Hungarian occupation of Transcarpathia sheltered the Carpatho-Ukrainians from much of the German or Soviet-scorched earth tactics. However, by no means were these western Ukrainians exempt from other horrors of the war. Hundreds of thousands of Jews were handed over to the Nazis. Although the Slavic Ukrainians did not suffer the same atrocities as the Jewish Ukrainians, the Nazis still had little regard for any Ukrainian people. In fact, the Nazis viewed all Slavs as subhuman, subjecting them to disgusting brutalities.

Captain Erich Hoch of the Third Reich championed these Nazi degradation tactics. On March 10, 1944, acting under the direct orders of his Reichskommissar "to inflict the utmost severity towards the native population," the Nazi officer repeatedly raped Lina, daughter of the patriot Andrii Volodymir Kravenko. The fruit of the violence inflicted upon Lina was Andriy Kravenko.

He was born after the German-Hungarian occupation and just before the Soviet invasion. Lina and baby Andriy had little time to bask in their independence. The Soviet invasion offered little hope of peace. In order to crush any thought of an independent Ukraine, the Soviets gathered all former Ukrainian nationalists or questionable members of the intelligensia, and shipped them to Siberian concentration camps. As the daughter of a renowned Ukrainian patriot, Lina would be arrested by the Soviet police. However, before she was taken away, Lina secured safe passage for her son. On the same day Lina Kravenko boarded a train destined for the frozen mines of Siberia, an elderly village woman and her husband traveled north of Hovr Hoverla up the Carpathian mountainside to the foot of the Tabennisi monastery with baby Andriy.

Andriy Kravenko's monastic education differed little from the original teachings of Pachomius. No monk slept lying down. Instead of beds, the monks rested on sloped chairs which allowed them to rest, but still remain in a prayerful posture. At their meals, each monk covered his head with his hood, revealing little or none of a brother's face during the meal. Talking was strictly forbidden at mealtime. Furthermore, a monk's eyes were not allowed to wander at mealtime.

The monks lived three to a cell, grouped in trades. After demonstrating exceptional literacy and language skills, Andriy moved in with two scriveners. The monks assembled together twice a night and for mass on Saturdays and Sundays. Schooling consisted of Bible reading and learning the scriptures by heart. For scriveners, this was taken one step further by copying texts by hand and translating them into different languages.

The young boy excelled in his studies and trade, mastering Aramaic, Coptic, Greek, Yiddish, Russian, French and English, in addition to mastering his chores. However, the Tabennesiot Order became problematic for Andriy the young man. Upon reaching puberty, Andriy challenged the drive and resolve of brothers his own age. With the occurrence of some minor incidences, the Order placed Andriy with the men. His two roommates, Brothers Barnabas and John, were thirty years his elder. The change proved adequate for a few years until Andriy again challenged his brothers, this time his elders.

Young Andriy held himself to a higher standard than others. His problem stemmed from holding others to the same standard. On occasion, Andriy berated Barnabas and John for resting in a slovenly position or resting at all. Andriy chastised the fun-loving Barnabas in particular for his excesses in food and drink. When others, who labored arduously with Andriy, could not keep pace with the young man-child in the gardens or on the stone walls, Andriy sent them away in disgrace, citing passage after passage of scripture describing inadequacies of the weak in spirit and body. Despite his harsh outbursts, such as striking Barnabas for clearing his throat while dining, the monks tolerated Andriy's rancid behavior until a fateful spring night on the top of Hovr Hoverla.

Every spring a band of thirteen monks paid homage to St. Pachomius by climbing Hovr Hoverla and spending the twenty-four hours of his feast day deep in prayer near the peak of the Carpathian Mountains. The monks prayed in solitude. For practical safety reasons concerning lions or bandits, the monks designated one brother a "watcher." The watcher protected the monks, who were deep in prayer, by overseeing the mountainside as a shepherd tending his flock.

Andriy had never been the watcher nor even accompanied the chosen monks to Hovr Hoverla. His fellow monks believed and prayed that such a religious experience would mend Andriy's tortured soul. In fact, Barnabas had insisted that Andriy must be given a chance to experience the spirituality of such a journey. Andriy led his brothers up the treacherous trails to an area near the peak of Hovr Hoverla. The twelve other monks scattered along the mountainside where each found his place of solitude. Through the night, Andriy walked silently over and back amongst his brothers. As he tended his flock, Andriy passed time by reciting text after text to himself. Hour after hour passed as Andriy cited passage after passage. It was no coincidence to Andriy that in the early morning hours upon the exact time he was reciting the Gospel of Thomas passage "Woe to the flesh that depends on the soul; woe to the soul that depends on the flesh," he found Barnabas lying flat on his belly like a snake in the grass. Beside Barnabas laid a local harlot infamous for exchanging sexual favors for food.

By mid-morning the watcher rounded up his brothers for the hike back to the monastery. Yet on this occasion, most of the monks had gathered together by noon. It was not until early in the afternoon when the monks found Andriy, postured in prayer, on a grassy knoll on the mountainside. Beside Andriy, the lifeless body of Barnabas had been delicately propped up, postured in prayer, despite the fact that the vertebrae in his neck had severed his spinal chord only hours ago.

Driven from the monastery by those who he had called brother, Andriy began the long journey into the civilization below the Carpathian cliffs. Fortunately, his monastic robes opened the arms and doors of villagers across Trans-Carpathia. Leaving the only place he had ever known as home, Andriy traveled east, away from his heritage. For eight months he moved from village to village until he reached to the Ukrainian city founded by Cardinal Richelieu at the edge of the Black Sea: Odessa.

Andriy Kravenko's five years in Odessa contrasted sharply to the leisurely life of shopping on Primorsky Boulevard or rollicking on Deribasovska Street. He lived alone in a flat by the docks. Kravenko's linguistic abilities helped him with several jobs on the docks until a local fartsovshchik drafted him into his black marketeering enterprise. The small-time black marketer, who called himself Karabas, was no rocket scientist, but he recognized the potential in Kravenko's unique linguistic talents. Karabas also knew how to exploit Kravenko's black-and-white morality.

After several years of manipulating the young Kravenko, a rival organization offered to buy Kravenko from Karabas. Although Karabas profited significantly from Kravenko, he could not refuse an offer from the notorious Komitet Gosudarstvenndi Bezopasnosti, known worldwide by its initials: KGB.

Kravenko spent eighteen years with the KGB, mostly in the field. Knowing indoctrination would be futile on this individual, the KGB ironically played upon Kravenko's ecclesiastical background. The KGB allowed Kravenko to purge the world of sinners, the weak flesh. The KGB merely directed Kravenko where to evangelize. Always an excellent student, Kravenko excelled under the KGB. Not only was he able to expunge from this earth who he deemed to be damned, Kravenko mastered field operations designed to tempt the weak individual's taste for sin, especially lust. Employing underage prostitutes to compromise businessmen or government officials was a Kravenko trademark, as was his intricate web of informers, or stukachi, as he called them.

Kravenko's strength still lay in his unflinching ability to render and execute a death sentence. The years at the KGB were not without controversy. Although Kravenko had one of the highest success rates of any KGB agent, a Kravenko operation also usually had one of the highest casualty rates. Although Kravenko's bloody operations irked some, the KGB could never argue with his results.

Then, of course, there was Kravenko's interference with the KGB operation in St. Peter's Square on May 13, 1981. The Polish pope was not popular with the KGB. Given the aggressive (and, in retrospect, highly successful) campaign which Karol Wojtyla waged against the USSR and the entire Eastern Bloc, Poland became an embarrassment. Having a Polish native as the leader of the entire Christian world did not help the USSR's struggle to control all of its satellite nations. Poland, as a Soviet satellite, was acceptable to the Western world. However, the birthplace of St. Peter's successor under the control of the Soviet Union was not. As far as the KGB was concerned, the proletariat's struggle required a solution to the dichotomy of a Polish pope. Deliberately setting up a Chinese wall around Kravenko for obvious reasons, Moscow utilized their Bulgarian operations to resolve the situation. If one of his stukachi had not tipped Kravenko off, he may not have been able to foil Mehmet Aci Agca's attempt on the pope's life. Fortunately for Kravenko, Moscow moderates prevailed over hardliners, denouncing the attempt as foolish and a distraction to the political objectives of the Communist Party. Kravenko's interference went unpunished, but his days were numbered.

When Gorbachev formally abolished the KGB in 1991, the Council of International Relations quickly snatched Kravenko away from what likely would have been a death sentence. Kravenko's skills, honed by the KGB, were much appreciated and well compensated by the CIR. The CIR utilized Kravenko mostly in the former eastern bloc. Kravenko's mission was simple: eliminate threats to the Council's political agenda. Whether the threat involved a rival corporate interest, a communist leader on the rise or an underworld gang kingpin, Kravenko executed his businessmen or Mafia leaders as if Russia and its former satellites were the Old West. Although Kravenko carried out all judgments without remorse or satisfaction, the nineteen bullets he put in Karabas' back and the one in his head at the Odessa seemed to prove a point.

Kravenko's current mission did not please him. It soon would be completed. He had been on loan to the Occidental Group and the fascist Elias St. Armand. He had been summoned back to New York City to clean things up. Dressed in priestly garments, Kravenko genuflected before the altar at St. Patrick's Cathedral and said under his breath, "I have cast fire upon the world, and see, I am guarding it until it blazes."

# FORTY-ONE

The pilot shot a look back at Roland Miller as his voice came over the speaker, "Touchdown at Fort Hamilton will be in fifty-seven minutes, sir."

Miller responded by giving a thumb's up to the pilot.

The military transport shook a little as it began to descend.

"You should get some sleep Farrell," Miller suggested to Peter.

"I can't sleep." Peter had dozed off over the Rockies out of sheer exhaustion, but had been awake for the past forty-five minutes, thinking.

He sat up.

"Are you all right, Farrell?" Miller inquired.

"She was right you know."

"What are talking about?"

"Detective Martinez."

"Yes."

"I have been led around this whole time."

"Maybe."

"There's no maybe about it."

The elder statesman did not respond.

"I was forced out of St. Louis, then I was blocked from flying to the east coast. Killing Dean Adams forced my hand to go somewhere else. Even if I did not hear about the Dean's death, I would not have been able to get on that plane. Then it was too easy to get out of the airport. But how could they have known I'd fly from Chicago to San Francisco?"

Miller continued to listen the young attorney babble.

"They must have known about Sara. They knew that I would go to her. Once I was in San Francisco, they had their patsy."

"Son," Miller interrupted Peter's analysis, "you need to focus on the present and the future, not the past."

"I am focusing on the future. My future could be as the man who shot the

President. The Shakespeare Killer assassinates the President. Better yet, I can see the headlines, 'President's Act Ended By Shakespeare Killer.'"

"We have that situation under control."

"Under control? The President is dead."

"Keep your voice down."

The roar of the engines drowned out any conversation, but Miller took no chances by grabbing Farrell's arm.

"What are you doing?"

As tight as the elder statesman's grip was, Peter wrenched his arm away from Miller.

"The situation is under control," Miller overemphasized the 'is.'

Peter stared at the man known as the "counselor to the presidents."

"The Secret Service is prepared for such contingencies. It will never be discovered that there was a shootout in the President's suite at the Kensington. That is being cleaned up as we speak. A doctor will confirm late tonight or early tomorrow that the President had a massive heart attack or an aneurysm."

"And the Vice President?"

"That's why we are going to New York."

"Why?"

"Vice President Algers is a part of the CIR, he may even be a part of Elias St. Armand's Occidental Group."

"This was a coup."

"I need to find that out, and I need to evaluate the Vice President's involvement."

"You're just going to walk up to the Vice President and ask if he killed any presidents lately?"

"The President told you that I was a part of the CIR. That is a half-truth. There was a time that I was very involved with the Council, because I was on its executive board. At that time, our influence and efforts concentrated on globalization on economic scales. The Bay of Pigs changed everything. The CIR's executive board came to the stark realization that in order to ensure economic stability, politically we needed to operate in a different manner."

"A different manner."

"Instead of shaping global policies with our economic influence, CIR's executive board decided it would dictate policies."

"What do you mean 'dictate policies'?"

"Channel events toward a desired outcome."

Peter stared at the elder statesman as he continued.

"It is not important to go into details, but the Board split into two factions. I, and several others, left. A violent struggle ensued over the next ten years to gain control of the Board. Since its reorganization, it has played a role in world politics that has transcended national interests."

"How can it still exist if the White House knows about it?"

"Sometimes the CIR's executive board can achieve results that an individual nation, limited by national and patriotic interests, cannot."

"You use them."

"And they use us."

"And now they want the White House."

"I do not believe the CIR was behind this."

"Why?"

"First, it is too crude. Second, it serves no purpose to kill the President. Fairchild did not like them, and they were not enamored with him, but their overall global interests were consistent with one another."

"Maybe their interests changed."

"Believe me, killing the leader of the free world serves no economic goals."

"Then why are we going to see them?"

"I think another struggle over the control of the CIR's Executive Board is happening, and Elias St. Armand is behind it."

Peter waited for Roland Miller to finish as the crew prepared for landing.

"Members of the board can confirm my suspicions."

"And if they do?"

"They'll help us stop St. Armand and Vice President Algers, if he is involved."

"How?"

"That will be up to you, Peter."

---

    Despite the twentieth-century steel and glass skyline of New York City, the city still flaunts its nineteenth-century opulence. The Ogden Arms is no exception. Nestled just outside the financial district, dwarfed by skyscrapers, the Ogden Arms is one of the city's most exclusive hotels. More a clubhouse than a hotel, rooms are rented on a monthly, or even yearly, basis. Suites are hard to come by at the Ogden Arms. It is not a matter of how much money you were willing to spend on accommodations, it is exclusively a matter of who you are. Reservations are made through the board of directors, and few had the connections to even make it that far. The Ogden Arms did not cater to rock stars, Hollywood idols, or flavors of the month. Only the real power brokers are invited to stay at the Ogden Arms.

    The Occidental Group's Elias St. Armand kept the presidential suite at the Ogden Arms. The irony was lost on him at the present time.

    "Damn!"

    Elias St. Armand, in his silk boxers, tank top, and black dress socks pulled up to his knees, stared at the television set. He grabbed a croissant from his silver breakfast tray. Furiously chomping on the flaky pastry, St. Armand stared at the morning television news, then flipped the channel for the umpteenth time. Still no news. What was taking so long? Surely one of the twenty-four hour news networks should be announcing a state of national mourning. And why the hell hasn't Tasha called, he thought to himself. She has never failed before. And those were much more difficult assignments: having to sneak into a palace, a drive-by in broad daylight, a military parade. Here, she had easy access to the room. The handgun matching the one Farrell had used was in the briefcase, which was already in the room. There would be only one checkpoint, which would be no problem, since the damn gun would already be in the room. And to top it all off, she probably had higher clearance than any chambermaid in the history of the hotel industry.

The plan was foolproof. She's in the room, eliminates the two agents with the silencer, then the President, drops the gun, then leaves. Simple and efficient.

As the morning news blared in the background, Elias paced the presidential suite's renowned Gold Room. With its twenty-foot gold-plated ceiling and excessive ornamentation, the room harkened back to the great wealth of the 1890s. The burgundy-colored carpeting richly accentuated the gold theme in the room. Each ivory-colored wall was adorned with gold-plated floral arrangements: roses, ivy, lilies, and fleur-de-lis. Each segment of each wall was lined with gold. A series of full-length French doors led to the balcony, but the autumn chill did not lend itself to opening the room to the outdoors.

Elias had begun to drift far away to the banks of the Berdawni River to the ancient Lebanese city of Zahle, home of his childhood. Zahle is, was, and always will be the heart of Lebanon as far as Elias was concerned. Located equal distance from the north to the south and from the east to the west, she is also the geographical heart of the country. Lying at the foothills of Mount Sanneen and overlooking the fertile Bekaa valley, the city also commands respect as a commercial center.

At one time, Zahle was the only Catholic city in all of Asia. Local savants traced the city's Christian heritage back to Paradise, the Garden of Eden, home of Adam and Eve. Others claim it was where Noah planted the first vineyard after the Great Flood. Zahle is, was, and always will be a special city. Zahle, after all, is the city of Saidet-en-Najat, Our Lady of Deliverance, the Blessed Virgin Mary.

It was his father who first told Elias of Saidet-en-Najat. Elias' father, a Maronite nationalist and Zahle's most respected politician, routinely took his son to the chapel behind the cathedral to pray before Saidet-en-Najat. The portrait of Our Lady of Deliverance was not a large painting, nor a particular valuable object d'art. However, there was something striking. It was in her eyes, powerful, yet sympathetic. At first glance one knew it was just a painting. However, the more time spent with her, it was as if she was in the same room as you, listening to your problems and fears. She welcomed and comforted all at once. Those same eyes listened intently. They lifted the sorrow, the heavy burdens that followed one into chamber of Saidet-en-Najat.

Consolation and support were not the only gifts Saidet-en-Najat bestowed on the people of Zahle. For if those were the only offerings, then the chapel in Zahle would be no different than any other place of worship around the world. Zahle was, is, and always will be special because of Saidet-en-Najat. Special because of her miracles. A young boy with only months to live is miraculously cured only days after his mother offers her prayers before Saidet-en-Najat. A blind woman regains her sight only days after her husband visits Our Lady of Deliverance. After an all-night vigil in the chapel by many of the townspeople, a small shepherd boy is found after being lost in the hills for three days. There also is the little girl who prayed for her mother to walk again after she had been stricken with polio. Ten years later, the mother walked her down the aisle at her wedding.

One of the more renowned miracles by Saidet-en-Najat is that of a father who prayed for his wife who had fallen into a coma after a difficult delivery. The mother delivered a healthy son, but had lost too much blood during the delivery. Less than an hour after the boy had been born, the mother slipped into unconsciousness. Moments later, the priest administered last rites. The father, a proud warrior, stormed from the room and ran to the chapel. The warrior chastised Saidet-en-Najat blaspheming the Virgin Mary and her Lord. In his rage, he even overturned the altar. Finally, he broke down and wept. As his tears streamed down his face, he collapsed, begged for forgiveness and to have just one more year with his beloved. Hours later, a child was sent into the chapel to tell the warrior that his wife had awakened from her deep sleep. The warrior was Henri St. Armand, Elias' father.

Henri St. Armand had been given his one year with his wife, Jodi. A year filled with happiness and new beginnings with their son, Elias. The year was also filled with giant strides for an emerging nation. Maronite nationalists, led by Henri St. Armand, among others, fought for independence from their Arab neighbors. Greater Arab-Syria remained Lebanon's deepest threat.

Although France had divided the two countries under its mandate, Syria never recognized Lebanon as a separate state. For Syria, especially King Faysal, Lebanon was part of an historical land which was part of a greater Arab homeland. As the Arab leader in the region, King Faysal sought to exercise autonomy over Lebanon in the Great Arab Revolt and to re-establish Greater Arab-Syria. Henri St. Armand and his Maronite patriots, with France's aid, defeated Faysal's forces at the Maysalun Pass outside Damascus. With Faysal and his Greater Arab-Syria defeated, Lebanon remained autonomous. These were the happiest of times for the St. Armand family, and for Lebanon.

They quickly came to an end. Fulfilling a prophecy, the year ended tragically with Jodi's death in her sleep exactly one year to the day that Elias was born. Henri bore no bitterness over the death. He begged for his year and lived every moment to the fullest. Every year for the next four years, he brought his son to the chapel before Saidet-en-Najat to give thanks for the prior year and for the special year the three had had together.

Elias remembered his sixth birthday all too well. It was on that date the State of Greater Lebanon under French mandate ceased to exist. A constitution liberated the country and the Lebanese Republic was born. Child that he was, Elias' memories had less to do with a birth of a nation and more to do with his father, who traveled from Beirut back to Zahle to be with Elias on his birthday. They had planned to go to the chapel, but the plans were irreparably altered. On the fifth anniversary of his wife's death, a sniper's bullet snuffed out Henri St. Armand's life. Greater Arab-Syria had taken Lebanon's proclamation of independence with the zeal one would expect. Syrian snipers stalking the Bekaa Valley hillside preyed on unsuspecting travelers. Henri St. Armand, who had fought so hard for his country's independence, never lived to see a free Lebanese Republic.

Elias St. Armand spent his entire birthday waiting for his father in the chapel. The priest found him close to midnight. Henri St. Armand was well known and it did not take long for Zahle to learn about their fallen warrior. The priest, the bearer of the bad news, attempted to comfort the child. But there was no consoling the child for he shed no tears. The child knelt before Saidet-en-Najat and stared into her eyes. As he fought back tears, the child vowed before Saidet-en-Najat that he would trade his life for vengeance for his father.

His jaw clenched, his hands in the form of fists, and the V-shaped vein in his forehead ready to burst, Elias St. Armand blankly stared up at the financial district's intimidating skyline. The hustle and bustle of the morning rush hour's din just beginning below him did not register. Nothing did. Then he heard it.

> *And this little news update from the west coast. The President has checked into a San Francisco hospital this morning. President Fairchild checked in early this morning at the same hospital in which he was making an unscheduled appearance at the Children's Ward. His spokesman merely stated that upon arriving at the hospital this morning, the President experienced some irregular heavy breathing. Upon pressure from his aides, the President checked himself in for what his doctors are calling "preventive testing."*
>
> *After opening up the polls yesterday in his home state of Ohio, Air Force One flew to San Francisco for what was called some post-campaign down time in California visiting Silicon Valley and Los Angeles. His spokesman assured the press corps that his west coast tour would be delayed by only a day and that he would not use this as an excuse to miss the Foreign Press Corps' Presidential Gala Friday in Washington, D.C.*
>
> *On a more serious note the Russian News Agency TASS is reporting that Russian Prime Minister...*

The rage disappeared from Elias St. Armand's face. He smiled. The President was dead.

# FORTY-TWO

"Peter!" Sara screamed with delight.

What had been a stern expression on his face quickly turned to glee as the love of his life ran towards him.

"Sara!"

The two embraced. Peter held her as tight as he could.

"What's wrong?" she immediately inquired sensing something from his clutch.

"Are you all right?"

"I'm fine. I take back all those barbaric things I've said about our military," she responded, speaking louder than normal as if wanting to be overheard.

"They have been perfect gentlemen."

"Where's Redwood?"

"He stayed back." Reassuring Peter she continued, "Some of Miller's men were taking him back to the cabin. He's fine; it's amazing the things he can do."

"Are you sure you are all right?"

"Worried about me, what about you?" Sara finally realized Peter had turned the topic of conversation away from himself as usual. "I didn't hear from you and could not reach you. These people knew nothing. I've been sick to my stomach."

"I'm fine."

Sara grabbed Peter and hugged him again.

"That drove me crazy. I don't," she paused, "won't do that again. You cannot run off like that again. We are not leaving one another again."

Peter took her face in his hands and stared into her blue eyes.

"That's what I have always wanted."

An F-14 Tomcat soared overhead.

Peter stepped back from Sara, finally taking notice of her olive green pants and khaki shirt.

"I like your new look," he said with a grin.

"Oh, I'm a mess," she replied.

"Did you enlist since the last I saw you?"

Looking down at her outfit, then flipping the hair out of her face, Sara smiled.

"Well, you know how I was sick to my stomach. I meant that literally."

Peter looked confused.

"Well, they flew me on one of those jet things," she continued, staring at the ground out of embarrassment.

Peter started to grin again.

"They fly so damn fast and there is only room for two people. I got sick to stomach twice. The pilot wanted to land both times, but I foolishly answered when he spoke to me. I really thought about pretending I passed out or something."

Peter's grin grew.

"Well I kind of made a mess of myself so they let me clean up." Finally looking Peter back in the eyes, "But I did tell them I would not dress all in olive green."

"You fashion plate, you."

They both smiled, finally.

Remembering the circumstances that brought them to the military hangar at Fort Hamilton in Brooklyn, New York, Sara began her inquiry.

"What happened to you, the meeting at the mission?"

The happiness in Peter's face quickly disappeared.

He casually looked around to see if anyone could overhear him. Recognizing that there was too much movement on the base for anyone to be interested in them, Peter coldly and calmly faced Sara.

"The President is dead," he said.

"The President of what?" Sara was understandably confused.

"The President of the United States. President Fairchild."

"But..."

"They did it, Sara," Peter grabbed Sara's arms firmly and told her, "They killed him."

"They? Occidental?"

"Occidental and whoever is behind Occidental. Sara, this is so much bigger than we thought."

Sara's astonishment turned to fear.

"Corruption is just a part of it. These guys are running the civilized world. I don't like this leader, let's get rid of him. I don't like the President's policies. No big deal! We'll appoint our own president. It's insane."

Realizing he was beginning to lose control again by the increasing volume of his voice, Peter surveyed his surroundings remembering what Miller had said to him on the plane.

He continued, "I don't know what we can do. The whole plane ride over here I kept thinking how hopeless all this was. How I've ruined your life. Ruined your life? I've probably signed your death warrant."

Sara took Peter's hand.

"Petie, one thing at a time. Are you sure? The President is dead?"

"I was there," he responded in a lower voice.

"Then why are you here? Why are we here?"

"See that man in the suit by the control panel over there?" Peter pointed to Roland Miller who stood by the officers and an enlisted man. The enlisted man appeared to be closing up some phone system from a briefcase.

"Isn't that Roland Miller?"

"Yes."

"Ambassador or what is it—Secretary Miller? I can't remember what his latest title even is."

"I don't know, but it's him."

"How?"

"He was there when it happened. We both were."

Sara interrupted, "Stupid, stupid, stupid. The President was in San Francisco, I forgot. Some last minute tour or something. We tried, I tried, to get on his schedule, but everything was too tentative, noncommittal. We only found out at the last minute that he was coming. We are always rejected, but not like that. Where did this happen?"

"The Kensington."

"And you got there how?"

"The President's people knew about me and grabbed me before I could meet with Elias St. Armand."

"So you never saw him?"

"Just as well. They said he would have killed me."

"So you were with Roland Miller?"

"And the President."

"And the President. Then what happened?"

"They told me all about Occidental and Elias St. Armand. Sara, it's not Democrats versus Republicans or liberals versus conservatives. It's democracy versus all of them."

Peter's voice had begun to carry.

Sara squeezed his hand. The two were completely engrossed with one another.

"Who is 'them'?" Sara asked.

"Good question," interrupted an older voice.

Sara was both startled and in awe. Still pissed off, Peter was not phased by the older voice. He ignored the voice and the man behind the voice.

"Miss Ahrens, I presume," Roland Miller introduced himself. "Roland Miller at your service."

Although impressed by the legend of the man, Sara suppressed her awe.

"There are people I report to that will need a lot of answers."

"I do not presume to circumvent your influence, ma'am. I know your reputation and have the utmost regards for you and your organization. In fact, I read a paper of yours that you co-authored for the Kyoto Conference. It impressed me."

Roland Miller was absolutely charming, disarming Sara before she could press him, but she did press him.

"How do we know that you are not one of 'them'?" Sara inquired.

"You do not," responded Roland Miller very matter of factly.

"Sara," interjected Peter, "he was there, he could have been killed, too."

"Maybe it was just meant to look like that."

"Believe me, young lady, there is no one who feels more responsible for this chain of events than I."

Without shedding a tear or letting his voice reflect his sorrow, Roland Miller glanced into the sky for a very brief moment as if seeking forgiveness from above. The moment did not pass unnoticed, but by no means did he draw attention to himself.

Roland continued, "The woman did not bring that weapon in on her own. The agents confirmed for me that Kerr's briefcase was opened and a hidden panel existed in the bottom. Judging from the woman's position in the room, the relatively short time she was actually in the room, and the fact that she could not have even entered the hotel with a weapon, the agents are reasonably sure that the weapon came from my protégé's briefcase."

"Reasonably sure?" Peter raised his eyebrow.

"The gun came from Kerr's bag," assured Miller.

"How could he have made it past security?" Sara could not believe what she was hearing.

"Just as I, John Kerr is exempt from many security checks."

"Exempt?" Sara commented still in disbelief.

"There are a few of us civilians who are considered 'beyond reproach.' Consequently, many standard security nuisances are ignored as a courtesy. They usually just make a check to make sure I am not holstering a gun somewhere."

An obviously disturbed Sara chastised the elder statesman, "So as long as I was chummy-chummy with the President, like you, I could just waltz right in the Oval Office and start blowing people away."

Sara obviously hit a soft spot.

Miller snapped back, "Young lady, this was not a normal security scenario. Even so, a gun could not have entered the hotel unaccounted for. And we have accounted for the gun. It was an agent's sidearm. The agent is missing.

Kerr or the woman, or both of them, removed the gun from the agent. Willingly or unwillingly, I do not know. I also know that it was a last-minute unscheduled visit at a place that had just been secured ten days ago by the Vice President's Secret Service detail. The missing agent was the agent who led the Vice President's detail ten days ago. I do not have the answers now. This was a worst-case scenario coupled with the ultimate treason."

Sara was not finished.

"Who planned the visit?"

"Kerr."

"This stinks."

Sara was finished.

Miller was not.

"I have known John Kerr for over ten years. There has never been even a hint of impropriety, let alone this."

"Ten years, I have shoes older than that," replied Sara.

"A lot has gone on in the past ten years, and Kerr has always been reliable."

"Listen," Sara's anger had converted to disdain toward the octogenarian, "for the last ten years you have not been exactly at the top of your game, have you?"

The frustration of the past couple days had taken its toll on Sara. She was tired of being dumped on and unwilling to accept excuses or apologies.

"Sara," Peter changed the course of the conversation, "we need to figure out what we're going to do."

"What are we going to do? Are you nuts, too? What are we going to do? Look around you. This is a military base."

Sara pointed to some of the soldiers.

"These are soldiers," she continued slowly. "They have guns. They will protect us."

"It probably is a good idea for her to stay here. There is no record of her arriving and no one would know she is here," Roland Miller directed his comment to Peter only.

"Hello? I am standing right here and what do you mean, 'for her'?" Sara turned to Peter. "Peter, you're staying here too?"

"Occidental still may believe I have their files. I may be the only one who can stop them."

Before Sara could speak, Miller started, "Whether Peter has or does not have the files is irrelevant; the key is whether they know he is alive. He is a loose thread, and the only loose thread that can tie all of this together."

"Sara, I am going to have to meet with some people. That's why we are here."

"I'm not staying here by myself."

Peter took Sara's hand in his and affirmatively stated, "Nope, we're done being separated."

"Like I stated earlier, she is probably safer here," Miller pointed out to Peter.

"Sara?" Peter looked for her approval.

"I'm not staying here by myself."

"Well, it is settled then. I will arrange for transportation and for a safe haven in Manhattan."

Roland Miller turned and slowly walked back to the hangar where the two soldiers still remained, one still carrying the briefcase with the encased telephone system.

After Roland Miller was out of earshot, Sara voiced her concerns about the man.

"Peter, are you sure about him?"

"Yes."

"Some of this just seems a little too convenient."

"Believe me, there was nothing convenient about dodging those bullets in that hotel suite."

"But him," Sara nodded toward Miller who was talking again on the attaché case phone, "and his right hand man?"

"Sara, the man is over eighty years old and he physically dove to push the President out of harm's way. I was there. A stuntman could not have coordinated everything that was going on."

"Still..."

"He's our only hope. We are way out of our league. It's not like we can drive up to Canada and hide the rest of our lives. I'm not asking you to trust him; just trust me." Peter took her hand. "We need each other, and now we need him."

# FORTY-THREE

Vice President George W. Algers knew Bob Fairchild did not like him. The President was not alone. In fact, most national polls showed him as a liability on the ticket two years from now. That, of course, was not the case seven years ago when Fairchild knew he could carry only the Midwest and the Northeast. That left California and the South. The popular California senator surely would carry her own state, and she did; so that left the South. And for the past thirty years, no one talked politics in the South without first talking to the Lone Star State's "Wild Bill" Algers.

William Wadsworth Algers II told nearly everyone he met that he never had to work a day in his life, and that is why he worked every damn day in his life. His father William Wadsworth Algers owned much of the land south of Houston. Bill Senior's cattle ranches quickly gave way to oil under "Wild Bill." Merely owning the land guaranteed family fortunes for generations to come. Despite the silver spoon heritage, Wild Bill had worked his father's ranch, "the Big W," going from ranch hand to head rancher by age seventeen. His father put him to work without letting anyone know he was an Algers, much less the "II." But that is the way they both wanted it. Father had challenged son, and son accepted. To everyone on the ranch he was simply known as "Wild Bill."

Before "Wild Bill," he was known as just Bill. But during his second week as a ranch hand, he climbed into the corral to tame a new bronco. He was only allowed into the corral to clean dung, but Bill could not help himself. Legend has it that he tamed the bronco on the first try. In the real world it took him ten falls over two weeks. The more experienced Big W cowboys dubbed him "Wild Bill." Bill Senior was a little more emblematic. He shot the bronco and had its head mounted in his ten-year-old's room.

Competition was in Wild Bill's blood. It was at the heart of everything. Taming his first bronco was the result of a dare. Taking the job as a ranch hand in the first place was a challenge Wild Bill could not pass up. Everyday was something different. From how much fencing he could mend, to how many cattle he could round up, and the always popular: how fast he could ride. But at the heart of his competitive streak was his father. Everyday he competed for his father's attention. Bill Senior was not an easy man to please, himself being a man's man, he was always regaling his own youthful accomplishments and indiscretions.

Wild Bill not only competed for his father's attention, he competed against his legacy. His father broke his first bronco at age eleven, Wild Bill at ten. His father had made his first cattle run to New Orleans at age fourteen, Wild Bill at thirteen. Bill Senior was able to out drink all his peers and then some at sixteen, Wild Bill at fifteen. Bill Senior had his first woman at age seventeen, Wild Bill at fifteen. Whatever rite of passage there was, Wild Bill strove to surpass his father's legacy.

Business was no exception. For when oil was first found on Ranchero Big W, Wild Bill grasped the significance of the opportunity better than anyone. He could not add to the family's fortunes by acquiring more land. His father had acquired more than was available. In ranching, land was everything. Land and politics. Bill Senior controlled the land and controlled the politicians. Oil provided Wild Bill the opportunity to distinguish himself from Bill Senior.

Bill Senior was no fool. He knew the value of oil and the opportunity it held for the future. What he did not know was how much oil was on his land. Wild Bill did. By the time Bill Senior ordered surveys of some land in Baytown, Wild Bill had already had results from the soil borings. Wild Bill knew the Galveston area was rich in oil. Bill Senior had no idea. Knowing his father had finally ordered soil borings of the suggested tracts, Wild Bill made his move to establish his own legacy. Wild Bill found out the name of the firm his father had hired to conduct soil borings, and then bribed them. In exchange for a handsome fee, the engineering firm swapped the Big W results with borings taken a hundred miles west of the test sites. Any evidence of oil was seen as an aberration, with little or no incentive to pursue. Wild Bill bought the land from his father and soon "discovered" oil. With one quick move,

Wild Bill had forged his legacy. "Discovering" oil was only the beginning. Wild Bill soon cornered all aspects of the petrochemical industry. Algers Oil, Inc. began producing synthetic rubber to supplement its oil refining. Algers Oil diversified further as it began to control shipping lines from Houston through Galveston Bay. In controlling much of the port, Algers Oil had a hand in every pocket in southeastern Texas.

Notwithstanding the fact that his entire fortune had its foundation in stealing from his father, Wild Bill Algers was a self-made tycoon. Of course, Wild Bill thought of himself as self-made. He knew his father would not have let him have that land if he knew it was rich in oil. He was right. Bill Senior wanted his children to stand on their own two feet, to make their own breaks in life. In due time, Wild Bill convinced himself that his father would have been proud of him for stealing the land, or making his own break, if you will. The only burr in Wild Bill's saddle was his son, George Wadsworth Algers. Wild Bill, jealous of his own relationship with his father and not willing to compete with a William Wadsworth Algers III, named his only son George. Late in life, he ranted on more than one occasion that he took one look at his son and knew he was not good enough for his and his father's name.

George was a constant disappointment to Wild Bill. Born a sickly child, he never gained the robust athletic build of his father or grandfather. Wild Bill also chastised George for needing a brace to correct his walk, glasses to overcome astigmatism, and corrective orthodontics which were referred to as "train tracks," Not only did his father consider George's physical attributes a handicap, but Wild Bill constantly rode his only son about his lack of intellectual capabilities. While both Bill Senior and Wild Bill were Phi Beta Kappa, George never rose above mediocrity. Wild Bill constantly deemed George's academic failure as a slap in the face for a child who was given every opportunity to succeed. A greater disappointment had to have been George's college enrollment into an Ivy League school. Wild Bill and Bill Senior had been football captains and honors students at Texas University. Tradition, and millions in alumni dollars, mandated that an Algers enroll at TU. Wild Bill never stopped burning from that betrayal.

After school, George failed to distinguish himself from any other executive in his father's company. The only distinguishing feature remained his name, a fact that infuriated his father. In addition, George never enlisted in any form of military service, even as a reserve. Wild Bill served as a marine in World War II, even though he was twenty-seven years old. Renowned for his medals earned at the Battle of the Marne, Bill Senior would spin tales about his service in the War to End All Wars for days. George, unfortunately, bore the "misfortune" of being too young for Korea and too old to be drafted for Vietnam.

George finally distinguished himself by his interest in the aerospace industry and NASA. Wild Bill considered it George's "moon phase," but Apollo II had a significant impact on the thirty-three-year-old Algers man-child. He begged his father to invest and pursue space research. Although it appeased his son, Wild Bill recognized the lucrative nature of government contracts. After all, he had been working with the government for years in the petrochemical industry. Soon the Algers name was tied to space research and design, with young George cutting ribbons all around southeastern Texas.

Even after the Algers' made a name for themselves in the aerospace industry, in part due to George Algers, Wild Bill kept a tight leash on his son. George remained a figurehead. A young face to look at for a burgeoning new space program. It made sense to Wild Bill, but there was no way in hell that he would let George ever make a decision.

After a time, Wild Bill even grew tired of George interrupting during board meetings. First it was discouraged. Then no longer tolerated. Finally, George Algers was banned from the meetings. When counsel advised that George's presence was required pursuant to the company charter, Wild Bill brought an empty suit to the next board meeting and flung it over George's seat. The issue was never raised again.

His father's contempt had a predictable effect on George. He was always known as just George as opposed to Bill Senior or Wild Bill. At one time, during high school, he attempted numerous "crazy" stunts such as loading a cow into the girls' restroom or pulling fire alarms in an attempt to have people call him "Crazy George." However, upon being caught and held in detention after school, his father dubbed him "Stupid George." He never made a name for himself, nor tried again. He knew nothing he ever did is his life could live up to Will Bill or the Algers name, so he did not try. The bar had been raised too high for George, and he saw little reason to even make the effort to achieve any name for himself. That is until he met Elias St. Armand.

From one side of the mirror, it appeared to be a strange twist of fate. The National Aeronautics Space Administration had come under fire for several space shuttle failures coupled with astronomical budget overruns. Public outcry demanded an accounting. Consequently, NASA assembled a committee consisting of aerospace industry heads, other industry leaders, a few politicians, and a few citizens. The committee would meet several times, spend millions in research, and issue a report stating that although NASA was not out of control, it needed to follow more stringent quality standards and adhere to its budget. An obvious choice to serve on the NASA Oversight Committee was Houston's very own George W. Algers. A surprising selection was Elias St. Armand. Although he was more than qualified as a successful industry leader with years of experience with government contracts, Elias St. Armand rarely, if ever, accepted such selfless appointments. Elias only did what was best for Occidental. Although he always said what was best for Occidental was best for the whole world, insiders knew St. Armand was always only out for himself. That is why it was so surprising that Elias accepted this appointment. Occidental had nothing to do with the aerospace industry. Be that as it may, Elias St. Armand accepted NASA's invitation to serve on its Oversight Committee.

George Algers did not meet Elias St. Armand until the second committee meeting in Washington, D.C. The two exchanged pleasantries before the meeting; however, after the meeting, Elias invited George to join him for dinner in Georgetown. Algers could not refuse upon hearing the names of the two other dinner guests, Dr. T. K. Weisskoph and Dr. Daniel Ostrander, both from the renowned Jet Propulsion Lab at the California Technical Institute in Pasadena, California. The two were not only pioneers in their field, deep space exploration, but the experts in the field. Deep space exploration was a pet project of Algers, and as opposed to ninety-nine out of one hundred other people, he actually knew who Drs. Weisskoph and Ostrander were. It was as if someone threw George a personal birthday party. Elias St. Armand was visibly bored with conversations centered on nuclear-powered electronic propulsion systems and laser transponders. George Algers was in heaven. A bond had been forged.

Whenever Elias ventured to Texas he never failed to visit George. George reciprocated when he was in New York or D.C. It was Elias who first turned George on to politics. Once again it was very subtle at first. Elias stroked George's ego, and fed him stories of how much more he could help the aerospace industry as a man of political power as opposed to just financial power. Wild Bill also joined the game. He did not think much of his son, but he did not think much of politicians either, so why couldn't George be a politician? Lack of charisma or a personality was the obvious answer, but Wild Bill knew money could overcome such obstacles. Therefore, with Elias St. Armand prodding and Wild Bill Algers pushing, George W. Algers ran for governor of Texas.

The primary was a shoo-in. With Wild Bill's political and financial backing firmly behind his son, other legitimate candidates stepped aside. With a nomination in hand, the Algers began one of the nastiest, ugliest political races in history. Somehow Elias' campaign consultants were able to dig up fresh dirt and smear the feisty conservative incumbent, Abby Sherman, throughout the campaign. By November the once strong, resilient Governor Sherman had been ripped to shreds. An Algers was now governor.

Wild Bill liked the fact that his son was governor because it kept him in Austin. However, George kept coming home to oversee his office's pet project: a new deep space research lab in Houston. Other than the Algers Deep Space Research Lab, George Algers served two very uneventful terms as governor. Economic prosperity and a decrease in crime guaranteed an unprecedented third term. Elias wanted George Algers to become the first three-term governor in Texas for other reasons. Elias was grooming George for a higher office.

That calling came in the middle of George Algers' third term. Although George's popularity was undisputed, he was hardly a national political figure. That all changed when his party scheduled its convention in Houston. As the presiding governor, and a sure bet to deliver his state in the upcoming presidential election, George nabbed one of the coveted speakerships. Things changed even more in the months preceding the convention. The Ohio governor, Bob Fairchild, had sewn up the presidential nomination, but the other spot on the ticket remained wide open. In the months preceding the convention, George Algers' name popped up on the political screen as a potential running mate. There were others who were more popular, visible, and loyal to the party, but Algers' name had been thrown into the ring. As the convention neared, George Algers gained more national exposure. Sunday morning talk shows featured him touting educational reform and how he had won the battle against crime in Texas. With two weeks left before the convention, Elias positioned George as only one of two viable candidates for the vice-presidency.

Fairchild's people had made it clear that they did not want Algers. They wanted Texas, but did not want Algers. Elias was informed ten days before the convention that Fairchild was picking California Senator Mary Cunningham in the hopes of pulling off a miracle and carrying California in the general election. George Algers was visibly disappointed, but Elias ignored the news. He stroked George's ego and focused him on his keynote address. Five days before the convention, Senator Cunningham issued a press release stating that if she were asked to join the ticket she would decline for personal reasons. After the election, Senator Cunningham paid a small fine concerning a tax issue involving her nanny.

At the convention, Fairchild named George Algers as his vice presidential running mate. The Fairchild-Algers ticket lost California, but swept the South on Texan coattails to carry the day. Vice President George W. Algers relinquished his seat in Austin and moved to D.C.

Even before Algers was sworn in, the battle to stay in office had already begun. Fundraising, fundraising, fundraising! Money poured in hand over fist. Algers also raised money for senators and congressmen. Elias instilled in

George the fear that without money, one had no chance to stay in office. Elias knew George would do anything to stay in power.

Other than the two votes he had to cast, George Algers' first six years as vice president had been uneventful. Both votes had concerned the Occidental Group, although neither named Occidental per se. The first vote concerned the Department of Agriculture's Promotional Market Program. The second vote concerned funding for ethanol subsidies. For the Promotional Market Program, Occidental received governmental subsidies amounting to $400 million to sell their products overseas. The second vote gave Occidental millions to promote ethanol. Elias told him that both votes would be close in the Senate which required him to cast the tie-breaking vote. Vice President George Algers cast tie-breaking votes in favor of both programs, in favor of Occidental, in favor of Elias St. Armand, and in favor of his re-election war chest.

George Algers had no ethical problems in casting Occidental votes. It was not as if this was the first time he had taken money in exchange for wielding his political power. Hell, that was the only reason his father helped him become governor in the first place. Wild Bill had George remove so many pesky environmental regulations that he thought he was going to have Sienna Club reactionaries camping on his front lawn for the rest of his life. Elias and his father were right; this is how things got done. Money talks, and it talks louder with six or seven zeroes. By the time he became vice president, George Algers had been prepared for the power of the almighty dollar in politics, even on this grand scale.

What he was not prepared for was Wild Bill's reaction to his vote on the ethanol subsidy. Needless to say, spending tax dollars to find an alternative for oil did not please many Texans, much less Wild Bill Algers. Wild Bill was furious. "Stupid" was the kindest thing he had to say about his son. Furthermore, Wild Bill's health was failing. A life of abusing his body, especially his liver, had taken its toll. His doctors did not declare him terminal, but they cut everything out of his life that he believed made life worth living. The more ornery he became, the more he disparaged his only son.

Back when George made his way through the Houston social circles or from boardroom to boardroom, his father's rantings were merely an embarrassment. Even as governor of Texas, Wild Bill's tirades were deemed "colorful" and actually helped George by adding some color to his drab personality. But on a national stage, as Elias pointed out, his father had become a liability. "Colorful" relatives may play well with the folks back in Texas, but soccer moms and the eastern elite would not understand the ravings of Wild Bill Algers, especially when he described his son as "stupid", "an ignoramus," "a space idiot," and "the only Texan who did not know a three letter word for petroleum."

Elias was right. His father had become a liability. George even thought about committing the old man. But Elias told him to be patient, that these things just have a tendency of working themselves out. Sure enough, Elias was right again. Although it was his liver that gave him problems, Wild Bill Alger passed away in his sleep when his heart gave out. With the death of his father, the constant oppression George suffered from had also died. The beratement, cruelty, and insults were buried with the old man. No longer would his father...

George Algers' cellphone rang.

Before he answered, George knew it could only be Elias St. Armand.

"Hello, this is George Algers."

"George, you better be ready," demanded Elias St. Armand.

"I am," George obediently replied.

"The meeting is in a half-hour, and the car will be out front in fifteen minutes. I don't want you late for this, George."

"I won't be late. I'm ready."

"This is too important for one of your little screw-ups, George. You hear me, George?" Elias was unyielding.

"I understand."

"No screw-ups."

"I understand."

"And another thing, when we get there, Aaron and I will do all the talking.

Not a word from you."

"Not a word from me."

"Not a word. Even if they ask you a question."

"Not a word, even if they ask a question."

"Not a word, even if they ask a question."

"But don't stand there like some Texas yahoo. either."

"I understand."

"Look presidential."

"It happened?" George Algers sounded as if he were going to have a panic attack.

"Now don't get all flustered, George." Elias paused, then continued, "We talked about this, George. I need you to be a man. It is your day to shine, George. We've come a long way since NASA, and now we are here at the finish line. I just need you to cross it."

"But it's too soon."

"George, get a hold of yourself. You knew this was coming. We talked about it. This is what you dreamed of. You will be the most respected man in the world. More than your father, more than your grandfather, or any other yahoo Algers you can dig up. A hundred years from now, the only Algers anyone will know will be the one they are teaching about in grade school, President George Wadsworth Algers."

George was silent.

"Ten minutes, George, now get your ass down front."

"I am on my way."

# FORTY-FOUR

Chamoun Al Khouri slowly got back into his rental car. He had fully expected to be strip-searched and maybe even detained an hour or two just to see how he would react. Without these inconveniences, he would be in New York City by midday, hours before an alternate would even be considered. Even the Montreal Airport was more secure than the American border patrol. At least at the airport he had to walk through a metal detector, and they checked his luggage against his claim ticket. Here, at the U.S. border, all they had was a dog smelling his luggage. Chamoun had no fear of dogs.

Chamoun's first memory, the earliest moment he remembered in life, involved a dog. A dog and his older brother, Antonios. His brother kicked a ball to him. The dog chased the ball. The boys played in a small field by his childhood home in Zahle, in the Bekaa Valley in northwest Lebanon. The year was 1964, Antonios was ten, Chamoun was only four, but he remembered the moment vividly, as if it happened again every time he closed his eyes. Antonios stood tall, but lanky, in his jeans and no shirt. Chamoun, small, a runt for the most part, wore blue shorts and red T-shirt. His T-shirt had some cartoon character on it but that was the only part of his memory that was foggy. The shirt was bright red, but the character was fuzzy. Antonios was clear. He was laughing, smiling, pointing, and instructing Chamoun how to use both the inside and outside of his foot while kicking the ball. The day was warm, the sun was bright, and the fun was apparent. He remembered every rock, every tree, but could not remember the cartoon character on his T-shirt.

Chamoun opened his eyes. There was much he did remember. He never forgot any moment in the year 1975. That was the year he was supposed to visit his brother at the monastery in the Akkar District. He was going to stay there for a week. His mother hoped Chamoun would follow in his brother's footsteps: follow God, not evil; follow love, not hate; follow peace, not war.

However, Chamoun knew Antonios better than his mother. Antonios may have been a disciple of the Lord, but he was also a patriot of Lebanon. Antonios protested the existence of the autonomous PLO Zone. For five years, Lebanon had to share land with the Palestine Liberation Organization, even though they were admitted terrorists, and they intended to stake out a portion of the land for an independent state of their own. Antonios may have been a man of God, but he was a child of Lebanon and loved his native land. As a patriot, Antonios protested. Only the clothes changed when he became a man of God.

At fifteen years of age, Chamoun was worlds apart from his brother intellectually, spiritually, and ideologically. The younger brother worshipped the older brother, but the gap in age and distance from one another dictated separate interests. While Antonios read scriptures, prayed for hours at a time, and organized the latest rally, Chamoun attended to high school, dreamed of becoming a World Cup soccer star, and stared too long at the pretty girls. In 1975, all that changed.

In 1975, Hell invoked its wrath upon Lebanon. The PLO question drove a wedge between the Lebanese people pitting once peaceful neighbors against one another. A deeper wedge was driven between neighbors in the name of religion. Christians and Muslims were driven by stirred passions inspired by the Crusades to fight over the land of the Phoenicians. Soon the Civil War would destroy the country, but in 1975, passions, not violence, ruled. Lebanese Christians pitted themselves against Lebanese Muslims. The instability invited the stabilizing forces of its neighbor, Syria. In 1975, Syrian military forces entered the country, never to leave.

The political turmoil provided a backdrop for Chamoun's 1975. That year, Syrian-controlled Saika forces slaughtered Antonios Al Khouri, a Maronite monk, brother of Chamoun Al Khouri. It happened at the massacre at Deir Ashashe. Chamoun never visited his brother in the Akkar District, nor became a monk as his mother had hoped. Everything changed in 1975. After his brother's death, Chamoun sought immediate vengeance. It would not happen. His brother's close friends, fellow Maronite monks, fellow patriots, prevented this from occurring; or rather, they delayed the inevitable. Brother

Michel was dispatched to give the tragic news of Antonios' death. He stayed for several days with the Al Khouri family. He convinced young Chamoun that a warrior was a noble path to choose, however, not the only path. Chamoun was bent on fighting, but Brother Michel did not feel that passion. Michel knew that Chamoun was an excellent student. Michel convinced Chamoun that not all wars are fought with guns. He told Chamoun that a patriot with a gun as his only weapon was not much of a warrior. Brother Michel instructed Chamoun that the most valuable patriot he could be would be a patriot that could fight with his intellect as opposed to a gun. For a gun fires but one bullet at a time, but an intelligent mind has an unlimited arsenal. Brother Michel preached the value of intellect in the war Lebanon fought. In so doing, he convinced Chamoun to stay in school and excel in his studies.

Brother Michel echoed many of Antonios' preachings to young Chamoun. Their monastery taught the same thing: freedom by embracing the truth. The monks believed in a free Lebanon: free from Syrian tyranny; free from Palestinian insurrection; and, free from Israel's invasion. Michel believed that this freedom could only be achieved if Lebanon embraced the truth that they are not a nation of one people, but of many peoples. Too many reject their Arab heritage. Too many reject their Phoenician heritage. Too many rejected the Muslim influence on their heritage. Too many rejected the Christian influences on their heritage. He preached that unless the Lebanese embraced the truth of their heritage, which is a melting pot of religions, cultures, beliefs, and customs, Lebanon was doomed to a prolonged affliction. Michel said that with freedom comes responsibility. And unless Lebanon can accept the fact the price of their freedom would be the responsibility that their neighbor may not share their same culture, religion, beliefs, or customs, Lebanon was doomed to a permanent baptism of fire. But before one can embrace the truth behind freedom, one must be educated to truth. For only education will breed freedom; ignorance only breeds hate. Michel always quoted Christ, "You will know the truth, and the truth will set you free."

Chamoun followed Michel's advice. He did not seek vengeance for Antonios; he sought knowledge. Knowledge that would help him further his brother's cause. Unfortunately, that knowledge was first sought in war-torn Beirut.

The civil war personified itself in the city. La Ligne Verte, the Green Line, separated Beirut in two communities: Christian East Beirut and Muslim West Beirut. The Green Line obtained its name from the greenery which grew in streets that were destructed and abandoned in the no-man's-land between the warring Christian and Muslim communities. Beirut, the Paris of the Middle East, the financial capital of the region, had been reduced to a war zone where self-made warlords and street gangs dictated economic and political decisions. For the few years Chamoun studied at the International University in Beirut, he would like to say that Hell had a name on this Earth, and its name was Beirut.

Chamoun studied medicine in Beirut. He wanted to change his country for the better, but lacked the political and spiritual drive of his brother. If he could not heal the spirit, at the very least he could heal the body. As a doctor he could practice his own version of healing in his country. In his studies, he learned more than he cared to. For a few months during an internship, Chamoun had worked in a morgue, assisting autopsies. The dead bodies did not bother him even though he was what some people would call an emotional person. Chamoun reduced the corpses down to a clinical state. The body was merely a composite of organs, muscles, bones, and tissues; nothing more. The corpse was not a person, merely a body of parts.

Although his studies and internship were located in a dangerous city, Chamoun remained safe. He was smart. He stayed clear of the Green Line. Sometimes that was not enough. He had heard too many stories of the "keepers." The "keepers" were men from the Muslim side of the Green Line who kidnapped people from the Christian side. Everyone knew who the "keepers" really were; they were Shiite Muslims who captured men and women for torture camps. Too many times Chamoun saw a corpse at the morgue with electrical burns on the body's fingers, toes, or genitals. The tortured bodies came from the other side of the Green Line, either dumped or exchanged for others. It was the morgue's job merely to identify the body, usually through posting photos or dental records. The bodies were those of students or

Christian rebels fighting the honorable resistance. Many of the bodies were young, too young. As disturbing as the bodies were with their obvious demarcations from torture, the causes of death listed on their death certificates made little sense. Young boys, who had obviously been tortured, even to a layman's eyes, were listed as dying from "cardiac failure" or "pneumonia."

Chamoun had never seen his brother's corpse. There was little left of Antonios' body, and therefore he was cremated immediately. Failing to see his brother's lame body was probably what impacted Chamoun the most when he saw Brother Michel's corpse on the table in his morgue. The lifeless body lying before him was that of a man he had admired and tried to follow. There was no secret that Chamoun had transferred the love, respect, and kinship he held for Antonios to Brother Michel. Consequently, Brother Michel's "cardiac failure" death dredged up every suppressed memory of Deir Ashashe and the mindless slaughter of innocent citizens, most notably that of his brother Antonios.

Brother Michel's body was riddled with bruises. His face had been disfigured almost beyond the point of recognition. His nose and jaw had been broken, his gums shredded, and both of his ears were missing. His chest and arms revealed burn marks, some electrical, some were from cigarettes. His fingernails and toenails were missing. The bones in his right ankle and left knee had been shattered. His hands had been left intact probably to allow him to write propaganda for his torturers. The physical abuse Brother Michel endured was overwhelming; however, that did not compare to how he actually died.

The inflammation of his nostrils and the appearance that Brother Michel had suffocated to death, troubled Chamoun. Tests established had also found extremely high levels of concentrations of acetylcholine in the nerve endings in his body, specifically his respiratory tract. His respiratory muscles had become so over-stimulated from the acetylcholine that they simply gave out, contracting and collapsing all the muscles which helped him breath. In layman's terms, Brother Michel's own muscles had choked him to death. It was evident from Chamoun's autopsy that after Brother Michel had been tortured for days, he had also been used as a guinea pig in some chemical warfare "experiments." Experiments which cost him his life, a life not worth living considering the torture he had endured.

Brother Michel's death robbed Chamoun of his soul. He was not enraged, but a cold hate fell upon him. A hate that did not need to be fed or fueled. His memories were fuel enough for the fire which forever burned inside of him.

As Chamoun drove south on Interstate 87 he felt the fire burn. He knew it would always burn. There were those who sought vengeance for Syrian and militant Muslim atrocities such as the massacre of the Christian village of Deir Ashashe or the secret tortures and experiments of the "keepers." They believed that they would be free from the fires in their bellies when Lebanon was free from occupation. Chamoun wanted a free and sovereign Lebanon, but he would not fool himself into believing that the end of the Syrian occupation would end his pain. The end of the occupation may end the pain of some patriots or Lebanese citizens, but Chamoun knew his pain would endure. For he would fight to the end, not the end of the occupation, but until the end of his life. As he drove south to New York City, he knew that the only thing that would end the hate deep inside of him would be his last breath.

# FORTY-FIVE

George Algers thought Elias could arrange anything.

The Secret Service detail assigned to him were the ones Elias had picked out for him. For this trip, the detail was kept to a minimum. A surprising minimum considering he was officially in New York City to visit inner city schools that were in the President's Inner City Outer Reading program. Elias was always able to arrange for this minimum detail when he wanted to meet with the Vice President away from D.C. Even though he knew he owed everything to Elias, it frightened George that Elias could arrange anything.

It was not as if he liked Bob Fairchild. They said everybody liked President Bob Fairchild. Well, George Algers did not. He definitely was one person who did not like Bob Fairchild. And Fairchild by no means held any love for Algers. He even admitted as much after that ethanol vote, when Fairchild asked him how in the hell a Texan could vote for a substitution for oil. The President's policy was clear: no more pork. And an ethanol subsidy certainly was pork. So one could safely assume that the Vice President would carry out the President's policy. It was a no-brainer, or so the President thought. After the vote, the President yelled at Algers for two hours straight, ranting about how it would look for a president to veto a bill his own vice president had voted for. The initial vote for the ethanol subsidy attracted little media attention, but a veto of the bill would be a media frenzy. They were stuck with the subsidy for two years. The two had not had a substantive conversation since the ethanol vote.

Even though the President and Vice President had not talked, the message from the President's office was abundantly clear. The President would not support a ticket that included George Algers. Whether it be for health reasons, personal reasons, or his father's death, George Algers was to make a graceful exit. He would be honored for serving his country and be allowed to return to Texas with "whatever dignity people believed he had," the President had told Roland Miller. In meeting with Elias St. Armand and George Algers, Roland Miller softened the blow the best he could. It was that very day that Elias had told George that he would be president within the next six months. What George Algers did not realize was how fast six months could tick off the calendar.

The skyscraper at 120 Broadway did not readily distinguish itself in the Manhattan skyline. However, its seventy-first floor conference room offered a tremendous view of Manhattan. From this perch the city was a game board where the occupants of the conference room could carve up blocks, trade them, sell them, or just remove them.

"Elias, come in," the familiar Blueblood Yankee voice of the Savile Row man commanded.

"Gentlemen," Elias paused, "not everyone is here."

The Savile Row man stood by the boardroom table, flanked by the familiar Englishman and two other older white men.

"Given your urgency, I am quite impressed by the showing, especially Otto here, who arrived only moments ago from Bonn."

"Is this some kind of joke?" Elias shot back.

The Savile Row man waited for Elias' tantrum to begin.

"You two knock it off." The Englishman stood up, straightening his charcoal grey Italian suit. "Where the hell is that button?" The Englishman fumbled around the end of the table. "Bravissimo."

Three HDTV screens rose from the table revealing two elder Asian men and one fair-haired man. Other than the fair-haired man, all of the men looked as if they were in their seventies or eighties. One of the Asian men may have been older. The fair-haired man appeared as if he could be in his mid-fifties.

Elias smiled.

"We are all here." The Savile Row man addressed Elias, "You have our undivided attention."

Elias introduced his team while they sat down at the other end of the table,

"There is no need for an introduction for," Elias paused, "President George W. Algers, or for that matter, Aaron Golde."

Aaron Golde nodded his head while Algers smiled awkwardly.

"And to my right is John Kerr of Miller and White, the final member of my Bi-lateral Commission."

The Savile Row man shook his head.

Even the peacemaker, the Englishman, appeared confused by the pronouncement, "Did I miss something?"

"I will get into that later. Gentlemen," Elias began to strut around the room, "you are probably wondering why I gathered you here."

Again the perplexed looks from one end of the table. The Savile Row man, still standing, was more annoyed than perplexed.

Elias continued, "I have come here to offer you something no man, not even Jesus Christ, has been able to accomplish. A feat no one army has been able to enforce. A feat that is attempted every four or five or six years as if it were a rite of passage for world leaders. A feat..."

"Elias, my dear fellow," the Englishman could take no more, "I can appreciate the dramatics; however, we are, as you are, all extremely busy men who never underscore brevity."

Unwilling to let the interruption interfere with how he had planned to unveil his plan, Elias merely waved his hand at the distinguished British gentleman and continued, "A feat only I can deliver." Elias paused, "Peace in the Middle East."

One of the Asian men began speaking Mandarin Chinese at a rapid pace. The other began speaking Japanese. The fair-haired man and the man called Otto remained unaffected by the news. The Savile Row man glanced at the other American.

"Gentlemen, the Middle East contains two-thirds of the world's proven oil reserves and well over one-third of its natural gas reserves. Unfortunately, it contains military proliferation in Iran, Israel, Syria, Algeria, Egypt, Libya, and the Sudan. Our friends in Israel soon will not be the only nuclear power. Thanks to my operation, Iraq is no longer an issue. Iran still has the technology base they need in order to build chemical, biological, nuclear, and radiological weapons; all with long-range delivery systems. Saudi Arabia has already bought long-range Chinese missiles. Egypt has intensified its covert missile and chemical-biological program. Gentlemen, this still is a powder keg ready to blow. I propose we let it blow a little more."

"Elias, you have our attention, but you are not making much sense," the Brit interrupted again.

Elias waved him off again and continued, "Actually, it is like what they do to prevent forest fires. Call it a controlled burn. I want Syria to burn."

Restless, the Savile Row man pulled his gold pocket watch from his navy blue pinstriped vest.

"Elias, why couldn't this wait until next month's meeting?"

"Because it is already happening," Elias responded.

The Savile Row man's head turned from his watch to Elias, "What do you mean it is already happening?"

"Congress has approved a financial aid package to Lebanon in the amount of thirty billion to repair the country's infrastructure. Of course, there is the contingency that Syria must pull out of Lebanon. Syria, of course, will not pull out and will continue to finance Muslim terrorist groups in Lebanon. As you know, Syria even turned down a three-billion-dollar bribe, ten percent of the aid, if they pulled out. And there still is the issue of war criminals hiding there and maybe weapons of mass destruction."

"Yes, Elias, we know that. But as you know, that money is not going anywhere because you have not been able to buy up enough votes to override President Fairchild's eventual veto of the bill."

"That no longer is an issue." Elias' response was quick and terse.

"What do you mean, no longer an issue?" the Englishman inquired.

"An assassin's bullet killed President Robert Hamilton Fairchild only hours ago."

The fair-haired man and the man called Otto remained unaffected by the news.

The Beijing representative smiled.

The Japanese representative shouted into his monitor.

The two Americans and the Englishman immediately rose, shocked by the news.

"Are you insane?" roared the Savile Row man.

"Clearly not," Aaron Golde finally addressed the Board. "Settle down, gentlemen, nothing has changed. Fairchild had always been a rogue. We merely have consolidated power."

Aaron Golde's gentle voice calmed the room to a degree.

Elias positioned himself behind George Algers. He put his hand on the Vice President's shoulder.

"I now have the White House," raising the palm of his other hand as if cupping something Elias continued, "and Congress."

Golde interjected, "Meaning, of course, there will be no presidential veto."

Enraged, the Savile Row man pointed his finger at Elias.

"You killed the President of the United States so you could piss away some money to Syria?"

"There will be some changes around here," Elias shot back.

"Gentlemen, gentlemen," the Englishman intervened.

Shaking his head at the Savile Row man the Brit continued, "Elias, we have heard no such news; surely you jest."

"The news has just been released that the President has taken ill and is confined in a San Francisco hospital."

"And?" the Englishman inquired.

Aaron Golde continued, "We have confirmed the attempt was made. If it had not been successful, surely all news reports would have confirmed that fact. However, since we know the attempt and know the President is 'confined', the only conclusion is that Roland Miller has been able to quarantine the situation."

The Englishman looked over at the other American who nodded.

"But he can't keep a lid on it forever."

Elias rubbed George Algers' shoulders.

"We will need confirmation," responded the Englishman.

"We are working on that now," responded Golde before he sat back down.

The Savile Row man sat down at the head of the boardroom table, behind him hung a large portrait of himself sitting in a burgundy leather chair in a fictional boardroom. He put his elbows on the table and clasped his hands together. Cocking his head to the side, a posture he always used to mock an adversary, the Savile Row man set his eyes on Elias St. Armand and said, "Now why would a Lebanese bastard like yourself want to give so much money to Syria?"

"The money is not going to Syria," answered Golde.

Still not taking his eyes off Elias, the Savile Row man retorted, "If you send money to Lebanon, you are sending it to Syria. It is a simple banking transaction. Whatever money goes through that puppet government in Beirut winds up in Damascus. Elias, you know that."

"That is why the money is not going into banks," snapped Elias.

Aaron Golde again addressed the Board, "Next week Congress will have another vote considering the thirty billion dollars in aid. The money which had been previously set aside to fund rebuilding Lebanon's infrastructure will be appropriated to finance Operation Cedar Strike, a multinational military invasion of Lebanon and Syria."

"A what?" the Savile Row man again responded in disbelief. The others listened to Aaron Golde.

"The situation parallels Kosovo, only in reverse which of course helps in the polls. Ever since the Israeli's pullout, Lebanese Christians have been victims of an ethnic cleansing of Lebanon by Muslim extremists. Of course, the numbers are not the same as they were in Kosovo; but on the other hand, Christians are the victims which, of course, will ignite and unite Western passions."

The other American spoke, "It will never work; the numbers are not there."

Golde continued, "Any numbers will do to justify the country's moral compass, the difficult part is to sell to the American public the necessity of the military action."

Elias interrupted his counsel, "We can work out the numbers after the invasion. We just need to get in there and wipe out the Muslims and the Syrians. We will be able to document all kinds of atrocities. We just need to tear the whole place down and restore it to its past glory."

"After Operation Cedar Strike, additional moneys will be funneled into Beirut from the United States, European Union, IMF, World Bank, and others. Within ten years Beirut will be the financial capital of the Middle East. With a firm U.S. presence in Beirut in the form of capital, technology, and of course, military aid, the region will not only stabilize, but flourish. Additional military bases in Iraq and Afghanistan will be required."

"No one will ever buy it," again stated the distinct Boston accent.

Aaron Golde walked to the window at the other end of the table. Turning to face the Board with the Manhattan skyline as his backdrop, he responded to the rumblings.

"It is not a matter of selling it or having people buy it. Peace in this region has been sought since the cradle of civilization. Everyone wants it. Everyone has always wanted it, except the power brokers who require instability to centralize their power. Attrition is removing some of these despots from power, but now we are in a unique place in history. Removing the unstable factors within these rogue nations is within our grasp. Israel is for it. Britain is in tow so NATO will comply. France, Russia and China," Aaron noticed that one of the screens had gone blank, "will not stand in our way. The time is now."

"How feasible is this?" inquired the Englishman.

"The Mossad have had a plan for over twenty years which they have revised yearly pursuant to technological advancements. Our military advisers have revised Israel's plans and have determined a ninety-six percent success rate with land forces stabilizing all borders within four days of air strikes. The whole operation would last ten days. Collateral damage, of course, could be excessive, but that is expected with these extremists."

"Ten days?" the Englishman repeated in disbelief.

"Ten days. The networks won't like it, but Syria will fold and deal quick as opposed to run and hide like Saddam. Of course the infrastructure will take years. Military bases would immediately be set up in Beirut and Tripoli."

The man with the Boston accent again spoke up, "Why would Americans tolerate American soldiers dying in Beirut again? It makes no sense."

The Savile Row man nodded in agreement.

"I believe it was Locke who said, 'There is nothing more aspiring than to see the easiness with which the many are governed by the few,'" misquoted Elias St. Armand.

Elias strutted again, this time over to the window by Aaron Golde.

"I will tell you why." He continued, "At rush hour tonight, in about eight hours, numerous sarin bombs will detonate in New York City killing thousands of this city's citizens. Nasty stuff that sarin gas. Thousands more will linger on their brink of death for days. The television ratings will be out of this world. Of course, it will be discovered that this was an act of terrorism sponsored by Islamic extremists based in Lebanon and financed by Syria. Operation Cedar Strike will be deemed a necessity, probably even a compromise of sorts, with those who will demand direct action against Syria."

Still sitting, and still with his hands clasped, the Savile Row man calmly said, "You're insane, simply put, you are insane."

Again Aaron Golde intervened, "This action has been as calculated as any other action this board has taken. The money has been there for months. After obtaining the necessary votes, the President was the only obstacle. Now he no longer is a factor in this equation. Granted, these final steps have moved at a rapid pace, but nothing can be further from the truth than to label these actions as irrational."

The Englishman spoke out, "Aaron, you know you could have consulted us."

"It was not necessary," Elias defiantly declared. "The four of us will be added to the Board of the Council on International Relations. I, of course, will carry George's proxy. My Bilateral Commission has had a ninety-five percent success rate in elections. Other than Minnesota, we carried the day yesterday. Occidental now owns a majority in the House and the Senate. With the addition of President Algers, we control American politics. Through Occidental I have helped this board on countless occasions. Now that my sphere of influence has increased, so shall my mandate."

"Cut the crap, Elias." The Savile Row man stood up again and spoke,

"He won't survive."

"Why?"

"All the evidence will show that the 'Shakespeare Killer' killed one more lawyer, the President."

With an ear-to-ear grin on his face, Elias left the boardroom with the others.

"Basically, you are telling us we have no choice."

Anxious not to have a line drawn in the sand, the diplomatic Brit jected, "If what you say you can deliver, of course, we welcome it with arms. Peace in the Middle East. Well, my friend's holdings in America will be worth ten fold in no time."

The Englishman patted the Savile Row man's back and continued, ' Aaron, you have dropped a lot on us and given us no time to react understanding is that this afternoon's event is inevitable?" His eye raised on the word 'inevitable.' "Be that as it may, it would be gracious if we knew how to elude this dreadful gas. Dear Otto traveled such a loi to be gassed."

"I suggest Otto leave," Elias cavalierly responded.

"It would not be a bad idea to leave the city; however, no one in thi will be affected. In order to maximize the repercussions, the event w place in a mass transit system," Aaron responded.

"There is no chance in delaying this until we have a little more digest and prepare?" the Englishman further inquired.

"We are unable to contact the individuals even if we desired to do

"This meeting is over," declared the Savile Row man as he pres button lowering the HDTV screens back into the boardroom table. C the man with the Boston accent exited the conference room through behind the Savile Row man.

"Elias, you and Aaron will stay in town. There is much we need out," the Englishman mentioned as the four members of Elias St. A self-proclaimed Bilateral Commission made their way to the front d

"I expect to hear from you this evening," responded Elias.

"Oh, Elias," the Englishman stopped the four with his voice and ued, "Whatever happened to your missing documents?"

Elias turned back to the Savile Row man and the Englishman. "There was nothing to worry about. The kid had mailed them to A whole time."

"Whatever happened to Farrell?"

# FORTY-SIX

"What time is it?"

"O-nine-hun...," the civilian-dressed military attaché assigned to Peter Farrell paused, "about 9:30."

"What is your name by the way?" Peter asked.

"Morgan, sir."

"Morgan?"

"Jack Morgan, sir."

"Jack Morgan," Peter paused, "this is Sara Ahrens."

"Nice to meet you," Sara politely responded shaking the military attaché's hand.

The three of them had plenty of room in the back of the limousine which slowly navigated the crowded Manhattan streets.

"I like the tinted windows," commented Peter in an attempt to make small talk.

"The tinted windows are bullet proof. The chassis is armor plated. Basically, this limo is a mini tank, reserved for foreign dignitaries and V.I.P.'s shuttling to and from Fort Hamilton to Manhattan."

On this particular trip, the V.I.P.'s were Peter and Sara.

"Where is this safe house anyway?" Sara asked.

"It is actually a hotel," replied Morgan.

"It's not gross?" Sara scrunched up her face with the word 'gross.'

"No ma'am, it's very upscale, but deserted."

"The base actually owns it, but rents two floors out for appearance sake. It has all the modern amenities and then some. No one would be able to gain entrance into the building with a weapon or perceived weapon without us detecting the device."

"Sounds pretty safe to me," Peter replied.

"Each floor is staffed with a dozen military personnel. Each room has a monitor channel where the guest can view visitors waiting at the front desk. A visitor cannot enter the facility without a guest pass. Anyone accompanying a guest must pass two photographic identification checkpoints in the lobby alone. A guest card is the only means available to access rooms, hallways, elevators, or stairwells."

"OK, I said it sounds great."

"Once we reach the hotel your safety is virtually assured."

"Virtually?" Sara asked.

"There has never been an incident at the facility."

"Let's hope we do not blow a perfect record," Sara said with conviction as the limousine slowly passed New York City's Grand Central Terminal.

---

One hundred and fifty years ago, 42nd Street was anything but the center of Manhattan. However, the New York Central Railroad, formed in 1853, built its transfer point at the 42nd Street location. When the decision was made to build a new Grand Central Terminal, none other than the "Commodore" Cornelius Vanderbilt himself dictated that this would be the location. Setting all ego aside, the Commodore could not have envisioned that Grand Central Terminal would become the world's most famous and busiest train stations, serving over five hundred thousand people every day commuting to upstate New York or to Connecticut or one of the many subway lines. Throughout its history, Grand Central ushered trains across America from New York to Los Angeles. Air travel finally regulated it to the voluminous commuter travel in today's world.

Rising between Lexington and Vanderbilt Avenues on 42nd Street, Grand Central's exterior is a tribute to the Beaux Arts. Trapped under the steel and glass skyscrapers, the south façade's clock stands defiant with the gods Minerva and Hercules at its sides. Above the clock, a winged Mercury—the god of speed, traffic, and the transmission of intelligence—takes flight with a soaring eagle.

Below the gods lie three entrances to the terminal. At one side entrance between the curb and the terminal's revolving doors, a newsman hacks dailies from the stacks of newspapers which barricade him neatly. He has carefully situated himself just below the terminal's steel awning to keep his wares dry. A slow and cool morning has him sitting down, protected only by a baseball cap and a navy blue hooded sweatshirt. The passersby, commuters, and tourists ignore the man and his newspapers as they enter Grand Central Terminal from one of south side's corner entrances.

Stepping inside, the marble splendor of the Main Concourse is revealed. The one hundred twenty-five-foot vaulted ceilings impress upon the traveler that he is waiting for his train outside, especially given the painted ceiling with the gold constellations of the zodiac embedded in a marine blue background. Modeled after the Gare d'Orsay in Paris, the platforms and waiting areas were combined under one roof with travelers descending down staircases from the Main Concourse to board their trains. The Main Concourse's majestic marble stairs descending from Vanderbilt Avenue also borrow from the City of Lights. Reminiscent of Charles Garnier's Paris Opera, the marble stairway, flecked with gold separates in two, allows a spectator to again take in the splendor of the Main Concourse without having yet to step on the main floor.

The main floor of the concourse is flanked by platforms and their tracks on either side. The marble and gold-trimmed ticket windows line the east side with commuters lined ten deep at windows to buy tickets to avoid the afternoon rush hour. Above the ticket windows, arrival and departure information changes every few minutes on the massive board, clicking as new information becomes available. In the center of the Main Concourse, the only object not moving among the flow of the sea of people is the circular information kiosk. Above the pamphlets, schedules, and individuals in the kiosk who are constantly harangued by impatient travelers, stands a golden ball with four clock faces telling time to travelers coming from any direction.

Off the Main Concourse floor, a stream of commuters flows down the escalators to the subway system. On one subway platform far below the elegant Main Concourse of the Grand Central Terminal, stands a man who had just spent part of his morning walking about the station undisturbed. The man, of obvious Middle Eastern descent but with no distinguishing features, is dressed in wrinkled, stained, and slightly soiled olive green slacks. A windbreaker covers up his T-shirt. The individual looks up and down the platform one more time before he boards the number six train back to Harlem.

———◦•◦———

As the limousine neared its destination, Sara interrupted the discomforting silence, "Peter, I almost forgot."

Sara pulled the folded piece of paper from her breast pocket.

"I found this surfing the web up at the cabin. Redwood didn't think it was anything. Actually he thought I was acting crazy."

Peter unfolded the piece of paper and began to read it.

"I think it's from your friend, Jimmy, back in St. Louis. See, Big Hank's nephew."

"I think you may have something, Sara."

Peter looked around the cab of the limo.

"What are you looking for?" Morgan asked.

"I thought you guys had all the 'modern amenities?'" Peter asked his military attaché.

"What are you looking for?" responded Morgan, this time in a less than helpful tone.

"Is there a laptop or some type of PC in here?"

Morgan pressed a button on the armrest which disengaged a panel behind the driver's seat. He pulled a laptop from behind the panel and handed it to Peter.

"Cool," Peter said as he opened the laptop.

"Does it have Internet access?" Sara asked.

"Of course." Morgan turned the screen toward him, touched the touch pad, and instructed, "There you go, you are online."

"Cool."

Peter had a new toy.

Peter began typing furiously. In any chat rooms discussing the "Shakespeare Killer," Peter typed the following message:

*Dear Big Hank's Nephew:*
 *Need to talk to you ASAP. Do not mail package I left you!*
*Please contact at this address as soon as possible.*
                    *-Saw You In BH's Courtroom*

"There, now we play the waiting game," Peter said as he finished typing.

"How long will it take?" asked Sara.

"Depends on what he is doing."

Peter squinted his eyes, then shoved his hand into his pocket.

"Here it is," declared Peter as he removed a business card from his wallet. Peter typed in the message one more time.

The Manhattan traffic had not relented and the large limousine was not exactly the type of vehicle that could dart in and out of traffic. The next fifteen minutes and one-quarter of a mile consisted of an awkward silence. Peter held Sara's hand.

The screen made a noise similar to a buzz, but a lighter pitch.

Peter opened the e-mail.

*Dear Saw You In BH's Courtroom,*
*Excellent name. Figured it could only be you. I assumed I was not going to hear from you. They got BH and I don't know what to do. Too late on the package, too. It left yesterday as we discussed. However, you said an extra copy never hurts so I made one for insurance reasons. Please advise.*
                    *–Big Hank's Nephew*

Peter's fingers worked fast and furiously.

*Dear Big Hank's Nephew:*
 *I did not know about BH. I am sorry. Obviously you know to*

*be careful. You earned a scholarship to wherever you want to enroll*
*for making copies. Can you scan them into a zip file for me? How long*
*will that take? I will also need you for distribution.*
                              *-SYIBHC*

After a moment or two, Peter received a response.

*Dear SYIBHC:*
   *When I said they got BH, I did not mean he was offered a new job; he*
*was terminated. If I follow in his footsteps, I will not need any scholarship.*
*I just need to know where to leave the remaining materials.*
                              *-BHN*

*Dear BHN:*
   *I understand where you are coming from, believe me. BH told me*
*I could depend on you. He also told me, and I am sure he told you, none*
*of the ugliness is ever going to get better unless each person helps to clean*
*up their block. Your block is just bigger than most.*
                              *-SYIBHC*

A response did not come right away. Sara, who had been reading over
Peter's shoulder, squeezed his hand. Jimmy's response followed.

*Dear SYIBHC:*
*You have no right to say that.*
                              *-BHN*

Before Peter could respond, Jimmy Powell sent another message.
*Dear SYIBHC:*
   *It will take me two, maybe three hours to scan these, maybe*
*sooner, if I find a capable sheet feeder. I will contact you then.*
                              *-BHN*

"I owe that kid," Peter exclaimed after he read Jimmy Powell's message.

"I am sure the hotel will have another laptop, or can Peter have this one?" Sara asked Morgan.

"There will be one in the room," Morgan responded, "but he can have this one, too."

"I'll take this just in case."

"Speaking of the hotel, here we are," Morgan said as the limousine pulled in front of a small, but elegant, hotel entrance on Madison Avenue between the Grand Central Terminal and St. Patrick's Cathedral.

Just as the limousine stopped and Morgan opened the door, there was a large crash. Morgan flew out the door. Peter and Sara were tossed about the cab of the limousine.

Peter and Sara heard gunfire. Peter pushed Sara to the floor of the limo and tried to survey the situation. There was now gunfire coming from the outside the door. Peering in the front of the limousine, Peter could see that the collision had shattered half the windshield. Peter heard screams from the street as he saw that the driver had been knocked unconscious; the military attaché in the driver's seat had been shot.

"Peter!" Sara cried out.

"I'm right here," replied Peter as he was on all fours above Sara on the seat.

"Morgan wants us to get out!"

There was a screeching of tires as the black sports utility vehicle backed away from the limo about fifteen feet.

"Farrell, now!" Morgan yelled at Peter.

Peter and Sara crawled from the limousine onto the sidewalk.

"Go down there!" ordered military attaché Jack Morgan as he pointed down the street toward a line of cars parked along the side of Madison Avenue

The first collision had knocked the limo sideways, perpendicular to the entrance of the hotel. Two security men from the hotel began to open fire on the other vehicle. Jack Morgan had barricaded himself behind the chassis of the limousine and also fired upon the attacking vehicle. Peter and Sara scurried away from the limousine, firmly holding each other's hands.

Peter stopped.

"I forgot the laptop," he said.

Sara pulled at him.

Peter looked back to see the laptop in pieces at Jack Morgan's feet.

"Come on, Peter," cried Sara as she tugged him along.

The black sports utility vehicle's wheels screeched again as it sped toward the limousine. Gunfire from Morgan and the security officers did not stop the oncoming vehicle. Morgan dove out of the way just before the vehicle came hurling into the front end of the limousine. Two men jumped from the vehicle and returned fire upon the security men from the hotel.

Sara and Peter had caught up to the rest of the screaming tourists, shoppers, and onlookers.

"There."

Peter pointed to East 45th Street. The light had just changed. People unaware of the violence on Madison Avenue crossed the street moving west on 45th Street. Peter saw exactly what he wanted to see, crowds. Crowds of people where Sara and Peter could hide.

# FORTY-SEVEN

George Algers sweated profusely. Despite Elias' assurances, he did not like how the meeting went. George thought it was a disaster. Everyone was shooting daggers at him. After all, he didn't kill President Fairchild; Elias St. Armand had him killed. He did not know that Elias would actually do it. George corrected himself; he did not know that Elias would actually follow through with his plans. After all, Elias always talked a big game. Would George want to be governor of Texas? Would George want to be vice president? Would George want to be president?

"Get me some water," the Vice President whispered back to one of his Secret Service agents.

"Mr. Vice President?" asked the school district's superintendent as she attempted to get Algers' attention.

"Yes?" George Algers responded.

"One of the children asked you how can we stop the violence in our schools," the superintendent repeated the child's question.

"Yes?" Algers responded again with a blank look on his face.

The superintendent leaned over again to the Vice President and said, "You know Mr. Vice President, what can we do about the recent shootings that have happened in our nation's schools?"

Still caught off guard, Algers responded, "Back in Texas, many of our teachers carry guns themselves and that seems to work."

The whole classroom became quiet.

Recognizing his blunder, the Vice President continued, "But what works in Texas may not work elsewhere. What is important to remember is that our administration is against gun violence, especially in schools."

The uneasiness in the classroom eased somewhat.

The superintendent offered, "How about we have the Vice President read us another story?"

The classroom erupted in cheers.

The Vice President smiled back to the kids then leaned back to the Secret Service agent.

"Where is that water?"

———✦———

Back on top of the 120 Broadway Building in the conference room overlooking Manhattan, the Englishman and the Savile Row man bickered until they were interrupted.

"Sir."

A middle-aged man in a two-piece grey herringbone suit entered the room.

"Yes," the Savile Row man responded as he turned toward the voice.

"Mr. Miller is here," the middle-aged man stated.

"Send him in, send him in," ordered the Savile Row man as he turned back to the Englishman. "It is about time."

The two men turned toward the door as Roland Miller entered the room.

"Ahh, the Michelangelo of modern American politics."

"Gentlemen," said Miller as he nodded at the two men.

None of the men sat down.

"We need answers, Roland," the Savile Row man demanded.

"How do I know that the CIR is not involved with Elias St. Armand?" Roland cautiously chose his words.

Frustrated again with another man who entered his boardroom with a brazen attitude, the Savile Row man raised his blue-blooded New York Yankee voice in response to the question, "Of course the CIR is involved with Elias St. Armand. Occidental has proven particularly useful in the United States as you are well aware."

He continued, "But if you are asking if we are involved with this harebrained scheme against President Fairchild, then you are as loony as he is."

The Savile Row man also chose his words carefully.

"How can I be sure the CIR had no advance knowledge of St. Armand's plans?" Roland asked.

"No one had any idea of what he was planning," responded the Savile Row man.

"Listening to the two of you is like listening to two old women from Sicily unwilling to reveal their secret olive oil recipes," interrupted the Englishman. Turning to Miller, the Englishman continued, "We only found out this morning about Elias' attempt on the President's life. Was he successful?"

"Yes," Miller responded without hesitation.

"The fool is going to cost us China and this could lead to the re-unification of the Soviet Union," the Savile Row man blurted out at the news of the President's assassination.

"Is Algers involved?" Miller asked.

The Englishman nodded again.

Roland Miller hesitated before he asked another name.

"John Kerr?"

The Englishman nodded a final time.

Miller shook his head.

"What are we going to do about Elias and his little 'Bilateral Commission?'" asked the Savile Row man, already knowing the Englishman's point of view but seeking Miller's input.

"Bilateral Commission?"

"It is what Elias calls his little Lebanese conspiracy."

Again Miller appeared to be confused.

"What are we going to do about him?" the Savile Row man asked again.

"Well," Roland Miller began, "George Algers is completely unacceptable."

"That's a given," responded the Savile Row man.

"What is the purpose of this Bilateral Commission?" asked Miller.

"His little group," responded the Englishman "wants to exercise power over the United States and the Middle East."

"I assume the CIR is not amused by Elias dictating foreign policy," Miller slyly chided the two board members of the Council on International Relations.

"The little imp has us by the..."

"We have hardly had any time to react to the situation," the Englishman interrupted before the Savile Row man could finish his sentence.

"The two of you have yet to decide how to play this out."
Miller challenged the two men equal in his age as well as stature.

"Do not belittle yourself, Roland. It's unbecoming," said the Savile Row man.

"As usual, you are correct, Roland," the Englishman admitted. "Occidental or this Bilateral Commission, whatever you want to call it, is a beast out of control. And the only way to slay a beast is to cut off the head of the serpent. Elias St. Armand must be retired, immediately and permanently."

"How long until the President's death notice?" asked the Englishman.

"Twenty-four hours, tops."

"Twenty-four hours until that idiot Algers becomes president," the Savile Row man said in disgust. "After that he'll be unreachable for weeks, months."

"Given the time frame, Roland, we will need your help," the Englishman interjected as he moved back to the window gazing at the art deco Occidental Tower halfway down the Manhattan skyline. "We cannot reach Elias in that time frame, but someone you know can."

Without showing a muscle of emotion, Roland Miller uttered aloud the name, "Peter Farrell."

---

The limousine carrying Elias St. Armand and Aaron Golde merged back into traffic. It had been John Kerr's first ride with the two men together in public. He had assured the two that all the loose ends would be tied up, and they would. Time was of the essence. Standing on the sidewalk, Kerr put his earpiece in and hit the speed dial on his cellphone.

"It's Kerr. What are your people doing?"
Kerr shook his head in disbelief.

"How the hell could your people have screwed this up, Watson? There were only three possible locations, so you knew it was going to be one of them."
Kerr shook his head again.

"Of course it's safe, I just don't have the time to get back to my office. We are on a tight schedule here. I need his body, and I need it fast. There is no more time for mistakes."

Kerr nodded, agreeing with the voice on the other end.

"It better happen in the next couple hours."

John Kerr threw the cellphone in the trash and checked his watch.

Across the street Andriy Kravenko watched Kerr hail a cab.

---

Peter kept looking over his shoulder as he negotiated 42nd Street's sidewalk with Sara in tow. Although he believed that no one had followed them from the incident in front of the hotel, he did not want to take any chances. He needed to find someplace safe. Safe for Sara.

"Peter."

Peter turned back to Sara, then pulled her to the side of an office building and out of the stream of people hustling up and down the sidewalk.

"Should we call the police or something?" Sara asked.

A man selling "authentic" Swiss watches gave Sara a stern stare as he closed up his briefcase and wandered further down the street to set up shop.

"With all those fireworks going off down there, I am sure the police are already there by now," Peter responded.

"What are we going to do?"

"I don't know," Peter answered honestly.

No one paid any attention to the two distraught individuals.

Peter repeatedly glanced down 42nd Street toward the hotel area. Sara observed Peter's neuroticism.

"Well, I know I'm not going back there," Sara commented as she watched Peter again nervously look down the street.

"We need someplace to regroup," Peter noted, still obviously shook up by another attempt on his life.

Silence again engulfed the two as the bustling crowd shuffled along in front of them.

"Peter, there."

Sara pointed across Fifth Avenue.

Set back from the enclave of skyscrapers stood the New York Public Library. Two majestic marble statues guarded the Fifth Avenue entrance. Between the south-side lion statue, Patience, and the north-side lion, Fortitude, the steps to the potential sanctuary invited the young couple. Patience and Fortitude were two virtues Peter presently lacked. Sara understood this fact as she led him across Fifth Avenue to the New York Public Library.

Sara almost had to tug Peter along as the two ascended the steps. Peter constantly checked behind them, around them and even in front of them for any trace of a hostile presence. The past sixty hours had rendered his nerves completely raw. The man climbing the stairs lacked his usual self-confident demeanor. This latest episode, the attack on Jack Morgan and his men, had left him frazzled. These emotions did not escape Sara's senses. She knew she had to make decisions for both of them.

As the two entered the Astor Hall Entrance of the library, Sara stopped and absorbed her surroundings. The entrance was encased in white, or more like ivory, marble. The vaulted ceilings hovered forty feet above all those who entered the library. The high arched windows allowed a warmth of light which invited all to climb the twin staircases to any of the slew of reading and research rooms.

"Peter," Sara faced the man she loved.

"Yes, Sara?"

"The way I see it," Sara began, "we need to get out of the streets where we can be recognized and kill some time before Jimmy Powell can get back to us."

"And?"

"And you love libraries, so what better place to hang out for a while?" responded Sara.

Sara grabbed Peter's hand and climbed the stairs pulling Peter behind her. There was no doubt about it. Peter did love libraries. The solitude, the serenity, the escapism, and the endless wealth of knowledge all drew Peter into libraries. It was one of the reasons he went into law in the first place. What other vocation paid so handsomely to research and write in a library?

Sara led Peter to the third floor. She had no idea where she was going, except for the fact that she was getting Peter further away from the streets of New York, figuratively and literally. The two entered the main reading room. They peaked to the left into the north wing. The rich wood interior, surrounded by volume after volume of books, was offset by the rows of computer terminals with patrons surfing the net or browsing through the library's unparalleled catalog. Little seating was available, so Sara led Peter over to the south wing. The south wing was the main reading area for patrons. The room was enormous and surrounded by countless leather-bound volumes exquisitely shelved along the perimeter of the room. An aisle partitioned the area down the center. An aisle divided the elongated tables that would have stretched the width of the room but for the partition. Copper-shaded lamps decorated the tables and cast essential light for readers. Handcrafted murals adorned the ceilings. The main reading room epitomized turn-of-the-century grandeur.

The two walked around the perimeter of the room. For a moment Peter had forgotten about the men stalking them. The two held hands as they made their way around the room.

"Peter," Sara whispered as she pointed to a coffee table book laying at the edge of one of the long reading tables. Sara sat down and began to thumb through the pages.

"It's your backyard," Peter commented.

"Look, it's Big Sur."

Sara tried to be quiet, but she was too excited.

"We never made it that far," Peter sheepishly admitted.

"My ocean."

Sara was possessive of the Pacific.

The two paged through photos of the Californian coastline, smiling at one another and occasionally squeezing one another's hand.

Peter lost himself in memories of a beautiful drive the two had down Highway 1. The original plan had the two drive down the coast from San Francisco to Big Sur. However, Sara wanted to stop along the way for a picnic.

Sara spent her childhood about an hour and a half south of San Francisco and a stone's throw from the beach. Most children grew up with ball fields and playgrounds. Sara had the ocean. Although there were several areas of beachfront, Sara never called it the beach. Spoiled by the California coast afforded Sara the luxury of calling a beach a place where hundreds, or thousands, gathered to swim or frolic in the surf and sand. At their picnic in the sand by a picturesque rocky cliff, the two had a friendly dispute as to the definition of a beach. Of course, Peter simply defined the beach as where the ocean met the sand. Sara jumped on this, telling him that defined some of the ocean floor, but you didn't see anyone setting up umbrellas at the bottom of the ocean. Sara continued to taunt the foolish midwestern boy throughout the picnic until he wrestled her down to the ground. As they lay in sand in each others arms, Peter knew that one day he would ask Sara to marry him.

The photographs of the California coastline also pricked Sara's lost memories. The sun, sand, rocks, and waves breathed life into the forgotten days of her childhood. Sara could picture her mother helping her find seashells, or the two retreating from the oncoming waves in their bare feet, or even standing above the rock line enjoying the mist from the breaking waves.

As Sara drifted in and out of her own little dream world, she could see by the smile on Peter's face as he pointed at some more pictures that the insane world they had left outside the library had been forgotten, if only for a fleeting moment.

———◦◦◦———

Sixty-two blocks to the north of the 120 Broadway Building, but in full view from pinnacle to pinnacle, the Occidental Tower was one of the tallest buildings in Midtown Manhattan. Its art deco style fit in nicely with the other Midtown skyscrapers. The view was unobstructed, contrary to some of the buildings downtown. Elias' grand office faced west with a panoramic view of Central Park, Rockefeller Center, the New York Public Library, the Empire State Building, and even a glimpse downtown. Smoking a cigar, Aaron Golde enjoyed one of Manhattan's most scenic views. Elias St. Armand stood off to the side of the office by a glass casing. In the case, lying on a crimson velvet stand, was a medieval ivory cross tied to a red ribbon. Elias opened the case and reached under the velvet stand. He pulled out a similar cross. The second cross was more grey than ivory, yet still polished. It also lacked the extravagant sharp medieval curves the first cross displayed. The second cross also was not as richly ornate with inscriptions as contained in the first. Finally, as opposed to the lavish ribbon attached to the first cross, only a thin strap of brown leather hung from the second cross.

"Have I ever shown you this, Aaron?" Elias asked Golde.

"That cross recently bestowed upon you?" replied the elder counsel.

"No, that is the church's fake one. They can probably churn those out as fast as plastic rosaries."

"What then?"

"This."

Elias laid the cross against his navy blue blazer's sleeve as he showed it to Aaron Golde.

"Looks rather plain compared to your new cross," commented the attorney.

"Beauty is in the eye of the beholder, and you never had much of an eye for beauty."

"You are about to tell me why this one is so beautiful."

"Yes," Elias exclaimed as he put the cross on over his head.

Elias continued, "Aaron this is the original Cross of St. Maro. The other one is merely a replica the Maronite Church hands out once in a great while. Ironically, they both came into my possession at about the same time."

"As an attorney, I am not going to ask you how the original came into your possession," chided Aaron Golde.

"The question is not how, but why?" Elias responded.

"Then why do you have the original Cross of St. Maro?" Golde politely asked.

"Legend has it," Elias began, "that only a few of the bones survived St. John Maro's death. Monks who had followed the man hid these relics. In order to keep them hidden, they fashioned them into an ordinary cross where they remained hidden for hundreds of years. The Cross of St. Maro did not reappear again until the First Crusade."

"As European princes and their vassals and slaves chased the Muslims from the Middle East, they happened upon these same Maronite monks from the Orontes River. So enthralled that their Lebanon had been freed from Muslim tyranny, the monks bestowed upon their liberator the Cross of St. Maro."

"The liberator of Lebanon was none other than Godfrey of Bouillon, Duke of the Lower Lorraine. Godfrey accepted the cross only because a visionary, Peter Bartholomew, had once told him he had seen a vision of Godfrey riding into a conquered Jerusalem wearing a cross."

"Now, given the fact that nearly every crusader had taken up the Cross, any cross, to fight this holy war, Bartholomew's vision was not exactly a long shot. Nevertheless, Godfrey accepted the Cross of St. Maro and his army marched into Jerusalem."

"The battle for Jerusalem started horribly for Godfrey's Crusaders. The Muslims stripped the countryside around the city of all crops and livestock. They poisoned all the wells. Inside the city walls the Muslims had gathered enough food and water for months. Not only were the Muslims better prepared for the siege, but they fought better. They beat back every advance by the Crusaders until despair had set in."

"Then, as legend has it, Peter Bartholomew appeared as a vision in Godfrey's dream, instructing him to wear the Cross of St. Maro into victory over the Muslims. Godfrey, of course, put on the Cross of St. Maro and engaged the Muslims. However, this time he conquered the city. The Muslims, of course, were all slaughtered."

"Of course," mimicked Aaron Golde.

Elias continued, "Upon recapturing Jerusalem, Godfrey of Bouillon was offered the throne of the Kingdom of Jerusalem. You know what Godfrey did, Aaron?"

"Do tell, Elias."

"He declined the throne. He said he would not wear a crown of gold where his Savior had been forced to wear a crown of thorns."

Elias looked at his reflection in the mirror donning Godfrey of Bouillon's

Cross of St. Maro as he continued, "You know what, Aaron?" he paused, "I would not have declined the throne."

# FORTY-EIGHT

Out of the library and fully refreshed, the two walked the streets of New York. However, after leaving their refuge for only a few moments, Peter's worst fears had been confirmed. Two men in suits and wearing earpieces spotted them. Peter grabbed Sara's hand.

"Peter?"

"They found us." Peter tugged Sara and pulled her through the crowds. The Times Square crowds were enormous, but Peter knew they would be found unless they found some place to hide. If there were two men, there certainly were more in the area with even more on the way since they had been spotted. It was easy to lose oneself in the crowds; however, unless the two of them merely wanted to keep going in circles they would have to leave the cover of the crowds.

Peter thought of places to hide. The subway station? Someone surely would be covering that area. Peter squeezed Sara's hand. Maybe back in the stores or restaurants. No, they could easily get cornered in a small place.

In front of one of the restaurant/bars, Peter hesitated to go in, then he saw some orange pylons at the corner. The two ran up to the corner. The two men followed a block-and-a-half away. But hundreds separated the hunters and the hunted. Several orange pylons diverted traffic around a New York City Electric truck and the work area that had been sectioned off. The warning lights on the truck blinked. Peter's first thought was to take the truck.

"Damn."

Peter looked through the passenger-side window. There were no keys in the ignition. Peter walked over to the uncovered manhole and looked down.

"I'm not going down there," Sara immediately told him.

Peter looked around. Hundreds of people were within twenty yards of him. All concentrated on the hustle and bustle of getting to their next destination.

"Come on. We don't have time to argue," Peter said as he helped Sara over the orange mesh fence.

Peter slid down the steel ladder. Sara quickly climbed down behind him. The intense smell of sewage and urine caused both of them to gasp for air.

The two descended into some kind of small underground hallway. The light from above allowed Peter to see a door to his right and a set of stairs to his left. Peter grabbed Sara's hand and headed for the stairs.

The two darted down the cluttered stairs. The emergency lighting for the exit sign lit up the stairs revealing flight after flight of trash, cardboard boxes, and urine stains. The cement stairs were steep and short. Each flight consisted of only five steps, a plateau, and then five additional steps descending in the opposite direction. Each plateau appeared to be an abandoned shelter for the homeless.

At every other plateau there was a small hallway with a door in the middle of the hallway. The door was always locked. The hallway was even more cluttered than the stairs. At the end of the hallway was another flight of stairs. The hustle and bustle of the city above them soon faded as they descended flight after flight after flight.

"Halt! Who goes there?"

From out of nowhere a man jumped up directly in front of Peter. Dressed in rags from head to toe, the man had been homeless for some time. Even in the dim light Peter recognized the blood-shot yellow eyes, toothless grin, unshaven dirty face. It was the face of countless homeless men he had seen and passed by on the street. However, this homeless man stood directly in front of him, thirty feet underground, clenching a pipe with both hands.

"Who goes there?" the homeless man asked again.

Peter stood his ground but made no sudden movements.

"Who are you?"

Immediately the homeless man stood at attention and recited, "I am Sir Lancelot, gatekeeper of the underworld, defender of the universe, guard of my domain."

Sir Lancelot stood at attention for another minute, then shifted his feet back to his attack position.

"Who goes there?"

"It is I, King Arthur," responded Peter.

"My king?" Lancelot inquired.

"And the fair Guinevere," Peter pulled Sara closer.

Lancelot clumsily went down on one knee and bowed his head, "My Lady."

Peter addressed the homeless man, "Brave knight, are there any more knights around?"

"No, my lord. The dragon from above chased them away."

"You must find them."

"I cannot leave my post, my Lord."

"An army is after us and I am trying to bring Guinevere to safety."

"I shall protect her," responded Lancelot as he again stood at attention.

"There are too many, brave knight. You must find other knights like you."

"The others are cowards. I shall stand my ground, my Liege."

Realizing he could not spend any more time arguing, Peter conceded, "Okay, brave knight, I must get Guinevere to safety. But I order you not to fight the army.

"What should I do my lord?"

Peter could not think.

"Count them," Sara chimed in.

"I shall count the army my fair lady."

Again Sir Lancelot bowed.

As Sir Lancelot remained genuflected, Peter and Sara skirted around him and raced down the next flight of stairs. As they descended further and further they could hear Lancelot shouting, "I shall count the evil army!"

Sixty feet below the streets of Manhattan, both Peter and Sara began to calm down. The last flight of stairs brought them to an area which could best be described as a concrete half room. There were no more flights of stairs. Although the emergency lighting from the stairs was not shining directly into the half room, Peter could see that on one end of the half room were the stairs; on the other end was a locked steel door. In between were the concrete floor, concrete ceiling, and two concrete walls. The fact that there was no trash, no urination stains, nor any remnants of anyone ever being down this far led Peter to believe that Sir Lancelot had been doing an excellent job at security. If only he could keep up the good work for a couple more hours.

The half room was moist, almost damp; however, there was no built up condensation or puddles. In a random act of futility, Sara tried the locked door again. Frustrated, Sara turned toward Peter. It was quiet. Not even Sir Lancelot's ranting and ravings thirty to forty feet above them could be heard.

"We will be safe here," Peter told Sara, saying what he believed she wanted to hear.

"Yes, but for how long?"

"Long enough."

With her hands on her hips and her head tilted, Sara stared at Peter.

Peter continued, "Long enough for those men to leave the area. Long enough for us to get some rest."

"Believe me, you are going to have to promise me a lot longer than that if I am supposed to catch up on rest."

"We'll hide out down here for a couple of hours, then resurface."

"How will we know that they have left the area?"

"In this city, they would have to believe that they lost us in the crowd and search up or down Broadway or anywhere between here and the base."

"What are we going to do then?"

"We have to get a hold of Jimmy Powell. Those files are the only thing keeping us alive."

"No, I mean what are we going to do in the meantime?"

"Sleep," Peter calmly said as he sat down on the cold concrete floor.

"Here?"

"I know it's not the Plaza."

"It's not even under the Plaza," retorted Sara as she smiled at Peter.

Peter smiled too.

As Sara sat beside Peter she continued, "How do you do it, Petie, always remain so content and confident that everything will work out?"

Before Peter could release one of his typical smug quips, Sara leaned against him and continued, "How do you know everything will turn out right? Is it this god of yours?"

"Sara," Peter started as he looked down on her, "I think your agnosticism is showing."

"Seriously, Peter, why do you believe in a god? Look at all the craziness in the world, meaningless death and suffering. People once revered for their principles, now revealed as leading a life of lies. Before I just thought there was no god. Now I know there can be no god."

"How can you know there is no God?"

"How can a god let all this happen?"

"It's not God doing this; it's people."

"I know, people like my father."

"Sara."

Interrupting him, Sara returned to her point, "But what about the Holocaust or all the death in Africa? How can your god do that?"

"It is not God; it's people."

"But why would he let them do that?"

"Free will."

"Well, he should have never given us that."

"I can think of more than a few who should not of had it."

"Be serious."

"Have faith, we maybe able to figure out how to make this world a better place."

Sara rested her head on Peter's lap and curled up beside him, then mumbled, "And then someone else will come along and screw it all up again."

The two were quiet for a minute.

In a drowsy voice, Sara started again, "If your god really does exist, prove it?"

"Now how can I do that?"

"I don't know. You're the one that believes in a god."

"Well it is not as if I can show you a picture from my wallet or something."

"Scientists can prove the Big Bang started the universe and they don't have a picture of the origin of the universe in their wallet."

Peter was quiet for a moment. With her eyes closed, Sara smiled at his silence.

"Well, let us take this Big Bang theory for a moment." The Jesuit in Peter Farrell began to rear its head. "If everyone agreed that the Big Bang created the universe, this consensus still does not reveal what caused the Big Bang. Something must have started all of this. My answer is God. I think believing in God also explains the complexities and miracles of life and nature."

"Does God answer your prayers?'

"I found you again."

Sara squeezed his legs with her head and arms.

"Do you think God answers everyone's prayers?"

"I think some answers are more clear than other answers."

Sara's voice was now barely above a whisper. Peter stroked her hair and smoothed it from her face.

"If you don't understand God's answer, how do you know God is listening?"

"Faith."

"I wish I had your faith, Peter."

Sara then fell asleep from pure exhaustion.

# FORTY-NINE

Just east of the 125th Street subway station in a seedy apartment over-looking the carnage known as East Harlem, Chamoun Al Khouri sat at the kitchen table staring at a box of aerosol canisters filled with lethal dosages of sarin. If it had not been for the death of Brother Michel or Antonios he may have never have come to know what sarin was or how it fatally cripples a man's respiratory system. Actually, he thought to himself, none of this would have been possible without his brethren in the Tigers.

A second man entered the kitchen, looked at Al Khouri and said two words, "*Trois heures.*"

Three hours.

Plenty of time to gather his thoughts. Chamoun felt as if he were looking into a mirror when he saw the other man. Yes, their features were similar and the eyes were identical. It was not that both had brown eyes that were blood-shot and yellowed by lack of sleep and nutrition, but the two had the same steel ice-cold glaze, as if only one thing was important and nothing else mattered. The other man's name was Youssef, or Ghazi, or Fares. He could not remember. It did not matter. Al Khouri knew the man by the look in his eyes. The eyes were those of a Tiger.

The Lebanese Tigers easily recruited Chamoun after the death of Brother Michel. Al Khouri sought unconditional vengeance. The Tigers sought bodies with no fear of death. Chamoun had been aware of the Tigers and other nationalist groups since the Palestinians had first began using Lebanon for guerilla raids on Israel. What attracted Chamoun to the Tigers, other than the fear they struck in their enemies, was their motto, "When the truth laid down with the gun, the Lebanese Tigers were born."

The Tigers led Lebanese Nationalists to victory in the "Hundred Day War" driving the Syrian army out of eastern Lebanon. But the Syrians and their supporters, with their superior weapons and numbers, always came back. Another important victory came at Zahle, defending the *Saidet-en-Najat*,

Our Lady of Deliverance, and the portrait of the Blessed Virgin Mary, against Syrian invaders. However, the Tigers' greatest victory, Lebanon's greatest victory, came on March 14, 1989. The Liberation War united all Lebanese against their Syrian aggressors. Syrian forces were driven from Lebanon. Chamoun smiled as he thought of that date, March 14.

He wondered to himself if there would ever be a place in history for him. Not in the near future. For as far as the outside world knew, Chamoun Al Khouri had been killed by a prisoner at the Answar I Detention Center in Khiam, Lebanon. His passport was Syrian. He was chosen specifically because there were no Interpol records of him or which would contradict a Syrian heritage. Everything would point to Syria, even the blood he used to draft the manifesto which would be the only traceable item from him left.

Chamoun Al Khouri unfolded the manifesto and again read it to himself:

*To the Downtrodden in Lebanon and in the World,*

*In the name of Allah, all merciful, all compassionate, and all powerful.*

*O free downtrodden people.*

*We are the sons of Allah's nation in Lebanon. Although small in number, our military power has dimensions the tyrannical arrogant world in the West cannot imagine. Every living, breathing fiber of every body in Allah's army is intertwined. Every body is a combat soldier when the cell of jihad demands, until there is no breath of life in that body. For every loss of breath to the call of jihad puts ever growing fear in our enemies' hearts. Fear will bring Allah's resounding victory against the United States and its allies.*

*O free downtrodden people!*

*The sons of Allah will not rest until the final departure of the tyrannical West from Lebanon and their imperialist influences cease in the region. The oppressive structure in our region must terminate, or hundreds like this soldier will give their last breath to this holy jihad.*

*O free downtrodden people now! Or Allah's vengeance will be unrelenting!*

# FIFTY

It had been a couple of hours since Peter and Sara had seen sunlight. Sara had slept most of the time with her head resting comfortably on Peter's lap. Peter was not sure if he had slept or not. He felt as if he might have dozed off, but did not know if it was more than a moment or so. His mind had been racing the entire time. Even when he closed his eyes, there was no rest. He needed to contact Powell. He needed to contact Roland. Most of all, he needed to contact every media source possible.

It was time to move.

The two began the long climb up to the surface world.

His concentration on the steps and concern over Sara slipping diverted his overreaching thoughts. Not completely, of course. First, they needed to make sure that they could surface without incident. More than likely the workers would be back. Furthermore, if Lancelot followed them up to the street, surely attention would be drawn to them. Of course, the municipal employees who would see them emerge without hard hats and fluorescent vests certainly would not let them waltz on by the orange security tape and construction cones. Maybe Lancelot would be a healthy diversion. And what were they to do once they emerged from the manhole? Surely their appearances, such as clothes and hair, had been recirculated to local and federal authorities and whatever other bounty hunters had been hired to find them. They had to change their appearances.

"Ohhh!" Sara slipped.

Peter helped her regain her balance on the narrow steps.

"Are you all right?"

His voice cracked as he held her arm and backside.

"Yes. I am just not awake yet," Sara replied.

Peter stared at her.

"I am fine, Peter, really. Let's keep moving and get out of this dreadful place."

Sara turned from Peter and continued her climb up the steep steps.

Maybe finding Lancelot would be for the best. He was roughly Peter's size, maybe a bit shorter and stockier, but maybe they could swap clothes. Something could fit Sara to change her appearance. There was also plenty of crap, well not necessarily crap, but other mush and grime in the bowels of Manhattan that they could smear their faces with and muss their hair. Sara, without a doubt, would object at first. And, of course, Peter would need to exchange shoes with Lancelot for the Dogman touch.

"Peter," Sara whispered as she stopped dead in her tracks.

Peter turned the corner to one of the level areas where the stairs were located on the other side of the platform. The manhole was up the next set of stairs. But in between the stairs to the manhole and Sara laid the unmistakable lifeless body of Lancelot, strewn on the platform in his own pool of blood with his arm fully extended on the concrete holding his sword made from tinfoil.

"It's Lancelot," said Peter.

"He's dead," Sara replied.

Peter walked over to the body. From the way he lay on the cement, it appeared as if he had been running toward the steps up to the manhole.

"He was shot several times," Peter concluded as he stood over the body.

"I did not hear any shots," Sara noted.

"Neither did I," Peter responded.

Peter knelt over the body.

"It must have been silencers. It looks like there are a couple entry wounds."

"Police don't use silencers."

Sara was scared again.

"From the amount of blood this happened a while ago."

Peter pointed his finger to the large pool of blood.

"He was protecting us," Sara said. The fear in Sara's voice had changed to admiration.

"They must have left at least an hour ago," Peter looked at Sara.

"He probably saved our lives."

Sara knelt beside the body, kissed her forefinger and index finger, placed them on Lancelot's forehead, and closed her eyes for a moment.

His head twitched.

Lancelot's eyelids and nose twitched next.

Sara jumped back from the body.

Peter quickly knelt by Lancelot's side and thrust his hand by Lancelot's nose and mouth.

"He's breathing, slightly."

"We have to help him," insisted Sara.

Peter took off his oxford and tied the shirt sleeves to Lancelot's arms.

"Here help me sit him up."

The two propped Lancelot up. Peter took Lancelot's arms and placed them over his head. Sara pushed the man onto Peter's back. Peter was able to lift him to the next set of stairs. Sara helped take some of the pressure off Peter by pushing upwards as they lifted Lancelot up the stairs.

When they reached the manhole Peter knew that they would not be able to carry Lancelot up the ladder. Even if the two would fit through the manhole with Lancelot on his back, it would not work. Peter reached for the first metal step. Lancelot began to slip. Peter backed down and set Lancelot back down onto the concrete.

"Sara, climb up and tell them we have someone who has been shot down here."

Without hesitation Sara climbed the ladder up the manhole.

As Peter heard voices from above, he stripped Lancelot's clothes from his upper body. Lancelot's bare chest revealed two bullet wounds. Blood was seeping from the holes. Both were in his right side, opposite of his heart which Peter could still feel beating. One wound looked as if it had broken through his rib cage. The other wound, lower and off to the side, appeared to have passed right through his body. This was the bloodier of the two wounds. Peter untied his shirt from Lancelot's arms, then tried to tear the shirt in half. All he managed to accomplish was ripping off a sleeve. He balled up the sleeve and pressed it firmly on Lancelot's chest wound. He applied the rest of his shirt to the belly wound and waited.

He did not wait long.

Peter's back was to the manhole's ladder; however, he could hear several people climb down the steps. Then he heard some form of bag drop to the ground.

"Jim, this is not a prank. There are two guys down here and one on the ground."

Peter heard the man's feet hit the ground.

"Did someone call the paramedics?" Peter shouted out as he tried to turn his head.

"Yes," the muscular African-American man who was taller and bigger than Peter said.

"What happened down here, Dan?" the man named Jim asked as he let himself drop to the cement from the ladder.

"He's been shot," Peter interjected "at least twice. I found these two bullet wounds, but have not had the chance to look for anything else."

"Let me see."

The man named Dan lifted up each of Peter's hands separately, inspected the wounds and placed Peter's hands back to applying pressure.

"Jim, he's not shittin' us. These are bullet wounds."

"Damn," Jim responded, dragging the 'ah' sound in 'damn'."

"What's your name?" Dan asked Peter.

"Peter."

"Peter, I want you to keep applying pressure for another minute or two."

The utility worker, who obviously had some kind of medical training, inspected Lancelot's head, checked his pulse, and felt his legs for any other injuries.

"Here's your bag, Dan."

Jim set the black leather bag down by his fellow workman.

"Jim, start giving him some oxygen," Dan ordered.

Dan began to clean and redress the chest wound. Jim applied a small mask over Lancelot's nose and mouth and squeezed the hand pump every few moments.

Lancelot started to choke.

"Not so fast, Jim," ordered Dan, "he just needs a little help."

Dan lifted Peter's other hand to tend to the other gunshot wound.

"Are you all right?" Dan inquired right before he started to clean the belly wound.

"Yeah, nothing happened to us," Peter responded as he stood up, his eyes still glazed over in disbelief once again.

"Can you climb up that ladder?" he asked Peter.

"Yes."

Lancelot started choking again when Jim placed the mask on again. His eyes opened for a moment then closed.

"I need you to tell the two guys up there that we still will need the paramedics, not the fire department," he paused, "but we will need a backboard."

"Is he going to make it?"

"His pulse is strong, his breathing is slight but steady, so," the man stopped himself and began again, "yes, he will be all right. Now get up there. Remember, paramedics and a stretcher."

Peter looked back at Lancelot. Lancelot lifted his arm a couple of inches and folded his thumb over his pinky finger. He showed three fingers. There were three of them. Peter raced up the ladder. He did not see Sara at first, but he was looking for the other workers.

"They say they need a paramedic, but no fire department, just a backboard."

"Already radioed that in," said one of the two other workers.

Sara looked concerned as she was wrapped tightly in the yellow New York Electric jacket. Peter grabbed Sara's hand and squeezed it tight.

"One of the guys down there has medical training. He is going to be all right."

The two workers peered down the manhole.

One of the workers, the short guy with red curly hair and glasses, informed

Peter and Sara, "That's Dan. He was a medic in Desert Storm, a marine."

Sara pulled Peter closer with her hand and whispered, "The police will be here any minute."

Peter began to back away slowly. He led Sara away from the utility workers' marked area. Once free of the caution tape, Peter and Sara ran across the congested street. They heard the short curly haired man squealing in the background.

———————

Located on Fifth Avenue between 50th and 51st Streets is the seat of power, prestige, and prominence for the Roman Catholic Archdiocese of New York. That, of course, is St. Patrick's Cathedral. Arguably the most significant building architecturally on the avenue, the James Renwick, Jr. creation, with its twin spires on Fifth Avenue, transcends all place and time. Although the Gothic revival style clashes with Midtown's steel, glass, and concrete structures, the nineteenth century cathedral has its home in the heart of New York City. National and international dignitaries are constantly humbled by the cathedral's majestic presence as if it sprang forth from the earth to serve global pilgrimages. Depending on the lighting, the high Gothic interior quickly morphs from the somber and reverent white marble and stone structure decorated only with striking stained-glass windows to a dazzling display of incandescent lighting shimmering with gold, silver, and bronze decorating the altar. But today it was cloudy, cold and wet. The Gothic tomb exuded no radiance; even the majestic stained-glass windows lacked sparkle on this overcast day.

"Click!"

A flash went off over Andriy Kravenko's shoulder, interrupting his prayers to Mary Magdalene as he knelt in the section of pews away from the altar.

"Aren't these flowers arranged beautifully?" one elder midwestern woman noted to another.

"They're gorgeous."

"We need more flowers at our church."

"Take another picture in case that first one didn't turn out."

"Good idea, Gladys."

"Click."

The flash went off again. Kravenko's head began to lift as if he had just been awakened from a deep trance or meditation.

The two tourists remained undaunted in their task to photograph every angle of the entire cathedral at whatever costs.

"Over here, over here, Gladys."

A trio of nuns three rows in front of Kravenko glared at the two midwestern tourists.

Kravenko bowed his head again and mumbled, "I am the Alpha and the Omega, the beginning and the ending, saith the Lord, Amen."

Kravenko paused and continued, "Behold I am coming with the clouds, and every eye will see me, every one who pierced me, and all the tribes of the earth will wail on account of me."

He paused again.

"Even so, Amen."

Kravenko then rose from the pew, genuflected before the altar and walked back down the aisle to exit St. Patrick's Cathedral. Before he exited, he slipped John Kerr's three-thousand-dollar Swiss watch into the collection plate.

---

Peter and Sara ran back to Times Square. The swarming masses provided cover again.

"There!"

With his right hand holding Sara's hand, his left pointed down the street to an O'Shaughnessey & Frey, the mega bookstore which sold everything from books, music, and prints to clothing and furniture. However, they also promoted their Internet-savvy cafes. Two stores down from O'Shaughnessey & Frey, Sara stopped Peter's quick pace.

"Peter, wait."

Peter stopped and turned around. The New Yorkers began to sidestep around the two. Sara led Peter out of the heavy stream of people to the side-walk by a display window.

"You're a mess."

Peter looked at himself. His T-shirt, arms, and hands were stained with blood.

"How did you get clean?" he asked Sara.

"I got cleaned up waiting for you. But here, take this."

Sara took off the bright-yellow New York Electric jacket and gave it to Peter.

Peter slipped on the jacket and the two strolled into the store.

The security guard at O'Shaughnessey & Frey gave the two a quick once over, but with all the colorful hair, tattoos, and ripped clothes that cruised through the doors on a daily basis, there was little fear that they would stand out. They walked to the cafe area which was just left of the entrance with a view of Times Square. The cafe had Internet terminals set up at one end as well as some on the mezzanine. Couches, chairs, and coffee tables littered the entire area without any semblance of organization. It appeared as if the large cherry-wood bookcases and magazine racks were the only furniture items that did not move on regular basis to comport with customers ever-adjusting needs.

Looking at Peter's bloodied hands, Sara instructed, "You wait over there. I will get us set up."

Peter ambled over to the display window. The busy streets of Manhattan seemed surreal given the moment in history, Peter thought to himself. New Yorkers, with their blinders on, hustled back from lunch or to that next meet-ing or to that next store right around the corner.

"Peter."

"Yes."

Peter snapped out of the trance.

"Were you day-dreaming?"

Sara handed Peter a to-go cup.

"Hot chocolate?" he asked.

"Of course," Sara responded with a smile as she continued, "I also bought some disks. We're upstairs."

Peter looked back before he followed Sara up to the mezzanine level.

The mezzanine level reminded Peter of a college, or better yet, a government library built in the fifties or early sixties. The cherry wood downstairs and throughout the store exuded a feel of academia. However, the atmosphere upstairs was completely sterile. There was one long line of desk sets enclosed to contain both the hard-drive and the terminal. Each station was numbered with an oval steel plate reminiscent of something one would see on a high school locker. Where the main level contained numerous different exotic lamps to give a cozy feel to every corner, the mezzanine was bright and glaring with its two rows of fluorescent lighting.

"We are number three twenty-seven," Sara said as she led the way.

"Here we are."

Sara quickly logged on.

Peter sat beside her and began typing.

> *Big Hank's Nephew:*
> *Are you there?*
>> *-Saw You in BH's Courtroom*

A couple moments passed without a response. Peter typed the message in again. Again there was no response.

> *SYBHC:*
> *It's about time. Been waiting for you. Thought you had reverted to snail mail. Everything is done. Give me an e-mail address to send it to.*
>> *-BHN*

"We better use mine."

Sara typed in her e-mail address.

> *SYBHC:*
> *It's on its way. Anything else?*
>> *-BHN*

Peter thought for a minute, then typed.

> *BHN,*
> *Download one file every hour to news agencies on the net. Use their chat rooms, bulletin boards, or whatever. You are better with that than I am. BUT MOVE AROUND. DO NOT STAY IN ONE PLACE.*
> *Go somewhere else for the first hour, then another place the second hour. It is not safe to stay at one place, be imaginative. Do not think that I am just being paranoid.*
> *SYBHC*

Peter and Sara waited.

> *SYBHC:*
> *I know you're not paranoid. I am the one who is paranoid. I haven't slept since I met you. How can I get in touch with you again? Same chat room?*
> *-BHN*

> *BHN*
> *Yes. But if you do not hear from me by midnight, unload everything and get lost, real lost.*
> *-SYBHC*

> *SYBHC:*
> *I understand.*
> *-BHN*

Sara logged onto the Sienna Club's server and pulled up her e-mail. "There it is."

Sara downloaded the document. Peter opened the package of disks and the two began copying the Occidental files onto disks. Peter put the first one in his billfold. The second one he set to the side. He started to download the third when he felt a strong hand on his shoulder.

"Mr. Farrell, you will need to come with us."

The man flashed some form of government I.D. badge in Peter's face. Three other men had also surrounded Peter and Sara. There were four total, not three.

All four men were large, nondescript, and wearing earpieces. One of them already had Sara by the arm. Another gathered the downloaded disk and the blank disks, leaving the cardboard packaging behind. Peter instantly looked over the edge. If he jumped he could easily land on one of the bookshelves and fall to the main floor without injury. But with one look at Sara, he knew he could not leave her again. Unfortunately, the government agents would not give him a choice.

# FIFTY-ONE

Two Middle Eastern men in their late twenties or early thirties boarded the number six train, the Lexington Avenue Local heading toward the Bronx. Neither their clothing nor facial hair or anything about them was memorable. The only distinguishable items about them were their plastic bags of noodles and spices from Chinatown. As the subway train pulled away from the platform at the Canal Street station, the two men excused themselves and made their way through the crowded car to the next car, the second to the last car on the northbound train. The two proceeded through the second car. It was less congested than the previous car, but all the seats were full. As they approached the end of the car, a middle-aged Middle Eastern woman, probably in her early sixties, nodded at her two preteen boys who quickly vacated their seats for the two men with the Chinese food. Any northbound number six train that these two men would have boarded for the next thirty minutes would have had a similar grandmother with teenaged grandchildren who would relinquish seats in the second to last car. They would have said God willed it, but the Lebanese Tigers guaranteed it.

Chamoun Al Khouri looked at his reflection in the bathroom mirror. Neither his ragged clothes, nor anything about his appearance registered. The only thing he could see were his tired, yellow-stained, bloodshot eyes. Growing up, his mother told him he had the warmest chestnut brown eyes. That was a long time ago. The years of pain and suffering that his eyes had endured and observed had taken its toll. The color brown never registered when he saw his eyes. Warm certainly did not describe what he saw in the mirror. For what was once warm had become cold, ice cold. If a man's eyes were the windows to his soul, Chamoun Al Khouri had to wonder if he had a soul. He wondered if anyone with a soul was capable of the cold hatred that consumed him. As he stared into the face in the mirror, there were no thoughts concerning the theoretical or theological justifications of a Holy War. The eyes betrayed no patriotic emotion which stirred in the essence of a Lebanese Tiger militia. The tired, yellowish, bloodshot eyes did convey the call for vengeance. Vengeance for the massacre at Deir Ashashe. Vengeance for the torture and meaningless execution of the benevolent Brother Michel. Vengeance for the blood shed by his brother, Antonios. As Chamoun Al Khouri stared into his eyes, he saw one thing, something these eyes had grown accustomed to over the years. In the mirror of the dimly lit bathroom of the East Harlem apartment, above the grayish bags and below the bushy black eyebrows, the yellowish-stained bloodshot eyes revealed only one thing to Chamoun Al Khouri: Death.

---

There were no ifs, ands, or buts about it, Sara was pissed off. She would have been more anxious or frightened if everyone around her was not so damn polite and accommodating. But she did not want something to eat or to drink or to read. She wanted answers. Actually, one answer to one question would be sufficient. What have you done with Peter Farrell?

The walls began closing in even though the conference room had to be at least as spacious as the Sienna Club's Auditorium. The boardroom's doors were locked; the phone did not work; and Sara certainly was not going to get any information from the stuffy life-size portrait of that banker on the wall. Sara thought that the portrait was disconcerting because of the painting's realistic eyes. Sara expected that the eyes would follow her everywhere around the room like some cheap slasher movie.

"Sara."

The voice startled Sara for a moment. It was Roland Miller.

"I knew you were in on this," accused Sara.

"Sara, I need to explain the situation to you."

"Explain one thing. Where is Peter?"

"Actually, he is upstairs."

Miller's candor surprised Sara.

"Sara, the people who found you were organized through a joint effort. You were not brought here by Elias St. Armand. In fact, the people who brought you here are trying to stop the Occidental group."

"I want to see Peter."

"Not yet," the elder statesman paused, "he is needed elsewhere right now."

"I need him now."

"Sara, we are all being asked to make sacrifices right now."

"You mean Peter is going to be sacrificed."

"No, no, no."

Miller placed his hands on the leather swivel chair at the head of the table with the banker's portrait glaring over his shoulder.

"Then how come I can't see Peter?" pressed Sara.

"He is being debriefed right now. We need to know everything he knows. Then he is going to set up another meeting with Elias St. Armand."

"Can't you people do your own dirty work?"

"Peter Farrell is still the wild card that Occidental wants. He is the only one who can draw Elias St. Armand out."

"So you are using Peter as bait."

"In a manner, yes."

Sara had grown accustomed to the elder lawyer's direct approach, but it still did not lessen the shock value in confirming Sara's fears.

"Sara, we need Peter to stop Occidental."

"How can you put him in danger after everything he has been through; everything you both have been through? He saved your life."

"Every precaution will be taken."

"Are those the same precautions that were taken to protect the President?"

"Sara, we are not putting him on a street corner with a bull's-eye around his neck."

"You might as well. All the 'quote unquote' protection in this city has failed."

"That is why you are leaving the city."

"I am not leaving without Peter."

"Peter will join you first thing in the morning."

"Why can't I just stay here with Peter and we both leave in the morning?" the young environmental attorney inquired.

"Because," Roland began, "your presence will only complicate matters."

"Not good enough."

"Peter has agreed to help on one condition. Your safety is his utmost concern. Consequently, your presence not only compromises our ability to stop Occidental, but it compromises our ability to protect you."

"Peter cannot make that decision for me."

"Frankly, my dear, Peter understands he has no choice in this matter, and neither do you."

Any respect that Sara Ahrens had for Roland Miller's directness disappeared.

---

Peter paced the high-tech conference room for twenty minutes. After they had taken Sara from him, Peter's blood pressure rose. Patience was a commodity that Peter had very little stock in. If it were not for Roland Miller meeting him twenty minutes ago, Peter would have likely gone after Sara. Miller assured Peter that Sara was and would be safe. Miller also explained that Peter had to meet some people. He said that the unfortunate turn of events this afternoon dictated that the meeting occur immediately and at these offices. Miller also promised Peter that once the meeting was over that he would be able to see Sara.

That was twenty minutes ago.

After trying the useless phones and the locked doors, Peter realized that neither he nor Sara was simply here for a meeting. Despite this, Peter Farrell had little reason to doubt the great Roland Miller. Miller was supposed to die in the Kensington suite with the president. In addition, the men who brought Peter and Sara to these commercial suites brought them alive with little show of force. That fact alone shows that these men are not part of the same organization that started the shootout with Jack Morgan's men. Whoever brought them here valued their lives a hell of a lot more than Occidental did. However, that was little consolation to Peter when at the moment he could not see Sara and reassure himself about her safety.

The doors perpendicular to the hallway leading to the elevator opened.

"The mysterious Peter Farrell, it is an honor."

The jovial Englishman entered the room and immediately shook Peter's hand.

An older more conservatively dressed American entered behind the Englishman and sternly shook Peter's hand.

"Mr. Farrell."

"I thought you would be taller, bigger, a little more muscular," chided the Englishman. "Maybe with a big 'S' on your chest."

"You have me at a disadvantage," responded Peter.

"Our names are unimportant for the time being," replied the Savile Row man.

The Englishman sat at the conference room table and leaned back toward the window with the Manhattan skyline behind him.

"Roland tells us that you are somewhat aware of the Council, the Council on International Relations," noted the Englishman with his hands folded behind his head.

Peter knew he was way out of his league.

"Wait a minute," the Savile Row man interjected with his face scrunched in disgust, "tell him about the girl."

"You were always the romantic one," the Englishman chided.

"Ms. Ahrens is fine." The Englishman popped up out of his seat and reached underneath the head of the table. "I love this."

As the Englishman pressed the button, a dual-sided high-definition television screen emerged from the table.

"In fact," the Englishman continued, "Voilà, you can see for yourself."

The video screen showed Sara in a smaller conference room walking toward the window. Peter peered out the window behind the Englishman.

The Manhattan skyline was the same. Sara was in the same building and fine. The Savile Row man took charge.

"We all have a problem and that problem is Elias St. Armand."

"St. Armand is not my problem; he is your problem," responded Peter.

"Well, if my memory serves me correctly young man, my problem just tried to kill you and your friend a couple of hours ago, despite military protection. Consequently, I believe the term, 'our,' is appropriate."

"Easy, easy," the Englishman intervened.

"How's Roland Miller involved?" asked Peter.

"He is Miller's problem, too," responded the Savile Row man.

"You mean he is not one of you?"

"I think it is fair to say that Roland Miller uses us and we use him. We have a healthy working relationship," responded the Englishman.

"What would the President's right-hand man need with you?"

The Savile Row man's face scrunched up again.

"You actually believe that the President is the most powerful man in the world? Wake up, boy!"

"There are certain global conditions that dictate, no necessitate, a consortium such as ours," the Englishman politely answered. "For example, your president may be bound by national interests to placate American voters, whereas our consortium allows us to pursue global interests free from electoral concerns."

"Are not your global interests the same as your financial interests?"

"A sound, stable economy benefits everyone," responded the Englishman.

"Try telling that to the debt-ridden Third World nations," Peter snapped.

"We do."

The conference room door leading to the hallway and elevators opened. It was Roland Miller.

"Roland," exclaimed the Englishman. "I like this one. He's feisty."

"That is what the President thought."

"We were just explaining to Mr. Farrell the necessity for our existence," the Englishman pursued the point.

"We do not have much time."

"Nonsense," the Englishman continued. "Before us, isolationism led to Hitler, Mussolini, and Stalin. Globalism was unheard of, other than armies trying to carve up a pie. Striving for global economic security has changed the course of history. Do you think the Berlin Wall fell because people were trying to stop communism? No, of course not. The economic apple dangled by the West sent the wall tumbling down."

"We need to focus on Elias St. Armand," interrupted Roland Miller.

"In a minute, Roland," gestured the Englishman. "We exist to insure that our global financial interests are protected."

"And basically government and economics of all nations must serve the interests of your multinational banks and corporations," responded Peter.

"Yes," the Savile Row man entered the discourse.

"It probably is not politically correct to phrase it like that. I think it is better stated," the Englishman elongated his neck and stuck out his chin, "what is good for the goose is good for the gander."

"What you want," Peter said, "or what your 'consortium' wants are less national regulations, less national protections, in order that you can control more nations, or more so to the point, have the ability to promote and enforce your loans to nations without having any devaluation concerns. In effect, by eliminating nations' abilities to control their own economics, you ensure that your loans will be repaid first with, of course, a hefty interest. Behind your exaggerated sense of self-righteousness, you are no better than a shylock or a loan shark."

"Let's discuss Elias St. Armand," insisted Roland Miller.

With half a smile on his face and swelling up inside with the enjoyment of his friend being bested by this young man, the Savile Row man stepped forward.

"Agreed."

"What is your relationship with Elias and Occidental?" Peter directed his attack at the Savile Row man.

"Actually Elias and Occidental have been very useful to us. His approach to politics lacks certain delicacies, but the results have been exceptional."

"How has he been useful?"

"Our Council has always included some very influential men in American politics. Elias, however, has expanded that influence all the way to a grass-roots level. Essentially, he has made voting a ritual rather than an exercise of freedom. He has driven voter turnout down, limited choices of candidates, and controlled the media. Hell, he just engineered a media-driven coup to capture the presidency. Unfortunately, that has come at a price."

"He has become too big for his britches."

The Englishman stroked his thumbs along the back of his braces.

"That, and the fact that not all of his interests are shared by all of us."

"Like what?" inquired Peter.

"Take the Gulf Wars. We could not let the Iraqis take that oil or disrupt the balance of power in the region. At first, Elias was dependable. He engineered a story about Iraqi troops pulling three hundred babies from their incubators and leaving them on the frigid hospital floors to die. More importantly, he had everyone concerned with Saddam's elusive weapons of mass destruction. He circulated stories through the embedded media and inundated Congress with additional stories. But he could not stop with Iraq. He started the same campaign to occupy Syria. He wanted us to invade Syria. The Council said 'no.' Elias still pushed and pushed. He kept lobbying for a new Middle East. A Middle East with 'unlimited potential,' he said. I, along with my European and Asian colleagues, disagreed."

"Elias would not let it go," the Englishman chimed in. "He wanted, wants to light the fuse on the powder keg."

"How can he do that?" asked Peter.

"He is closer than you know," responded the Englishman. "He has the votes in Congress through his Occidental files."

"The thirty billion dollars in aid to Lebanon," Peter was starting to catch on.

"A military war chest," responded the Savile Row man.

"But the President would never..."

Once Peter realized what he was saying he stopped.

Everyone stared at Peter.

"Wait, wait, wait," Peter started as he began to pace. "People are not going to stand for this no matter how many politicians say it is the right thing to do. There will be more protests; there's no way."

"You are probably right; people dumping tea in the harbor and all that stuff," responded the Englishman.

"That is why Elias needs all those consumers of Occidental products on his side," the Savile Row man continued. "He can do it."

"How can he do it?" Peter knew he did not want to hear the answer to his question.

"He told us."

"What did he tell you?" inquired Miller who obviously had not been informed.

"Elias St. Armand plans to stage another terrorist attack right here in New York City."

Both Peter and Miller's jaws dropped.

"Elias St. Armand plans to sacrifice thousands, perhaps tens of thousands, of American lives to stir up public outrage against Syria. St. Armand is Lebanese and he wants Lebanon to be his new capital in the Middle East. Syria occupies Lebanon. Syria supports terrorism. Syria is the best target."

"In addition to the fact that he is still none too happy with you about Syria and Lebanon," interrupted the Englishman.

"My colleague here is convinced that Elias is after me because of my approval of the general acquiescence to Syria's occupation of Lebanon." The Savile Row man turned to the Englishman and said, "Syria was an integral part to Desert Storm and we had to honor our agreement with them."

The Englishman rolled his eyes.

"When the Kosovo action occurred, Elias again requested that we take action in Lebanon. He requested it again with the Al Qaeda, the Taliban, and the Gulf Wars. We said we would look into the matter."

Roland Miller became fully engaged in the conversation, "How come we were not informed?"

"Everything escalated in the last couple of days," retorted the Englishman.

"Wait a second." Peter stopped pacing. "Aren't you going to stop this terrorist attack?"

"All we know is that it is going to happen tonight."

"Tonight?" Peter was slowly regaining his composure as well as appreciating his value to these men. "I want Sara safely out of town immediately. No airports."

"That is already being taken care of," responded the Englishman as he pointed to the television monitor.

Sara was no longer in the room.

"No airports," Peter reiterated.

"She's taking a long train ride to a safe place upstate," the Englishman countered.

"What assurances do I have?"

"None," responded the Savile Row man.

"None?"

"We need your undivided attention," the Savile Row man insisted. "We want to free your mind of any distractions from what we need you to do for us."

"We just cannot have you running after your little gal," the Englishman spoke up stressing the word "gal" in his best western accent.

"You want me to get to St. Armand?"

"Do not be so melodramatic, young man." The Englishman reached over to the head of the conference table again. "I love this part."

The Englishman pressed another button which opened the doors behind the conference room table again.

In walked the tall blond who had wrestled Peter in and around his apartment. The same man from the SUV who brought him and Sara to Elias St. Armand's boat.

"Mr. Farrell, I believe you have met Andriy Kravenko," the Englishman introduced in a melodramatic manner.

"He is one of Occidental's men," accused Peter.

"No, actually he was assigned by us to watch over this Occidental file situation," answered the Savile Row man.

"We need you to get Kravenko close to St. Armand."

"You are the only one," the Savile Row man continued. "Elias would be suspicious if Kravenko just showed up, but with you there is a chance to get close to him."

"Won't he just kill me on sight?"

"Do not flatter yourself, Farrell," the Englishman responded. "Granted, Elias St. Armand is no lawyer, but how would the press handle it if the Shakespeare Killer was going after this layman? When he is going to kill you is when he takes you out of the public eye."

"That's reassuring," Peter said. "I wish you would have said 'if.'"

"You are not ignorant, Mr. Farrell," the Savile Row man lectured. "You know as well as we do that you are still a wild card for St. Armand. You have turned into something that he cannot tightly fit into his box."

Peter did not like this. He did not like being used, much less used to lure a man to his death.

"Mr. Farrell," said the Savile Row man as he walked away from Peter toward Kravenko. "I thought you would jump at the chance to avenge your brother's death."

Peter did not take the bait and changed the subject, "What do you know about this act of terrorism?"

"Only that it will be on a grand scale and dramatic, like Elias himself," responded the Englishman.

"We expect it to be some biochemical device in a public place, maybe a place of public significance. It will be a place that will make Americans feel vulnerable again," finished the Savile Row man.

"There is not enough time to develop any type of intelligence on this matter," the Englishman added. "We have tried."

"The only option is St. Armand," the Savile Row man told the four men. "He is the only one with the answers."

"But if St. Armand falls, what stops the next Occidental man?" Peter inquired.

"Occidental is not some hydra," explained the Englishman. "If you cut off Occidental's head, it will fall."

"Which certainly helps you," Peter noted.

"This may be the only chance to stop Elias St. Armand," the Savile Row man candidly admitted. "You are correct, young man. However, if Elias succeeds, there is no stopping Occidental. Elias St. Armand will conduct global policy as if he were a spoiled child: helping those who are nice to him and punishing those who fall on his bad side. However, when Elias falls and you retrieve the Occidental files, we will be able to tame the Occidental beast."

"He does not have a copy of the files and he only had a couple of them," Roland Miller interrupted.

Peter Farrell let the statement stand uncorrected.

"So the Speaker's file was just a bluff." The Savile Row man started smiling at the Englishman. "Well, no matter, now that we know these files exist, our man Kravenko will retrieve them."

Peter looked and felt disgusted.

"Can I change?" he asked tugging the NYE worker's coat that he still wore.

"No," the Savile Row man responded.

"I want to see Sara before I go," Peter requested.

"There is no time," the Savile Row man again refused Peter.

"Do go." The Englishman gestured to Farrell as if he were dismissing him.

"Remember, Farrell," the Savile Row man cautioned, "it is in your best interest and your friend's best interest to get Kravenko to St. Armand."

Peter received the message loud and clear. If he did not do what he was told, Sara's life was in jeopardy.

# FIFTY-TWO

The security guard at the front desk was in a state of complete shock. "But, sir, I told you, you can go up to the reception on the twentieth and they can help you with any appointment you may have."

With a stern voice Peter again told the security guard, "You call reception, you call whomever you want, as long as word gets upstairs that Peter Farrell is here to see Elias St. Armand."

"It won't do any good."

"Just pick up the phone."

"But..."

Kravenko, with his jaws clenched and barely opening his mouth barked, "Pick up the phone."

The security guard picked up the phone.

"There is someone here to see Mr. St. Armand."

The guard paused.

"I told them that."

He paused again and rolled his eyes up to the ceiling.

"I told them that, too."

There was another pause. The guard looked more uncomfortable.

"He is dressed like a bum and says he is Peter Farrell."

There was very little pause this time.

"I am at the main desk in the lobby."

The guard looked back and forth as he waited.

Peter checked out the lobby. Art deco was de rigueur. Marble, black, gold, amber, and blue reigned supreme. The sheen of the entire lobby also was enhanced by a chrome lining which was actually stainless steel. Mirrors also accented the sharp angles in the lobby which actually made the entire room appear smaller than the portion of the city block it occupied. Lighting was kept to a minimum. It was a very intimate setting for a corporate headquarters.

Peter half expected to see a giant thirty-foot buffed-up statue of Elias St. Armand wrapped in a loin cloth holding a golden globe over his head. The lobby, free from such a gaudy display, was a pleasant surprise.

Peter looked at Kravenko and noticed the scratch up the side of his face from when they fought on Halloween.

"You're not going to hold that against me are you?" asked Peter, pointing at the wound.

Kravenko touched the scab.

"He who touches pitch blackens his hand."

"Well, I guess that takes care of that."

"Gentlemen," the security guard spoke as he still held the phone to his ear. When Peter and Kravenko turned to the security guard, two muscle-bound men clad in four-thousand-dollar Armani suits stepped up from nowhere.

"Follow us," one said.

Shades of the blue suited and brown suited justice agents on steroids flashed through Peter's head. The two security men were virtually identical in size: both huge; both bald; both clad in Armani; and finally, both of their mannerisms were robotic. The only distinction lay in the fact that the guard who spoke had a goatee, and the other did not.

The two guards led Peter Farrell and the assassin named Kravenko to the third elevator bank, a smaller one than the other two, consisting of only two elevators as opposed to the six elevators in the other two banks. In between the two elevators appeared to be a rectangle consisting of black opal marble encased in chrome. There were no buttons. The bulky guard with the goatee placed the palm of his hand on the piece of encased marble. A moment later one of the elevator doors opened revealing a spacious room decorated in burgundy leather and brass studs. Antique cushioned wooden benches rested on both sides of the elevator with a Persian rug on the floor and another door across from the entrance. Again there were no buttons other than those on the phone next to the bench on the right. Fifteen of these large guards could have fit into the elevator comfortably. As the doors shut behind them, Kravenko lifted his arms and the guard with the goatee removed the Glock automatic pistol from Kravenko's holster. The other man frisked Peter and determined that he had no weapon.

The elevator ascended quickly to the sixty-first floor. The doors opened revealing an unparalleled office suite. To the right of the elevator were two doors presumably leading to a boardroom of sorts. But to the left, a spacious two-storied room unfolded. There was a huge glass bay window overlooking the city, mostly Central Park and inland. Straight ahead, a spiral staircase adorned by a gleaming stainless steel railing and steps descended from what appeared to be a parlor or living quarters upstairs. Elias St. Armand, clad in a smoking jacket, tailored shirt, and ascot, descended from above as Peter took in the rest of the eclectic office suite. As well as general office equipment, such as a desk, bookshelves, file cabinets, computers, fax machines, and a copier, most of the room appeared to be dedicated to various trophies which included: a suit of armor, a full-scale taxidermied white Bengal tiger, several sets of tusks hanging from the walls, as well as numerous colorful or weathered tapestries, two aquariums, one contained miniature sharks, about a half dozen glass casings raised on pedestals, several vases, and a trophy case containing photos, memorabilia, and trophies. The electronic blinds for the large windows across the room opened the entire area. Otherwise the suite would look like a very expensive garage sale.

"Welcome, gentlemen."

From his demeanor, one would think Elias St. Armand was hosting a cocktail party.

"Can I offer you a drink? You look like you can use one, Mr. Farrell."

Elias St. Armand walked over to the bar.

While Peter Farrell had been consuming his surroundings, Kravenko had surveyed the entire situation from a different perspective. As Elias St. Armand walked away from the four men, Kravenko delivered a crushing blow to the base of the skull of the goateed guard, incapacitating him. The muscle-bound goateed guard instantly fell to the ground. The other guard was a half step in front of Farrell. Hearing the slight commotion, he quickly whirled around brandishing his sidearm. However, the second guard never had a chance. Before his gun was completely raised, Kravenko cracked the man's jaw with the same powerful hand that leveled the first guard. Kravenko delivered another blow to the man's throat with the same right hand. Finally, the assassin grabbed the back of the guard's head and rammed him into the wall beside the elevator. Neither guard was conscious.

"Now, that was not necessary."

Elias St. Armand appeared amused by Kravenko's display of hand-to-hand combat.

Kravenko continued his work. He lifted the goateed security guard's legs and dragged him between the elevator doors of the elevator all four had just exited. He took the other guard's arm and lifted it toward the black opal panel, then pressed the guard's palm to the panel. The doors of the second elevator opened. Kravenko then dragged the guard's body to the doors and placed the crumpled body between the second set of elevator doors. Access to the suite through the two elevators had been blocked.

"I see that my little monk friend is acting like a Trojan horse," Elias commented as he poured some cognac into a snifter.

St. Armand's calm demeanor sharply contrasted Peter Farrell's delayed shock. He was not sure if Kravenko was about to attack him next, or whether Elias St. Armand remained the target.

"Do come in," Elias continued as if all that happened was that the wind blew a shutter closed.

Regaining his composure, Peter was still unsure of what he was to do. He had helped his mime sidekick gain entry to the Occidental suite and access to Elias St. Armand. Now he did not know what was going to happen next. Elias St. Armand was the first to grasp the essence of the moment.

"You have no idea why you are here, young man, do you?"

Kravenko led the way toward St. Armand. Peter followed.

"You are here because I wanted you here," summoned St. Armand.

Peter thought that either St. Armand had no idea that Kravenko was here to kill him, or that Peter was in way over his head. Despite the gruesomeness of the act, he hoped it was the former.

"Your choice of allegiance leaves a lot to be desired, Mr. Farrell."

Peter wondered if the megalomaniac knew that Roland Miller and the

Council sent him. There was no one else in the room. Why was St. Armand so confident in himself, so arrogant?

"I could have had you eliminated a dozen times. Just in the lobby, I decided to let you live a little bit longer. However, you have the good fortune in timing, in that you are arriving so close to my moment of triumph."

"I am here to offer you a deal," Peter started to believe he was in way over his head and started grasping at straws.

"There are no more deals with you." His tone was completely dismissive.

"You missed the boat, son. Aaron had such high hopes for you." St. Armand paused and then nodded at the Ukrainian assassin. "I might have to rework something with Mr. Kravenko, but your days of negotiating have expired."

Kravenko lowered his weapon.

"But I have the Occidental files," insisted Peter.

"So?"

"Every hour one of the files will be released on the Internet. Sexton was only the first, many will follow."

Peter believed he was starting to gain momentum.

"So?"

Despite his training, Peter could not contain the look of surprise on his face.

"The indiscretions, or transgressions, of some politicians will be irrelevant in a few minutes. You do not understand, young man. Occidental is just a stepping stone."

Elias St. Armand paused to relish in his own moment.

"You are here because you were a pivotal, no, I would go as far as to say, crucial part in obtaining a greater glory."

"Greater glory?"

"Of all people, you should understand, Mr. Farrell," lectured Elias St. Armand as he lifted the glass casing enshrining the Cross of St. Maro.

"Me?" Peter replied, raising his eyebrows.

Lifting the authentic Cross of St. Maro from beneath the faux cross, Elias began his rehearsed monologue, "Do you know what this is?"

"The Cross of St. Maro," responded Peter. Sitti's speech was not lost on the young lawyer.

"I'm impressed."

Peter continued, "But what does that have to..."

"Maro was a contemporary of your St. Patrick," interrupted St. Armand to prove his point.

"As with your little leprechaun Patrick, St. Maro attracted followers by his wisdom and fortitude. These two men, no, demigods, also drew upon a divine power to rid their lands of serpents and demons. As Patrick cast the snakes from Ireland, Maro banished the pagan Muslims from Jerusalem and the holy land of Phoenicia."

"I will bring them home from the land of Egypt and gather them from Assyria; and I will bring them to the land of Gilead and to Lebanon till there is no room for them," chimed Kravenko.

"Exactly."

Elias St. Armand waved his arms as if he were at some Baptist revival. The bones of St. Maro clinked against his watch.

"This is..." Peter began.

"And so shall I deliver Lebanon," Elias forcefully stated as he put the Cross of St. Maro around his neck.

"I lived up to my end," Peter continued.

"You have not even begun to realize your place in history, Peter Farrell."

"My place in history?"

"Tomorrow, the United States will be at war again."

"War?"

"War. A very lopsided war. The United States of America will unilaterally engage in repeated strikes on Syria, depleting their military of half its force by week's end."

The young attorney was expressionless.

"You think that I am crazy?" the billionaire asked. "Crazy, no," denied Elias St. Armand as he answered his own question, "A zealous patriot, yes."

Although the tone in his voice had lowered an octave or two, his mannerisms remained emphatic as if he were conducting an orchestra, or more likely as if he were speaking to thousands of devoted followers.

"Lebanon is the only satellite state in the world; the only former democratic state at the mercy of another state's totalitarian regime. There are no more Soviet satellites. There are no more colonies in the British Empire. Even the satellites in Yugoslavia have achieved independence. There is only one satellite state and that is Lebanon."

"Syrian troops entered Lebanon in 1975. Forty thousand of these Syrian troops remain in Lebanon with the aid of an untold number of secret police and intelligence agents. These Syrian troops, secret police and agents have committed atrocities against the Lebanese people on a much grander scale than anything in Kosovo. Anyone who has ever posed a threat to the Syrian regime in Lebanon has been killed, imprisoned, or forced into exile."

Elias took a breath as he stood in front of the thirty-foot bay window with the backdrop of New York City behind him. The gigantic stainless steel gargoyles protruding from the Occidental Tower protected St. Armand's back as he continued his oration.

"The domination of Lebanon is at the brink of no return. Syria has flooded Lebanon with over a million immigrants. Syria has been more successful than Serbia in this regard because of its ability to keep the influx of Syrians into Lebanon while cleansing Christian Lebanese from their own country. The anti-Christian, anti-Lebanese, anti-democratic, Syrian regime has even begun rewriting Lebanese history. Lebanese children are being indoctrinated with the conquests of Arabic and Islamic fairy tales as well as Syrian dogma. They are slowly but surely disenfranchising Christians and any Lebanese patriot from their country. Syria is not holding a troubled nation together but creating a province for Greater Syria."

"I am a student of history and I will not allow six thousand years to be erased. Lebanon has never been a part of Syria, and it will not become a Syrian province now. To the contrary, Syria will once again become a part of Greater Lebanon in the new Middle East."

St. Armand glanced at Kravenko and continued his sermon, "men of

God," he looked back at Peter, "men of principle, are the easiest to manipulate because their next move is always foreseeable. You have been the perfect pawn. Without the death of the President at the hands of some fanatic, the fanatic of course being you, I would never have been able to launch my campaign. Sure, Aaron had a contingency plan to pull you out if you came with us, but everything just worked out too perfect. Perfect for me. Perfect to vindicate St. Maro by freeing Christian Lebanon from Islamic control."

Peter knew he needed to provoke this pompous ass into revealing more. He thought that Kravenko would have killed St. Armand by now unless he needed more information from him. Peter cared about whatever catastrophic event Elias St. Armand had planned, but his thoughts were more on having Kravenko do whatever he had to do and getting back to the CIR to ensure Sara's safety. The CIR, Elias, and Occidental had control over too many things to engage in idle threats. For that matter, everything they said they were going to do, they did. Peter had to keep reminding himself that the President was dead; and more importantly, the man standing before him had the President killed. For Peter, there was the realization that a man like this had the ability to set in motion a war. However, now was not the time for fear. He had to help Sara.

"I think it's obvious that your master plan has already failed," Peter taunted the man who believed he was the manipulator of the free world.

"Failed?"

Elias St. Armand would play this game with the young attorney.

"Yes, failed."

"How?"

"Well, obviously I am here," Peter stated, but starting to sound if he were making it up as he went along, which he was.

"And your point is?" Elias paused.

"If I killed the President in some fanatical suicidal rage, how is it that I am in New York as opposed to dead in San Francisco?"

"Don't flatter yourself. You will die soon enough."

"But any coroner or prosecutor worth a dime would be able to figure out that I was not killed at the scene of the assassination or even at the time of the assassination.

"Details," Elias St. Armand dismissively responded.

"Details are important, crucially important in criminal investigations, much less the assassination of the President of the United States."
Elias opened the door beside the bay window, stepped one foot on the veranda, turned and snapped back at Peter, "Ever hear of the Warren Commission?"

Peter followed St. Armand onto the empty veranda. Kravenko stayed by the door as if the two silver majestic gargoyles overhanging each side of the veranda forbade him to enter their nest.

Elias St. Armand continued.

"The important undisputed details are that you were in the same room when the President was slain; and that a gun linked to you in other murders was the one that killed the President. The public will not need any other details. The rest will fall into place."

Peter was starting to believe the maniac.

"But that pales to what is about to occur in about fifteen minutes."

"In fifteen minutes?"

"In fifteen minutes, the details of the President's death will take a backseat to the next battleground in the war against terrorism."

"And that is?"

"Do you know what an organophosphate nerve agent is? That is a rhetorical question of course. I have learned a lot about them lately. A nerve agent, like Sarin, affects enzymes causing them to be over-stimulated. First, you breathe it into your lungs. The muscles in your throat and chest contract and then begin to collapse. Respiration becomes slow, then ceases. Your blood pressure also falls and your heart begins to  pump irregularly. A lethal dose of a half a milligram can kill an adult in thirty minutes."

All Peter could think to himself was that this son of a bitch was going to gas innocent people.

"Come here, Mr. Farrell."

Peter, still in a state of shock, joined St. Armand at the edge of the veranda.

"I know it's hard to see from this angle, but if you look straight down below you can see Grand Central Terminal. Rush hour central. A half million people pass through that building daily."

Peter could not believe what he was hearing.

Elias St. Armand checked the time on his Rolex.

"In thirteen minutes, two Syrian terrorists will release about twenty kilograms of sarin into the atmosphere of the Main Concourse of Grand Central Terminal. Thousands will die. Tens of thousands more will suffer irreparable injuries. Fear and rage will rule. And this time, the sword of vengeance will be swift and decisive. Syria will pay..."

As Elias continued, Peter had lost his ability to breathe. The words "She's taking a long train ride to a safe place" rang through his skull. His heart sank.

Sara.

Peter turned toward Kravenko. Kravenko nodded as he had come to the same realization that Sara could likely be one of the innocent victims in twelve minutes. Peter raced past Kravenko toward the elevator.

Elias St. Armand had no idea what had just transpired. More to the point, no one had ever left his presence in such a manner.

"Stop him," ordered St. Armand.

Kravenko took a couple steps toward Peter.

Peter dragged the body of the goatee laden muscle-bound guard from between the elevator doors. He then entered the elevator. The elevator door did not move. Peter took a half a step out of the elevator and gave Kravenko a puzzled look.

Kravenko raised the palm of his hand toward Peter.

Peter lifted the goatee man's arm to the black panel beside the elevator door and pressed his palm against the panel. As the hand fell to the ground, Peter jumped into the elevator.

The door began to shut when St. Armand picked up the receiver to the telephone.

"Well, he's going nowhere."

Kravenko spun around and shot the phone right out of Elias St. Armand's hands.

Elias finally realized his control over Kravenko had its limits.

"You of all people understand that it is God's will to restore Lebanon to its glory. The Bible demands it. The book of Isaiah states 'Is it not yet a very little while until Lebanon shall be turned into a fruitful field, shall be regarded as a forest.'"

Without hesitation Kravenko replied, "Lebanon would not suffice for fuel, nor are its beasts enough for a burnt offering."

Elias began to back pedal around the other side of the desk as he spouted out, "It shall blossom abundantly, and rejoice with joy and singing. The glory of Lebanon shall be given to it...They shall have the glory of the Lord."

As he followed St. Armand, Kravenko, his voice low but forceful, retorted, "The violence done to Lebanon will overwhelm you; the destruction of the beasts will terrify you, for the blood of men and violence to the earth, to cities and all who dwell therein."

Stepping backwards, Elias stumbled over the rug and braced himself on the glass casing that carried the faux Cross of St. Maro.

"Wait!" Elias shrieked.

Kravenko raised his pistol and his voice, "Open your doors, O Lebanon, that the fire may devour your cedars!"

Elias fell to his knees before Kravenko. With one last gasp, he pleaded again.

"I have a relic that could be from Pachomius."

The look on Kravenko's face was one of pity and disgust.

"I can get it for you, and you can also have back the Cross of St. Maro." Elias lifted the saint's bones from around his neck and presented them to Kravenko as one last gesture begging for his life.

With Elias St. Armand kneeling before him, Kravenko bowed his head and closed his eyes for a moment while he recited, "In the invocation of saints, the veneration of relics and the sacred use of images, every superstition shall be removed and all filthy lucre abolished."

As he stated the word "abolished," he pulled the trigger. Elias St. Armand's body fell to the ground. Kravenko picked up the Cross of St. Maro and walked to the elevator.

The East 125th Street subway station was no different than other subway stops other than the fact it was located between Harlem and East Harlem in one of New York City's less touristy areas. The renowned skyline of the city was absent in this tenement area. The area's African-American and Latino populations suffered poverty similar to Compton or the South Side of Chicago. Drugs and violence were the rule, not the exception, in this area. The East 125th Street Station, with its abundance of pay phones, bustled as the business center of sorts for pushers and dealers. The placement of a subway station in the area was symbolic, in that it was the only escape for those trapped on this part of the island who were prevented from crossing the Harlem River into the Bronx by the Willis Avenue Bridge, or into Queens by the Triborough Bridge. Jumping the gates of the subway offered a reprieve, or at the very least, a brief furlough from the desolate troubled neighborhood. For Chamoun Al Khouri, the East 125th Street Station represented the first step in what would be a glorious day for Lebanon.

Al Khouri and his compatriot descended down the second flight of steps to the platform. Neither looked conspicuous for their surroundings. Both wore olive-colored slacks that were wrinkled, soiled, and stained. The stitching on the cuffs had been torn so that the pant legs flapped over their worn tennis shoes. Both men also sported dirty T-shirts. Over his shirt Al Khouri wore a heavy flannel shirt, unbuttoned, but covering his entire torso. His fellow patriot's dirty T-shirt was almost completely covered by the navy blue windbreaker zipped up to his chest. Both men carried plastic bags within plastic bags. Within the second set of bags, and covered under several newspapers, lay six aluminum canisters.

As the number six train, the Lexington Avenue Local, pulled up to the platform, the Lebanese freedom fighters patiently waited at the end of the platform. They would be taking the second car. Each step in the journey had been meticulously planned. Every detail must be followed. It was nearly rush hour, and the trains were already full. People squeezed in and out of the subway cars. However, the cars at the end of the train were always less crowded.

The second car of the number six train was an exception. Although there were few places to sit, no one had to stand. Immediately as Al Khouri and his compatriot boarded the train, two other Middle Eastern-looking men rose from their seats, then disembarked. Right on cue, Chamoun Al Khouri, the avenger of Deir Ashashe, sat in the seat that had been saved for him. In ten stops they would arrive in Grand Central Terminal. In ten stops, the wheels would be set in motion to avenge his brother Antonios' death. There was no turning back. No last word from a contact giving him final approval that the mission was a go or abort the plan. That would have had to happen long ago. Soon the Tigers would be victorious. Lebanon would be free. And Antonios would be able to rest in peace. And so would Chamoun Al Khouri.

# FIFTY-THREE

Roland Miller stood side by side with the Savile Row man staring out the full-length window at the steel and glass jungle. The Englishman hung up the phone. He nodded to the Savile Row man. The Savile Row man played with a cigar.

"Do you think they will make it in time?"

Roland's voice was serene with a feigned compassion.

"Does it matter?" responded the Savile Row man.

"What do you mean 'does it matter?'"

Roland turned to the Savile Row man.

"The Occidental files are no longer lost, and Elias will no longer be an issue."

"And the thousands Elias promised to kill?"

"Irrelevant in the long run, just collateral damage," the Savile Row man bluntly responded as he lit his cigar.

"What about Algers?"

The Englishman joined the two men by the window just as Miller had posed the question and interjected, "That has just been taken care of."

"Who will it be?" asked the Savile Row man.

"Scholfield," replied the Englishman.

"I could think of better choices," responded the Savile Row man.

"I can think of worse," stated the Englishman.

"Much worse," chimed Miller as the three elder men stared out the window down at the masses huddled below.

"That Farrell of yours has potential," the Englishman noted, more as an inquiry than an observation.

"He does at that," Miller confirmed.

"If he survives."

The Savile Row man ended the conversation with a large puff of Havana smoke.

They told her that Peter was safe and no longer in danger. Sara didn't believe them. Sara had a hard time believing Roland Miller. Miller assured, no promised, her that Peter was fine. Peter trusted him, but Sara could not distinguish Miller from the other old men. They all had an exaggerated sense of their own importance. First, the old crotchety W.A.S.P. His tie was tied so tight, the flow of oxygen to his brain must have been cut off. He had no business barking orders to her in such a dismissive manner. He treated her as if she were a little school girl. The dirty old Englishman was no better with that fake Italian accent and overstated mannerisms. He probably wished she was a naughty little school girl. And finally Roland Miller. Sara could not believe he pandered to the other two. For all she knew, this Council of International Relations could just be a part of Occidental. What had Peter's brother said? Trust no one. How could she trust these old men?

They said that Peter would meet her tomorrow up in the Adirondacks. She was told that Peter's debriefing would go well into the night, and the city was not safe for her. So it was the consensus of the elders that Sara would be sent upstate until Peter completed the debriefing. The security breach earlier with the limousine dictated the less conspicuous mode of transportation of traveling by train. Also because of the lapse in security, the frothy Englishman insisted his personal guards be used. Since they had all arrived that morning in New York from London, no one would be able to recognize them. Consequently, with four bodyguards in tow, Sara found herself waiting impatiently on track thirty-four in Grand Central Terminal for the 5:15 train to Albany.

George Algers closed the door to his hotel suite, alone at last. All those miserable children and their annoying questions. It had been a horrible day all around.

There was a knock on the door.

"Come in," said Algers, still irritated and now morose. He had not had a chance to take his jacket off.

"Sir," a Secret Service agent, not one of his regular crew entered the room. "What is it now?"

"These just arrived for you."

The Secret Service agent handed the Vice President two blank envelopes then left the suite.

George set the envelopes on the coffee table and removed his coat. As he walked toward the bedroom he loosened his tie. He stopped in his tracks. What if something was wrong. Elias never called him. He didn't say he would, but surely he would have called by now. What if the envelopes were from Elias?

The Vice President turned around and walked to the coffee table. He picked up the first envelope. After reading its contents, he fell into a sitting position on the sofa. In disbelief he read the letter again.

> *Dear George:*
>
> *Tonight before the prime time news I will resign from office citing health reasons because of my age. Because of this, I find myself finally being able to actually say what I want to, without worrying about the consequences.*
>
> *As you know, I knew your father and grandfather very well. It sad-dened me when Bill passed away earlier this year. In fact, it saddened me so much that I had my personal physician review your father's medical records. We determined that there are some inconsistencies that will need to be explored.*
>
> *Whether we explore these inconsistencies formally, informally, or not at all is up to you.*
>
> *As a Texan, I know you will do the honorable thing.*
>
> > *Very truly yours,*
> > *Senator John Jay Knox*

Algers opened a second envelope. It was a photocopy of a death certificate. It was the death certificate for William Wadsworth Algers II. The cause of death was listed as "myocardial infarction caused by amphetamines, trace amounts of which were discovered in a second autopsy."

George Wadsworth Algers put his hands over his face and began to cry.

---

On any given day over five hundred thousand tourists, workers, or commuters pass through majestic Beaux Arts-influenced Grand Central Terminal on 42nd Street between Lexington and Vanderbilt Avenues in Manhattan. Protected from being swallowed up by the surrounding city by Roman deities Mercury, Hercules, and Minerva, Grand Central Terminal analogizes itself to the heart of the city. The analogy applies to function as opposed to pathos. Grand Central Terminal brings people into the city through its veins and distributes them throughout the city through its arteries. Not the vision of literary prose, but a vital organ nonetheless. Although a heart reinvigorates blood with oxygen as it passes from vein to artery, the same cannot be said about the thousands of commuters in a mindless trance as they move from train to subway, subway to subway, and subway to train. As they move about the terminal, no one notices the two pathogens that have entered the heart of New York City. Chamoun Al Khouri, the avenger of Deir Ashashe, and his compatriot had just arrived at Grand Central Terminal.

---

"Getting off soon, Sam?" the beat cop asked Samuel Smith.

"About an hour," Smith replied.

"Have a good night if I don't see ya," the beat cop smiled.

"Same."

The police officer stopped, pointed his nightstick at Sam Smith and added, "But stay out of trouble, Sam."

"Wouldn't have it any other way."

They both laughed.

Samuel Smith had been selling papers at the corner of 42nd and Vanderbilt Avenue since shortly after the First Gulf War. Otis had been on the beat for the last five years covering the sidewalks and adjacent areas to Grand Central Terminal. The two liked one another. But the two also had an understanding.

Sam always gave Otis a free daily on his coffee break, and Otis maintained an extra presence around Sam's corner so that some kid would not rip him off. Sure, Sam had his German Shepherd, "Saddam," but having a policeman hang around was a better insurance policy. After all, if some kid ripped off his money, what was he going to do, wheel after him?

Sam Smith did not lose his legs in the First Gulf War. He saw a lot of crap there, but war did not cost him his legs, stupidity did. In his youthful and reckless days just following the war, he was either on one side or the other of a bar. He bartended four or five nights a week at a dive bar in Queens. The other nights he was either barhopping in Queens or in one of the other boroughs. After one night of debauchery, shortly after he passed out fully clothed in his bed, a loud noise woke him. In his inebriated state, he mistakenly believed the car that backfired in the street below was an intruder trying to break into his apartment. His nightstand drawer contained a souvenir Colt .45 automatic pistol from the war. The customized hairpin trigger and lack of safety features were considered "bonuses" when he smuggled the weapon home. A combination of his lack of dexterity skills and absolutely no sense of judgment left him without the use of his legs after the fumbled weapon discharged severing his spinal cord at his waist.

After several months of self-pity, drugs, and alcohol, a Veteran's group set him up with his corner at Grand Central Terminal. They also gave him the dog. The name, "Saddam," was Sam's idea. Sam used the name because he liked the idea of having a dog collar around Saddam. The things he saw in the Gulf still made him question if God could exist. What that man did to his own people with biochemical warfare. He still could not get the faces of some of the nerve gas victims out of his mind. He was lucky that none of that shit got him. Now Sam had Saddam himself, and Otis, of course, protecting him.

———

Peter Farrell had no idea how far behind him Kravenko was, but he had a fair idea of what he was doing. Unfortunately for Elias St. Armand, Sara's safety was Peter's only priority. He exited the art deco Occidental Tower and raced across Lexington Avenue almost decorating some cab as a hood ornament.

As Peter entered the next building, he realized he had no idea where exactly he was going. He only knew a direction from the view from Elias' office window. For all he knew in his rush to get to Sara, he could have exited the Occidental Tower in exactly the opposite direction of Grand Central Terminal. There was no time for error. Peter grabbed the first person he saw.

"Where's the train station?"

The poor girl he grabbed was a teenager. With her brown shoulder-length hair, plaid lumberjack-style shirt and black purse clenched in her white knuckles, she was someone's daughter or sister visiting the big city for the first time. She cried immediately when Peter grabbed her. Peter surveyed his surroundings. The adrenalin and anxiety allowed him to digest only so much. He was at the beginning of a long hallway, crowded with people. But it was not just a hallway; it was a long market with breads, meats, delis, produce and exotic or "fine" foods for sale on each side of the jam-packed aisle. Racks of breads or counters separated the white-shirted, black-slacked staff from customers. Peter cut in front of a long blond-haired woman in her late twenties carrying a shopping bag full of a day's worth of shopping in the Big Apple before returning to Westchester County.

"Where's the train station?" Peter shouted at the butcher behind the meat counter.

The din of the mass of shoppers lessened the impact of Peter's voice on the butcher. However, Peter did not exactly go unnoticed.

"Hey, pal," the butcher snapped back, "this lady was first."

"But," stammered Peter as he stared at the butcher.

The blond shopper tapped Peter's arm and said, "Grand Central is down the hall and down the escalator."

A stunned and reactive Peter Farrell thanked her before he dashed through the market, parting people with his left arm and elbow, which led the way.

Grand Central is a terminal, not a station, because the trains terminate there mainly on stub-end tracks. However "terminate" is hardly the word to describe one's journey upon disembarking at New York City's Grand Central, especially upon entering the Main Concourse. The grime-infested concourse marked by its black ceiling, which had been damaged by smoke and water, had been renovated. The twenty-five-thousand-square-foot mural depicts a turquoise night backdrop for Zodiac constellations and two thousand five hundred gold-painted stars where a half a century of New York City grime had once ruled. But the majesty of the Main Concourse only begins with the constellation-laden ceiling. The concourse itself has expanded by the simple removal of the clutter that included billboards, TV monitors, and vendor signage. In their places are sparkling chandeliers and classical sculptures. Cleaned and unobstructed, the soaring arched windows fill the concourse with daylight, again adding to the burgeoning feeling of space in the Main Concourse. The colossal marble floor also opens the entire area. Each end is adorned by a mezzanine level with restaurants that are accessed by grandiose marble stairways garnished with brass railings. However, at the center of the Main Concourse, isolated like an island in a marble sea, is the circular information desk. Atop the information desk stands a brass clock with four opal faces greeting this meeting place for generations of New Yorkers. It was 4:55 p.m.

---

Sara had grown accustomed to the four agents who accompanied her. She did not know what kind of agents they were or had been—Secret Service, FBI, CIA, or NSA. All she knew was that they were heavily armed and bound to protect her at all costs, or so that is what Roland Miller had told her. Sara still did not trust him completely, but she had little reason to doubt him in this case and even less options if she did. Her comfort level increased when the agents actually took her to the place that Miller said they were taking her: Grand Central Terminal. She always hated those women in the movies who blindly entered a car or left with someone who everyone did not completely trust only to find herself killed off in the next scene. Sara felt that she had passed the "next scene" test. She made it to the train station as promised and made it to the next scene. Although she was always on her guard, the possibility of one of her bodyguards/agents doing anything in the middle of one of the busiest metro centers in the world was highly unlikely. After all, she did make it to the next scene, as opposed to taken across the river and ending up on some embankment in New Jersey, which of course crossed her mind more than once.

From where they were standing on the platform for track 34, Sara could observe the hustle and bustle in the marble-laden Main Concourse. Businessmen and women rushing to catch their trains to Westchester County or Connecticut or even up to the Adirondacks where she was heading. She disagreed with Miller that no one would be able to find her up there because "they" knew how to find her at Redwood's cabin. In fact, she would not be going if it was not for Miller's assurances that not only would Peter would be safe, but that Miller's men would stay with Redwood until this was over. Miller's men said that Redwood did not need the help, but they had no problem staying with him. Miller had even let her see Peter to show that he was all right. Although Peter appeared physically fit, his mannerisms and pacing revealed otherwise. Whatever he was discussing, no arguing, with those men about, Peter was furious. Sure she had seen him embroiled in heated debates on politics and religion, but the passion he displayed in that boardroom was more than a debate. Peter was angry. Peter was angry at the two men in the room with him.

Sara was confused as to why Miller would not tell her the identities of the men with Peter. His explanation that these were men who could not only develop, but implement, an exit strategy was not helpful. Of course they were powerful men because they had the means to track Peter and Sara down.

"The train will be leaving in twenty minutes," noted the head agent, the one who grabbed Peter's shoulder at the bookstore.

Sara looked at him blankly, still deep in thought.

"That means we will board in five minutes," he continued.

"Yeah." Sara snapped out of her thoughts. "When will Peter be joining us?"

"I have been told, as you were, that Mr. Farrell will be joining us first thing in the morning," the no-nonsense agent answered as he continued to shift his eyes around the platform area.

Partly wanting to hear a voice other than the one in her head, but mostly to confirm that there were no inconsistencies in the agent's story, Sara continued to question him.

"How is he going to meet us first thing in the morning if the train takes three hours?"

"As you well know, Mr. Farrell will be transported by a private jet in the morning which will travel considerably faster than a train."

Sara was not endearing herself to the agent.

"I'm not good enough for a plane?"

"As you know, the present situation requires a less conspicuous method of travel than accessing airports."

"But Peter will fly tomorrow," Sara began.

"Miss, I am here to protect you. Mr. Farrell is of no concern to me now."

"Everyone expects this all to be over by tonight?"

Sara looked for an answer from the agent, but the agent just walked away.

With all of the frantic commuters rushing about, Sara could hardly believe that after tonight all of this would be over.

———◈———

Entering from the Lexington Avenue/42nd Street end of the Main Concourse via the stairs and escalators from the subway, two ragged men with brownish-olive complexions stopped for a moment. The two carried plastic bags in both hands. Entering the renovated Main Concourse, the two were reminiscent of relics from another era in the train terminal's colorful history. However, it was clear to Chamoun Al Khouri and his compatriot that they usher in a new era, one filled with terror and fear.

The two split up at the foot of the east balcony. Each knew what he had to do. No words would need to be spoken. No words had been uttered since leaving the Harlem apartment.

# FIFTY-FOUR

Although Peter was in excellent physical condition, the anxiety over Sara's safety as well as the mad dash from Elias' Occidental suite rendered him breathless for a moment as he entered the Main Concourse of Grand Central Terminal. The undaunting task before him required him to take a breath. Tens of thousands of people darted and moved back and forth in front of him as he stood at the foot of the East Balcony. Generally, Peter handled pressure well. More accurately, he thrived on it. His mind was always thinking of the next step. If this happened, then he would do that; if that happened, then he would do this. Always thinking, trying to stay one step ahead of the situation. However, that skill, that gift, eluded him now. His mind, his edge, escaped him. He could not think clearly with Sara's life mercilessly in the hands of these suicidal terrorists. Fleeting visions of the thousands of other potential innocent victims entered his thoughts, but they were quickly replaced by the image of Sara. He was not being callous toward anyone else; he just could not let anything happen to her. He could not live without Sara. They had already wasted too much time. Too much time because of Occidental. Too much time because of his own stupidity. If only he could get her back. If only he could think.

While racing down the market concourse on his way to the terminal he should have remembered that they said that Sara was taking a train to a safe place "upstate." That meant that any trains to New Jersey or Connecticut were out of the question. Furthermore, "upstate" probably did not mean Westchester County, or probably anything south of Poughkeepsie. That left trains that were heading toward Albany or around that area. It probably would take only a minute or two to check the boards to see what trains were heading toward Albany. It would then only take another couple of minutes to check the corresponding tracks that were listed. However, only after Peter stood at the foot of the East Balcony surveying the situation for a moment or two, did this revelation appear to him.

Just as Peter took a step to canvas the concourse, a strong hand grabbed his shoulder. Peter spun around. It was Kravenko.

"I have to find Sara," Peter uttered.

Kravenko shook his head.

"I have to find Sara," Peter repeated.

"No," Kravenko simply said.

"She's here."

"Yes."

"So I am going to get her out of here," Peter emphatically stated as he began to look around again.

Kravenko grabbed Peter's shoulders and spun him around so that the two were face to face again.

Peter knocked Kravenko's arms off his shoulders.

"Many will die," Kravenko calmly but sternly stated.

"But Sara won't."

"Many will die," it was Kravenko this time repeating himself.

"I don't have time for this," Peter countered as he turned his head again, this time toward the exits to the tracks.

Kravenko grabbed Peter's shoulder and repeated, "Many will die."

Something caught Peter's eye before he turned back to Kravenko.

"But we have no idea who these people are," Peter reasoned before he focused his attention back on what had caught his attention.

Peter turned back to Kravenko.

"It's like finding a needle in a haystack."

Now Kravenko surveyed the crowd.

"There!" Peter directed Kravenko. A homeless man was walking the perimeter of the Main Concourse carrying two plastic bags. He was not a complete throwback to the dark ages of the Grand Central Terminal, but he also was not that out of the ordinary in this day and age. What struck Peter was what the man was doing with his plastic bags and the cans he had in his hands. He was not collecting cans. To the contrary, he took cans from his plastic bag and put them back into the waste containers. It took Peter a minute before he realized the man was placing the lethal sarin canisters into the trash receptacles. Dispersing the deadly gas from various canisters throughout the Main Concourse certainly would expose more people to the gas than from one centralized local area.

Peter looked at Kravenko and began his first step toward the terrorist. Kravenko gestured with his head for Peter to go after Chamoun Al Khouri. Peter nodded in return and dashed off toward the avenger of Deir Ashashe. Kravenko did not run. The other Lebanese Tiger had ducked into the track, probably to place a sarin canister closer to those commuters waiting by the train on the platform. Kravenko did not run but took long strides, masquerading any appearance that he was chasing after anyone. Keeping a quick pace, Kravenko still managed to get to the waste can imbedded in the inner wall of the Main Concourse without bumping or startling anyone. His stride was catlike in execution, an uncanny combination of stealth and speed. He reached his hand into the receptacle and pulled out a canister having the size and weight of a can of soda pop. There was only one. After pocketing the canister, Kravenko casually but quickly turned the corner to enter the train platform. Passengers milled around. There was no sign of the Al Khouri's compatriot. Then the foursome by the end of the train moved. There he was. Standing with his back to Kravenko by the train's last car, and more importantly by a trash can. Stealth gave way to speed as Kravenko's four long strides pierced the sparse crowd.

Without warning there was a scream two tracks down from Kravenko. The Lebanese patriot was startled, but it was too late. It was over before anyone knew better. As Al Khouri's accomplice turned toward the shriek, Kravenko descended upon him. In one swift action, Kravenko wrapped his left arm around the terrorist's neck. His right arm clamped onto the left side of the man's forehead. With a quick snap, the terrorist reign of terror ended. With the crowd still distracted from the commotion two tracks away, Kravenko secured the terrorist's plastic bag of canisters and released his lifeless body onto the tracks four feet below the platform.

———⊱•⊰———

Peter Farrell's mad dash across Grand Central's Main Concourse was intermittently interrupted by commuters determined not to miss their trains. A rotund man turning away from the information desk nearly flattened Peter halfway to the West Balcony. The fleshy fellow's bellowing voice spewed expletives, startling everyone in the immediate area including Chamoun Al Khouri.

The terrorist took no chances, spinning around to flee. However with his first step Al Khouri knocked a young co-ed to the ground. Her fellow collegian, a naïve freshman from Keokuk, Iowa, shrieked in terror as she thought the two were being mugged.

The co-ed's scream startled everyone on the platform waiting for the train on track 34. Sara Ahrens and her bodyguards were no exception. One of the guards drew his weapon; another stood close to Sara while the other two tried to sum up the situation.

The large man's mitt was not quick enough to grab Peter's arm as he darted around the man's stomach in pursuit of Chamoun Al Khouri. The ten steps between Peter Farrell and Al Khouri were reduced to six steps, but the terrorist, who was now on his feet again, stumbled out of the Main Concourse toward the shops underneath the West Balcony.

When Peter reached the base of the marble staircase, Al Khouri entered the tunnel exiting the Main Concourse. Peter reached his hand into the waste receptacle. Beneath the gum, candy wrappers, pop cans, and paper cups partially filled with cold coffee, Peter felt a heavy metal canister. It had to be it. Peter gently pulled the can out of the trash receptacle. Peter had no idea how gas could escape from the can. He worried about hitting a button on the side or accidentally flipping a switch which would release the deadly Sarin gas killing all those around: the rotund man chasing after Peter; the co-eds comforting one another after their brush with big city life; and Sara who could be just around the corner.

———◆———

Sara could not believe her eyes. There he was, only forty feet away. Sara forgot about the young girl's scream which drew her attention to the Main Concourse in the first place. Sara forgot about everything except what unfolded before her eyes, a man with his arm in a trash can. It was Peter.

---

Chamoun Al Khouri distanced himself from the man chasing him. He was ten steps ahead of the man grabbing the sarin bomb from the trash can. Confusion set in. The plan had unraveled. Something had gone wrong. Deir Ashashe must have its vengeance, but would today be the day? Chamoun turned backward to see if he was still being followed. He was. He could not be caught now. Not after everything he had been through. Not after Antonios. Not after Brother Michel. The pain had to end.

---

The small aluminum can containing the sarin was no bigger than a can of soda. It even weighed a little less. The silver-colored can was unmarked. It had to be it. Peter flipped the can over to reveal a plastic digital timer attached to the bottom. The timer counted down from the two hundreds. Two hundred eleven. Two hundred ten. Two hundred nine. Peter realized he had a little over three minutes to deal with these canisters. After a quick look back for Kravenko, Peter dashed after the terrorist. Two hundred five.

He was running away. Sara wanted to yell out, but her bodyguards might do something stupid. If Peter ran toward her, these gun happy security agents might just mistakenly go after Peter. What was Peter doing in the trash can? What was he doing at Grand Central Terminal? They were to meet tomorrow. He must have been there for her. There are no coincidences. Nothing in the past couple days has been a coincidence. It has all been planned or staged. Sara knew that both of them were at the train station because it had been planned. Something was being orchestrated and Peter was in trouble. She had to help him. Two of the security men had started to walk over to the next platform. Another stood by the train. The other, close by her side, was barking orders into a cellphone. Sara tore off after Peter.

One seventy-five.

Al Khouri was completely perplexed. The American had taken the bomb out of the receptacle and chased after him, bomb in hand. He did not even try to defuse the simple device. The American was crazy. More so, the American was destroying everything. Had the American collected the other sarin bombs? There was not enough time. But if there were other American agents involved, the whole plan would fail. He could not be caught. Someone had to avenge Deir Ashashe. It must not end this way.

"Hey, jackass, watch where you are going," the short and stocky Italian-American Mets fan yelled at Chamoun Al Khouri just before the two were about to collide. Al Khouri scrambled around the Mets fan into the shopping area by the ramp leading out to 42nd and Vanderbilt Avenue.

One forty-three.

Two men wheeling their travel cases blocked Chamoun Al Khouri's path up the ramp to the street exit. To his side was another trash can. Al Khouri reached into his plastic bag for another canister, but instead of setting the timer and placing it in the trash, he put the Sarin bomb back in the bag with the others. The two seasoned travelers before him had moved, giving Al Khouri plenty of room to start up the ramp.

Before Al Khouri could start toward the exit, his body crumpled to the ground. Peter had hurled himself into the terrorist knocking Al Khouri down as well as another man dressed in black jeans, T-shirt, and blue jean jacket. The jean jacket man's lunch spilled from his brown paper bag onto the floor. Mixed with the peanut butter sandwich, chips, and apple were five silver canisters with plastic bottoms. The digital timers had slashes running through their dials. They had not been set. As Peter raised his fist to strike the terrorist, he heard Sara's voice and hesitated.

One twenty.

"Peter!" Sara screamed.

One nineteen.

The young man in the jean jacket grabbed Peter's arm before he could hit Chamoun. That was all Chamoun needed. The terrorist cocked back his right leg and kicked Peter in the face, sending Peter's whole body backwards, crashing into a woman's legs and her department store paper shopping bag. Al Khouri rolled over onto his knees, then feet. He ran toward the exit ramp.

One hundred seven.

As the stars and sting from his face began to fade, Peter heard Sara calling again. He also saw the terrorist escaping. The canisters on the ground were not set, and it was unlikely that anyone would pick up something that looked like a bomb. Surprisingly, he had held onto the one can in his hand. The two red nines told Peter that he did not have much time. He also could not be sure if the terrorist had any more gas bombs. Sara was only a couple steps away.

"Don't let anyone touch these," Peter yelled at Sara as he pointed at the silver canisters.

Peter recognized a couple of men running toward him. He recognized that they were the Englishman's agents by their clothes. They were catching up to Sara. She was safe.

Al Khouri regained his ten step lead by the time Peter started after him again. He tried to run up the left side of the forty-foot brick ramp. That side, with its polished brass railing, was crowded with people holding onto the rail. Peter was gaining on Al Khouri.

Eighty-six.

Chamoun Al Khouri reached the exit first. The snap of the cold wind chilled the beads of sweat on Al Khouri's forehead as he emerged from Grand Central Terminal onto the 42nd Street sidewalk. Chamoun's third step onto the sidewalk was his last.

Seventy-two.

Peter bolted out the exit door, tackling Chamoun Al Khouri. The two twisted bodies tumbled into Samuel Smith and his paper stacks. The fall tossed Sam's body from his wheelchair to the sidewalk's curb.

Sixty-three.

Both Peter and Al Khouri, stunned by the collision, did not react quickly.

Peter was flat on his back. Al Khouri was on all fours beside him trying to get back the wind that had been knocked from him. Peter moved first, and landed a roundhouse left hook into Al Khouri's kidney area. Chamoun Al Khouri collapsed and squirmed. Peter rolled the terrorist's limp body over and climbed on top of him. With the canister still clutched in his fist, Peter delivered two blows to the terrorist's face. Al Khouri no longer moved. Realizing what he was using as a weapon, Peter quickly pulled his arm back and checked the timer on the Sarin canister.

Forty-six.

Peter knew he had to throw the bomb down a sewer somewhere. While still sitting on Al Khouri's stomach, Peter patted down the terrorist's jacket. There were no more canisters. Peter checked the timer again.

Thirty-nine.

As Peter looked at the timer, Chamoun Al Khouri reached up and grabbed the top of the canister. Before Peter could react, Chamoun Al Khouri's index finger pressed down hard on the red digital numbers.

Zero.

Sarin gas shot out of the other end of the canister smothering the terrorist's face.

"It's gas!" shouted Sam Smith as he balled up protecting his nose and mouth from the lethal nerve agent.

Everyone ran.

Peter sat motionless, only moving his head away as if the canister caused a horrendous stench.

Kravenko kicked the canister from Peter's hand and smothered it with his coat. A little smoke seeped from the outside of the jacket, but the clothing contained most of the gas. What did escape dissipated in the damp cold New York City wind.

Chamoun Al Khouri had bore the full force of the sarin gas in his face, in his mouth and nose, through his throat, and already into his lungs. Chamoun's nose began to run uncontrollably. His eyes watered and his pupils began to constrict. Chamoun felt the tightening in his chest. He knew what had already begun and was reluctantly prepared for the end. No more pain for the loss of his brother, Antonios, and all the others at Deir Ashashe. No more memories from the morgue from behind the Green Line in Beirut. The memory of the tortured lifeless body of Brother Michel would no longer haunt him. Chamoun had difficulty breathing. He could also feel the drool seep from his mouth. He no longer owned his body; sarin did. Chamoun Al Khouri knew he was going to lose consciousness soon. He let his mind drift back to the arid Bekaa Valley. He was kicking the ball to Antonios. The dry air made it difficult to breathe. He was just a little boy now, dressed in a bright red shirt kicking a ball to his older brother. The hot dry air was so hard to breathe, but the Bekaa Valley was so peaceful. The dog chased after the ball. His brother laughed. The little boy smiled. He finally remembered the cartoon character on the little boy's bright red shirt. It was a smiling mouse with big round ears.

Peter moved off of the terrorist and sat a few feet away. His eyes were irritated. He knew he had been exposed. He was in shock.

"Lay down," commanded Kravenko.

Peter lay back onto the sidewalk. People were screaming and running around. He also heard a dog barking a few feet away. And he heard Sara scream his name. He also felt his nose itch; it began to run.

Kravenko ripped off part of Peter's shirt. Peter felt a needle puncture his chest. He could hear Sara.

"Is he going to be all right?" Sara shouted at Kravenko. The lifeless body of Chamoun Al Khouri hopefully did not supply the answer.

Kravenko ignored Sara and administered another shot to Peter. Atropine. Then another shot. Pralidoxime.

"Peter, you are going to be all right."

The cracking of her voice betrayed the words of comfort.

Sara held Peter's hand as his chest tightened. It was difficult to breath. He could hear Sara, but could not speak. His throat began to collapse.

"Peter hang in there."

Sara focused her fear. The fear turned to anger. She was not going to leave him this time. And he certainly was not going to slip away if she had anything to do about it. Not this time.

Peter released his grip. He was tired. It was hard to fight. It was hard to breath. He drifted back again to the picnic on the California beach, Sara's backyard as she called it. He could feel Sara's arms around him as they kissed with the waves creeping closer and closer to the two lovers. As he stared at her and held her hand, he could still feel the embrace. She smiled and said something, but he could not hear her. He only heard the waves. He felt her squeeze his hand.

"Damn it Peter! You promised me that there would always be a tomorrow!" Sara shouted as she clasped his hand in hers.

Other than the firm grip of Sara's hand, Peter's last feeling was a stinging sensation in his throat.

# EPILOGUE

*Good evening everyone. This is Stone Beanery wishing you well tonight on America Tonight.*

*Tonight on America Tonight, we go back to the nation's capital where another senator and three more congressmen resigned from office today. For all of you keeping score at home, it's eleven senatorial resignations and thirty-eight congressmen who have resigned from office in the past week. These mass resignations have breathed new fire into the turmoil surrounding Washington after the deaths of President Robert Fairchild and Vice President Algers. Despite the Algers' family's constant denials of the rumors that Vice President Algers committed suicide because he could not handle the pressure of becoming president upon hearing of Fairchild's fatal aneurysm, this story still has legs, especially here on America Tonight. More on that later.*

*Overshadowed by the upheaval in D.C., the nation also has lost one of its modern robber barons in Elias St. Armand. Sunday night on America Tonight, we will air a special on St. Armand entitled "The Passing of a Philanthropist." The special will be followed by another One on One talk with Christina Cook. Christina has an exclusive interview with Rose St. Armand, who has a lot to say about her late husband. "Misty, what is heating up on the West Coast...*

As Peter turned off the television in the War Room adjacent to the Oval Office, he commented, "You do have a sixty-three percent favorable rating in the polls." His voice was still hoarse.

The cut from Kravenko's emergency tracheotomy was visible, but at least Peter no longer had to wear bandages on his neck. His throat was no longer sore but his voice was scratchy. Sara told him it was sexy. Peter took whatever he could get.

"The market is up, the weather is beautiful, and the holidays are almost upon us. The American people have confidence in your handling of the situation," chimed in Roland Miller.

"Given the fact that voter turnout dove below fifty percent this past election, I just think the American people still don't care."

"I do," Peter Farrell quickly responded.

President Madeleine Scholfield smiled. She liked having Peter around. He brought the good out in others.

"Peter, you should round up your nieces and go home," the President ordered. "We have a busy weekend."

Jenny could not stay in St. Louis after John's death so she, Catherine, and Maggie moved in with Peter and Sara in Georgetown. Little did Sara know when she accepted Peter's proposal that she would have an instant family. To help with the transition, Peter and Sara brought Jenny and the kids to the White House every Friday. Despite the gorgeous weather the past two Fridays, the girls had relegated themselves to the White House bowling lanes. The girls thought it was so "cool" that a house had its own bowling alley. Even though Catherine and Maggie missed school and their friends, the distraction served everyone's purpose for the time being.

"I'll get them in a minute."

Peter wanted to talk to the President for a minute.

"Knox keeps pleading for leniency," Roland Miller interjected. "What should I tell him?"

Citing his advanced years, Senator Pro Tempore John Jay Knox also resigned, abdicating his position for the constitutional succession for the presidency. He had already made a deal with the devil, now it was merely a matter of saving some face. Knox knew he could not remove the black Occidental cloud that hovered over him, but he thought that stepping aside and ensuring a smooth transition of the presidency would count for something. It did.

"There has been too much blood shed," commented the President.

"So I should tell him he is a free man?"

Roland Miller could not act melodramatic if his life depended on it. Miller knew Knox had paid his dues.

"Free?" The President threw a glare at Miller. "Strip him of everything. No assets, no power, not even his voice. He can have his pension and his name, but I want everything else he owns. I also do not want to see him in this town or even hear about him. You make that clear to him."

With all the turmoil over the past two and half weeks, Peter had heard that stern voice from President Madeleine Scholfield on a number of occasions. He had also heard a much more reassuring voice from her. Twice she had addressed the American public on television. Both times she carefully, if not painstakingly, explained to the American people that their government would be undergoing an integrity check on the grandest scale. At first, the polls applauded her intentions, but doubted her ability. However, as the number of resignations increased, so did the President's approval ratings.

"I'll inform Knox now," Miller announced as he left the room in the opposite direction of the Oval Office.

Peter and President Scholfield were finally alone.

"Is Sara still angry?" inquired the President. The President had angered Sara when she refused to allow Sara to have her father publicly rebuked. President Scholfield explained to Sara that the judiciary could not afford to expose her father. Every one of his decisions would be strictly scrutinized and possibly overturned irrespective of whether bias involving Occidental could be shown. The fear of any attorney who had ever lost a case before Judge Ironsides Ahrens appealing that decision and clogging up an already over-taxed judiciary convinced the President that there had to be a better way. There was. An independent judiciary tribunal, a star chamber, was formed to investigate not only Ahrens' judicial decisions, but any other Occidental judge as well. The President appointed Sara as an investigator for the star chamber so she could help undo whatever her father may have done. Although Sara gained some solace in working off her father's penance, she still had not forgiven him, nor was she likely to do so in the near future.

That is why Peter still had Judge Ahrens' letter. Kravenko must have slipped it in with things when he saved Peter's life. Peter carried the letter with him all the time with the hope that Sara would finally want to read her father's last words to her. That time had not yet come.

"Her anger is not directed at you," Peter responded.

The President arched her eyebrow at the thought that this made a difference, but understood the naïve attorney's misguided attempt at consoling the President of the United States. The President ignored the subtle disrespect.

"She is a remarkable woman, Peter. You are a lucky young man."

"I tell myself that every day," noted Peter with a slight smile.

"Peter, you seem troubled. Are you still concerned that Aaron Golde has not surfaced?" The President paused as she turned from Peter to look out onto the White House lawns. "Roland assures me that he has been taken care of and that was all I officially need to know."

The official word was that Aaron Golde retired and was traveling in Europe.

"Taken care of?" Peter uttered in almost a questioning tone, "you mean like what was left of Kerr's body in the East River?"

"I know you do not mean to show any disrespect, Peter, but removing this cancer from the government is going to take some time."

"Is this cure any different than the disease?" retorted the young attorney.

"If you really thought that, you would not be here."

The door snapped open. The newly-appointed Press Secretary Sachi Watson entered.

"I am sorry to interrupt, Madam President."

"It's all right, Sachi," the President responded.

"I just wanted to double check on our response to the North Korean buildup," inquired the new press secretary.

With the hints of instability in the government, military intelligence revealed that North Korea mobilized its southern forces into the DMZ.

"No change," assured the President.

The press secretary began to back out of the room.

"Wait," interjected the President, "tell them that if North Korea or any other rogue state does anything the United States deems a violation of international law or that threatens our national interest, our response will be swift."

The President paused, then stood and continued, "You tell them that we will act multilaterally if we can, and unilaterally if we must."

Press Secretary Watson smiled and left the room. Peter and the President were again alone.

"Peter, can I count on you?"

The rhetorical question was meant as a challenge to the young lawyer.

"You are right," responded Peter. "I would not be here unless I believed in what we're doing."

After a pause Peter continued, "My reservations do not apply to you, my sense of duty, or even Roland; it is just all the horse trading without any due process."

"Peter, I understand you are somewhat of a history buff. Even the Founding Fathers found it necessary to suspend some liberties in achieving independence. Alien and sedition acts were *de rigueur*. Our history is replete with such examples in times of emergency."

"As long as you are aware of my reservations."

"Peter," the President lectured, "we may not be a good democracy, but we are the best one."

"We need to get better," retorted the young attorney as he felt his cellphone vibrate.

"We will," responded the President.

"It's him again," Peter glanced at the same door Miller left through.

"You stay, I want to check on Sachi."

"Thank you, Madam President."

President Scholfield waved with the back of her right hand as she left Peter alone in the Oval Office.

"I'm here," Peter answered his cell.

"My dear Peter, why so curt?" asked the Englishman.

"What do you want?"

"Oh, I am going to enjoy working with you, I only wish I was younger."

"We are not working together."

"*Au contraire.*"

"Why did you call?"

"We fear our mutual friend Roland may be a bit long in the tooth." The Englishman paused, "We like you Peter. More importantly, we know how to communicate. And as we have seen, it is in everyone's best interests to keep communication lines open."

"What do you want?" repeated Peter.

"Merely to say that we will be in touch, *arrivederci.*"

<hr>

Andriy Kravenko entered a spacious third-story flat on Rue de Castellane only a hundred meters from the Madeleine. He had just returned from a short sabbatical at the ancient rock-hewn Church of St. George in Lalibella, Ethiopia. After removing a small package from the pocket, Kravenko placed his jacket over the side of an armchair in the foyer. Without hesitation, he walked down the long hallway, past several rooms, to the room at the end. Beyond the door was the bedroom of a minimalist. There was a bed and a closet. There was nothing on the walls. No mirror, paintings, pictures, or even a clock.

Kravenko opened the closet and walked to the back wall. A hidden button revealed a hidden room.

The concealed space was dimly lit. Pencil-thin lights illuminated tables that bordered the entire room. Kravenko passed a table that contained numerous texts, one of which resembled the Book of Kells. Lying on another table were various statuettes, including four bronze lions from the Forbidden City. Kravenko opened the package and set the Cross of St. Maro on another table between two other crosses fashioned from bones: one from the Priory Church of St. Bartholomew the Great, and the other from Aachen.

Kravenko exited the hidden room in his bedroom. It was a quiet night in Paris. Soon that would change.

<hr>

The hour was late. A row of tourists milled about the Lincoln Memorial. Despite their presence, the atmosphere was somber, even reverent. Peter Farrell stood at the feet of the colossal president. Although he had memorized it, Peter read the inscription chiseled over the ivory statue again:

IN THIS TEMPLE
AS IN THE HEARTS OF THE PEOPLE
FOR WHOM HE SAVED THE UNION
THE MEMORY OF ABRAHAM LINCOLN
IS ENSHRINED FOREVER.

"I knew I would find you here," Sara said as she entered the memorial. "I wanted to tell you the good news. After forty years of exile, Redwood is coming back to Washington."

Peter felt a warmth and comfort in hearing Sara's voice.

"We need him."

"You're spending a lot of time here."

"I like this place," Peter told his fiancée as he put his arm around her.

"You've always had a thing for Abraham Lincoln," she quipped, "but I am getting worried, since you've been here a half-dozen times since we came to Washington."

"I have always wondered if another person could have kept our nation together as he did during the Civil War," Peter pondered.

"We will never know," he continued.

"I hope we never have to find out," added Sara.

The two stood gazing up at the president for a minute or two as another small group of tourists entered the Memorial.

"Come on."

Sara took Peter's hand in hers and led him through the enormous pillars toward the steps.

As the two walked down the stairs, Sara began again, "You know Abraham Lincoln once said 'I have an irrepressible desire to live till I can be assured that the world is a little better for my having lived in it.'"

"It applies to you, Peter." Sara gazed at the man she loved. "The world is better for you having lived in it."

The two reached the bottom of the steps where the Reflection Pool lay before them glistening with the image of the Washington Monument pointing back toward Lincoln.

Peter turned back toward the illuminated Lincoln Memorial and remembered his telephone call with the Englishman, "I think it's too soon to close the book on me."